Robert Williams Buchanan

The Coming Terror

And Other Essays and Letters

Robert Williams Buchanan

The Coming Terror
And Other Essays and Letters

ISBN/EAN: 9783744721714

Printed in Europe, USA, Canada, Australia, Japan

Cover: Foto ©Andreas Hilbeck / pixelio.de

More available books at **www.hansebooks.com**

THE COMING TERROR,

AND OTHER ESSAYS AND LETTERS.

THE COMING TERROR

AND OTHER ESSAYS AND LETTERS

BY

ROBERT BUCHANAN

' In interiore homine habitat Veritas.'—AUGUSTINE.

' *Sir To.* Dost thou think, because *thou* art virtuous, there shall be
no more cakes and ale?
' *Clo.* Yea, by Saint Anne—and ginger shall be hot i' the mouth too!'
—*Twelfth Night.*.

' Leave nothing sacred—'tis but just
The Many-headed Beast should know.'—TENNYSON.

NEW YORK:
UNITED STATES BOOK COMPANY,
SUCCESSORS TO
JOHN W. LOVELL COMPANY.
1891.

NOTE TO THE SECOND EDITION.

— ◦◦◦ —

SCARCELY is 'The Coming Terror' issued to the
world than a Second Edition is called for—which
is satisfactory enough, as showing that even the
trades-union of Criticism cannot quite kill an outspoken book by a non-union man. Here and there,
indeed, to my astonishment, the work has received
words of actual approval, qualified, of course, with
a suggestion that it need not be taken quite seriously ;
but, as I write, the good old three-decker newspapers
are beginning to take listless aim with their heavy
guns at my cockle-shell. The *Times* sends a sleepy
projectile, which falls, as usual, far short of the
mark ; the good old ship *Observer* deigns to fire a
random and rusty shot, while thundering heavily
and internally about 'gospel according to Buchanan'
and 'angry philippics'; and *The Speaker*, a new boat
of the top-heavy species, tries to run down the cockle-
shell on the score that the conduct of its pilot is 'un-
gentlemanly.' Altogether, I have to congratulate
myself on a fair measure of old-fashioned abuse.
To have been saluted amicably by the Wooden

Walls of Cockneydom would have been proof positive that my little vessel contained nothing but sailing orders for the lumbering Literary Fleet and complimentary messages from Headquarters to the blundering gentlemen in command.

I resent only one imputation, — that I have written, and write, 'in a temper.' If it were true, it would not be surprising, but it is, in point of fact, not true at all. I am, let me assure my critics, a singularly calm person, and if I aim at a whole Fleet of leaky Vessels, it is quite coolly and good-humouredly. I know, quite as well as my severest censor, that I am fighting against heavy odds, with no chance whatever of winning the battle. I know that War, Prostitution, Providential Legislation, the New Journalism, the New Morality, will fling out their bunting long after I am sunk and drowned. I know that I shall be shot in the back, beaten down, swarmed over, and generally overcome, by the conventional Marines. *Après?* I am rather amused than angry. 'Woe to you when the world speaks well of you,' says the prophet.

I must warn my readers, however, against one particular method of the enemy—the method christened by Charles Reade 'the sham sample swindle.' By quoting some of my phrases without their context, one or two of my critics have attempted to show that I am hostile and unjust to everybody,— that I call Zola 'a dullard,' denounce Tolstoi, and side with Philistia against other great personalities.

Readers of this book will discover how far and how earnestly I justify the very men I am accused of decrying, and a reference to contemporary chronicles will further establish the fact that I alone, among English authors, have demanded, even for the writers with whom I disagree, perfect liberty of literary expression.

Since much of my complaint is against Journalism as at present conducted, I can expect little or no mercy from that quarter ; and I ask for none. What the Roman Catholic Church was for many centuries, what the Protestant Church became during the period of its decadence, the Church of Journalism is to the present generation,— shallow, dogmatical, cruel, and inquisitorial. To secure its praise and sympathy, means both moral and intellectual degradation. Yet, as the reader is aware, I have not been slow to avail myself of its pulpits, and entering its temples, to denounce its own temporizers and money-changers, to be denounced in turn as a dreamer and a madman. I am possibly the one, and certainly the other ; for I still believe in the strange gods whose marble images bestrew the world, and I still look upward to the heavens, not downward to the drains, for the Light which is Life.

That 'The Coming Terror' is a Jeremiad and not a gospel, may at once be admitted. Yet Jeremiah was, in his small way, a gospeller as well as a prophet. He endured 'reproach and derision

daily,' his townsmen of Anathoth threatened to
slay him if he did not cease exposing abuses, and
even his own family ' dealt treacherously ' with him.
The same fate awaits every man who fails to flatter
authorities, or who reminds society of its follies
and its imperfections.   Even Thackeray, elegantly
preaching the Gospel according to St. Jeames, was
described by the superfine Reviewer of his period
as ' no gentleman.'

ROBERT BUCHANAN.

April 20th, 1891.

PREFACE.

I MUST apologize to the serious reader for preserving, in the present permanent form, at the request of many correspondents, the following passing comments on public events and social phenomena. My aim is selfish, yet two-fold. Firstly, these comments may be useful by-and-by to readers of my less desultory contributions to literature; secondly, I am enabled, in republishing them, to restore one or two passages which were too outspoken for the columns of the daily newspaper of the period.

From the first moment I began to write I have been endeavouring to vindicate the freedom of human Personality, the equality of the sexes, and the right of Revolt against arbitrary social laws conflicting with the happiness of human nature. Had I paused there, I might have secured the suffrages of a friendly minority. But, unfortunately, while defending Freedom on the one hand, I have been defending Society on the other, under the impression that social organization is not always, and not necessarily, tyrannical. From my point of view, the average Home is not invariably (what the gentlemen of the Hall of Science describe it to be) a 'Harem,' nor is the average Morality inextricably associated with 'the piggish virtues of the Georges.' I am, therefore, out of harmony with the minority as well as with the majority, and am little likely to find favour with either party: either the Convention-

alists who assume that everything existing is right, or
the Reformers who believe that everything existing is
wrong.

At this moment of publication a great wave of Mock-
Morality is threatening to destroy much that is beautiful
and pleasurable in Life, in Literature, and in Art. Nearly
every natural function, certainly every natural enjoyment,
has been arraigned as criminal, and the vice of incontinence
in matters of the Body has been confused, by the blind
leading the blind, with the passion for freedom in matters
of the Soul. Not for the first time in the history of the
world, Man has discovered that he is naked. So ashamed
is he of his unclad organism, that he is content to adopt
any kind of hypocrisy as a garment. The ulcerous rags of
Asceticism, the dingy cloak of Pessimism, the tin-drawers
sanctioned by the Vatican, the cheap slop-suit of current
Socialism, and the quasi-military breeches adopted by the
Salvation Army, have all been found acceptable, even
necessary; for if any idea is established among philanthropists nowadays, it is that Man is naturally an indecent
animal, and that his propensities are, of necessity, brutal.
This idea is dominant not only in circles professedly puritan,
but in circles professedly free and eclectic,—for the Calvinistic preacher and the advanced Moral Reformer are agreed
at least on one point, that the World is ugly, and that Man
is a Beast. Hence the new Gospel of Total Abstinence from
the Beautiful and the Enjoyable; hence the creed that all
conduct, all emotion, all Life, all Literature, all Art, must
have its sanction from the scientific discovery without, not
from the conscience within; hence certain unnatural ordinances of Marriage and Divorce, the restriction on all true
freedom of Relation between the sexes, the licensing laws,
the inquisitorial Councils, the new Journalistic Police, the
death of free Literature, and the paralysis of free Art. Instead of sunshine and fresh air, Humanity accepts the
Dingy Science *in excelsis;* in lieu of a God proved to be

non-existent or paralytic, it clamours round its Providence made Easy.

County Councils, Vigilance Associations, Arbitrary Trades-unions, the new Science of Self-Exposure, and the new Literature of sexual pathology, are all but steps on the way to the dreary millennium of State Socialism, to the period of the greatest Tyranny of the greatest Number. Every institution, however peaceful, however beautiful, is to be destroyed and trampled down under the hob-nailed boots of Demos. Intellectual activity itself will soon be regarded as a dangerous form of Competition! What the world will become when the State superintends all living functions and governs all living acts may be gathered from the direful prophecy of social nullity painted, with blind and misplaced enthusiasm, in a book called 'Looking Backward.' Is it to be wondered at that so many men, dreading the catastrophe, turn Tories in despair?

The main contention in the following pages is that no amount of political or social tinkering will complete the process Nature chooses to work out by her own slow methods of conscientious evolution, and that, by the present growth of quasi-providential restriction, by the emergence of Mob Morality and Mob Rule, those sublime methods are being indefinitely retarded, even occasionally reversed. In proportion as we limit the freedom of the Individual, we retard the progress of the Race, destroy human character, debase human intelligence, and arrest the development of the social conscience. Sanitation in both the physical and the moral world comes of free oxygen, free sunshine, and free exercise. Knowledge comes of personal experience and suffering, not of political or moral dogmas, all hollow as the dogmas of any and every Church. In a word, no organization of human beings, no union, secular, priestly, or apostolic, can help one man to 'save his Soul alive,' or, what is the same thing, to save the Souls of those he loves.

The glory of the Age is its recognition of the responsibilities of human Brotherhood; the disgrace of the Age is its attempt to confuse philanthropy with tyrannous legislation. Seen from the standpoint of common justice, our present condition of Society is one actively stirred, in every fibre, by the science of Humanity. Ways and means may differ, but Tory and Liberal alike are striving, and not ineffectively, for the common good. If the balance of private philanthropy and beneficence were to be ascertained even now, it would be found, perhaps, that the weight of 'good works' was on the side of those who are trying to conserve whatever is just and noble in our constitution; that in all matters of private tolerance and kindliness to human beings in the mass, the Tory was more generous than the Liberal, and the Liberal more sympathetic than the Radical. The old feudal system itself was wiser, and far pleasanter, than the new Despotic Socialism. The last scientific and political Providence, like the old Christianity, postulates an utterly non-existent and absolutely unreal Human Nature; it legislates for men and women as they never were, and demands a perfection of obedience which would convert them into moral parasites. Men grow by happiness and freedom, by the exercise of every natural function; men dwindle when they become merely portions of a Political Mechanism. The result of Socialistic Legislation is seen nowadays in a thousand disastrous forms—some of which I have endeavoured to describe in the following pages; while, on the other hand, I have not been afraid, at the risk of seeming inconsistent, to point out the folly of anti-social forms of Individualism,—forms which show the Individual anatomising his own morbid secretions, parading his own obscene discoveries, shutting out the common sunlight, and finding in Nature only the Calvinistic phenomena of Darkness. Disease. and Death.

R. B.

CONTENTS.

THE COMING TERROR:

A Dialogue between Alienatus, a Provincial, and Urbanus, a Cockney.

THE COMING TERROR:

A Dialogue between Alienatus, a Provincial. and Urbanus, a Cockney.

Urbanus. I have often wondered, my dear Alienatus, at the very scant respect you seem to pay to lawfully constituted authority, and to those who have been termed, and rightly, the leaders of mankind. This attitude of irreverence, combined with a disposition to enter into combat with any individual, however ignoble and unworthy, who throws down to you the gage of battle, has prejudiced many intelligent people against you. For myself, I love a quiet life, and cannot understand the temperament which disturbs itself with social and political shadows ; and I think, if you will permit me to say so, that your position in the world would have been very different if you had, like certain other poets, led ' a philosopher's life in the quiet woodland ways '—in other words, let the squabbles of the world alone, and confined your attention to literature pure and simple.

1—2

ALIENATUS. That is possible ; but literature *quâ* literature has ceased to interest me very much.

URB. You surprise me ! Literature, to my thinking, is the one star of peacefulness in a very troublesome world. A play of Euripides or Shakespeare, a poem of Theocritus or Tennyson——

ALI. Quite so ; all these are charming, and I hope I am not insensible to their attractions. At least twenty years of my life have been devoted to the study of what is best and most beautiful in written books. But I have long since come to the conclusion that all Art is a trifle compared with the terrible problems of the world ; and so far as Poetry is concerned, it only interests me at the point where it is identical with the higher idealism—Religion. Besides, you are aware that in my opinion Poetry has long been the synonym for mere verbalism, that the area of modern Verse is a dark plain of dulness, vacuity, and verbosity. At the present moment, indeed, I can hardly understand the type of intellect which sits apart in the pursuit of mere self-culture of any kind, and takes no trouble to understand the mystery of actual existence.

URB. My dear fellow, that mystery is insoluble. We can know nothing.

ALI. Pardon me : we can know everything that is necessary.

URB. The wisest men who have lived assert the contrary.

ALI. Pardon me again : the really wise men have offered us not merely supposition, not merely negation, but verification.

URB. Verification !—of what ?

ALI. Of the soul of goodness in things evil, of the reality which abides under all phenomena, of the absolute reality which, for want of a better name, we entitle God.

URB. In other words, the Unknowable ? the Unrealizable ? the Inconceivable? the Unthinkable ?

ALI. What is unthinkable is non-existent, for Thought is the only absolute Existence. But suffer me ! If we go on like this, we shall get into the deep waters of the metaphysicians. Let us confine ourselves, on this occasion at least, to the limitations of experience. What sort of a world do you, from your point of view, find it ?

URB. An excellent world, if meddlers would let it alone. A delightful world, if quidnuncs would not constantly remind us of its imperfections. He who walks through it with his eyes alert will find it, on the whole, sweet and reasonable enough. He who persists in star-gazing is sure to stumble into some open grave. Just reflect, my dear fellow, how short a time is given us to realize our powers at all. Is it not the height of folly to spend that time in asking questions of the Sphynx ?

ALI. You think, then, that the pleasures of consciousness are all-sufficing ?

URB. It is sufficient to know that they are all

we can possibly compass in the space of life at our command. To be fairly happy ourselves, to make others fairly happy, is the utmost we ephemera can achieve.

ALI. But *after?*

URB. After life ? Why, a blank to be filled up by no process of human reasoning.

ALI. Then you are a materialist ?

URB. Say, rather, a Pantheist.   I have read Spinoza—a delightful soul sent to teach us dilettanti the poetry of simple mathematics, and to affirm by beautiful syllogism the divine religion of intellectual negation.   '

ALI. Stop there.   Come back to the world. Curiously enough, its fascination for *me* lies in the very imperfections you would wish to conceal.   I should not care to live—indeed, it would be impossible for me to live—if I thought the secret of life inaccessible to human reasoning, and it is through a realization of imperfection that I attain moral security.

URB. That's a paradox, but I think I understand you.   You mean to say that the very imperfection of our faculties is a proof that there is a perfection outside that imperfection ; the Unknowable is proved by the very limits of our knowledge ?

ALI. Something of that sort.

URB. Thus, if I shut my eyes and see only blankness, that blankness establishes the fact of something beyond me !   Well, go on.

ALI. Let me return to my own conception of Life. It consists outwardly of the phenomena of imperfection, urged by some mysterious force upward to a point which at present seems incomprehensible and unattainable. It consists inwardly of a sensation corresponding to those phenomena, equally imperfect, and equally obedient to a mysterious force. I dismiss for the present all metaphysical argument as to the identity of the phenomena without and the sensation within. All I would imply is, that both the physical and the spiritual motion is in an upward direction.

URB. All philosophers admit it. Even Schopenhauer does so, under certain qualifications—that is, he sees the world advancing intellectually and morally, but only towards a *cul de sac* of general despair. To be very good is to be very miserable. Luckily, *I* am not good !

ALI. My own conception of Life consists of three processes—Feeling, Knowing, and Divining ; in other words, of sympathy, verification, and exaltation. Most men stop at the first process ; a limited number of men reach the second ; few attain the inspiration of the third. Sympathy is perceptive and retrospective ; verification is sympathy sanctioned by science, by experience ; and exaltation, the last process in this moral chemistry, is prospective and prophetic.

URB. Granted. At what are you driving ?

ALI. At my old hobby—the construction of a

Science of Sentiment, capable of justifying Life and explaining phenomena. Let us now alight from the airy balloon of a generalization, and come down to the solid ground. I predicted to you some time ago, by the method just described, that the Belshazzar's Feast of modern civilization could not go on for ever ; that some day we should discern the fatal Handwriting on the Wall. Well, there it is, burning before our eyes, as it has burned for the last decade, ever growing brighter and more terrible. It betokens another cataclysm rapidly approaching. Terrified by the first warning, men have endeavoured to prepare against the advent of a new Reign of Terror.

URB. Possibly, with your prophetic faculties, you can tell me what shape that Terror will assume ?

ALI. The shape it has assumed always, that of Anarchy, that of the Demogorgon, who is all-creating yet all-destroying. In simpler words, Humanity will arise and rend itself. The present Order will vanish, like a house built on sand, but with it will vanish every vestige of a social cosmos. The triumphant majority of human beings will trample down all the rights of minorities, all the privileges of individuals, all the moral differentiation of the human race. No man will breathe freely in his own dwelling. No personal life will grow, upward or downward, its own way. There will be universal legislation, expressed in a creed which shall base the salvation of the State on the destruction of the individual.

URB. By what tokens do you assume the existence of this tendency ?

ALI. Firstly, by the frightful increase of social legislation, expressed in the Acts of tyrannical Parliaments, and in the powers given to civic bodies ; secondly, by the apotheoses of political and scientific demagogues ; thirdly, by the increased corruption and *mouchardism* of an irresponsible Press ; fourthly, by the completed sinfulness and tardy repentance of those ' governing ' classes who no longer govern ; fifthly, by the gradual deterioration of our jurisprudence, once the symbol of our independence ; sixthly and most decidedly, by the universal conversion of religious Catholicism into the Calvinism of Science.

URB. I hardly follow you. Let me ask you, to begin with, to explain the paradox which represents Legislation and Anarchy as convertible terms ?

ALI. I had thought that a student of our one sane living philosopher would have needed no such explanation. Mr. Spencer has illustrated in his own masterly way that legislation is only beneficent when it is reduced to the narrowest possible compass consistent with human safety. The tyranny of a majority, however beneficent in intention, becomes of its own nature anarchic. Anarchy, politically speaking, is a condition of things representing the triumph of communities over the wills and wishes of individual men. There is the anarchy of Despotism, the anarchy of Parliaments, the anarchy of the Bureau. Every one of these means the destruction of natural rights and privileges, the stifling of personal aspiration, the death of individual enterprise and endeavour.

URB. Pass by your charge of over-legislation. I had an illustration of it the other day, when I heard it proposed, at the County Council, that two or three zealous elderly gentlemen should be told off to go 'behind the scenes' of an evening, and see if the ballet-skirts were 'moral.' Come to your Demagogues. Surely the apotheosis of the Demagogue is the aggrandisement of the Individual?

ALI. The Demagogue lives by pandering to the follies, jealousies, and prejudices of the democracy which makes him possible. I will not cite Mr. Gladstone ; my respect for him is too great to allow me to criticise his occasional moral misadventures. I will go to the very dregs of politics, and cite the senior member for Northampton. Mr. Labouchere has many gifts, but neither sincerity of purpose nor reverence for human aspiration is among them. He has gained his popularity, his vogue, by becoming, firstly, the Paul Pry of journalism, and, secondly, the Scapin of politics. He has violated the privileges of private life, by haunting the back kitchens of the aristocracy and counting the candle-ends of the governing classes. A *mouchard* by temperament and education, he has become by accident a legislator. The climax of his audacities was reached only the other day, when openly, in the House of Commons, to the manifest satisfaction of a crowd of fellow-demagogues, he proposed to pollute the ears of his fellow-members by opening up the moral cesspool of a foul and disgraceful scandal. Here was anarchy indeed about to transform itself into the very fibre of legislation. Fortunately, even the bear-garden of St. Stephen's is not yet turned into a commission of moral sewers.

URB. Poor Labouchere! He has his good points. Remember the toys for the Children's Hospital.

ALI. I am not condemning the man, but the state of public sentiment which makes him politically possible. He has been praised publicly for his services in exposing the vices and follies of the aristocracy. Just another turn of the wheel, and he would consign all aristocrats *quâ* aristocrats to the guillotine. If ever the Revolution comes, he will be its Robespierre, while the impassive and impeccable Parnell may become its St. Just. But just alter the circumstances. Suppose a Demagogue were to arise among the Tories, and to devote his energies to proving, which would be easy, the vices and follies of the proletariat, or, again, the vices and follies of the *bourgeoisie*. Would not such a person be cried down as a nuisance, as an irrelevant person, wasting his time and his opportunities? It is just as base to throw filth at one class as at another. To do them justice, our aristocrats have never posed as morally impeccable, and from time immemorial their cavalier peccadilloes have been far more venial than the cynical Puritanism of the plutocrats who serve Mammon and cheat on 'Change.

URB. Of course I do not approve of scandal-mongering, but do not forget that the man you condemn has been called the ' Friend of Ireland.'

ALI. Poor Ireland! Has she a friend indeed under the sun? Mother of demagogues and desperadoe , how is she shamed in the sight of the world! No one living loves Ireland and Irishmen more than I ; no one rejoices more that an unhappy nation has burst its bonds. But I have lived in the distressful country, not merely for months, but years, and I have witnessed with my own eyes the terrorism of organized communities over the lives of individual men. I do not speak, mind, of assassination, of boycotting, of political conspiracy, but of the endless petty tyrannies exercised in ordinary life by the will, the caprice, the malice, or the ignorance of the majority. I am not now alluding to the Land League, or to any political organization. I am speaking of the temperament which converts Irishmen, wherever they gather together, here as in America and the colonies, into tyrannous and anarchic group . As the nation is, so is every village in the nation—the abode of men

whose sole aim in government would be, under
Home Rule, to stifle every free thought and free
action in independent members of the community.
What they have achieved now by conspiracy, they
would rapidly achieve by legislation, and in a short
time no rational Irishman would dare to call his
soul his own.

URB. You foresee, then, in Ireland, the
imminence of the new Terror?

ALI. Here, as well as there, I perceive an indifference to all sanctions, save those of the
arbitrary will of the majority. The enormous increase of taxation, the ever-increasing transference
of responsibilities to the shoulders of the ratepayer,
the burdens put upon every description of private
enterprise, the rapid growth of State prerogatives,
the embargoes placed on moral and intellectual
liberty, the moral censorship of literature, are
portentous signs of indifference to the natural
rights of Man.

URB. Surely we have witnessed of late years an
extraordinary movement in the opposite direction.
Take one sign from the Continent—the resignation
of Prince Bismarck, and the humanitarian attitude
of the young German Emperor.

ALI. Is it possible that so transparent a piece of
legerdemain can deceive the eyes of any rational
man? If I desired to select any modern nation
as an illustration of my contention that over-
legislation is moral anarchy, I would select the

German Empire, a régime of blood and iron,
cemented by the sacrifice of thousands of human
beings.   The man Bismarck was a Demagogue who
based his calculations on the mad hunger of the
masses for Nationality.   He succeeded by sheer
brute force in consolidating an authority which
made the people militant and left no vestige of
real freedom in the land.   He erected the new
German Empire at the expense of the liberty, even
the moral intelligence, of every individual Teuton.
In the name of Christianity he destroyed the right
of each human being to save his soul his own way.
His strength was the will of the people ; his success
was the proof of their collective unintelligence.
With the gains wrung from the sweat of the
nation's brow, with the willing tribute given by
communities gone mad with nationalism, he bought
the press, while violently gagging and suppressing
every expression of honest and enlightened opinion.
And what has come of it ?   What is the harvest
of the blood-seed sown on the battle-field in the
names of Christ and Death ?   Social stagnation,
literary dumbness, political anarchy ; for now, after
all this waste of life, arises the phantom of Demogorgon, prompting the new Emperor on his throne,
and suggesting that a tottering Despotism should
be fortified by the suffrages of a tyrannical
Socialism.   'The game of Nationality, the farce
of war, is played out,' says the little Cæsar ; ' let
me now summon the " Socialists," who will per-

suade my people to rivet the fetters on their own hands, while curbing free activity and enterprise in all directions. Let me represent now by Divine right the tyrannies of trades-unionism, pseudo-co-operation, and " beneficent " legislation. Let me assume the sacred prerogatives given to me by a priesthood of atheists using the old shibboleth of Christianity.' What will be the result ? A new kind of tyranny, another Providence made Easy, a fresh departure in the region of governmental despotism. The Teuton, already a slave militant, will become a slave social, and on his gyves will be engraved the words ' The Necessity of Organization.'

URB. Curious language, coming from you, a professed Socialist !

ALI. The higher Socialism is not trades-unionism. The object of the higher Socialism is less to organize under political agencies than to widen the area of personal freedom as far as possible, so that in proportion to the liberty of action granted to individuals would be the comfort and security of the community. As I have often contended, true Socialism is only another name for Individualism. When it combines, it is against the tyranny of kings, of parliaments, of bureaus, of majorities ; but the law of its combination is that free action, free thought, free speech, is the prerogative of every one of its members, even of its kings and parliaments.

URB. You will come to chaos there, my friend !

Motto, 'The common good, and every man for himself.'

ALI. The motto, after all, is not such a bad one. The common good is achieved only when every individual is allowed to work out his well-being and salvation through his own activities. Human nature can never be saved by any kind of special Providence, mundane or supra-mundane ; its strength or its weakness must be based upon the natural laws of evolution. Futile is the legislation which seeks to reconstruct society by equalizing the good and the bad, the worthy and the unworthy, the strong and the weak.

URB. Then your so-called higher Socialism is not destructive ?

ALI. Oh, but it is !

URB. I thought so. You yourself, for example, have argued strongly against monopolies in pro-perty and land, and you have said, if I remember rightly, that the will of the people has the right, at the expense of individuals, to redress centuries of wrong-doing.

ALI. Certainly. The voice of conscience has a right to be heard, whenever class caprice or local legislation acts in defiance of absolute ethical and political principles.

URB. Name a few of these principles, if you can.

ALI. You will find them very excellently set forth in that old-fashioned Book containing the Ten Commandments. Not one of those Ten Commandments limits irrationally the moral freedom of the individual.

URB. I'm not so sure about that. The seventh, for example? I have never yet been quite able to realize the caprice of a Providence which fills us with certain passions, and yet damns us for their gratification.

ALI. Still more difficult, I say, is it to realize the legislation which, while recognising the commandment, adopts measures for its safe infraction. Next to War, perhaps even more than War, Prostitution is the bane of modern communities. Like War again, it is recognised as a necessary evil. Now, there is no such thing as a necessary evil.

URB. How would you propose to get over the difficulty as regards the daily and hourly breach of the seventh commandment?

ALI. By clearly explaining what that commandment means; by showing that the thing forbidden is only adulterous where it infringes on the absolute rights of other individuals. Meantime, the new Reign of Terror will reach its full fruition, when the legislator decrees that human passions, and their indulgence, are of necessity immoral, when the adamantine laws of Marriage contract are made still more onerous, when the inherent Puritanism of Science, supported by the suffrages of a cynical majority, doubles and trebles the penalties to be paid by poor human nature for natural mistakes. Scientific Puritanism, you will discover, is only the

2

old Inquisition under another name. At certain periods of human progress (see Mr. Lecky *passim*) not only natural appetites, but natural affections, were looked upon as suggestions of the Devil. Love was identical with lust, and so degraded became the moral consciousness, that the male avoided and feared the female, even in the person of a mother or a little female child. We have got a little beyond that now, but we have yet to recognise the fact that the passion of Love is not a phrase to include the criminal aspects of adultery. The anarchy into which moralists as well as politicians are now drifting may be illustrated by a reference to the last work of Count Tolstoi, at once the most influential and the least consistent of modern novelists—a writer who, more than any other living, touches the quick of human evil and defines the limits of human freedom. Yet never was the inhumanity of the Puritanical bias more painfully illustrated than in this book of the most beneficent of recent legislative teachers. In the 'Kreutzer Sonata,' a study of the morbid anatomy of marriage, Count Tolstoi contends, against experience, against instinct, against all verification, that those marriages are happiest which resemble most a placid and non-passionate friendship between the sexes ; that, in other words, the passion of Love is a fatal preliminary to any abiding relationship between man and woman. With cold and pitiless hands, the writer breaks the golden bowl of

Romance, and tells us that Passion is of necessity
evil, illustrating his thesis by a picture of such
foulness as might have emanated from the diseased
imagination of a mediæval monk. In some of his
contentions I, of course, agree—in his crusade
against mere animalism, against the legalization
of Prostitution, against the carefully protected
impurity of men. But to hear from such a teacher
that the most divine thing in Life, young Love and
young Romance, the Soul's Ecstasy, the Body's
Sacrament, the World's Desire, is only foulness
and foul vanity, makes one despair of human
wisdom. Teaching like this is only another
form of the legislation which is substituting everywhere for natural law an unnatural system of
repression. When the new Reign of Terror is
completed, we shall breed our human beings as
we breed our cattle, by the sanitary rules of a
scientific legislation, and under the beneficent
inspection of some suffragan St. Simeon Stylites.

URB. Such a system of selection has indeed
been suggested, that we may avoid the evils of
hereditary disease and over-population. I confess
that I agree with you in regarding its possibility
with a certain feeling of horror. It is not to be
disputed, however, that these evils, particularly
that of the propagation of diseased and inferior
types, will have to be reckoned with somehow.

ALI. Undoubtedly, and the way our legislation
reckons with them is by protecting diseased and

inferior types at the cost of the hale and superior. Do not misunderstand me, however. I have always contended that physical defect, so far from being necessarily evil, is often a defect in the line of growth. The idea of scientists, that a perfectly strong and healthy breed of men and women would of necessity be a higher development, is as absurd as that other idea which attaches a fictitious importance to the laws of heredity. Weak and diseased men are often the salt of humanity. Strong and healthy men and women not unfrequently, by some mysterious law, produce degraded offspring. Meantime, the phrase ' Heredity ' has become part of the scientific shibboleth which converts feeble thinkers into social tyrants.

Urb. You seem very severe on Science generally.

Ali. Heaven forbid ! (True Science, like true Religion, is not to be confounded with empirical tyranny. So long as our men of science concerned themselves with discovery and verification of the facts of Nature, so long as they loosened the bonds of Humanity by proving that these bonds were for the most part self-imposed, so long as they waged destructive war against Superstition and touched no one of these Verities which are the birthright of thinking men, they were saviours and benefactors.)Their organization into a Priesthood of personal/inquiry, into a social Inquisition, was a proof that they had yielded up prerogatives in

favour of an intellectual despotism. The true
scientist is reverent like Faraday, and cautious like
Darwin. The false scientist is the incipient moral
demagogue ; one of the Beadles of the Nation ; the
thinker who sacrifices the love of pure and gentle
individual progress to an insane love of *forcing*,
by systems of repression, the tardy work of Evolution. I have criticised, in another connection, the
attempt of Professor Huxley, a very familiar type
of the scientist militant and political, to limit and
even to deny altogether the natural Rights of Man,
and I have been rebuked a little flippantly by
this gentleman for presuming to assert that true
Socialism is not the Socialism of the Day. This
good man, while indirectly defending the *status quo*,
denies absolute political principles altogether, and
would substitute for human freedom the half-
verified discoveries of a small scientific Providence
—a Providence whose cardinal principle appears
to be : let political reformations alone, and impose
on the individual who is struggling for freedom
as many restrictions as possible. To talk of the
rights of men is, according to this Daniel come
to judgment, about as wise as to talk of the rights
of wild beasts, *e.g.*, the man-eating tiger. More
than most publicists, such men as he are hastening
on the advent of the New Terror.

URB. Well, come to your third token of the
tendency to save the State at the expense of the
Individual. I think you cited the New Journalism.

Surely if freedom of speech is found anywhere, it is in the columns of that Journalism.

ALI. I have failed to discover it.

URB. Indeed.

ALI. The New Journalism, above most things, is tyrannous and anarchic. So far from being the free speech of individual men, it is the voice of the Demogorgon proclaiming the era of completed literary ignorance. Next to the tyranny of Parliaments is the despotism of the newspaper. Practically irresponsible, feeding the weak appetites of the community with the garbage of the latest news, sending its *mouchards* into every house, imposing its espionage on every public individual, weaving its tissue of scandals and of falsehoods, judging everything and every man by the hastily erected standard of the humour of the hour, the New Journalism, an importation from America, has paralyzed literature and destroyed free thought and free feeling all over the world. The man who used to think now takes his thought from the current printed cackle of the moment. The man who used to read now skims the surface of current news and deems it information. In proportion to the anarchic tongue-confusion of this last Tower of Babel is the deadening of all sense of decency, the loss of all sense of individual liberty.

URB. Heyday! would you have no gossip in newspapers at all? You forget that we moderns are in far too great a hurry to read treatises and voluminous tomes, or even sober newspapers.

ALI. The hurry of which you speak is that of the social River shooting to its fall. All light, all peace, all peacefulness, all the stillness of the home, all the beauty of life, is covered by this common cloud of ignorance, and destroyed by the Americanised Newspaper. By the New Journalism the individual thinker is tortured and cried down. It is Babbage's Organ in the Street.

URB. People must read something!

ALI. Better to read nothing than to read what deadens their very sense of freedom, and pulls them out into the clamour of the common hue and cry. Take up one of these journals at random, and what do you find? Firstly, the publication of a Scandal so infamous, and described so infamously, that the very air of Nature is polluted as by a cesspool, the stench of which penetrates as poison into every household of the land; and secondly, close to this inhuman parade of filth, made in the name of a repressive moral legislation, a *plébiscite* of readers on the moral and intellectual qualities of the ' Best Books,' or the ' Best Men.' Could the completed sinfulness of ignorance go further?

URB. The idea of the *plébiscite* was, I suppose, merely that of gathering information as to what books were most read, and what teachers were most in vogue.

ALI. Just so ; literary truth and honour were to be gauged by the mind of the general reader, merits were to be assessed by the suffrage of creatures base enough to subscribe to this very journal of abominations. Observe, moreover, that I include in the phrase ' the New Journalism ' even certain publications which appear at longer intervals than does the daily paper : the monthly reviews of human inanity, the quarterly reviews of dead or dying prejudices. Here is a case in point. A review once fairly sane, but now puzzle-headed, publishes an article entitled ' Tennyson— and After,' in which, after a cold and cruel calculation that one of the noblest poets of the hour must in the course of Nature shortly disappear, the writer firstly suggests a possible successor to what, if so great a soul had not adorned it, would be a barren honour, and, secondly, points the finger of scorn at men who, so far as I know, would reject that barren honour if it were given. Thus, to paraphrase the present Laureate's words, it is not sufficient for the singer ' to leave his music as of old,' but over him, even while he breathes, even while he still brightens the sunshine, ' begins the scandal and the cry.' That, perhaps, is a mere trifle—the mere cackling of a goose in the Pantheon. But what shall we say of the Journalistic Demagogue who, confident of the prevailing anarchy, sure of the reigning madness and folly, offers to turn his review, his journal, his

magazine of stolen goods, into a Confessional—into
a place of vantage where he may sit listening to
all the obscene details of human sin and misery,
and so sitting, dispense an uncleanly absolution ?

URB. The New Journalism has never loved you,
my dear Alienatus. Henceforward, I fear, it will
love you even less.

ALI. I never craved its love or feared its hate.
Yet understand me. When I speak thus of one
form of Journalism, and cite these instances of its
folly and criminality, I am not blind to the fact
that elsewhere, despite this last manifestation of
mob-rule, Humanity is kept alive. There have been,
and there are, great journalists—men full of even
prophetic vision ; many of these men have sunk
into the vortex, never to emerge again ; a few
survive, crying ' peace ' to the anarchy around
them. It would be strange, indeed, if in the crowd
of souls not one upturned his forehead to the
Light.

URB. Then you do not denounce Journalism
altogether ?

ALI. I might as well, like Canute, denounce the
rising tide. After the Coming Terror has reached
its height, these waves which now threaten to
submerge us will settle down. What is best, what
is truest and gentlest, in Journalism as in Life, will
certainly survive. Not, however, before Thermidor,
the hot month, which shall consume the *mouchard*
and the scandal-monger, and scorch up the sham-

priest and sham-philanthropist.   Even now we
may see how these organs of public opinion turn
like wild beasts and rend each other.   Even now
we may see how the venomous press turns *en masse*
on those journals which still remember the laws of
literature and preserve their self-respect.   Fortunately, such journals still exist, to point the way
to literary reformation.

URB. I fancy they are many—the others few.
But (may I confess it ?) I find the many very dull.
I like hot spice in my daily literature.

ALI. You are a Philistine—no, I beg your
pardon, a Cockney.   Ah, well, after all, the
Cockney triumphs!

URB. If Boston is the 'hub' of the universe,
Cockayne is the 'hub' of civilization.   Come to
your governing classes, and to your jurisprudence.

ALI. Our governing classes no longer really
govern ; if they still occupy the high seats of
Olympus, it is in impotence of Godhead, trembling
at Demogorgon—Socialism, the Mob, the Plébiscite.
Some of them, in sheer despair, spring down to
join the anarchists.   Our jurisprudence, once
founded on faith in the Divine Order, once rational
and honest, is now rapidly disintegrating under the
influence of atheists who hourly take the oath to
God, and the cruel catholicism of superstition is
rapidly being supplanted by the cruel Puritanic
bias of modern materialism.   Personally, I have
been much censured for having proclaimed my

astonishment that an agnostic Judge should
sentence a criminal to death in the name of a
Deity in whom he, the Judge, does not believe.
Such an act, in my opinion, is of the very nature
of Jesuitical insincerity. I would go further, and
assert that no official of avowed infidelity should
hold office in a Christian land. Observe, however,
that I am not vindicating Christianity, but merely
pleading for moral consistency. The day indeed
is not far distant when, under the New Terror,
the term Christianity will be abolished.

URB. How so ? And what term would you
suggest in its place ?

ALI. Any term which fitly expressed the truth.
We are no longer Christians. Why continue to
use the name ? I know what you would say,
that the word ' Christianity ' expresses all that is
noblest and best in our civilization. That is so ;
but it expresses far more—the supernatural superhuman element in which we have ceased to believe.
If Christianity had been only a creed of rigid
morality, of brotherly kindliness and goodness, of
altruism, it would have perished centuries ago.
Its survival is due to the assertion made, or re
puted to have been made, by its Founder, that
this world, so far from being perfectible, is only
a preliminary to another world, or worlds, of infinitely higher perfection ; that Man is not perish-
able, but individually immortal ; that, in simple
words, Man has an eternal Soul. How many of

our lawyers, our legislators, our publicists, even our clergymen, believe *that?* Yet everywhere the Name of God is used to endorse profane documents, the shibboleth of supernaturalism is employed to sanctify legal fiction. If Jesus Christ walked in the streets to-day, and worked, or pretended to work, miracles of healing, he would be arrested as an impostor and a charlatan, testified against by witnesses who kissed the New Testament, and sent to prison, possibly by a clerical magistrate who had taken the oath that the accused was Divine. You smile. You think I exaggerate the importance of consistency and honesty in such matters? But no law, no jurisprudence, no legislation, can be safely built upon a Lie. If we are Christians, we belie our creed, we forswear ourselves, every hour of our lives. If we are not Christians, we are rogues and liars.

Urb. You would, then, abolish Christianity?

Ali. I would abolish all tampering with terms; I would use words to symbolize the truth. I would have the word 'Christianity' confined to the area of its actual believers. I would not allow it to cover, with a mantle of compromise, a Nation which still believes in such paganisms as, for example, the paganism of War. But let us turn for a moment to another point illustrative of the disintegration of jurisprudence under the action of anarchic Parliaments. You observed, no doubt, the recent extraordinary action of the Home Secretary in the

case of that *cause célèbre*, the murder at Crewe.
Now, the point to which I would solicit your
attention is, not the mental aberration of the
gentleman at the Home Office, but the enormity
of the legislation which transfers a public duty to
the shoulders of a political official ; not to the
process of reason by which the Home Secretary
arrived at his lame and impotent conclusion to
execute one of the brothers and to spare the other
and the more guilty, but to the monstrous and
almost incredible fact that a salaried State
Secretary, holding office in the name of a political
majority, has the power to decide absolutely, in
the face of an English Jury, on a question of life
or death.

URB. Such, you are aware, is the law.

ALI. It is the law I am indicting. I have
followed its records, and watched the process by
which human conscience has tried to leaven the
brutality of those legal principles among which
Mr. Justice Stephen has included the 'lawful'
thirst for 'revenge.' It is not so far a cry, as
many think, from the cruelty of the old Roman
law against Parricide, to the new English law
against similar offences. Then, as now, it was
thought expedient to teach tenderness and affection by a process of judicial torture. Then, as
now, the ethics of punishment were primitive,
violent, and irrational. Then, as now, it was part
of the judicial method to illustrate the sinfulness of

slaughter by an official exhibition of the same blood-shed which, in non-official exhibitions, awakens so much natural horror.

URB. I am aware that you have frequently protested against the Death Penalty.

ALI. It is not my purpose at present to enter on the broad question of the expediency of capital punishment under any circumstances whatever. The point to which I desire to draw your attention is the present condition of our *legislation*, as illustrated by the condemnation of the boy-murderers at Crewe. These wretched youths, under circumstances of frightful provocation, took their father's life. They were tried before a jury of twelve intelligent Englishmen, representing, according to English law, the rest of their countrymen, and they were found guilty, but with 'a recommendation to mercy.' Mercy? To whose mercy? Their God's? Their human Judge's? Surely, in this connection, the very word 'mercy' was fatuous and absurd. What the jury meant by that miserable formula, which Officialism compelled them to adopt, was simply this : 'These boys certainly committed parricide, but the facts we have investigated establish that their guilt was qualified, and that they do not deserve to pay, and shall not pay, the full penalty of their crime.' What follows? The chosen representatives of the people having decided that the prisoners are *not* to die, the salaried official straightway puts on the black cap

and condemns them to die, adding another miserable
formula, that he will convey to 'the proper quarter'
the jury's recommendation to mercy. Surely
common-sense must decide that it was the Judge's
business, either to quash the verdict altogether as
against the weight of evidence, or to adopt the finding of the jury and at once to pass some such lesser
sentence as would meet the requirements of the
case? But the Law said 'No!' The Law said
that the formulas of official imbecility should be
pursued throughout. The Law said that the
verdict of English citizens, the true and only
representatives of public opinion and public justice,
shall be referred to a *petit maître* at the Home
Office, to be decided *ex cathedrâ* then and there.
The Caiaphas of the bench transfers his responsibility to a small political Pontius Pilate. 'Shall
these men die? The voice of the people cries
"Spare them," but it is for thee, O Pilate, to
decide.' Well would it be for all of us if the new
Pilate Punchinello, like his nobler prototype, had
washed his hands of the whole business. He could
not do that. He might, nevertheless, have remembered that his position as arbitrator was only
another miserable formula. He might have
recognised the fact that the sentence of mercy
had *already* been pronounced, by the only men
authorized by the nation to pronounce it, and that
he, as a political official, was only the mouthpiece
and the servant of the English nation.

URB. I suppose he acted according to his lights?

ALI. Possibly. We have had 'hanging' judges and 'hanging' Home Secretaries, all existing in the miasmic fog of our jurisprudence. Fortunately for humanity, we have no longer our 'hanging' *Juries*, for at the present stage of our enlightenment it is difficult to get together *twelve* human beings equally devoid of the reasoning faculty and the sentiment of humanity. On the breath of no one individual, however just, however powerful, should hang an issue of life or death. Review again this tale of Parricide, in the light which shines everywhere save in the sunless cave of Officialism. The murdered man was, we know, a husband and a father; he had a wife whom he tortured and tried to kill, and he had children who were maddened by the sufferings he inflicted on their mother. ' True,' the old Roman law would say, and is still saying ; ' but he was, above all, a *father.*' I endeavoured a little while ago, you remember, to suggest the outlines of a Science of Sentiment ; such a Science may serve us now. Sentiment as Science affirms that the man who brings children into the world voluntarily assumes the highest of all human responsibilities. These children were created by his will, not their own, and the first duty which emerges from their creation rests on *him*, not *them*. He has to establish his fatherhood, ethically, by acts of help and love. If he fails in these, if by deeds of cruelty and repres-

sion he condemns his own unhappy issue to misery
and despair, he has forfeited the privileges of
human paternity. Now, the father of these poor
boys was, ethically, no father at all. He was only
a strange man in the house, wilfully responsible
for all its daily sorrows. Peruse the record of his
infamous misdeeds ; turn to the record of all that
his children suffered at his hands ; then ask yourself if the crime for which his sons were condemned was truly Parricide ? It was Homicide,
truly ; but it was only the homicide of a strange
man.

URB. Rather a sentimental view of the case.

ALI. The Cant of Sentiment upholds that fatherhood in blood is all-sufficient. The Science of
Sentiment discovers that fatherhood in blood may
be merely the result of human selfishness, cruelty,
and lust. Those who bring children into the
world are conjuring up the very Spirit of Life, and
woe to them if that Spirit should be offended !
The day, indeed, is not far distant when human
Conscience will decide that to increase the number
of created beings, heedless of the responsibility
which comes with their birth, or without the power
and means to condition them into well-being, is a
crime even worse than any passionate deed of
extermination.

URB. Are you not a little inconsistent ?
Almost in the same breath that you advocate
the liberty of the subject, you admit the necessity

3

of such legislative restrictions as would lessen the
liberties resulting in over-population.

ALI. By no means. I advocate no legislative
restrictions.

URB. Yet you fully realize the baseness of bringing human beings recklessly into the world, in
defiance of the responsibility incurred by so
doing.

ALI. Fully ; but no legislation can touch that
baseness. The law of Nature itself must rid us of
it. ((The modern tendency of Legislation is, on the
one hand, to superintend natural processes, and, as
I have expressed it, to *force* the work of evolution ;
and on the other hand, by lessening personal
responsibility, to preserve, artificially, inferior
types.) Our preposterous Poor Laws are not only
fostering what is worthless, but destroying that
individual charity which, like mercy, is twice blest
—blessing him that gives and him that takes.
Officialism is the robe of Lazarus, covering a
thousand open sores. Our poor have recognised
this, in their loathing of such protection as that
of the workhouse.

URB. Then you would have unlimited private
charity, and unlimited population ?

ALI. Both should be regulated by the moral
growth of individuals. Wise charity and sympathy
will not multiply the worthless, by freeing them of
all the rewards and punishments of personal
activity. Unlimited population will be checked

by one thing only—the realization on the part of individuals of moral responsibilities. In other words, Progress must move upwards from the subject, not downwards from the legislator. That the unnatural motion is now superseding the natural proves the certainty of my coming Reign of Terror. ⸢That New Terror will, at least temporarily, be the submergence of individual freedom and activity under the waves of political and social anarchy—legislation, if you like the name better. ⸥ Let me enumerate once more a few of its characteristics, already touched upon and illustrated :

1. Political Tyranny of Majorities, culminating in Providence made Easy, or so-called Beneficent Legislation.

2. The Destruction of Personal Rewards and Punishments, the general paralysis of Individual Effort.

3. Espionage in all the affairs of Life, public and private.

4. Trades Unionism, and Supreme Despotism of the Public Will ; Protection of the Unfittest.

5. The New Socialism, organizing to suppress free action in all matters of contract and personal activity.

6. The New Journalism, flaunting over the grave of Free Literature, and clothed in completed Ignorance.

7. The New Jurisprudence, practically con-

founding the empirical laws of expedience with the absolute laws of ethics.

8. Moral Sanitation, extending from things civic to things ethic and personal, while placing written books and painted pictures in the same category as works of drainage and lighting.

9. The New Ethics, scientific, saturnine, yet Puritanical, and :

10. The New Priesthood of Science, regulating the growth and development of the species, the freedom and activity of mankind, by the arbitrary laws of empirical and materialistic discovery.

URB. And the result ?

ALI. That of the *Plébiscite* in France, of Deutschthumm in Germany, of legislative Tyranny all over the world. No man will be a free agent ; every man will find his life's work done for him by beneficent legislation ; he will breed according to legislative enactments ; he will be fed, clothed, and protected, not by his own hands, but out of the common purse. Property of all descriptions will be abolished. While the iron bands of Morality will be drawn tighter, so that neither man nor woman can breathe freely, Morality and Immorality will be licensed equally. There will be no books, for there will be no book-readers. Life will be superintended in all departments according to Acts of Parliament. The legislative politician, already the bane of public life, will become the authorized representative of organized Anarchy.

There will be no class distinctions, not even the
distinction between wise and foolish, good and bad,
for all men will be equally wise, good, and apathetic.
Religion, born of human emotion, fostered by
human necessity, will become extinct as the dodo ;
or if it survives, will be dealt with by the
authorized Inspectors of Lunacy. England will
be well lighted, well drained, moral, conventional,·
an excellently-regulated Machine. Prostitution,
of course, will remain, and War, since the new
Legislation recognises them as disagreeable necessities ; but they also will be providentially superintended.

URB. Well, after all, you have described a
Cosmos, not a Chaos. Anything is surely better
than the poverty and misery which now surround
us, than the system which gives superfluity to the
rich and starves the innumerable poor. My dear
Alienatus, I thought you a Socialist and a
Radical ; I find you actually arguing for the
status quo.

ALI. That shows how little you understand me
—how little you understand human nature. I
have defined true Socialism, not as the arbitrary
will of those who would altogether destroy institutions and crush freedom of individual action, not
as the rule of the Mob and its mouthpiece the
Demagogue, but as the combination of free
individuals to limit general legislation wherever
it paralyzes personal endeavour and destroys

personal rewards. I am therefore a true Socialist; that is, a man eager for the common good, but one who believes that good can only be attained by such complete freedom in life, morality and religion as is compatible with the general growth and welfare. In the same sense, I am a Radical; but to be a Radical, one who reforms at the *root*, and not the branches, is not to be a reckless destroyer of good and beautiful institutions. When I contend *contra* Professor Huxley for the natural freedom and equality of men, I do not mean that all men are equal in power or in intelligence—to say as much would be the height of folly; what I do mean is that every man has *per se* a right to his own unfettered activities, and their results, and that, as a corollary, no system of society is to be upheld which paralyzes these activities by vested interests arbitrarily created. I am for Freedom in full measure, but not for the Freedom which is anarchic. As a member of the social organization, I cheerfully submit to the necessary conditions which make Society possible. As a free individual, I refuse to submit to Society in matters of private conduct and private opinion. Legislation may drain the street in which I dwell; it shall not touch the faith in which I live, or brand me as reactionary and immoral because I demand free liberty of action in all matters which do not infringe on the liberties of other free individuals.

No man, no body of men, shall legislate for my Soul. All spiritual qualities cease to exist, when they cease to be spontaneous. All conduct ceases to be moral, when it becomes conventional—*i.e.*, when it fails to represent the activity and the ambition of the individual. I cannot be made good or bad by Act of Parliament. Legislation may convert me into an animal mechanism ; but I prefer annihilation itself to that contingency.

URB. And this new Reign of Terror ? Do you think that it will last ?

ALI. God knows ; but while it does last, everywhere there will be stagnation, which is Death. Man, having deposed the gods, will have to reckon with the last god, Humanity, that final apparition of the Demogorgon. Woe to him, if in dread of the Shape he sees as in a mirror, he becomes his own slave ! Woe to him if, to appease his thirst and hunger for the loaves and fishes of the earth, he sacrifices to Social Despotism the freedom of his living Soul !

ARE MEN BORN FREE AND EQUAL?

A Controversy.

ARE MEN BORN FREE AND EQUAL?*

No more crowning illustration of the incapacity of the scientific mind to grasp philosophical propositions could possibly be found than the criticism of the Socialistic theories of Rousseau, just published by Professor Huxley in the *Nineteenth Century*. Admirably as he is equipped for the light skirmishing of popular knowledge, Professor Huxley fails altogether to understand the great French idealist, just as surely as he fails, in his perversion of Herbert Spencer, to grasp the meaning of our greatest English philosopher ; and both in the matter of his argument and in the manner of its expression, he exhibits the logical insecurity of the specialist transformed into the dilettante. Great wisdom and insight, attaining to almost prophetic vision, cannot be combated by the random shots of mere intelligence, and all the Professor's cleverness, all his liberal culture,

* The following letters appeared in the *Daily Telegraph* in January and February, 1890. They originated in the attempt of Professor Huxley to discredit Mr. Spencer's theory of absolute political ethics.

does not save him from the fate of those who
criticise great propaganda unsympathetically, and
from the outside. So serious a social issue, however, hangs on the advocacy by a distinguished
man of retrograde and anti-human political theories,
that it may be worth while to point out the fallacy,
nay, the absurdity, of Professor Huxley's main
contention.

Nothing is easier, as we all know, than to
ridicule the extravagances into which Rousseau
was carried by his discovery, *viâ* Hobbes and
Locke, of the natural equality of men, by showing
how his splendid imagination ran riot among ex-
traordinarily fanciful pictures of primitive perfection.
He was careful, nevertheless, to warn us that these
pictures were possibly imaginary and illusory—
as Science has, indeed, proved them to be—and
were rather premonitions of what would be than
visions of what had been. When, however, he
asserted that men were born free and equal, and
that Civilization had destroyed to a perilous extent
their natural freedom and equality, he never meant
to say—as Professor Huxley makes him say—
that the physical and intellectual faculties of
individuals were uniform in quality. His thesis
was a sane and a sublime one, already recognised
in our jurisprudence, that so far as moral rights
were concerned, all human beings, by the law of
nature, stand in the same practical category. Gifts
of genius and of insight, although the birthright

of individuals, confer no prescriptive rights of moral
exemption ; they distinguish certain men, as colour
and odour distinguish certain flowers, as fleetness
and beauty distinguish certain animals, but they
do not free the possessors from the ordinary conditions of physical and moral being, to which conditions all men alike are born.   Shakespeare the
Seer resembles Hodge the boor in all the characteristics of an eating, drinking and sleeping animal,
and, further, as a unit in the body political and
social.   The two are equal by nature in all the
fundamental conditions of life, in all the limitations
of human vitality.   But Rousseau went a great deal
further than this.   He contended that intellectual
culture,   or   civilization,   so   far   from   necessarily
improving the individual man, not unfrequently
led to moral deterioration—a monstrous assumption from the point of view of specialists like
Professor Huxley, but a perfectly tenable one
from the standpoint of those who set instinct and
insight above special acquirement.   The history of
mankind, more particularly the biographies of great
men, is full of incidents which establish the paradox that a wise man is frequently a fool, and that
a man of strong reasoning power is often a moral
weakling.   It is questionable, in fact, whether the
advance of the race in Sociology, in Art, in Literature, in Science, has been accompanied with any
real advance of the individual—whether, to put
the issue into other words, any amount of personal

culture renders a man superior to his fellows in those primary sympathies and affections which condition the lives of the lordliest and the least intelligent. Humanity has doubtless developed in power and knowledge, but individual men remain very much what they have been from the beginning of society. To grasp this point thoroughly, and to understand whither the mighty insight of Rousseau was directed, we must understand that in the eyes of the philosopher of Geneva, as in those of the founder of Christian ethics, moral qualities were absolute, while intellectual gifts were merely relative and subsidiary. Let us take, by way of analogy, one day of a great and wise man's life, and contrast it for a moment with another of a life which is neither great nor wise.

William Wordsworth, Poet and Recluse, gets up in the morning, washes and dresses, and after a walk in his garden goes in to breakfast. Reads the news from London, and à propos of some new production of Keats or Shelley, avers that it 'contains no more poetry than a pint-pot.' Goes for a long walk over the mountains with his sister Dorothy, and being full of matter for a new poem, scarcely perceives that his companion is wearied out and waning in health. Towards afternoon, feels again the pangs of a hungry animal, and returns to feed. Possibly, like his pet terrier, has a little nap after dinner. Wakens, and listens to a little music. In the evening, does his correspondence, and adds a few touches to a manuscript poem. A starry night : he stands at his door and surveys the constellations. Certain fine thoughts flow through his mechanism, as the wind agitating an Æolian harp. Feels convinced that there is a benevolent Personal God, and that, on the whole, it is a very beautiful and excellently regulated world. Prays to the Giver of all Good, and, being tired and sleepy, goes to bed early and sleeps the sleep of the Just.

Now, in all this, as possibly in most of the days of other Poets and Philosophers, there is nothing, except the power of writing fine poetry, to distinguish Wordsworth from the uneducated mountain Shepherd who lives in the neighbourhood, and who knows only one book—the Bible of his fathers. The Shepherd gets up, washes, dresses, and after driving his flock from the fold to their pasture, either returns to eat or feeds on bread and cheese on the mountain side. He reads no news, but meeting some neighbour, hears the latest gossip from the market town. Spends the day loafing on the mountain, and when he is hungry and thirsty eats and drinks again. If the weather is fine, has a nap among the heather. Drives home his flock in the evening, and sits down for a smoke among his family. Glances out at the shining night and feels—or, possibly, does not feel—a certain sense of awe and loneliness. Remembers what his father has taught him, that there is a God up yonder. Prays to that God, and throwing himself down on his humble bed, sleeps the same sleep as his neighbour the poet at Rydal Mount.

These two men have all day fulfilled the same primary functions, and in every process of their day there is more resemblance than divergence ; in other words, the preponderance both of action and feeling is in favour of natural equality. ' Ah, but,' cries the hero-worshipper, ' you have left out the one sign distinguishing one from the other —that of superior intelligence, that of the poetic gift.' I think Wordsworth himself would have been the first to admit that, apart from the accomplishment of written speech, the Shepherd's insight, sympathy, and affections might have been fully equal to his own ; for if the poet of Rydal has taught us anything, it is that the poor and uninstructed, the ignorant of men and books, are among the most beautiful souls of Humanity. The gift of song is glorious in a man, as it is in a nightingale, but it does not necessarily make him better as a human being, and certainly does not free him from the weaknesses and necessities of his human inheritance. Being a gift, it belongs rather to God than to himself. It certainly gives him no privilege of moral superiority.

Be that as it may, my illustration may help the reader to understand what Rousseau really meant when he proclaimed the natural equality of human beings. [He meant that men are born equal, inasmuch as they are subject to the same laws and entitled to the same advantages.] He meant that no man, however·powerful, had a right to accept any pleasure which any other man might not receive on the same terms. He meant that worldly knowledge, including book knowledge, is at the best a limited thing, seeing that all man knows is ' that nothing can be known.' He meant that class distinctions, class prejudices, class pride, class privileges, are the merest appropriation of un-limited selfishness, infringing the rights of Humanity at large. He meant that men would be happier without physical luxury, and purer without in-tellectual pride. True, in picturing his ideal state he went too far, but, going as far as he did, he reached and he defined the limits of the area of social and political freedom. He attained the apogee of his prophetic life when he wrote the ' Savoyard Vicar's Prayer,' which embodies the noblest of his teaching, and answers still the inner-most yearning of the heart of Man.

How far Professor Huxley is from understand-ing the Religion of Equality may be gathered from several of his own expressions. We already know that, speaking as a scientific specialist, he rejects Mr. Spencer's masterly definition of absolute political ethics ; but he goes farther, and finds nothing absolute in any ethics whatever. No man of philosophic perception could have affirmed that 'the equality of men before God is an equality either of insignificance or of imperfection ;' no man of political insight could have suggested that universal suffrage is synonymous with *Laissez faire*. Professor Huxley describes himself as among those 'who do not care for Sentiment and do care for Truth,' forgetting that there is no real Sentiment which is not a truth's adumbration, and assuming, in the true spirit of the age, that what is sentimental must necessarily be false. The series of questions with which he cross-examines modern revolters on the thesis that 'all men are born free and equal,' is surely a *reductio ad absurdum* of the quasi-scientific manner. No one ever talked, as he makes his witnesses talk, of 'the political status of a new-born child,' no one ever contended that, because freedom is born within the human flesh, it becomes an actual factor before that flesh is conditioned into moral intelligence. But it is when we reach the Professor's own conclusions that we discover what his derision of Equality and Freedom really means. His defence of the *status quo*, of the topsy-turvydom of modern society, of the condition of affairs which gives Jacob all the fruits of the earth and leaves Esau to starve in the wilderness, is founded on the plea of 'practical expediency'—a plea on which even Nero might have justified himself to what he termed his conscience in planning the conflagration of Rome. 'There is much to be said,' Professor Huxley thinks, echoing poor

Carlyle, 'for the opinion that Force, effectually and thoroughly used so as to render further opposition hopeless, establishes an ownership which should be recognised as soon as possible!' 'For the welfare of society, as for that of individual men,' he continues, ' it is surely essential that there should be a statute of limitations in respect of the consequences of wrong-doing !' Surely here we have teaching worthier of Mr. Jonathan Wild than of a popular professor in a State whose very religion is founded on the *à priori* assumptions he despises. Science itself should have instructed Professor Huxley, just as surely as Religion does its votaries, that the penalties of wrong-doing are exacted even to the uttermost generation. Is there a statute of limitations to the law of heredity, to the law by which the sins and follies of the fathers are visited upon their children ? If no such statute prevails in the physical, why should it do so in the social and political worlds ? Only one thing can cure evil, and that is the destruction of it at any cost, at any sacrifice. So long as it exists it is a canker and a curse. Assume that our social system is founded on wrong-doing—and Professor Huxley has admitted it—by what possible standard of ethics would he keep it permanent ? Because it ' exists,' and because, since it exists, it is ' expedient.' Talk of the ' sham sentiment ' of Rousseau ; it becomes sublime doctrine by the side of the sham reason of his critic, who, while

4—2

scorning and despising the gospel of *Laissez faire*, in the same breath preaches the essence of that gospel !

In a second letter I will, with your permission, endeavour to explain more fully than is at present possible the ethical standpoint of those propagandists who, in suggesting crucial reforms of our present social and political systems, base their arguments on the absolute principle of the natural freedom and equality of men.

I am, etc.,

ROBERT BUCHANAN.

[To the above letter Professor Huxley first replied as follows, but in the meantime an editorial article had appeared commenting somewhat adversely on my suggestions.]

To the Editor of the ' Daily Telegraph.'

SIR,

I have read Mr. Robert Buchanan's letter, which has been kindly sent to me. I would not on any account interfere with so characteristic a development of latter-day Rousseauism—so many people fancy that it is dead and buried, and that I have wasted my time in slaying the slain.

I am, faithfully yours,

T. H. HUXLEY.

3, JEVINGTON GARDENS, EASTBOURNE,
   January 24.

To the Editor of the ' Daily Telegraph.'

SIR,

I had hoped, in the present discussion, to avoid current politics altogether ; for it is impossible to touch on political issues—especially in the columns of a daily newspaper — without awakening a storm of prejudice and misunderstanding. I shall still endeavour to steer clear of contemporary broils, although your own comments on my first letter do certainly invite polemical treatment. Will you permit me to say, however, that I am more astonished at your indirect championship of the doctrines of expediency than at your quite irrelevant diatribe on the personal character and conduct of Rousseau ? Perhaps, however, you do not quite realize that your attack is less upon the religion of modern Socialism than upon the Creed of Christianity itself? The strongest, or, at any rate, the most accepted, argument against that creed has been that it is, although theoretically excellent, practically impossible. Society has refused from time immemorial to be ruled in the conduct of life by either its principles or its precepts. Men hoard up riches in this world, and when one cheek is smitten they do not offer the other. They pray in the Temple, but they curse and cheat in the market-place. Interrogated on this inconsistency, they explain that adherence to the absolute

tenets of their religion would be suicidal. Even
some of our most Christian teachers have protested that the Christ was too superhuman, too
transcendently impolitic, to be followed quite all
the way along the thorny path of self-abnegation.
So that when you say that Rousseau's doctrine
is refuted at every point by the facts of life, you
should add that Christianity also is so refuted ;
and you would be, from the political and historical point of view, perfectly right. The Founder
of Christianity, however, carefully distinguished
between the adherence we may find it expedient
to give to Cæsar and that higher adherence we
must give to God. He paused at first principles
and went no further, hoping against hope that
those first principles were seeds which would grow
surely in the conscience of humanity. ' Love one
another' was his highest and holiest admo-
nition—one which we, in this Christian country,
carry out by allowing wealth to accumulate and
men to decay ; by permitting, as in the case
of the deer forests of Scotland, the accidental
wealth of one or two men to mean the destruction
and expatriation of thousands ; by suffering, as
in Ireland, a landlordism without even the excuse
of capital, to drive a whole Nation into despair
and into crime.

You ask me, naturally enough, if somewhat
flippantly, to name those absolute ethical principles on which I and far more able propagandists

would base the reconstruction of Society, while at the same time you seek to stultify my advocacy by suggesting that it is doubtless purely sentimental, and must conflict on every side with the results of daily experience. Now, it would be idle as well as impertinent for me, at the very time when the/sanest and clearest intellect known to us at present on this planet has occupied itself with the exposition of absolute principles in ethics (to the great mental confusion of scientific Philistia and Professor Huxley), to attempt in my perfunctory way to define those principles. For their definition I must refer you to Mr. Herbert Spencer's more recent writings—luminous as all that comes from that crystal pen, unanswerable as most of the arguments that come from that master mind. Mr. Spencer himself has told us, in words of dignified remonstrance, that his exposition has been misunderstood and perverted at every point by Professor Huxley ; and so, if we examine the matter closely, we shall find the case to be. Mine is a far humbler task, to explain as far as possible to the hasty readers of a great daily newspaper, in as clear and popular language as is at my command, a few simple points of that propagandism which proposes to redress centuries of wrongdoing, and possibly to reconstruct society.

One word, before I proceed, concerning your own estimate of the teachings of Rousseau, which estimate varies little, if at all, from that of Professor Huxley. Forgetful altogether that I began by agreeing with Rousseau on the subject of first principles, and *not* by approving the hastily-designed political and social structure he based upon them, you resort to the stereotyped mode of polemics, that of attacking the great doctrinaire's personal character. Here, however, you unconsciously support my main thesis—that great intellect has little or nothing to do with moral goodness, and that Rousseau, in much of his conduct, was a sort of philosophical Jack Shepherd. It should be remembered, however, that Rousseau made no concealment whatever of his moral distemperature and social larcenies ; that standing, as he expressed it, before the Judgment Seat, he made a clean breast of his sins and weaknesses, whereas most other men have chosen to hide, rather than to discover, their moral littleness. While I doubt the expediency of such revelations, I believe them to have been made in all sincerity, and I am also quite sure that the record of most men, if so made public, would shock propriety as much as the record of Rousseau. The one charge which you revive against the husband of poor Thérèse—that of abandoning his children to the foundling basket—is, though horrible enough, capable of some defence, in so much as the suppression of personal instincts it involves is quite consistent with the theory that the care of offspring should devolve upon the community at large. It is superfluous, however, to extenuate the conduct of a man who was in the private concerns of life scarcely a sane agent, who was swept into endless folly and inconsistency by sheer force of temperament. For the rest, the good old fallacy resuscitated by you, that Rousseau was personally responsible for the excesses of the Revolution, was killed and buried long ago. The Revolution was the direct consequence of the wrong-doing of Society, causing the collapse of an ancient and effete political system, and had little or nothing to do, either directly or indirectly, with literature. It came from the masses who had never learned to read, and who sought not books, but bread. Rousseauism, and all the other 'isms' of the pre-Revolutionary period, were the amusement of the aristocracy of culture, and were to the masses of the French nation, previous to the promulgation of certain catchwords by the leaders of the national movement, about as intelligible as double Dutch. You suggest, moreover, that the points which I mention as illustrative of Rousseau's insight are mere 'truisms' which no one denies or ever did deny, and that the really important matter in Rousseau's teaching is the constructive portion of the 'Social Contract.' Had this been so Rousseau would have been forgotten long ago. It was his perception of those very 'truisms' which made him a Prophet and a Seer.

It is his insight into first principles which makes
him living to this hour. How many of us admit
even now, or prove by their conduct to their
fellows, that moral goodness is better than intellectual power ?   How many of us feel in our
hearts and illustrate in our lives that luxury and
pride, arrogance of knowledge or of birth, are evil
things ?   How many of us proclaim that the war
between nations, like the war between individuals,
daily mocks the commandment which said, ' Thou
shalt not kill '?   Truisms, say you ?   Truisms to
which almost every institution of our society, every
glory of our civilization, gives the lie ; truisms in
the teeth of which a successful soldier may rise up
and recommend to us, as General Wolseley did
the other day, the example of a nation of atheists
and martinets as one worthy of English imitation ;
truisms which no one practically admits to be true ;
truisms which, when advanced to justify the enthusiasm of Humanity, you and other publicists smile
at, and relegate to the regions of sentimental
superstition.   Why, Christianity itself has become
a truism—a fetish to swear by when we rob our
neighbour and corrupt our neighbour's wife.   Its
excellent moral principles are admitted, even by
those who dismiss its dogmas, as so firmly established as scarcely to be worth discussion.   What I
and other propagandists want, however, is for that
religion, which is essentially the religion of equality,
to be tried in practice.   It has never been tried

yet, save by a few isolated individuals from Father
Damien backwards. Who knows but that, after
all, it might serve ; that it might be better at
any rate than the Gospel according to the Printer's
Devil and St. Mammon's current Epistle to the
Philistines ? Who knows but that, with a little
scientific adjustment, it might prove almost as
practicable as the political creed which tells us
that the *status quo* of the Impenitent Thief, who
still holds the plunder his ancestor stole, is to be
respected and consolidated, according to a certain
' statute of limitations '?

The true political problem, placed before themselves by those propagandists who, like myself, are
Socialists only in the good and philosophical sense,
and who are not, like mere Communists, enemies
of all vested interests whatsoever, is to regenerate
Society without destroying that part of its structure which experience proves to be sound. The
principle that men are born free and equal does
not imply, as its opponents frequently suggest, that
absolute intellectual equality is possible, or that
men, being free, are free to do exactly as they
please ; it merely means, as I have said, that each
unit of society has equal rights of membership, and
complete liberty of action within the scope of the
common organization. Absolute individual freedom is of course impossible, as citizenship, *i.e.,*
equality and fraternity, implies due recognition of
the rights of others. The difficulty, then, is how

to adjust the relations of human beings in such a
manner as to secure the utmost amount of liberty
and equality possible. While the degrees of
power and wealth can never be exactly the same,
and while due allowance should be made for
the rewards of individual energy and industry,
care should be taken that the accumulation of
power and wealth from generation to generation should not lead to the aggrandizement of
one class at the expense of another, or to the
security of any one individual through the social
destruction of any of his fellows. This means,
translated into other words, that the rights of
acquired property are subservient to those of the
general prosperity ; that such luxury as an individual possesses in excess of his rational needs is
conditioned by the destruction of certain other
individuals to whom that luxury might have provided the necessaries of life.) Here we reach,
without turning aside into a very difficult region
of political economy, a first great principle—that
every working member of society has a right to
a share of those necessaries which alone make
existence possible. Can it be argued, in the face
of the statistics of existing poverty, with the
knowledge of the daily and hourly shipwreck of
human lives, that the necessaries of life are so
distributed ?

Here, again, we touch one of those ' truisms '
which everyone admits, but few or no men act

upon ; and we shall find, indeed, that each principle of just Socialism is in the nature of a truism.
We have already learned, however, *contra* Rousseau, that social freedom is limited, unlike natural
or moral freedom, which is absolute. Certain
rights of property would still remain intact, under
any disintegration caused by the first principle, or
truism, already named. ' I do not want to touch
your treasures,' said even Robespierre, ' however
impure their source. I am far more anxious to
make poverty honourable than to proscribe wealth;
the thatched roof of Fabricius need never envy
the palace of Crœsus.'

The second principle which I would name, as
founded on the natural freedom and equality of
men, is equal freedom of *opportunity.* This freedom is being to a large extent secured by the
spread of national education, since no man can
fulfil the rights of citizenship to whom social
neglect and selfishness have denied the very vocabulary of civilization. It is possibly impracticable
at present that every man should have exactly the
same start in life, the same chance of securing
social prosperity; but what the Socialist propagan-
dum demands is some sort of approximation of
starts and chances. The present arbitrary division
of classes is founded on an arrangement which
overworks and denies rational leisure to large
classes of the community in order that other
classes may ' eat, drink, and be merry.' Equal

freedom of opportunity, then, means just distribution of labour—means that Society should not be divided into idlers and drones, that all men should share to a certain extent in the practical work of the world.] Is this the case ? In the face of the ignorance and misery of our labouring classes, of the lives blackened out of human likeness by cruel and endless toil, of our sempstresses spinning out the thin thread of life for a few pence, can any sane man suggest that freedom of opportunity is, under our present social system, possible ?

True, there will always be idlers, and possibly, until the Millennium, there will always be drones. The problem of the higher Socialism is to limit the number of both, by rendering the prizes and the honours of civilization open to all. How to solve that problem? Surely we should go a long way to its solution if we averaged the hours of leisure to all men, and so recognised that want of rest is as certain a sign of pauperization as want of bread.

Here, perhaps you say, is a manifest contradiction, since I postulated in my first letter that natural freedom and equality were, being absolute, altogether independent of relative culture or intellectual acquirement. What I did say was in no sense contradictory, being merely that intellectual culture did not necessarily imply moral advance. For a state of natural freedom and equality, however, the primary vocabulary of civilization is

essential.   A blind man cannot see the sun, and a
man-beast of burthen cannot perform the rational
duties of society.   I contended, however, that the
accumulation of mere knowledge meant nothing,
morally speaking—indeed, knowledge is specialism,
and is only valuable in so far as it discovers
those laws which become the common property
of all.   Thomas Carlyle would certainly be called
a man of culture, of wide and phenomenal information, quite apart from his quasi-prophetic faculty ;
yet what was the culture worth which led him to
rail against all mankind, and to revenge the natural
freedom and equality of a troublesome liver by
abusing the world at large ?   To St. Thomas of
Chelsea, the nigger was 'a servant' by grace of
God ; Macaulay, a 'squat, low-browed, commonplace object'; Coleridge, a 'weltering, ineffectual
being'; Wordsworth, a 'small diluted contempti-
bility'; Keble, of the 'Christian Year,' a 'little
ape,' and Keats's poems 'dead dog'; Charles Lamb,
a 'detestable abortion'; Grote, a person with
a 'spout mouth'; Cardinal Newman, one without 'the intellect of a moderate-sized rabbit';
Mr. Gladstone, 'one of the contemptiblest men,
a spectral kind of phantasm'; and Mill, his dear
friend Mill, a 'frozen-out logic-chopping machine.'
True, great genius is great wisdom, and from this
point of view great genius is very rare.   Yet who
can help thinking, in glancing over the lives of our
cleverest and greatest men, that increase in special

knowledge too often means increase in obtusity, in
folly ?   Even the gentle Darwin, a soul at peace
with all men, and wise, surely, in his generation, has
told us that the only imaginative delight of his age
(when all his splendid faculties still remained
intact) was to read trashy novels, that he 'hated'
Shakespeare, and that to turn to a play of Shakespeare 'made him sick !'   Reading these records of
men, justly esteemed for their power and knowledge, one is almost disposed to exclaim, with
Voltaire, that 'the good folk who have no fixed
principles on the nature of things, who do not know
what is, but know very well what is not, these are
our true philosophers.'

To illustrate all the principles which the higher
Socialism accepts as absolute would be utterly
impossible in the space of a newspaper letter.   I
will mention only one other, of the most paramount
importance at the present juncture.   A corollary
of the thesis that men are born free and equal,
morally speaking, is the certainty that no unnecessary or arbitrary limits should be made to
freedom of private action and private conduct.
Mr. Spencer has pointed out, with his own un-
equalled lucidity, the dangers which Society is at
present running from over-legislation in matters
social.   The tendency of even modern philanthropy is to class groups of men and women in
comfortable pigeonholes, and to arrange for them
down to the smallest details the functions and

duties of life ; and Science itself, like a gigantic
Mrs. Pardiggle, is assuming the airs of a social
censor and peripatetic district-visitor. Heaven
forbid that the services which true Science has
done to spread the common particles of Light, and
to remedy human ignorance and human wretchedness, should be overlooked or forgotten! But
moral legislation based on empirical knowledge, like
religious legislation based on barren dogma, may go
too far. Talking the other day with a London
physician of great experience, and in full sympathy
with the scientific reorganization of society, I was
surprised to hear him express the opinion that the
' model ' dwellings prepared for the working classes
had been far from an unmixed blessing ; that they
were comfortless and cheerless for beings who were
often unable to provide necessary food and fuel,
and that they destroyed in a great measure the
sense of personal independence. Elsewhere, indeed,
we are threatened no longer, as of old, with the
religious tyranny of the Priest, but with the presumption of the moral and social Legislator.
County Councils, Vigilance Committees, Societies
for moral sanitation, have encroached upon the
liberty of the subject, even to the extent of deter-
mining what he may read and know. Not content
with regulating his physical well-being, they have
endeavoured to regulate the amount of Light and
Knowledge he may enjoy ; and hence the deathless bigotry of English Puritanism, collaborating in

5

despair with the new-born bigotry of scientific discovery, is limiting human freedom in almost every walk of life.

I have named three principles, on the triumph or failure of which depends the future of Society : equal freedom to share the necessaries of life, equal freedom of opportunity to advance, equal freedom to shape individual thought and action within the necessary limitations of political organization.   If the *status quo* admits these principles, and if they are allowed free scope of activity, then nothing more is to be said.   The higher Socialism contends that they may be recognised generally, even as ' truisms,' but that, in most of the affairs of life, in nearly all its practical conduct, they are entirely disregarded.   Large bodies of the community have practically no food to eat, no freedom to earn even common sustenance ; still larger classes, though they may gain the common necessaries of life, are, by the cruelty of their labour for bare bread and from the pressure of the organization around them, forbidden the opportunity to advance a single step ; and classes even yet larger are, by the spirit of temporizing and compromising (approved as we have seen by even scientists like Professor Huxley), denied the natural freedom of human beings, on the plea that, under a political ' statute of limitations,' the force originally founded on wrong-doing ought to be respected !

Well, Rousseau's sublime paradox still holds :

' Man is born free, and everywhere he is in chains.'
It is useless, or it seems useless, to argue against
those who, like Professor Huxley and your
wandering-witted ' Hereditary Bondsman,' contend
that the freedom and equality of Nature means
(what it was never supposed even by Rousseau
to mean) that all men are alike, that there is no
such thing as differentiation of power or character,
and that one man, however degraded and uninstructed, is as good as any other. This is
merely the *reductio ad absurdum* (very useful to
the holders of vested interests) of the argument
which proves that every member of the community
has a born right to share the common benefits and
privileges of Humanity ; that, in other words,
neither the aristocracy of power nor the aristocracy
of culture is entitled, beyond the necessities of the
common preservation, to limit the action of human
freedom, human enjoyment, and human opportunity.
Men advance more surely by freedom than by
restraint, necessary as certain restraints may be.
Before the outbreak of the English Revolution,
personal prerogative, the arbitrary will of one
sincere political bigot, had strangulated English
Liberty. Englishmen arose *en masse*, and Liberty,
in the political sense, was saved. Before the
outbreak of the great French Revolution,
Catholicism had almost destroyed the conscience
of a great Nation. The inevitable cataclysm came,
with what terrible accompaniments we all know.

5—2

At the present hour, at the very time when the free thought of England is at its brightest and best, when the scientific and historic methods have disintegrated the whole mass of religious superstition, another great upheaval is imminent, to the peril, perhaps the destruction, of our whole social system.

> ' Le passé n'est pour nous qu'un triste souvenir ;
> Le présent est affreux, s'il n'est point d'avenir,
> Si la nuit du tombeau détruit l'être qui pense.'

So sang Voltaire. A colossal Hand, which some call the hand of Destiny and others that of Humanity, is putting out the lights of Heaven one by one, like candles after a feast. It behoves us, then, to watch heedfully that the same Hand, having emptied the heavens, does not touch the lowly but life-illumining lights of Earth. The fairest of these lights is Liberty, is the principle of natural freedom and equality, without which individual growth would be impossible, and social organization, as men now understand it, an impossibility.

I am, etc.,
ROBERT BUCHANAN.

P.S.—Some idea of the absurdities of Over-legislation may be gathered from the regulations of Saint Just, quoted in Von Sybel's ' History of the French Revolution ' : No servants, no gold and silver utensils, no child under sixteen to eat meat, nor any adult to eat meat on three days of the decade ; boys at the age of seven to be handed over to the national school, where they will be taught to speak little, to endure hardships, and to train for war ; divorce to be free to all ; friendship ordained a public institution, every citizen on attaining majority being bound to proclaim his friends, and if he had none, to be banished ; if any one committed a crime, his friends were to be banished, etc. This, it must be admitted, is the Code of Nature with a vengeance !

[My second letter caused Professor Huxley to break his vow of silence, and answer as follows :]

To the Editor of the ' Daily Telegraph.'

SIR,

I have already offered a cordial welcome to Mr. Robert Buchanan on the occasion of his *début* in the theatre of political speculation ; and the sincerity of my wish that he may continue to exhibit the results of the poetic method, in its application to the dry facts of natural and civil history, is nowise affected by the circumstance that he considers me to be an advocate of ' retrograde and anti-human political theories,' a defender ' of the topsy-turveydom of modern society,' and, altogether, a scientific Philistine of the worst description.

I do not address you for the purpose of combating these opinions, or even to set forth some pleas for mercy which might weigh in my favour with any judge less confident of his competency. I would not even be so indecent as to linger too long on this side of annihilation ; but, unless I be worse than other criminals, I trust you will permit me to send a few words to the scattered remnant of the people in whose minds the ana - thema just fulminated has not extinguished any little credit I may have hitherto possessed. It appears that there are 'three principles on the triumph or failure of which depends the future of society : equal freedom to share the necessaries of life ; equal freedom of opportunity to advance ; equal freedom to shape individual thought and action within the necessary limitations of political organization. If the *status quo* admits these principles, and if they are allowed free scope of activity, then nothing more is to be said.'

Now, it seems to me that the political principles of which I have been a tolerably active advocate all my life, and of which I hope to remain an advocate so long as I have the power to speak or write, may be expressed, though somewhat clumsily, by just these words. Perhaps I deceive myself, but it really is my impression that I am hardly open to the charge of having failed to assert freedom of thought and action any time these five-and-thirty years. Unless I am dreaming, I have done what lay in my power to promote those measures of public education which afford the best of opportunities for advancement to the poorer members of society ; and that in the teeth of bitter opposition on the part of fanatical adherents of the political philosophy which Mr. Buchanan idolizes, the consistent application of which reasoned savagery to practice would have left the working classes to fight out the struggle for existence among themselves, and bid the State to content itself with keeping the ring.

As to equal freedom to share the necessaries of life, I really was not aware that anybody is, or can be, refused that freedom.* If a man has anything to offer in exchange for a loaf which the baker thinks worth it, that loaf will certainly be given to him ; but if he has nothing, then it is not I, but the extreme Individualists, who will say that he may starve. If the State relieves his necessities, it is not I but they who say it is exceeding its powers ; if private charity succours the poor fellow, it is not I but they who reprove the giver for interfering with the survival of the fittest. Logically enough, they ask, Why preserve Nature's failures ? That a philosophy of which these are the unvarnished results should rouse a humanitarian enthusiast, whose sincerity is beyond question, to be its champion is singular ; though not more singular than the vilipending of Saint Just for

* What, no one ?

over-legislation, by a worshipper of Rousseau. An
ingrained habit of scientific grovelling among facts
has led me to the conclusion that Jacobin Over-
legislation was a direct consequence of Rousseauism.
These gentlemen guillotined the people who did
not care to be free and equal and brotherly in their
fashion. If anyone doubt the fact, I would advise
him to read M. Taine's volume on the 'Jacobin ·
Conquest of France,' which is all the more interesting just now, as it affords the best of com-
mentaries on the Parnellite conquest of Southern
Ireland.

The source of a great deal of the wrath which
seems to have been raised by my essay appears to me
to lie in the circumstance that my critics are too
angry to see that the point of difference between us
consists, not in the appreciation of the merits of freedom in the three directions indicated, but in regard
to the extent of those 'necessary limitations' of freedom to which all agree. My position is that those
limitations are not determinable by *à priori*
speculation, but only by the results of experience ;
that they cannot be deduced from principles of
absolute ethics, once and for all, but that they
vary with the state of development of the polity to
which they are applied. And I may be permitted
to observe that the settlement of this question lies
neither with the celestial courts of Poesy nor with
the tribunals of speculative cloudland, but with
men who are accustomed to live and work amongst

facts, instead of dreaming amidst impracticable formulas.

I am, sir,
Your obedient servant,
T. H. HUXLEY.
EASTBOURNE, *January 27.*

To the Editor of the 'Daily Telegraph.'

SIR,

Unwilling to occupy your space, or to try the patience of your readers needlessly, I abstained, in my letter of the 27th, from dealing with a topic of some importance suggested by a sentence in Mr. Robert Buchanan's second communication. On reflection, however, I am convinced that, in the interest of the public, the omission was an error, and I ask for an opportunity of making reparation. This is the sentence :

'The true political problem, placed before them selves by those propagandists who, like Mr. Spencer, are Socialists only in the good and philosophical sense, and who are not, like mere Communists, enemies of all vested interests what-soever, is to regenerate society without destroying that part of its structure which experience proves to be sound.'

Mr. Spencer, therefore, is declared by Mr. Robert Buchanan to be a 'Socialist' 'in the good and philosophical sense.' The other day the

Newcastle Socialists declared that their doctrine concerning land-ownership was founded upon Mr. Spencer's early teachings, and that these had never been really disowned by him. If they are right in this contention, and if, in Mr. Buchanan's eyes, their Socialism is of the 'good and philosophical' sort, then, of course, it may be proper to call Mr. Spencer a Socialist. I offer no opinion on this delicate subject ; but I may be permitted to say that, hitherto, I have laboured under the impression that, whether he is always consistent or not, Mr. Spencer belongs to a school of political philosophy which is diametrically opposed to everything which has hitherto been known as Socialism.*

The variations of Socialism are as multitudinous as those of Protestantism ; but as even a Bossuet must be compelled to admit that the Protestant sects agree in one thing, namely, the refusal to acknowledge the authority of the Pope, so I do not think it will be denied that all the Socialist sects agree in one thing, namely, the right of the State to impose regulations and restrictions upon its members, over and beyond those which may be needful to prevent any one man from encroaching upon the equal rights of another. Every Socialistic theory I know of demands from the Government that it shall do something more than attend to the administration of justice between man and man, and to the protection of the State

* 'For 'Socialism' read 'Communism,' and this is true.—R. B.

from external enemies. Contrariwise, every form
of what is called 'Individualism' restricts the
functions of government, in some or in all directions, to the discharge of internal and external
police duties, or, in the case of Anarchist Individualism, still further. Scientifically founded by
Locke, applied to economics by the *laissez-faire*
philosophers of the eighteenth century, exhaustively
stated by Wilhelm von Humboldt, and developed,
in this country, with admirable consistency and
irrefutable reasoning (the premisses being granted)
by Mr. Auberon Herbert, I had always imagined
Individualism to have one of its most passionate
advocates in Mr. Spencer. I had fondly supposed,
until Mr. Robert Buchanan taught me better, that
if there was any charge Mr. Spencer would find
offensive, it would be that of being declared to be,
in any shape or way, a Socialist. Can it be
possible that a little work of Mr. Spencer's, 'The
Man *versus* the State,' published only six years
ago, is not included by Mr. Buchanan among the
'more recent writings' of which he speaks, as,
perhaps, too popular for his notice ?

However this may be, I desire to make clear to
your readers what the 'good and philosophical'
sort of 'Socialism' which finds expression in the
following passages is like :   .

'There is a notion, always more or less pre-
valent, and just now vociferously expressed, that
all social suffering is removable, and that it is the

duty of somebody or other to remove it. Both
these beliefs are false' (p. 19).

'A creature not energetic enough to maintain
itself must die' is said to be 'a dictum on which
the current creed and the creed of Science are at
one' (p. 19).

'Little as politicians recognise the fact, it is
nevertheless demonstrable that these various public
appliances for working-class comfort, which they
are supplying at the cost of the ratepayers, are
intrinsically of the same nature as those which,
in past times, treated the farmer's man as half-
labourer and half-pauper' (p. 21).

On p. 22, legislative measures for the better
housing of artisans and for the schooling of their
children; on page 24, for the regulation of the
labour of women and children; on page 27, for
sanitary purposes—meet with the like condemnation. And the whole position is neatly summed
up in the answer to the question, 'What is essential to the idea of a slave?' put at page 34. It is
too long to cite in its entirety, but here is the
pith of it:

'The essential question is, How much is he
compelled to labour for other benefit than his own,
and how much can he labour for his own benefit?
The degree of his slavery varies according to the
ratio between that which he is forced to yield up
and that which he is allowed to retain; and it
matters not whether his master is a single person

or a society. If, without option, he has to labour for the society and receives from the general stock such portion as the society awards him, he *becomes a slave to the society. Socialistic arrangements necessitate an enslavement of this kind :* and towards such an enslavement many recent measures, and still more the measures advocated, are carrying us ' (p. 35).

The words which I have italicised, as it seems to me, condemn Socialism of all kinds pretty forcibly; and I further suggest that they appear to be somewhat inconsistent with the acceptance of even a 'good and philosophical' form of that creed. But Mr. Robert Buchanan's profound study of Mr. Spencer's works may enable him to produce contradictory passages. I invite him to do so.

I am, Sir,

Your obedient servant,

T. H. HUXLEY.

EASTBOURNE, *January 29.*

To the Editor of the 'Daily Telegraph.'

SIR,

I have certainly expressed myself very ill if I appeared to be accusing Professor Huxley of wholesale Philistinism, using the word 'Philistinism' to imply a class of intelligence outside of all sympathy with advanced ideals. No one can recognise more fully than myself the service which Science has of late years done for Free-thought and for Humanity, and it was precisely because Professor Huxley was classed, and classed deservedly, among the most distinguished of those Scientists who have sacrificed leisure and comfort for the sake of their fellows, that I was aghast to find him ranging himself once, but I hope not for ever, with the opponents of human progress.

On what plea, may I ask, does Professor Huxley, in classing not only the uncrowned and unhonoured poet, but also the crowned and honoured philosopher, as equally impracticable, arrogate to himself the exclusive mastery of current and historical 'facts'? Seemingly upon the plea that both philosophers and poets dwell in mere cloudland; while he alone, with mailed feet like those of Perseus, walks, dragon-slaying, on the common ground. It is idle to defend the Philosophers, but I think even the Poets have shown their capacity to realize practical problems. One of them, whom all the world honours, sounded the trumpet-note of human freedom when he wrote the 'Areopagitica.' Another of them, less appreciated and far less noble, struck off the bonds of Calas and touched the quick of human doubt when he sang of the Earthquake at Lisbon. Both these men were particularly distinguished —the second no doubt a little barbarously—by their consummate mastery of 'facts.' As to Mr.

Spencer, a philosopher *pur et simple*, he has
marshalled in his ' Principles of Sociology ' and in
the compilations published as practical addenda to
that work, an array of social and historical evidence
unequalled certainly in this generation. Professor
Huxley, on the other hand, burrows so deep among
what he considers ' facts ' that he becomes a sort of
moral troglodyte, and loses knowledge of the upper
sunshine and fresh air.

' An tenebras Orci visat vastasque lacunas.'

And when he emerges into common daylight what
has he to tell us ? Not the grand truths which he
and others have won honour by advocating, but
trivial *ipse dixit* statements, not to be verified in
any daylight whatever. His one ruling idea concerning men is that they must be ' governed '—
washed, cleaned, assorted, parcelled out and labelled,
educated up to the theory that there is a political
' statute of limitations,' and that the force of a
special governmental Providence is a thing not
to be resisted.

Just look a little closer at his statements, that
' there is much to be said for the opinion that
force effectually and thoroughly used, so as to
render further opposition hopeless, establishes an
ownership that should be recognised as soon as
possible,' and that ' for the welfare of society,
as well as for that of individual men, there should
be a statute of limitations in respect of the consequences of wrong-doing.' Let us ask ourselves,

in the first place, by what means men are to
determine the hopelessness of opposition ? The
history of the Christian origins, of Society before
the English or the French Revolutions — nay,
above all, the story of Science itself, of its martyrs
and its conquerors—is the record of struggles
which, from the point of view of contemporary
experience, were altogether ' hopeless.'   Even the
last French Empire, with its triumph over a
generation, with its glorification of the gospel
according to Belial and Baron Hausmann, threatened France with utter despair, crammed and fed
France with all the physical comforts of sensualism
and what Carlyle called ' Devil's dung.'   Then
look   at   results ;   look   at   the   conscience   of
Humanity hoping against hope, rejecting all the
Devil's moral prescriptions ' to be quiet and yield
to the powers which be and must be,' but disintegrating the evil of political institutions by sheer
persistency of opposition.   Whenever Professor
Huxley can show that there is no hope on the
earth or above it, then assuredly, and not till
then, we will sit down with him and ' grovel
among facts.'   Meanwhile, we can only grieve
that the religion of Science, hailed by all of us as
the birth of a new day, is fossilizing already into
a religion of despair ; that the New Politics of
the Expert is a chaos, not a cosmos, has not even
the glimmering of a cosmos.   And the ' statute
of limitations '?   Reduce it to common·sense, and

what does it mean? It admits that modern Society is founded on ancient wrong-doing, that Jacob robbed Esau long ago ; but it asserts that —on the corollary, of course, that 'opposition is hopeless '—Esau, having discovered the theft, and returned to claim his birthright, is to go back to the desert. Biblical History, being much shrewder than modern Science, tells us that he did nothing of the kind. The life corporate of Society, as Science and Philosophy alike agree, is practically an enlarged version of the life of the Individual. Thus, then—to make an illustration—I was knocked down and robbed of all I possessed, twenty, thirty years ago, by a person stronger than myself. For all these years I have been a pauper and an outcast through my enemy's wrong-doing. To-day, after endless suffering, I discover my enemy, a rich and prosperous man, a member (say) of the City Council and the Vigilance Committee, enjoying the unearned increment as well as the original capital he stole. I go to him quietly and say, 'You robbed me years ago ; I am not malicious, and you may keep what has accrued, but I want you, my dear sir, to restore me my original capital.' Am I to be answered, to be silenced, by the statement that the robbery took place such a very long time ago ; and that, my case being hopeless, ownership established had ' better be recognised as soon as possible '?

6

'As to freedom to share the necessaries of life,' says our new Daniel come to Judgment, 'I really was not aware that anybody is, or can be, refused that freedom,' and he illustrates his contention by saying that 'if a man has anything to offer which the baker thinks worth a loaf, that loaf will certainly be given to him.' What a mockery of, not to say 'grovelling in,' facts, have we here! What a putting of the cart before the horse! Society begins by paralyzing a man, by denying to him ordinary light, leisure, instruction, the power of 'having anything to offer'; it converts him into a mere pauper by refusing him the common vocabulary of civilization, and then, when he asks for bread, Society replies, 'Certainly; what have you to give me in exchange?' What Freedom and Equality mean is that every man should be invested with the power *enabling* him, by fair labour, to produce something which is a loaf's value. Is this the case? If it is so, then I am stultified, and the Professor's 'facts' are victorious.

So much for the Professor's general statements. In the postscriptal letter published this morning in your columns, Professor Huxley suggests that I am possibly much mistaken in calling Mr. Herbert Spencer a 'Socialist,' and after quoting certain passages from the philosopher's writings, invites me to quote from the same writings passages which are contradictory. So far as the

Land Question itself is concerned, and the attitude of the Newcastle reformers thereupon, I presume I need not go further than cite the following passage from ' Social Statics ': ' Equity does not permit property in land. For, if one portion of the earth's surface may justly become the property of an individual, held for his sole use and benefit, as a thing to which he has an exclusive right, then other portions of the earth's surface may be so held, and our planet may thus lapse into private hands. It follows that if the landowners have a valid right to its surface, all those who are not landowners have no right at all to its surface.' Mr. Spencer has not been in the habit of disclaiming his own dicta, and the Socialists of Newcastle need have no fear, I fancy, that he will disclaim this one. But, Professor Huxley insists, Mr. Spencer's later utterances are those, not of Socialism, but of Individualism, entirely overlooking the fact that the terms Socialism and Individualism are *not contrary terms, but two facets of the same proposition.* \\

So far as Socialism in our own country is concerned, I ought to know something of its inner nature, for I was born in its odour of popular unsanctity. My father was one of Robert Owen's missionaries, and the personal influence of Owen —one of the greatest and best of doctrinaires— influenced all my early life. Now, Owen's first and cardinal dictum, the one on which he insisted with almost wearisome iteration, was that Man, though born free and equal in the sphere of moral rights, ' was entirely the creature of circumstances,' and the main mission of his life was the mission of Socialism generally—to modify those circumstances so as to produce, practically, a new Moral World. I have yet to learn that such Socialism conflicts to any unnecessary extent with Individualism ; indeed, the history of the movement is full of amusing episodes illustrating the entire freedom of its believers in such matters of personal conduct, and even of opinion, as did not imperil the machinery of the social organism. The well-known and well-meaning Mr. Galpin went about clothed in a simple sack, and the divergences of individual opinion on moral questions led to strange manifestations at New Harmony. Across the Channel, and in France particularly, the story of Socialism is the story of infinite eccentricities. From the personal absurdities of St. Simon down to those of Auguste Comte, from the amazing performances of the speculative Enfantin to those of his pupil and practician Bazard, it is easy to perceive that Socialism postulates the right of a man to do what he pleases so long as he takes his turn at the task-wheel, and does not interfere with the privileges of his fellow-believers.

It is not for me to explain Mr. Spencer, who can so admirably explain himself. It is quite possible that he may disclaim being called ' a

Socialist,' since the word (as Professor Huxley well knows) is so connected in the public mind with an idea of state tyranny; but I wrote advisedly of 'the higher Socialism,' not of the lower, just as I might write of the higher Christianity, to distinguish it from the lower, the historical, and the dogmatic forms of that creed. Professor Huxley's particular instances, in which he finds either an anarchic Individualism or an absurd contradiction, may be very summarily dealt with.

Mr. Spencer has stated, in the first place, that it is quite impossible to remove 'social suffering' altogether, a statement grounded on his experience that, so long as men are men, there will be individual victory and failure. I fail to see how that conflicts with the opinion that the chances in the competition should be equalized as far as possible—in one way, as we have seen, by preventing individuals from monopolizing the land. Strangely enough, Professor Huxley stigmatizes with the charge of dangerous Individualism the very man who says that Society should protect itself at all points from the encroachment of individuals! 'A creature not energetic enough to sustain itself must die,' says Mr. Spencer again, which is surely true, and in no way at variance with the theory that the social organism must be restrained from cruelly *crushing* any creature out of life. Socialism contends that it is not want of energy, but want of opportunity, that pauperises men and destroys individual vitality.

Professor Huxley's next citation from Mr. Spencer—that 'it is demonstrable that various appliances for working-class comfort, supplied at the cost of the ratepayers, are intrinsically of the same nature as those which in past times treated the farmer's man as half-labourer and half-pauper '—and that in proportion to a man's helplessness without social aid and superintendence is the degree of his ' slavery '—would, I conceive, be subscribed to by most Socialists.   For what men want is to start the social reformation at the beginning and forwards, not at the end and backwards.   What the 'good and philosophical ' Socialist says is clear enough : ' I do not particularly care for Governmental interference with my private life and comfort, though I recognise the necessity of political and civic government, down to such general details as draining and lighting.   What I do want is to have the weeds cleared away which prevent my progress as an individual member of society.   You cannot help me much by compelling me to labour, without option, for the common benefit, while, at the same time, you confirm the institutions which allow large classes of men not to labour at all.   I will not become a " slave to your society," because I do not recognise that society as founded on absolute political ethics.   I was born a free man, not a slave.'   I do not fancy that Mr. Spencer disagrees

on any essential point with the 'good and philosophical' Socialist.

Let me put the matter plainly. Professor
Huxley misunderstands the higher Socialism as
thoroughly as he misunderstands Mr. Spencer.
He is 'trimming,' while Mr. Spencer is recon-
structing. The triumph of Socialism, historically
and morally, is the triumph of Individualism.
Ecclesiasticism, for example, has gone down like a
house of cards, because the free thought of
Individualism—*id est*, Socialism—said, in face of
huge majorities, that Ecclesiasticism was an interference with the right of private judgment in
matters personal and spiritual. Protestantism
decayed, from the moment it became, instead of
the protest of a minority, the tyranny of a
majority. Socialism itself, the lower Socialism,
has collapsed in many of its organizations, because
it forgot its first principles of freedom and equality ;
because (to take Professor Huxley's illustration) it
suggested to the Revolutionists the idea of sustain-
ing common freedom and equality by guillotining
each other, and because, as in the case of Enfantin
and his group, by upholding a scientific and sensuous priesthood as 'the Living Law of God,'
it adopted the insane vocabulary of superstition.
'Father,' said Bonheur to Enfantin, 'I believe
in you, as I believe in the sun. You are to
my eyes the Sun of Humanity.' Well might
Lafitte exclaim to such enthusiasts, ' You post

your advertisements too high—one cannot read
them.'

Unhappily the leaning of most new creeds, as
of all the old, is in the direction of social tyranny.
And why ? Simply because poor human nature
finds it hard to understand, and far harder to carry
out, absolute ethical principles. Socialism, like all
other human efforts to secure the greatest happiness
of the greatest number—like Christianity, like the
Religion of Humanity—has failed again and again.
But if Professor Huxley's dicta of quasi-providential or Governmental interference with the
conduct of life were to be universally accepted,
Humanity might well despair for ever ; for with
the destruction of Individualism would end the
last hope of the higher Socialism. Over-legislation
would restore slavery to mankind, and preserve the
semi-disintegrated feudality which is still so large a
portion of our political system. The philosopher,
not the quidnunc, holds the secret of wise legislation. The creed of the higher Socialism, not the
creed of those who believe that Socialism conflicts
with Individualism, is that which follows the Law
of Nature, by basing individual chances on the
natural freedom and equality of men.

To find Professor Huxley fighting for the *status
quo* in Politics is to me a far sadder sight than to
find him (for such a miracle may some day happen)
fighting for the *status quo* in Religion. Religion,
after all, can take care of itself. But the man

who argues in favour of Force as a proof of ownership, and of a Statute of Limitations in matters of secular wrong-doing, will one day have to cast in his lot with Ecclesiasticism and the Bishops. There is no way out of the dilemma, for Church and State stand or fall together. I shall watch with curiosity the process which may lead to the conversion of another Saul.

I am, etc.,

ROBERT BUCHANAN.

January 31.

To the Editor of the 'Daily Telegraph.'

SIR,

Your readers must take Mr. Robert Buchanan's censures of me and my opinions for what they are worth; I am not concerned to defend myself against them. Mr. Buchanan thinks that 'Socialism and individualism are not contrary terms, but two faĉts (? faces)* of the same proposition.'

Hence, it would seem to follow that when Mr. Spencer declares that 'Socialistic arrangements necessitate enslavement,' he also means that 'individualistic arrangements necessitate enslavement.'

And I must leave that instructive development

* 'Facts' in my letter was a misprint for 'facets.'

of absolute political ethics—together with the question whether Mr. Buchanan is entitled to cite a work which Mr. Spencer has repudiated—to be further discussed by those who may be interested in such topics, of whom I am not one (!).

I am, your obedient servant,

T. H. HUXLEY.

EASTBOURNE, *February* 3.

To the Editor of the ' Daily Telegraph.'

SIR,

Suffer me, like Professor Huxley, to say one last word, and that word shall be one of cordial acquiescence in the suggestion that the enslavement of Society is also the enslavement of the Individual. I have yet to learn that an individual, save in the sphere of absolute thought and ethics, is not in a certain sense the ' slave ' of his own organism. Just as a society is held together by its laws of life, so is a man held together by identical laws. He cannot escape from the general discharge of functions and interchange of currents which condition his vitality. The microcosm is a society just as much as the macrocosm. So far the Scientist and I are agreed. We only part company at the point where the scientist treats both Society and the Individual as mechanical only, independent altogether of those absolute principles which, while they fail to ' interest ' Professor

Huxley, are attacked so vehemently in his system of 'Providence Made Easy.'

I am, etc.,
ROBERT BUCHANAN.

[This discussion ended with the following energetic letter from Mr. Herbert Spencer :]

To the Editor of the 'Daily Telegraph.'

SIR,

Though the recent controversy carried on in your columns under the title 'Are Men Born Free and Equal?' has chiefly concerned certain political views of mine, I have thus far remained passive, and even now do not propose to say anything about the main issues. To Mr. Buchanan I owe thanks for the chivalrous feeling which prompted his defence. Professor Huxley, by quoting passages showing my dissent from what is *currently understood* as Socialism, has rendered me a service. I might fitly let the matter pass without remark, were it not needful to rectify a grave misrepresentation.

Describing the position of the penniless man, Professor Huxley says: 'It is not I, but the extreme Individualists, who will say that he may starve. If the State relieves his necessities, it is not I, but they, who say it is exceeding its powers; if private charity succours the poor fellow, it is not I, but they, who reprove the giver

for interfering with the survival of the fittest.'
And the view thus condemned by implication he
has previously characterized as 'the political
philosophy which Mr. Buchanan idolizes, the
consistent application of which reasoned savagery
to practice would have left the working classes
to fight out the struggle for existence among
themselves.'

Professor Huxley is fertile in strong expressions,
and 'reasoned savagery' is one of them ; but in
proportion as the expressions used are strong,
should be the care taken in applying them, lest
undeserved stigmas may result. Unfortunately,
in this case he appears to have been misled by that
deductive method which he reprobates, and has
not followed that inductive method which he
applauds. Had he looked for facts instead of
drawing inferences, he would have found that I
have nowhere expressed or implied any such
'reasoned savagery' as he describes. For nearly
fifty years I have contended that the pains
attendant on the struggle for existence may fitly
be qualified by the aid which private sympathy
prompts. In a pamphlet on 'The Proper Sphere
of Government,' written at the age of twenty-two,
it is argued that in the absence of a poor law 'the
blessings of charity would be secured unaccom-
panied by the evils of pauperism.' In 'Social
Statics' this view is fully set forth. While the
discipline of the battle of life is recognised and

insisted upon as 'that same beneficent though severe discipline, to which the animate creation at large is subject,' there is also recognised and insisted upon the desirableness of such mitigations as spontaneously result from individual fellow-feeling. It is argued that privately 'helping men to help themselves' leaves a balance of benefit, and that, 'although by these ameliorations the process of adaptation must be remotely interfered with, yet, in the majority of cases, it will not be so much retarded in one direction as it will be advanced in another.'

'As no cruel thing can be done without character being thrust a degree back towards barbarism, so no kind thing can be done without character being moved a degree forward towards perfection. Doubly efficacious, therefore, are all assuagings of distress, instigated by sympathy ; for not only do they remedy the particular evils to be met, but they help to mould humanity into a form by which such evils will one day be precluded' (pp. 318, 319, 1st edit.).

Professor Huxley's ingenuity as a controversialist, great though it is, will, I fancy, fail to disclose the 'reasoned savagery' contained in these sentences. Should he say that, during the forty years which have elapsed since they were written, my views have changed from a more humane to a less humane form, and that I would now see the struggle for existence, with resulting survival of

the fittest, carried on without check, then I meet
the allegation by another extract. In the 'Principles of Sociology,' sec. 322, I have explained at
some length that every species of creature can
continue to exist only by conforming to two
opposed principles—one for the life of the immature, and the other for the life of the mature.
The law for the immature is, that benefits received
shall be great in proportion as worth is small ;
while for the mature the law is, that benefits
received shall be great in proportion as worth is
great—worth being measured by efficiency for the
purposes of life. The corollary, as applied to
social affairs, runs as follows:

' Hence the necessity of maintaining this cardinal
distinction between the ethics of the family and
the ethics of the State. Hence the fatal result if
family disintegration [referring to a view of Sir
Henry Maine] goes so far that family policy and
State policy become confused. Unqualified generosity must remain the principle of the family
while offspring are passing through their early
stages ; and generosity increasingly qualified by
justice must remain its principle as offspring are
approaching maturity. Conversely, the principle
of the society guiding the acts of citizens to one
another must ever be justice, qualified by such
generosity as their several natures prompt ; joined
with unqualified justice in the corporative acts of
the society to its members. However fitly in the
battle of life among adults the proportioning of

rewards to merits may be tempered by private sympathy in favour of the inferior, nothing but evil can result if this proportioning is so interfered with by public arrangements that demerit profits at the expense of merit.'

Still more recently has there been again set forth this general view. In ' The Man *versus* the State,' pp. 64-67, along with the assertion that ' society in its corporate capacity cannot, without immediate or remoter disaster, interfere with the play of these opposed principles, under which every species has reached such fitness for its mode of life as it possesses,' there goes a qualification like that above added.

'I say advisedly—society in its corporate capacity, not intending to exclude or condemn aid given to the inferior by the superior in their individual capacities. Though, when given so indiscriminately as to enable the inferior to multiply, such aid entails mischief ; yet in the absence of aid given by society, individual aid, more generally demanded than now, and associated with a greater sense of responsibility, would, on the average, be given with the effect of fostering the unfortunate worthy rather than the innately unworthy ; there being always, too, the concomitant social benefit arising from culture of the sympathies.'

In other places the like is expressed or implied, but it is needless to cite further evidence. The

passages I have quoted will make sufficiently clear
the opinion I have all along held, and still hold ;
and everyone will be able to judge whether this
opinion is rightly characterized by the phrase
' reasoned savagery.'

HERBERT SPENCER.

LONDON, *February* 7.

FINAL NOTE ON THE DISCUSSION.

It will be seen that much of the question, ' Are
men born free and equal ?' became merged in the
other question, ' What is Socialism ?' My answer
to that question—*i.e.*, that true Socialism was a
combination to protect the rights of individuals—
was paradoxical enough to puzzle my friend Mr.
Spencer, and I had neither the time nor the
opportunity to explain my meaning fully. I have
no more sympathy than Mr. Spencer himself (as I
have shown elsewhere) with any kind of tyrannous
organization, whether framed in the name of
vested interests or in the name of the people.
True Socialism—the Science of Sentiment—to
which I adhere, fetters no man's moral activity,
limits no man's character, restricts no man's
evolution :

> ' No man can save another's Soul,
>   Or pay another's Debt.'

And what the individual man cannot do, cannot be
done by any organization of men. Thus I stand,
with Mr. Spencer, for the spread of the sense of

moral responsibility, for individual effort and energization; while Professor Huxley stands for the *status quo*, for Beneficent Legislation, for Providence made Easy. As little as either of these teachers do I see hope or find comfort in the savagery of false Socialism, in the Anarchy of Ignorance, in the terrorism of the emerging Demogorgon. Far as I follow Mr. Spencer, however, in his masterly abstract statements, there is a point where even a disciple and a friend may hesitate. I cannot calmly leave the regeneration of things evil to the slow and certain evolution of the corporate conscience; I feel that there is much to be said for the advocates of a more active social reorganization, and I am not so convinced as Mr. Spencer of the necessary sacredness of contracts, or of the wisdom of holding them inviolable. It would not be difficult, I think, to define the limits within which even State Socialism is expedient and beneficial. Nothing certainly can be more terrible than the existing condition of things, both social and political, and all efforts to mend that condition, be they ever so revolutionary, have my sympathy. It is quite clear, therefore, that I do not follow the Prophet with my eyes shut, and I can quite understand that Mr. Spencer must have considered me, in more than one expression of opinion, a Devil's Advocate.

R. B.

7

ON DESCENDING INTO HELL:

A Protest against Over-legislation in Matters Literary.

'Tell me, where is the place that men call Hell?
Meph.—Under the heavens.
Faust.—Ay, so are all things else ; but whereabouts?
Meph.—Within the bowels of these Elements
Where we are tortured and remain for ever.
Hell has no limits, nor is circumscribed
In one self place : but where we are is Hell ;
And where Hell is, there must we ever be
And, to be short, when all the world dissolves,
And every creature shall be purified,
All places shall be Hell that are not Heaven.
Faust.—I think Hell is a fable.
Meph.—Ah ! think so still, till experience change thy mind.'
MARLOWE'S *Faustus.*

ON DESCENDING INTO HELL.

To the RIGHT HON. HENRY MATTHEWS,

Home Secretary.

RIGHT HON. SIR,

You are, I understand, a Roman Catholic; I am a Catholic plus an eclectic. I have the highest respect for the creed in which you believe, since it is perhaps the most logically constructed of all human creeds ; but while I admire the logic I do not admit all the premises, and cannot consequently follow you to all its conclusions. Is it too much to hope, however, that even Roman Catholicism has shared the fate of other beliefs, and been shorn of many of its imperfections ? Its history represents it as at once the friend of literature, and literature's mortal enemy ; it has preserved for us much that is precious, together with many husks of uncleanliness which might have been more wisely destroyed, and it has formulated the Index, before which, from generation to generation, Free Thought has trembled. It washed the sin-stained robes of St. Augustine with one hand, and it burned Giordano Bruno with the other. All that is over, and just

now, in the eighty-ninth year of this century,
Roman Catholicism stands face to face with its
old enemies, Free Thought and Science, with whom
less than a miracle might even yet effect a reconciliation. For the creed of Persecution is also
the creed of spiritual Insight : the carnal wolf's
clothing, perhaps, still hides the Lamb of God.
If in its supreme moment of eclipse the suffering
Church were to admit its sins and reform its
terminology, Humanity might almost accept its
blessing — forget Torquemada, and remember
Bishop Myriel.

An opportunity occurs now in England. A
new Inquisition, with which the Roman Church
has fortunately nothing to do, proposes to shut
all carnal books, and to punish all men who write,
read, and sell them. For issuing to the public the
writings of an able Advocate on the Devil's side,
an unfortunate Publisher of Books lies now in
prison.* The flourishing Puritan, apt pupil of
old Rome in persecution, has decided that Free
Thought is to be silenced, and the Arbor Scientiæ
cut down and burned. It is the story of Castilio
over again, and John Calvin survives in the spirit,
to make a martyr's bonfire. Now, then, I believe,
is the time for the Church Catholic, the Church
persecuted and purified, to confess her sin, and cast
in her lot with the Humanity she once hated,
saying, ' Even as my Saints and Monks preserved

* Written in 1889.

for men the banal humanities of Greece and Rome, even as (while stifling the literature of speculation) they saved for the world the literature of the flesh, letting my children nourish themselves on the bread thereof and cast the leaven away, so will I now proclaim that even the Literature of Hell shall not be hidden quite below the depths of argument.' If the Church escapes this opportunity, it will be her own misfortune; if she takes it boldly, she will gain at least one day's triumph. More than any Church still surviving, she believes that her arguments are overpowering. Since she has found it quite useless to suppress her enemies by force, why not suffer them to have their say in open daylight, before the world? By her instrument, a Roman Catholic Home Secretary, she may do this, and she will be wise to do it. Let her by your means, sir, open the prison of one of whom those who love her not have foolishly made a Martyr. Let her proclaim from the housetops, 'Men, speak out your utmost, lay bare Nature to its depths; your liberation will be my justification, for although you descend into Hell you will only be following my Master, who left his Cross, a flaming symbol, even *there.*'

May I, as briefly as possible, review the case to which I solicit your earnest attention?

A certain

M. ÉMILE ZOLA,

whom superficial criticism persists in classing among

the votaries of pleasure, is a dreary and dismal
gentleman whose mind is solely exercised on
questions of moral drainage and social sewerage.
He goes so far as to assert that Modern Society is
full of disease germs scattered through the air from
the social deposits ; and to prove his case, he takes
us, when we are willing to be improved, right down
into the sewers and the catacombs.   I went there
lately with him ; and held my nose.   The very
raiment of my guide, when we emerged into the
daylight, was redolent of offal ; it looked and smelt
unclean, and I got away from it as soon as possible,
not before I had recognised, however, that the man
was right in some measure, and that the drains
were bad.   Now, it never occurred to me for one
moment that poor Zola ought to be *given into
custody*, but a crowd of very clean persons loudly
clamoured around us, and messages were sent for the
nearest policeman.   Before the stern myrmidon of
the law could be found, Zola had disappeared, but
an unfortunate and innocent deputy, told off to
conduct the public in the absence of his principal,
was incontinently laid hold of by one Dogberry,
haled off before Justice Shallow, and then and
there condemned as a public nuisance.   Moral :
Leave the drains alone ; let the world wag, even if
typhoid fever should flourish.   Moral number two,
very acceptable to the average insular intelligence :
Conceal from all clean people, especially young

people, the fact that there is such a thing as sewerage at all.

I have never held (and I do not hold now) the opinion that drainage is a fit subject for Art, that men grow any better by the contemplation of what is bestial and unpleasant ; indeed, I have always been puritan enough to think pornography a nuisance. It is one thing, however, to dislike the obtrusion of things unsavoury and abominable, and quite another to regard any allusion to them as positively *criminal.* A description even of pig-sties, moreover, may sometimes be made tolerable by the cunning of a great artist, and this same M. Zola, though a dullard *au fond,* for the simple reason that he regards pigsties as the *only* fore-ground for his lurid moral landscapes, appears to be so much better and nobler than myself, in so much as he loves Truth more and fears consequences less, that I have again and again taken off my hat to him in open day. His zeal may be mistaken, but it is self-evident ; his information may be horrible, but it is certainly given in all good faith ; and an honest man being the rarest of phenomena in all literature, this man has my sympathy—though my instinct is to get as far away from him as possible.

In trying on more than one occasion to do justice to his sincerity, while seriously finding fault with his method, I have had to be constantly reminded that he is *a Frenchman;* and a French-

man, from our insular point of view, is synonymous
with everything that is unclean and detestable.
Despite the fact that we have derived for hundreds
of years all our 'ideas,' such as they are, from
France, despite the fact that Frenchmen have
been the pioneers of Freedom and Free Thought
all over the world, we still preserve the old superstition that a Frenchman is born a 'light' person,
whose sole conception of life is derived from his
experiences as a *boulevardier*.   The English race
has no 'ideas' whatever ;   indeed, it abominates
'ideas,' and is thoroughly practical and pragmatical
in its views, of social subjects especially.   True,
when once convinced of a great principle, it can
hold to it, as our Puritans did when they got the
lambent torch of Protestantism from Geneva, as
our philosophers did when they caught the reflex
of the Fiery Cross of Free Thought in Paris ; but
we work by tenacity, like the bull-dog, while
Frenchmen, like the greyhound, work by sight.
We have had to get even our Byrons and our
Shelleys second-hand from the Revolution.   We
have fought inch by inch against the obtrusion
of every new 'idea'; then at last, accepting it, we
have held to it like grim Death.   Thus, in religion
and even in philosophy, we have been practically
converted, but on one point, that of social statics
and their expression in literature, we are invul-
nerable.   We won't be reformed in our morality.
We decline to listen to anyone, especially a priest

or a Frenchman, who affirms that human nature is not virtuous by instinct and by predisposition. We repudiate all 'ideas' connected with the existence of moral Hell. We still our consciences, approve our Social Evil, and refuse to inspect our drains. While doing the best to give one half of the community a foretaste of Hell upon earth, we affirm that this is the best of all possible worlds, and that English civilization is the only possible civilization consistent with the welfare of a troubled planet.

In this spirit of disingenuous optimism, we have organized

OUR LATTER INQUISITION

—a curious conclave, composed of all phases of character and opinion ; with Justice Shallow as chief Inquisitor, and Messrs. Dogberry and Verges as watchmen in ordinary. Decree number one : let all 'deformed' individuals, and especially all Frenchmen, be 'run in' and 'charged.' Decree number two : books being the Devil's engines, all books are to be 'inspected,' and if found guilty of any 'ideas,' summarily burnt or expurgated. Decree number three : any publisher of a book calculated to destroy our cardinal principle, that this is the best of all possible worlds, is to be seized, fined and imprisoned. Decree number four : that public virtue is impossible without the sanction of the police, and (as a corollary) that public taste is a thing strictly within the determination of the watchmen and custodians of our virtue. Decree number five : that our system of sewerage is to remain in the region of Supernatural Mystery, and that any literature touching upon it is to be condignly abolished *Imprimantur*, the revised New Testament, the 'Lamplighter,' and the tracts of Christian knowledge. *Condemnantur*, all poems, all fictions, which expose the Gehenna underground, or attack the moralities which shine above it. *Expurgantur*, Shakespeare, Dryden, and Byron (the last delicately, for he was a lord). Signed, Shallow, Grand Inquisitor ; Countersigned, Dogberry, Chief Constable in Ordinary. In the intervals of our pleasant Inquisition, we listen blandly to a droning Military Person who beguiles our leisure with prospects of a general Conscription, and who holds up the German system of providential and governmental superintendence in all departments of life and thought as the beacon of modern Civilization !*

A few words concerning the character of

MR. VIZETELLY,

the imprisoned publisher, may assist you to take an impartial view of the situation. His entire life had been spent in the service of art, journalism and literature. Bound over as an apprentice to his father, James Henry Vizetelly, who had one of the

* See Lord Wolseley's utterances, *passim.*

largest printing businesses in the City of London,
he acquired his own freedom by servitude, though
members of the family had been freemen of the
City for several generations. Subsequently Mr.
Henry Vizetelly was apprenticed to Orrin Smith,
the well-known wood engraver, and proved his best
pupil ; the works containing wood engravings
signed ' H. Vizetelly' are nowadays sought after
by connoisseurs. Mr. Vizetelly's connection with
journalism dates from the foundation of the
Illustrated London News. The first 'idea' of
that publication germinated in the brain of Mr.
Herbert Ingram, who thought of establishing a
kind of *Illustrated Police Gazette.* Mr. Vizetelly
prevailed upon him, however, to make the publication more comprehensive in its scope, wrote the
prospectus, and largely contributed towards launch-
ing the first number. This was the foundation
of illustrated journalism. Soon afterwards Mr.
Vizetelly, having somewhat abruptly severed his
connection with the *Illustrated London News,* went
into publishing. He was the first to introduce
'Uncle Tom's Cabin' and the poems of Edgar
Allan Poe to the English public. He also did a
great deal to popularize the immaculate Mr. Longfellow in England. The 'Evangeline,' illustrated
by Sir John Gilbert, was due mainly to his
endeavours ; also the 'Hyperion,' illustrated by
Birket Foster. For the latter he visited all the
localities mentioned in the work (accompanied by

Foster), and sketches were made on the spot to serve as illustrations. This 'Hyperion' is very rare nowadays, and fetches a high price. About the time of the Crimean War Mr. Vizetelly started the *Illustrated Times,* and gathered round him a number of clever writers—then mostly unknown to fame, but many of whom have since made their way in the world—Thackeray, the Brothers Brough, the Brothers Mayhew, Sala, Edmund Yates, Sutherland Edwards, Frederick Greenwood, and many others. Among the artists were John Gilbert, Birket Foster, Julian Portch, and Gustave Doré (then first introduced to the English public). Whilst starting and editing this new publication, Mr. Vizetelly devoted considerable time and energy to furthering the general interests of his profession. He acted as Honorary Secretary to the Association formed for the Repeal of the Paper Duty, and in regard to the abolition of the Newspaper Stamp he took decisive action by issuing several numbers of the *Illustrated Times* without the stamp. The Board of Revenue prosecuted him, claiming a fine of several thousand pounds. This was never enforced, however. The question was taken up by public men, and soon afterwards the Stamp impost was abolished. In 1865 he became Paris correspondent of the *Illustrated London News*—went through the siege of Paris and Commune for that journal—organized a service of sketches by balloon post, so that the paper was able to supply a more complete pictorial record of the siege than appeared in any other journal. He afterwards represented the *Illustrated London News* at Berlin and Vienna—acted as British Wine Juror at Vienna, 1873, and Paris, 1878 — wrote a number of text-books upon European wines, after visiting all the wine producing districts on the Continent, Madeira, Canary Isles, etc. These books are standard works of reference.

As an author, Mr. Vizetelly has also written on Berlin and Paris. His 'Story of the Diamond Necklace' completely unravelled what was long considered a historical puzzle—supplementing and correcting Carlyle's well-known essay in many important particulars. He has also contributed numerous articles to *Household Words*, under Charles Dickens, and was on various occasions a correspondent of the *Times, Daily News*, and *Pall Mall Gazette*. He started his present publishing business in 1880, and thereby, as I shall show, did much yeoman's service for first-class literature.

That, Right Hon. Sir, is the record of the man whom the Vigilance Committee, trading on the prudery of the English community, casts into prison. His crime is that he has not presumed the business of publishing to include the prerogatives of a *censor morum ;* that he has published in the English language what nearly every educated person reads in the French ; that, in a word, he has introduced to the uninitiated the works of Émile Zola and one or two writers of doubtful decency. Even if we admit his error in this last particular, do not his long services far outweigh his indiscretions? Has he not been a brave sergeant in the army of English journalism? But I decline to admit his error. I affirm that Émile Zola was bound to be printed, translated, read. Little as I sympathize with his views of life, greatly as I loathe his pictures of human vice and depravity, I have learned much from him, and others may learn much; and had I been unable to read French, these bald translations would have been to me an intellectual help and boon. I like to have the Devil's case thoroughly stated, because I know it refutes itself. As an artist, Zola is unjustifiable; as a moralist, he is answerable; but as a free man, a man of letters, he can decline to accept the fiat of a criminal tribunal.

The details of an interview with Mr. Coote, Secretary of the Vigilance Committee, compel me to add a few words touching the conduct of

THE PERSON FOR THE PROSECUTION;

and to begin with, I take leave to say that Mr. Coote's assertions were simply infamous. ' I think it served Vizetelly right,' said this Secretary of the Vigilance Committee; 'look over his catalogue, and form your own opinion.' May I ask,

Sir, if you *have* looked over his catalogue? *I* have done so, and with the following result. Besides the works of Zola, Flaubert and Daudet, many of them admirable in every sense of the word, Mr. Vizetelly has issued to the English public the works of Count Tolstoï and of Fedor Dostoieffsky ; an admirably edited series of the Old Dramatists ; Mr. Sala's 'America Revisited,' 'Under the Sun,' 'Dutch Pictures,' and 'Paris Herself Again'; the immaculate M. Ohnet's 'Ironmaster'; Mr. Greenwood's 'In Strange Company'; M. Coppée's 'Passer-by' (Le Passant); the stories of Gaboriau and Du Boisgobey ; a whole library of brilliant social romances, including tales by Cherbuliez, Theuriet, About, Féval and Mérimée ; and, to crown all, his (Mr. Vizetelly's) own excellent works on 'The Diamond Necklace' and 'Wines of the World.' These, among other publications equally worthy and inoffensive, form the *bulk* of the catalogue for which the Secretary of the Vigilance Committee would keep an honourable man in prison. Does Mr. Coote ever *read* anything outside the literature of the 'Lamplighter' and the 'Old Helmet'? Does he see no difference between even 'La Curée' or 'Madame Bovary' and the sealed-up books sold sometimes in Holywell Street ? It seems to me that it would be as rational to consult the first area-haunting policeman on the ethical quality of literature, as to accept the evidence of

8

a censor who is either a mischief-maker or an ignoramus.

It is no exaggeration to say that the whole existence of the so-called Vigilance Committee is an infamy, and that the treatment of Mr. Vizetelly is merely a specimen of Dogberry's evidence and Shallow's justice. The misfortune is that Mr. Vizetelly, instead of taking his stand like a man on his total work as publisher, pleaded in the first instance ' guilty.' Possibly he knew British judges and British juries better than I do ; but the result is lamentable, and I repeat my question, where is the persecution to stop? Does any sane man imagine that it is really corrupt books that destroy Society, and that any suppression of literature will make Society any better? No; these books, where they are corrupt, merely represent corruption already existing — are merely signs and symbols of social disease. The argument that they bring ' blushes to the cheek of a young person ' is irrelevant. They are not written for the young person ; and if they are, the young person will get at them, now and for ever, in spite of the policeman. Criticise them, attack them, point out their deformities and absurdities as much as you please, and as much as I myself have done; but do not imagine that you will purify the air by *suppressing* literature, or that you can make people virtuous by penal clauses and Acts of Parliament.

And the harmless Ohnet, and the stainless Coppée, and the good Theuriet, and the great Tolstoï, and the sublime Dostoieffsky, not to speak of the full-blooded Old Dramatists and the genial Mr. George Augutus Sala, are all practically condemned to Limbo in the lump, under the shadow of Mr. Vizetelly's awful 'Catalogue'! This precious Dogberry of a Vigilance Committee is left to straddle with his watchman's Lanthorn, and shriek 'Deformed! Deformed!' over the mutilated remains of Art and Literature. To-morrow, perchance, he will toddle up to Burlington House, and insist on either seizing or clothing all the 'improper' pictures of nude ladies, and we shall soon have the President of the Royal Academy committed to prison for daring to paint a Venus without a bathing costume, or an Ariadne without a petticoat.

For my own part, I hold the matter so serious that I am appealing to you, on the highest grounds of all, religious grounds, for Mr. Vizetelly's immediate release. If there is any manhood among English writers, they will see that the matter is one involving their own liberties, now and in the near future.* If there is any consistency

* That there might be no doubt on this head, the Vigilance Committee, in a letter published June 25, 1889, warned English authors to 'look out,' and not to go too far, or they, too, might get into trouble! But there wasn't much danger—not one contemporary English author except myself protested against the persecution!

8—2

among English publishers, they also will contend for freedom and immunity from constabulary supervision. Special Providence, as embodied in the form of an amateur moralist-detective, is on their track. We shall see our beloved ' Ouida ' run in to Bow Street, and ' Ouida's ' publishers whimpering by her in the dock. Every publisher of the atrocious works of Shakespeare will stand in the pillory. As for Mr. Vizetelly, he may indeed have cause to cry *peccavi* if neither authors nor publishers come to his aid. He is seventy years of age, he is a *littérateur* as well as a publisher, and, according to the latest accounts, he is suffering greatly. If it were only for his introduction to the public of one great and perhaps unequalled book, ' Crime and Punishment,' I should regard him, not as a criminal, but as a martyr and a public benefactor. Here is a good chance, Right Hon. Sir, to show that the mantle of Beaconsfield has fallen on a Tory Home Secretary ! Benjamin Disraeli might have had a thousands faults, but he never forgot his literary inheritance, and in a case like the present he would have defended the freedom of letters against a whole army of canting busybodies and prurient 'Vigilance Committee-men.'

For all this civil interference with spiritual prerogative, Right Hon. Sir, must be very distasteful to the Church of which you are a distinguished representative. In matters spiritual, which to a great extent are matters literary, that Church has always upheld her own tests as final, and often, while she has burned a religious heretic, she has afforded sanctuary to a carnal offender. She trembled, it is true, before Galileo and other rectangular dogmatists of scientific discovery, but she never feared pornography, or thought that it could overthrow the higher standards of human nature. One of her most logical postulates, indeed, has been that Man is evil by inheritance and by predisposition, and that only by Faith or Spiritual Knowledge can he be saved. Hence her gentleness to the literature of Heathendom, her complacency in dealing with purely human Art and Letters. While preserving the Christian documents she was quite content to leave Humanity its Sappho, its Lucretius, its Juvenal, its Catullus, even its Aristophanes. For though she was persuaded to make short work of schismatics, who after all have little knowledge of life, she was ever kindly to the poets, the most incontinent of whom knew life thoroughly. She went with Dante into Hell, and she ascended with Calderon up to Heaven ; but loving also her cakes and ale, she preserved the *gaudriole* for the amusement of her monks. She has, in short, been a friend to *belles lettres*, even the most pornographic. In these respects, as in many others, I sympathize with her. Far less human and sympathetic has been her gloomy half-sister, Protestantism. If Protestantism had its way we should have no books except One, which is excellent, no doubt, but not always amusing. In a word, this is a quite tenable proposition : that Literature has more to fear from the Church which canonizes and exalts one Book, than from the Church which asserts that Human Nature shall not be at the mercy of *any Book whatsoever.*

The days are long past when even the Church, Roman and Catholic, had any real cause to be afraid of human flights of fancy, or any anxiety to suppress them ; more than one of her monks has chuckled over Pantagruel, and I know that certain of her priests have followed with feverish anxiety the temptations of a certain Abbé Mouret. Putting certain little fanciful dogmas aside, the Roman Church is far more tolerant to human necessities and human weaknesses than any of her offshoots— nay, than even her grim Arch Enemy, the Church of Science ; and than this last Church she is in one respect infinitely wiser, that her last word is one of pity and comfort for human backsliding.

The pity of Science is the pity of Despair ; the pity of the Church is the pity of Faith and Hope, and of Regeneration.

True, you say as of old, ' Unless a man believes in my confession of faith, he shall surely perish— but if he believes he shall be saved,' an assumption which Scientists amuse themselves with, to their own final consternation. For, translated into the language of common-sense, your dogma means that foulness, sin, physical disease, hereditary taint, have no power to touch the Soul—that he who believes in the Supreme Love and Pity shall, despite them all, save his Soul alive ; whereas that other Church of Science teaches what I contend to be a foolish heresy, that the Soul can be saved only by the Body in which it dwells, that by the law of heredity the Body may destroy and eliminate even Man's immortal part.

As I write an illustration comes to my hand. A certain Scandinavian writer, who is to M. Zola what the dustman of a suburb is to the scavenger of a city, has written a play called ' Gengangere '—that is, in French, ' Les Revenants,' and in English ' Ghosts.' To get his material he had literally, like others before him, to enter Hell, nor do I blame him, though I doubt his moral. Picturing an individual whose nature is poisoned through and through by hereditary taint, who is morally and physically diseased because he inherits from an unclean paternity, he leaves this individual in the corruption of hopeless idiocy, gibbering at the Sun. No one ray of Hope brightens the tableau, but the cruel consuming Sun drinks up this wasted life like a drop of dew. A solemn and an awful truth, says Science. But apart from the question (never yet fully reasoned out by physiologists) of how far the spark of life *eludes* the taints cast upon it, of how far, for example, even the loathsome sores of syphilis may be crystallized after a generation into cells of prismatic thought (as is possibly true in certain examples of meningitis), the lesson we are taught in this doleful drama leaves moral questions entirely within the domain of *physiology*. Now, I, personally, refuse to exist in that most melancholy domain ; and here, again, human evidence is with me. One miserable infant, almost a fœtus in size and development, became the Arouet whose voice rang round the world and liberated Calas. The strumous Keats *faced* the Sun, and cast it glaring on his canvas as ' Hyperion.' Unhealthy men, tainted men, weakly men, have dominated the world of art and literature, where Michael Angelos and Benvenuto Cellinis have been the exceptions. I have known a man reduced by the fault of his progenitors to a state bordering on mental decrepitude, and yet that man was sane and wise, a beautiful soul, happy, and a peacemaker. I decline, then, to believe that Original Sin and Hereditary Taint, though they exist loosely in your dogma and tenaciously in that of Science, can cast me down into nothingness. I *know* the Soul eludes the Body at every stage of our development. I find every day that perfectly balanced structure, the *mens sana in corpore sano*, is utterly deaf to the music tainted and polluted structures hear. A perfectly healthy man is frequently a monster, generally a mere machine, and not till that boasted body of his is twisted and tortured, carbonadoed and shaken to pieces, does he become spiritualized.

Now, why should the Church, which goes as far as this with me, and declines to accept any text but that which is spiritual, fear

THE DEVIL'S EVIDENCE,

the argument for the Body, the special plea of cheap Science? If the Church does not fear it, the new Inquisition does. A Vigilance Committee casts Mr. Vizetelly, the publisher, into prison, for simply permitting a scientific scavenger to produce his frightful documents ; while a no less vigilant Lord Chamberlain refuses under any circumstances to let ' Gengangere ' be performed in English upon the English stage. No ; these things must be veiled, the argument on the other side must not be stated, the descent into Hell must never be alluded to, except by those who are supposed to keep the Keys. Surely there is no truth which Science or Art can bring to light, which Infallibility should fear? Surely Satan should be permitted to argue out his case? ' No,' say the Vigilance Committee and the Lord Chamberlain, ' no, a thousand times; since sewerage is a Mystery, and children and young persons might overhear the argument and be contaminated—that is to say, converted.' A foolish fear ! a feeble superstition ! The argument will out somehow, in spite of all Inquisitions. Human nature will not suffer its own salvation or damnation to be discussed *in camerâ.* The matter must be fought in open day.

Sometimes, Right Hon. Sir, your Church has feared the truth, and on every occasion when she has done so, the result to herself has been lamentable. Yet it is to the Truth, the Eternal Verity, that she makes her appeal, pledging herself to its infallibility. Now, I could go through her dogmas one by one, and show that they are constructed impregnably on the instincts of human nature; only she herself, unfortunately, has misunderstood them, and hence the hideous historical record which constitutes the popular indictment against her. Yet, amid all follies, all contradictions, all cruelty, all schism, she has kept one particular glory—her patience with physical deterioration, her Faith that *no carnal sin or carnal knowledge can really wreck the Soul.* She has often been afraid of phantoms of her own conjuring, never of flesh and blood; 'ideas' have terrified her, but men and women have always been her sympathetic study.

In that masterpiece of English eloquence, the 'Areopagitica,' the trumpet note of which is now faintly heard in literature, our great Epic Poet has marshalled every argument, produced every proof, in favour of the Liberty of Unlicensed Printing. Nobler words never flowed from the lips of man. Wise on this as on all other vital questions, Milton, a Greek god in the gray robes of a Puritan, through which his roseate nakedness shone in celestial beauty, spoke more than one word for the poor Devil. *He*, at least, knew that there is weakness in Humanity as well as strength, and that the primitive instincts are perennial ; for had he not painted Eden on Adam's marriage day, when

> ' To the nuptial bower
> He led her blushing like the morn,'

and had he not pictured to us the amatory exploits of Zephyr and other kindred spirits ? True, he appears to reserve to his friends of the Parliament the right of destroying such books as are wholly prejudicial to decency and harmful to the State ; ' and yet, on the other hand,' he adds, ' as good almost kill a good man as kill a good book : who kills a man kills a reasonable creature, God's image, but he who destroys a good book kills reason itself, kills the image of God as it were in the eye.' Even as the holy Chrysostom nightly studied Aristophanes, so did the blameless Milton nourish his mind on the still more scurrilous pages of our own comic dramatists. ' I cannot,' he contends, ' praise a fugitive or cloistered virtue ; assuredly we bring not innocence into the world, but impurity much rather : that which purifies us is trial, and trial is by what is contrary.' ' Banish all objects of lust, shut up all youth into the severest discipline that can be exercised in any hermitage, ye cannot make them chaste that came not thither so.'

Who is to decide for us what is good, if our own
nature and inspiration are powerless to help us?
Is it to be the Pope of Rome, or any deputy
Cardinal, or any Scottish Elder of the Kirk, or
some member of a newly-created City Council, or,
finally, Mr. Justice Shallow of the law courts?
There are zealots who would burn the works of
Shakespeare, as there were zealots who cursed and
anathematized the works of Burns.   To a certain
order of intelligence, *all* literature is profane,
dangerous, inexpedient.   Large portions of the
community believe any stage play whatsoever is
an abomination ; large portions warn us that the
reading of any work of fiction or fairy tale is sinful
and pernicious.   Whither then might we turn for
guidance, if not to the Supreme Church which,
after burning her own effete Index, may affirm the
perfect

LAWFULNESS OF ALL HUMAN EVIDENCE,

knowing that she can, by the strength of her
adamantine logic, refute every carnal lie ?

I can assure you, Right Hon. Sir, that it is in
no spirit of levity that I, who have little love for
Roman Catholicism, suggest a way in which the
Church Infallible may yet be saved.   That way is, as
I have suggested, to perform a latter-day miracle
and cast in her lot with the Church of Free
Thought and Free Speech.   For I regard this
proposed Suppression of Literature as an encroach-

ment of Puritanism (which has always hated literature) on the one hand, and of Pragmatic Science upon the other. Puritanism affirms with gloomy pertinacity that we are lost if we are not strictly moral, *i.e.*, moral from the Puritan point of view ; Science avers with vehemence that its raw and half-verified discoveries are to regulate the conduct of our lives, and promises, if things are so ordered, that Humanity will in due course, after an era or two, arrive at the perfectly-balanced Mind in the perfectly-balanced Body—a Teutonic condition to be found even *now* in the Fatherland ! Neither Puritanism nor Science, however, affect the Church's prerogative by one hair. The one takes too much care of our conduct, the other is too anxious about our health. The Church alone, at this supreme crisis, when an innocent man is cast into prison, when the suppression of literature is threatened, and when neither Puritan nor Scientist cares to utter one word of public pro-testation—the Church alone, I say, can command the situation, and deny the right of synods or vestries to silence any voices, even those from Hell. Her spiritual terminology is, after all, far nearer to the pantheism of Servetus, than to the dismal anthropomorphism of John Calvin. 'I have no doubt,' said the Spaniard, ' that this bench, this table, and all you can point to around us is of the substance of God ;' adding, when it was objected that on his showing the Devil must be of God's substance too, ' I do not doubt it ; all things whatever are part of God, and Nature is His substantial manifestation.' For which and other pestilent heresies, Servetus, to the huge joy of John Calvin, was burned alive, roasting first for two hours in the flames of a slow fire, and begging piteously that they would put on more wood, or do something to end his torture.

Now, all such cruelties and abominations, together with all the schisms and heresies of the Churches, have arisen (1) from the human anxiety to be too rectangular, too *scientific*, and (2) from the disposition of novices in discovery to force their opinions upon their neighbours. Just as little as Metaphysics could tell the Church of the real nature of God, while tempting its hearers to tear the human images of God asunder, can Physical Science tell us of the real nature and destiny of Man. Humanity, at the present issue, pines to free itself from *all* arbitrary assumptions ; it yearns for the liberty to inquire, in its own way ; and it is out of lay books, to no little extent, that its knowledge must be derived. *Das mehr Licht hereinkomme!* it cries with Goethe, the Pagan. Just as certainly as the light which leads astray may (as Burns protested) be ' light from Heaven,' so may the light which guides and saves be light from Hell. To drape one half of the human figure is not to prove the whole structure to be celestial ; to ignore the existence of Evil is not to ensure the triumph of Good. The literature of Hell is God's literature too.

How well has suppression worked in other countries ? Take Italy, for example, a country of which both Providence and Priesthood have taken such particular care ; the chosen home of the Index and the winking Virgin ; the region of Pompeii and of *oggetti osceni*, into which neither women nor children are suffered to enter. There, obscene things are carefully hidden, literature is' wistfully burked—with such stupendous good to the community that dirt and disease and libertinage flourish up to the very gates of the Vatican. Then take France, with which Providence has always been in more or less of a temper, where literary freedom has run to licence, and where Art is synonymous with independence, not to say looseness, of morality. In France, the domestic affections flourish to wonderment, and the idea of family relationship is strangely sacred ; insomuch that even in polluted Paris, on the stage, the one sentiment which ' brings down the house ' is the sentiment of parental or filial love. Then take Germany, strangled by the governmental Providence, and reaching to its apex of licensed infamy in Berlin : a free nation without a free thought, smothered by its own strength of Nationality, straddled over by a Martinet of pipes and beer ; the Fatherland which every German adores, and escapes from at the first opportunity. Then take England, still free, in spite of the god Jingo ; still merry, in spite of the Rev. Mr. Grundy and his wife ; yet the chosen home of the ' young person,' the land where literature is under the protecting wing of Mr. Mudie, and where the moribund drama gasps and struggles Desdemona-like under the smothering pillow of the blindly jealous Lord Chamberlain. It is with England, of course, that the present inquiry is most concerned. With a literature un-equalled for breadth and power, with Shakespeare throned and crowned, and Milton uttering the trumpet notes of freedom, England still languishes without ideals or ideas. She has had her Jonathan Swift and her Henry Fielding, but she has never had her Rousseau—never possessed one man since Milton to stand fearlessly between the two opposing forces of Superstition and Freedom, and to utter the gospel of reconciliation ; to denounce the Priestcraft of Religion with one breath, and the Priestcraft of Science with the next ; to go down into Hell's most sulphurous depths, and to learn that the only light even *there* is Light reflected from Heaven.

For nothing in Roman Catholicism is so beyond contention as the dogma that Hell *is*—a belief which it holds in common with all creeds called Christian. It remained for a great thinker, Emmanuel Swedenborg, to establish the fact that Hell is not merely a locality, but also an omnipresent ' con-dition.' I know scarcely one great English classic, from ' Othello ' to ' Tom Jones,' from ' Tom Jones ' to Burns' ' Address to the Deil,' which has not illustrated the theory that

HELL EXISTS,

and that the Devil, who is often very humorous and entertaining, should have a hearing. Since we have adopted Satan's original suggestion, and eaten of the Tree of the Knowledge of Good and Evil, I do not think we can alter our food *now*, and get back to the ambrosia of Eden. The fact that, ashamed of our nakedness, we have made ourselves an apron, does not justify us in covering all our flesh with old-fashioned steel armour. The knowledge we have secured, at the cost of our innocence, is not to be ignored. The freedom we have gained, at the price of our moral peace, is not to be abandoned. In other words, we cannot save ourselves *now* by ignorance, nor can we be saved by providential suppression. Every man who would be strong for the world's fight must visit Hell, and become acquainted with its literature ; when he is certain to discover, if my own experience is any guide, that the angels there are real, though fallen.

Even this same Zola is a prophet after your own liking, if you will only bear with his banalities. He prophesies Death and Doom, if purity and self-sacrifice do not arise again to save the world. His text is older even than your Church—' the

wages of Sin is Death.'   He takes us from death-
bed to death-bed : some vile and loathsome, like
that of poor Nana, some divinely beautiful, like
that of little Jeanne.   There is a saint and a
martyr even in that hotbed of pornography, ' Pot
Bouille ' ; and when I think of the poor blind
bourgeois father, copying folios for a few pence
that his wife and daughter may wear finery, and
then dying broken-hearted when he finds all his
life is founded on corruption, I weep at another
Crucifixion.   To state this is merely to contend
that fine things may be found even in an Inferno :
that Proserpine's flowers did not all fall on the
ground from Dis's waggon, but that some were
borne with her right down into Hades.   Surely
Zola should content those who believe in corruption
and deterioration.   The Gospel according to the
Sewers is *your* Gospel of Original Sin.   The
scientific dogma of hereditary taint is *your* dogma
of the Fall.   True, in many particulars, your creed
is the nobler, and will last the longer.   You tell
us that we may be saved by Faith, redeemed by
obedience to the primal Law, and so, indeed, we
may.   But we shall never be redeemed by closing
up all books, by pretending (in the face of our
knowledge to the contrary) that there is no such
thing as Sin at all.

The point for which I have always contended
is that both cynical pessimism and coarse realism
are alike infinitely *absurd*.   A thoroughly unclean

book is almost invariably a thoroughly foolish one. Zola, for example, is, at his coarsest, merely a subject for laughter; the dirt sticks to him who writes, not to him who reads, and makes the writer look ridiculous. The sense of the absurd, in fact, is the *granum salis* which keeps literature wholesome. Even *Justine* becomes innocuous, even Petronius becomes harmless, when so disinfected. Yet when I look at Rabelais in his easy chair, I need no grain of salt, for I am thinking only of the broad humanity of the man. Even Sterne's dirty snigger is forgotten in his quaint humanities. *Nihil humani a me alienum puto;* nothing in literary humanities injures me one hair. My eyes are yonder on Mount Pisgah, and though I yearn for the region of stainless snow, I know my way lies through this mud.

In all these respects, and in others, I follow the Roman Catholic Church. There is only one difference between us, that while she fears one form of Rationalism, that which deals with certain dogmas and symbols for which she has an insane though natural affection, I, adding eclecticism to catholicism, fear no doctrine, no book, and no man. I shall say my say for or against the Devil, as any free man has a right to do, but I shall never contend *that he has no existence.*

In this our England, we have numerous priesthoods or deputy Providences, without counting the sad and cloistered priesthood of old Rome. We have, for example, the priesthoods of Episcopacy, of Dissent, of Good Society, of Art and Letters (or Dilettantism), of cheap Science, and, most potent, yet least responsible of all, the Priesthood of the Press, or Journalism. Now, there is not one of all these bodies which is not thoroughly convinced that its own view of the Universe is right, which does not, when occasion offers, persecute and torture unbelievers, which would not, if suffered to do so, summon the executioner or the constable ; and if these same priesthoods were to be called together in full synod, and asked to decide the fate of Literature, the general verdict would possibly be one of Strangulation or Castration. The clergy of all denominations hate each other, the Good Society people suppress each other, the Dilettantes detest all curtain-lifters who are not Dilettantes, and the Journalists are the terror and the scourge of every original thinker under the sun. All, however, are agreed on one point—that, in this most respectable country, there must be no descending into Hell, that Literature especially must be kept clean and wholesome, fit for family perusal. Hence we have been blest for many years with an expurgated literature, in the category of which, I rejoice to say, may be found such books as bring Heaven down to Earth and glorify human nature. Let it be granted, indeed, that a book founded on heavenly intuitions, such a book as the Poems of Tennyson, as the 'Cloister and the

Hearth' of Charles Reade, as the 'Esmond' of Thackeray, as the 'David Copperfield' of Dickens, as the 'Westward Ho!' of Kingsley, as the 'Lorna Doone' of Blackmore, as the 'Woodlanders' of Thomas Hardy, as the 'Greene Ferne Farm' of Richard Jefferies, as the 'Angel in the House' of Coventry Patmore—such a book, with the sunshine and fresh air upon its leaves—is worth a thousand times all the Devil's documents put together. We thank God for it, and it has God's blessing. But there are moments when even the best of us crave more—crave the bitterness of knowledge, the sight of the charnel-house, the glimmer of the deep, dim lights of Hell. For, as I have said, Hell *is*, and we must know it, and to know it is, in the end, to abominate and to avoid it. We are not celestial beings yet. We are earthly and human enough to fancy that the diet of celestial beings is very often insipid. We want the records of human sin and pain. We crave for the elemental passions. We tire even of plum-pudding, and thirst to eat husks with the swine. We miss the tasty leaven, in super-celestial food. And so, when we are sick of a surfeit of holiness, we turn to Farquhar for gay rascality, to Swift for brute-banality, to Byron for lightsome devilry, to Goethe for intellectual concupiscence, to Heine for the persiflage which scorns all sanctities and laughs at all the gods, and to Zola for gruesome testimony against sunlight and human nature. When this is done, after we have seen the Satyr romp and heard the hiccup of Silenus, after we have seen Rabelais charging the monks on his ass Panurge, and left Whitman loafing naked on the sea-shore, do we turn again with less appetite, with less eager insight, towards the shining documents of Heaven ?

Of all the great writers who have been canonized by Humanity, there is scarcely one who, under the proposed Inquisition of Messrs. Shallow and Dogberry, would not have been 'run in,' pilloried, fined, or imprisoned. The author of 'Pericles' would do his six months as a first-class misde- meanant, in company with 'the author of 'Œdipus' and other foreigners of reputation. Sappho, for one little set of verses, would be tied to the cart's- tail, in company with Nanon and Mrs. Behn. In one long chain, the dramatists of the Elizabethan age would go to the moral galleys, followed by the dirtier dramatists of the Restoration. Fielding and Smollett would find no mercy, Richardson himself would only escape with a warning not to offend any more. To come down to contemporaries, I think Mr. Browning might be adjudged an offender against the law of modest reticence, and Mr. George Meredith a revolutionary in the region of sensuous passion. Not all his odes to infancy, not all his apotheosis of the coral and the lollipop, would save Mr. Swinburne. But the authors of the 'Heir of Redclyffe' and 'A Knight Errant' would

rise up to the stainless shrines of literature, and
Mr. Slippery Sweetsong might become the laureate
of the new age of Moral Drapery and Popular
Mauvaise Honte. How good, then, would
Humanity become, bereft of Shakespeare's feudal
glory, denied even a glimpse of frisky blue
stockings under the ballet-skirts of Ouida !
Morality would be saved, possibly. All would be
innocence, a moral constabulary, and good society.
We should have choked up with tracts and pretty
poems and proper novelettes the mouth of a sleeping Volcano; but when Ætna, or Sheol, or Hell, had
its periodical eruption, what would happen *then ?*

I shall not attempt in the space of a brief letter
to penetrate into the *philosophy* of this great
question ; but it will occur to you that Milton's
famous protest against the suppression of books
was echoed indirectly, centuries later, by Mill's
notable plea for Liberty, in which it was contended
(1) that the opinion we wish to suppress may be
true ; (2) that it may, at any rate, contain a
portion of truth ; (3) that vigorous argument
concerning opinions really and wholly true is the
only way of saving these opinions from becoming
conventional and prejudicial to intellectual activity ;
and (4) that without such argument, even good
moral doctrine would cease to have any vital effect
on character or conduct. I rather fear, remember-
ing a certain estrangement which resulted from a
quasi-Rabelaisian joke of Carlyle at Mill's expense,

that the author of the 'Essay on Liberty' would have drawn the line of indulgence at naughty books—just as Locke did, much earlier. But these are brave words of Locke : ' It is only light and evidence that can work a change in men's opinions, and light cannot proceed from corporal sufferings or any *outward penalties ;*' furthermore, ' the power of the civil magistrate consists only in outward force, while true and saving religion consists in the inward persuasion of the mind, without which nothing can be acceptable to God.' Mill's main contention is that it is well or ill with men just in proportion as they respect *truth.* The main contention of suppressionist philosophers is that if the majority can crush out vice by law, it is vicious not to do it, even if a little truth has to be sacrificed too. But how shall we decide what is vicious ? Shall not the history of persecution warn us to be careful how we judge ? And in so far as books are concerned, is not the record of every generation filled with the names of books labelled vicious by the contemporary majority, and afterwards pronounced soul-helping by the verdict of posterity ? The suppressed books form in themselves a Bible of Humanity. If it were only for the sake of one or two little chapters, say the Epistle of Shelley to the Muggletonians or the Song of Songs (not of Solomon, but) of Heine, I should regard that BIBLE of HETERODOXY with devout affection.

Personally, I claim the right of free deliverance, free speech, free thought, and what I claim for myself I claim for every human being. I claim the right to attack and to defend. I claim the right to justify the Devil, if I want to. I can be suppressed by wiser argument, by deeper insight, by greater knowledge, but not by the magistrate, civil or literary. I would stand even by Judas Iscariot in the dock, if his Judge denied him a free hearing, a fair trial. The Truth, if she is great as we assume her to be, must prevail. The evidence of the Devil is necessary to secure the triumph of God; if it were otherwise, the Devil, not his Judge, would be Omnipotent. And the evidence which proves vice and proves virtue must be from *within*, from the Spirit which you cannot cast into prison, but which chooses not unfrequently to chain and shackle itself. Meantime, it is Mr. Coote and the Vigilance Committee, not Mr. Vizetelly, who lie in ignoble chains. We want more light, not more Darkness; more knowledge, not more ignorance; not more government, but more freedom of speech —more production of documents, more verification. Let your Church, Right Hon. Sir, turn round upon herself and say *this*, and we shall witness the last miraculous conversion. *Help* her to say it. Justify literature, justify free thought, by releasing Mr. Vizetelly from a bondage which its an insult to literature. You have only to lift your hand. You have only to say, ' God is, and

He fears nothing, good or evil, that He has created.'
This would be the last and crowning proof of one
man's wisdom; of the Church's infallibility, which
is insight ; of her function, which is the reconciliation and interpenetration of good and evil ; and of
her prerogative, which is the right of Spiritual
Judgment independent of the dim and doubtful
lights of the Civil Law. The police magistrate
cannot save us from Evil, which is in ourselves,
but, even now, Religion *can*.

In this country, I believe, only two classes are
specially pornographic : those who never read at
all, because they cannot or will not, and those who
are sufficiently wealthy to buy and read *éditions de
luxe*. Mr. Vizetelly's publications cannot affect the
former classes, and their existence is a matter of
indifference to the latter, who finger their Casanova
at leisure, and pay readily for costly works like
Burton's translation of the Arabian Nights. The
point of the persecution, therefore, appears to be
that Mr. Vizetelly's books are sufficiently attractive
and cheap to reach those classes who are pornographic in neither their habits nor their tastes—
young clerks, frisky milliners, *et hoc genus omne*.
Now, these people are precisely those who are
robust and healthy-minded enough, familiar with
the world enough, to discriminate for themselves.
Whatever they choose to read will make them
neither better nor worse. The milliner will frisk
without the aid of a Zola, and the young clerk will

follow the milliner, even within the protective shadow
of a Young Men's Christian Association. Wholesale
corruption never yet came from corrupt literature ;
which is the effect, not the cause, of social libertinage. Do we find morality so plentiful amongst
the godly farmers and drovers of Annandale, or
among the ' unco' gude ' of Ayrshire or Dumfries-
shire—thumbers of the Bible, sheep of the Kirk ?
Stands Scotland anywhere but where it did, though
it has not yet acquired an æsthetic taste for the
Abominable, but merely realizes occasionally the
primitive instincts of *La Terre?* Dwells perfect
purity in Brittany and in Normandy, despite the
fact that Zola there is an unknown quantity, and
Paris itself a thing of dream ? Bestialism, animalism, sensualism, realism, call it by what name you
will, is antecedent to and triumphant over all
books whatsoever. Books may reflect it, that is
all ; and I fail to see why they should not, since it
exists. I love my Burns and like my Byron,
though neither was a virtuous or even a ' decent '
person. My Juvenal, my Lucretius, my Catullus,
and even my *porcus porcorum* Petronius, are well
read. My 'Decameron,' with all its incidence of
amativeness, is a breeding nest of poets. Age
cannot wither, nor custom stale, La Fontaine's
infinite variety. But I take such books as these
as I take all such mental food, *cum grano salis*, a
pinch of which keeps each from corruption. Even
the fly-blown Gautier looks well, cold and inedible,

on a sideboard, garnished with Style's fresh parsley.
But I have never found that what my teeth nibble
at has any power to pollute my immortal part.   I
must stand on the earth, with Montaigne and
Rabelais, but does that prevent me from flying
heavenward with Jean Paul, or walking the mountain tops with the Shepherd of Rydal ?   Inspection of the dung-heaps and slaughter-houses with
Jonathan Swift and Zola only makes me more
anxious to get away, with Rousseau, to the peaceful height where the Savoyard Vicar prays !   By
Evil only shall ye distinguish Good, says the
Master ; yea, and by the husks shall ye know the
grain.

The man who says that a Book has power to
pollute his Soul ranks his Soul below a Book.   I
rank mine infinitely higher.

                          ROBERT BUCHANAN.

NOTE.—Since the above letter was written I
have heard that Messrs. Vizetelly have ' suppressed' their translation of Murger's ' Vie de
Bohème,' a book as good and wholesome, to my
mind, as life itself ; and that Messrs. Chatto and
Windus have burned their ' stocks' of Rabelais
and Boccaccio.   *O tempora ! O mores ! O sæclum
insipiens et inficetum !*   What next ?—and next ?
and next ?   O yes, the seizure of the pictures
painted to illustrate the merry Vicar of Meudon,
and the unfettered circulation, in every journal,

of the last dirty details of the Divorce Court. And simultaneously comes the legislation which would confine the ragged street-child to the slums, and denies it one glimpse of happiness in the wicked Theatre! Only those who really know the facts, who have been familiar with the blessing a single Drury Lane Pantomime used to bring to a thousand homes, can understand the cruelty and futility of this last example of providential legislation.

R. B.

THE MODERN YOUNG MAN AS CRITIC.

THE MODERN YOUNG MAN AS CRITIC.

FRANKLY, I do not know what the Modern Young Man is coming to ! The young man of my own early experience was feather-headed, but earnest ; impulsive and . uninstructed, but sympathetic and occasionally studious ; though his faults were many, lack of conviction was certainly not one of them. He dreamed wildly of fame, of fair women, of beautiful books ; and when he read the Masters, he despaired. A great thought, even a fine phrase, stirred him like a trumpet. For him, in his calm and waking moments, female purity was still a sacred certainty, and female shame and suffering were less a proof of woman's baseness and unworthiness than one of man's deterioration. He lifted his hat to the Magdalen, in life and in literature. The human form, even when wrapt in the robes of the street-walker, was still sacred to him; and he would as soon have thought of laying sacrilegious hands upon it as of vivisecting his own mother. In Bohemia he had heard the bird-like

10

cry of Mimi ; in the forest of Arden he had
roamed with Rosalind. For him, in the light-
heartedness of his youth, the world was an en-
chanted dwelling-place. The gods remained, with
God above them. The Heaven of his literary
infancy lay around him. Out in the darkened
streets he met the sunny smile of Dickens, and
down among the English lanes he listened to the
nightingales of Keats and Tennyson. But *now*,
with the passing of one brief generation, the world
has changed ; the youth who was a poet and a
dreamer has departed, and the modern young man
has arisen to take his place. A saturnine young
man, a young man who has never dreamed a dream
or been a child, a young man whose days have been
shadowed by the upas-tree of modern pessimism,
and who is born to the heritage of flash cynicism
and cheap science, of literature which is less literature than criticism run to seed. Though varied in
the genus, he is invariable in the type, which
includes the whole range of modern character,
from the young man of culture expressed in the
elegant humanities of Mr. Henry James and Mr.
Marion Crawford, down to the bank-holiday young
man of no culture, of whom the handiest example
is (as we shall see) a certain egregious Mr. George
Moore. The modern young man, whether with or
without education, has no religion and no enthusiasm. Nourished in the new creed of Realism
and ' Art for Art,' he is ready, with De Goncourt

and Zola, to 'throw a woman on the dissecting-
table,' and cut the beautiful dead form to pieces,
and content, with Paul Bourget (*ridiculus mus* of a
social mud-heap in parturition), to take Love ' as a
subject,' and call it a cruel enigma. Even the
insufferable Gautier was superior to all this ; he
was not too clever to live, not over-full of insight
to write. But the modern young man is the very
paradox of prescience and nescience, of instruction
and incapacity. He writes books which are dead
books from the birth ; he formulates criticisms,
which are laborious self-dissections, indecent ex-
posures of the infinitely trivial ; he paints, he
composes, he toils and moils, and all to no avail.
For the faith which is life, and the life which is
reverence and enthusiasm, have been denied to
him. The sun has gone out above him, and the
earth is arid dust beneath him. He has scarcely
heard of Bohemia, he is utterly incredulous of
Arden, and he is aware with all his eyes, not of
Mimi or of Rosalind, but of Sidonie Risler and
Emma Bovary. He has looked down Vesuvius,
out of his very cradle. In Boston he has measured
Shakespeare and Dickens, and found the giants
wanting ; in France he has talked the *argot* of
L'Assommoir over the grave of Hugo ; even in
free Scandinavia he has discovered a Zola with a
stuttering style and two wooden legs, and made
a fetish of Ibsen ; while here in England he
threatens Turner the painter, and has practically

(as he thinks) demolished the gospel of poetical sentiment. And yet, curiously enough, he has done nothing, he has given us nothing; for he *is* nothing. He is appearing before us, however, in so many forms of pertinacious triviality, that it behoves us to take a passing glance at him, and to inquire, however briefly, into the phenomenon of his existence. To study that phenomenon completely would far transcend the limits of a brief article; so I must confine myself at present to the consideration of the young man in one capacity only, that of Critic, though he is nothing indeed if not critical, as we shall see. From the day when Goethe sent forth his 'plague of microscopes' to the day when Matthew Arnold defined poetry itself as a 'criticism of life' (committing poetical suicide in that preposterous definition), everybody has been critical, and of course our young man is no exception to the rule. Of the Modern Young Man as Critic, then, I propose to furnish some few easily selected illustrations, subdividing my types as follows: (1) The Young Man who is Superfine; (2) the Detrimental Young Man; (3) the Olfactory Young Man; (4) the Young Man in a Cheap Literary Suit; and (5) the Bank-Holiday Young Man—the last pretty much the same as discovered in real life and classified by Mr. Gilbert. All these young men have drifted into literature, and, though there is an immeasurable distance between the distinction and culture of type number one and

the unkempt barbarity of type number five, they
have all certain characteristics in common—an
easy air of omniscience in dealing with the great
problems of Life and Thought, an assumption of
complete familiarity with the ' facts ' of existence
(they are all, in a word, wonderfully ' knowing'),
an open or secret disrespect for average ideals, a
constitutional hatred of ' conventional morality,'
an equally constitutional hatred of ' imagination,'
and, above all, a general air of never having been
really young, of never having loved or worshipped,
or been mastered by, anything or anybody, on the
earth or above it.

Taking the types in their intellectual and natural
order, for I propose to work down the scale from
the highest note to the lowest, I can find no better
example of the Superfine Young Man than Mr.
Henry James, well known as the author of several
minor novels and numerous minor criticisms.
Highly finished, perfectly machined, icily regular,
thoroughly representative, Mr. James is the educated young or youngish American whom we have
all met in society; the well-dressed person who
knows everybody, who has read everything, who
has been everywhere, who is nebulously conscious
of every astral and mundane influence, but who, as
a matter of fact, is most at home on the Boule-
vards, and whose religion includes as its chief
article the well-known humorous formula—that
good Americans, when they die, go to Paris. No

one can dispute Mr. James's cleverness ; he is very
clever. He is, moreover, well-spoken, agreeable,
good-tempered, tolerant. He can even, upon occasion, affect and seem to feel enthusiasm—can talk
of Tourgenieff as 'lovable,' of Daudet as ' adorable.'
For the first quarter of an hour of our conversation with him we are largely impressed with his
variety, his catholicity; after that comes a certain
indescribable sense of vagueness, of superficiality,
of indifferentism; finally, if we must give the thing
a name, a forlorn feeling of vacuity, of silliness.
With a sigh we discover it ; this young man, with
all his information, with all his variety and catholicity, with all his wonderful knowledge of things
caviare to the general, is, *au fond*, a fatuous young
man. Startled at first by our discovery, we turn
away from him ; then, returning to him, under dis-
hallucination, we perceive that he does not really
know so much, even superficially, as we imagined ;
that his easy air of omniscience is a mere cloak to
cover complete intellectual indetermination. For
him and his, great literature has really no existence. He is secretly indifferent about all the gods,
dead and living. He takes us into his confidence,
welcomes us into his study, and we find that the
faces on the walls are those, not of a Pantheon, but
of the comic newspaper and the circulating library.
He appears to recognise the modern Sibyl in
George Eliot; and why, indeed, should he not take
that triumphant Talent seriously, when the inspira-

tion of his childhood was the picture-gallery in
Punch, when he sees a profound social satirist in
Mr. du Maurier, and when he can fall prone before
the masterpieces of that hard-bound genius *in posse*
Mr. Robert Louis Stevenson? These, then, are
the glorious discoveries of the young man's omniscience—George Eliot, Alphonse Daudet, Flaubert.
Du Maurier, Mr. Punch, and the author of ' Treasure Island.' With these, one is bound to say, he
is, like all well-bred Americans, thoroughly at home.
He says charming things concerning them. He
finds more than one of them (adopting that hideous
French phrase) ' adorable.' He becomes the little
prophet of the little masters, and he publishes a
little book* about them—a book full of the agreeable art of conversation, such as we listen to in a
hundred drawing-rooms. Nor is it at all out of
keeping with this elegant young man's character
that his talk about his literary ideals is, when it
is most admiring, most patronizing. He keeps in
reserve a latent scepticism even concerning the *dii
minores* of his microscopic religion ; nay, he suggests to us that his remarks concerning them are
merely lightly thrown-out illustrations of his own
superabundant sympathy—that, if you really put
him to it, he *might* read Shakespeare with appreciation, and *could* share the boy's enthusiasm about
Byron.

Very characteristic of Mr. James is his neat

* ' Partial Portraits,' by Henry James.

little paper on Alphonse Daudet—a quite marvellous example of ' how not to commit one's self in
criticism,' how to burn incense with one hand and
snap the fingers of the other.   He begins by
saying that ' a new novel by this admirable genius
is to my mind the most delightful literary event
that can occur just now ;' he ends by ' retracting
some of the admiration ' he has ' expressed for him,'
and saying that he has ' no high imagination, and,
as a consequence, no ideas ;' and finally, as an
afterthought, to conciliate his Famulus Mr. Facing-
both-ways, he cries, ' And then he is so free !' and
' The sight of such freedom is delightful.'   This
inconsistency, it will be admitted, is rather hard on
an author of whom Mr. James also remarks : ' If
we were talking French, nothing would be simpler
than to say that Alphonse Daudet is *adorable*,
and have done with it.'   The ' admirable genius,'
a book from whose pen is ' the most delightful
literary event that can occur,' who is so ' free,' and
whose delight and freedom consists in ' having no
imagination, no ideas,' must be a little puzzled by
such treatment ; but, after all, it is only the
superfine young man's way of telling us that he is
really so omniscient as to have no clear opinion at
all on that or any subject.   In one of the best
things in the book, a conversation about ' Daniel
Deronda,' in which the interlocutors are a literary
gentleman and two talkative ladies, he is seen at
his best or worst—now panting with admiration

for George Eliot's genius, again inferring that she
had no genius at all, trimming, finessing, explaining,
blaming, excusing, till the poor puzzled reader ex-
claims in despair, ' Oh this Superfine Young Man !
What *does* he mean ?   What *does* he feel ?   Why
does he not speak out his mind, and have done
with it ?'   This, however, is not Mr. James's
method.   His desire is to convince us at any
expense that he sees every side of a question, is
familiar with every *nuance* of a subject ; and in
the eagerness of this desire he is paralyzed out of
all conviction.   His perceptive faculties are good
enough, naturally ; his temper is highly agreeable
and his style affable in the extreme ; but his
courage is as non-existent as his opinions.   So
clever yet so half-hearted a gentleman never yet
committed himself to criticism.   Not less amazing
than the fact that he should consider a drawing-
room discussion on ' Daniel Deronda ' really worth
recording, is the fact that he should labour under
the impression that he has really pronounced any
dictum on any subject.   One can understand the
critics who *have* opinions, wise or unwise.   One
can follow with amusement the subacid sneers of
Hazlitt, the florid flourishes of Macaulay, the
sledge-hammer blows of Carlyle, the screaming
invective of Mr. Ruskin, because all these writers
have something to say and contrive to say it ; but
when we enter the *salon* and encounter the superfine young man, who is neither bitter, nor florid,

nor brutal, nor shrewish, but is in all respects
perfectly well-behaved, we are not amused or
edified—we are bored.   It matters little whether
he is pattering to us about George Eliot, or about
'his friend' Tourgenieff, or about Alphonse
Daudet, or about the caricatures in *Punch*, or
about the Art of Fiction—the effect is invariably
the same.   No sooner is one opinion advanced
than it is qualified with another ; scarcely is one
view taken when another is substituted ; an
endless succession of personal pronouns—'*I*
think,' '*I* will admit,' '*I* consider,' '*I* suspect,' etc.,
covers a total absence of critical personality.   The
young man's very religion is 'qualified.'   His mind
is bewildered by its dreadful catholicity.   He has
not a spark of hate in him, because (with all his
admirations and 'adorations') he has not a spark
of love.   As was said long ago in another
connection, ' How sad and perplexing it must be to
be *so* clever !'

One regrets not a little that the final impression
left by a young man of such cultivation should be
one of dulness, of silliness ; yet so it is, and it is
only another proof that education is sometimes a
very misleading thing.   I can quite imagine that
Mr. Henry James, had he read less, travelled less,
known less, might have become a highly interesting writer ; but early in his career he appears to
have quitted America for Europe, and to have left
the possibilities of his grand nativity behind him.

To be born an American is surely a great privilege ; yet nearly all Americans of talent flit moth-like towards the garish lights of London or Paris, and hover round these lights in wanton, not to say imbecile, gyrations, till they pop into the glare, drop down singed and wingless, and are forgotten. No individual is so catholic as an average American of culture ; no individual is, *au fond*, so worldly, so supremely trivial ; and Mr. Henry James is this average American *in excelsis.* A good deal of this is, of course, matter of temperament ; a good deal more, matter of training. Youngish men like Mr. James have refined their perceptions to so thin a point that they are only fit to commemorate the judgments of the drawing-room on the one hand and the smoking-room on the other. The air of free literature asphyxiates and paralyzes them. Outside of society and Paris, they are far too clever, far too educated, to breathe or live at all.

It is Mr. James's privilege, or perhaps his misfortune, to write for the English public ; but I strongly suspect him of a hidden longing to cater for the public which is Continental. If he were not doomed by his nationality to be a superfine young man, he would perhaps choose to become a Detrimental one, like his friend M. Paul Bourget, who dedicates a book to him and claims at least two-thirds of him as thoroughly Parisian. The Detrimental Young Man, to whom I now come by a very natural transition, is quite as pertinacious as Mr. James, though far less cautious ; fully as omniscient, but not nearly so self-assured ; far more audacious, but in reality quite as dull. He is a refined or superfined sort of naturalist, to whom the coarse method of Zola appears very shocking, and who, before he ' dissects ' the human subject, is careful to *wash his hands;* nay, he goes further, and washes his subject too, that the spectator may be spared disgust and pain as far as possible. An elegant young man, with a certain amount of surgical skill, he affects to have studied profoundly the morbid anatomy of the female character ; but, alas ! we soon discover that his elegance is merely that of a man about town, while his science is only a device to hide the tastes of the *boulevardier.* Two or three feeble novels, and a few flabby criticisms, form his literary credentials ; so that he would be scarcely worth considering if he were not the type of a very numerous class. Like his fellows, he parades a ' method '; like his superiors, he vaunts the dogma of *L'Art pour L'Art,* which, in other words, is Art without the aspirate, without any heart at all. The world is beginning to discover, by the way, that the moment a writer begins to talk about his Art he is forfeiting its privileges. It is quite true, moreover, that Art has nothing to do with Morality, directly ; but it has a great deal to do with it indirectly ; for (as I attempted to show years ago) if a work of Art is beautiful, it *must* be moral. This, of course, is not saying that it may not offend against conventional canons. But all the palaver about Art of such writers as Flaubert was merely a feint to disguise a radical defect in sympathy, an incapacity for imagining greatly and feeling either deeply or profoundly; and it will be found generally that the writers who echo the palaver are, like Flaubert, workers in *mosaic*—artists who, instead of working under special inspiration or with inspiring passion, take little bits of subject and piece them together, sometimes with very charming effect, but never with the genius of great literature, The talk of Art for Art is, in short, disingenuous, being used almost invariably to excuse or to justify trivialities of invention and temperamental want of creative insight.

What kind of a person the Detrimental Young Man is may be gathered from a reference to one of his well-known stories, ' Un Crime d'Amour,'* a work so far critical that it seems to embody the writer's theory of social life. It is the very commonplace history of a *boulevardier's* love for his friend's wife, his seduction of her, and the consequent misery and dishallucination. In the opening chapter we are introduced to the only three *dramatis personæ*—the husband, the wife, and the lover. ' Le petit salon était éclairé d'une lumière douce par les trois lampes—de hautes lampes posées dans les vases de Japon, et garnies

* By Paul Bourget.

de globes sur lesquels s'appliquaient des abat-jour simples de nuance bleu pâle.' This 'nuance bleu pâle' is the only thing which differentiates 'Un Crime d'Amour' from other idylls of adultery, and the only quality which distinguishes M. Paul Bourget's 'method' from that of other foolish young men. It permeates the story and the style, it sicklies o'er the countenances of the adulterers and the author, it is used in lieu of honest daylight to give artistic seeming to a theme which is radically prurient yet absurd. In one consummate chapter we are treated to a detailed description of the furnished house which Armand, the lover, takes for his mistress, and in which, dazzled by the 'nuance bleu pâle,' 'elle venait de sentir, sous les caresses de cet homme qu'elle aimait si profondément, une émotion inconnue s'éveiller en elle.' Then the same 'nuance' travels on to the husband, who in course of time, poor fellow! gets very blue indeed; rests on the wretched woman, who deceives her lover as well as her husband and then cries, *in articulo mortis,* 'C'est cette souffrance qui m'a sauvée, c'est par elle que j'ai jugé ma vie ;' and finally transfigures the Detrimental Young Man himself, while he informs us that 'une chose venait de naître en lui, avec laquelle il pourrait toujours trouver des raisons de vivre et d'agir : la religion de la souffrance humaine.' This is the moral, that experiences of the sort I have described make even a detrimental young man alive to the fact that

treachery and seduction turn life into Dead Sea
fruit and lead married ladies into much trouble.
We have heard it a thousand times before, we shall
hear it a thousand times again ; for our modern
young men are honest enough to admit that Love
is not a thing of cakes and ale. No; it is the prerogative, it is the glory, of the Detrimental Young
Man to pose himself in the pale blue 'nuance' of a
picturesque unhappiness. In his sad perception of
the sorrows of *crim. con.* and the dreariness of infidelity, he resembles our own glorious Ouida ; and
he resembles that classic of the Langham in other
respects—in a feverish appreciation of millinery
and upholstery, in a love of subdued lights and
soft odours, in a rapturous inspiration to paint the
splendours of the bedpost and the mysteries of the
bath-room. Indeed, if we could imagine Zola and
Ouida collaborating on a story to be afterwards
revised by Mr. Henry James, we should get a very
good idea of a work by M. Paul Bourget. We
should have all the nastiness *plus* all the niceness,
and the whole carefully supervised by a master of
the superfine.

In another novel, 'Cruelle Énigme,' the
Detrimental Young Man goes further, and for the
edification of his friend Mr. James, to whom the
work is dedicated, 'throws a woman on the dissecting table,' and vivisects her, arriving, after
much more millinery, at the conclusion that Love,
like life, is 'a cruel enigma.' The poor woman

deceives everybody, even the very young lover
whom she adores, and is, in fact, just the familiar
tame-tigress of French fiction; but she is specialized
again for us by the pale-blue 'nuance,' producing
in this case an anatomical study much in the
manner of the eccentric artist Van Beers. All
this might be very interesting, no doubt, if there
were any Science in it. Readers who know what
Balzac has done in this way would certainly not
deny the attraction to be found in the morbid
pathology of the female character. But Balzac
was a man, not a *boulevardier;* and even Zola
is a Man deformed. One page of the 'Human
Comedy,' or one chapter of 'La Joie de Vivre,' is
worth all that M. Paul Bourget or Mr. Henry
James ever wrote or dreamed of writing. And if
I return without apology to our Superfine Young
Man in this connection, it is not that I am un-
aware of the ethical distinction between him and
the Detrimental Young Man. But there is an
ethical resemblance also, though it does not lie
upon the surface. It is the business—it may,
for all I know, be the boast and pride—of Mr.
James and his compeers to translate the fiction
of the French Empire and Republic into a vocabulary suitable for the perusal of young American
ladies ; and young ladies, in England and America,
read their dreary books—compared with which
the literature of the 'Lamplighter' and the 'Old
Helmet' is edifying. To call *them* immoral would

be exaggeration; they are not vital enough to be immoral. But they, too, parade the pale-blue 'nuance' which is to redeem insipidity and impertinence, and turn commonplace into Art. In their cold-blooded self-sufficiency, in their indomitable triviality, in their stupendous dulness and omniscient vacuity, they suggest Zola (a dullard *au fond*) under ruthless expurgation and Gautier without the flesh. For, the modern French theory of writing being that nothing is too trivial for a subject so long as it gives opportunity for narrative and analysis, French novelists escape dulness by choosing subjects which, though trivial, are suggestive or unclean ; and our Art for Art novelists of English race choose, in secret emulation, subjects which, though trivial almost to fatuity, are prurient in their supreme affectation of moral catholicity.

But let me put it in plainer words, in clearer English. There is neither flesh and blood, nor virility, nor manly vigour, in these young moderns, either in France or England ; they breathe no oxygen ; they display no intellectual or moral health. They hang about the petticoats of young women, in the 'nuance bleu pâle' of a moral atmosphere of their own making. Contrast a book like 'Un Crime d'Amour' with a book like Murger's 'Vie de Bohème,' and note the difference between two generations. Compare the 'Sappho' of 1887 with even the 'Dame aux Camélias' of

11

1850. To go even a little further back, the jaded
young man of Alfred de Musset still preserved his
hallucinations. Rolla saw his ideal naked, not on
the dissecting-table, but *alive*—

> ' Et pendant un moment, tous deux avaient aimés !'

He was not a nice young man, with his shirt-
collar turned down *à la* Byron, and his addiction to
absinthe ; but, compared with this modern young
man, he was a gentleman, a poet, and a dreamer.
And then, if you will, compare such books as ' The
Portrait of a Lady ' with the early girl-studies of
Trollope, a novelist ever thin and trivial enough, in
all conscience. *There* was the fresh flush of English
life, the breath of English homes ; *here* we get only
the simper of the superior person, the drawl of the
superfine young miss etherealized into a heaven of
small sensations, small intuitions, and small, in-
finitesimally small, conversation. It is nothing to
the purpose to explain that Mr. Henry James is a
strictly moral writer in the ordinary sense of the
word, and that M. Paul Bourget is a highly
immoral one. My own impression is that the two
gentlemen are more nearly akin, both in mind and
morals, than either would care to admit. Though
one is superfine, while the other is detrimental,
both are omnisciently silly ; neither has one spark
of the vitality, one flash of the insight, which made
young men write books a generation ago.

Whose children are these ? Who is responsible

for the appearance of these young men in society
and literature ? I think their literary genealogy,
though here and there obscure, may be traced with
quasi-Biblical accuracy on both sides of the
Channel. *There,* our own Byron begot Alfred de
Musset, and Alfred de Musset begot Dumas *fils,*
and Dumas *fils* begot Daudet, and Daudet begot
Paul Bourget. *Here,* Richardson begot Jane
Austen, and Jane Austen became the mother
of Theodore Hook, and Theodore Hook begot
Anthony Trollope, and Anthony Trollope begot
Henry James. In either succession there was
a gradual process of deterioration, resulting at last
in what physiologists call 'an exhausted breed ;'
nor is the present threatened intermarriage between Parisian impertinence and English triviality
likely to improve the stock. Meantime, the great
masters, Balzac and Hugo, Fielding and Dickens,
appear to have left no lawful descendants. Look
back again at the Paris and the London of a
generation ago ! How fresh and living, how full
of wild enthusiasm and delightful temper, was
literature ! Here and yonder, the breeze blew
lightly from Bohemia. Art was sunny, life was
free. The young Frenchmen swaggered like
Fluellen, forcing all and ready to honour the
green leek of Romanticism. The young Cockneys
swarmed everywhere, full of the new gospel of
Dickens and a robustious Fairyland. Young
writers were neither cynical, nor cautious, nor

11—2

'knowing'; they were mad with the exuberance of their vitality. Since the old boys were childishly reverent and happy, why should not the young boys be so too? In those days there was little or no thought of 'dissecting' women, only of loving and honouring and embracing them; no care to hang round the skirts of young ladies, analyzing their intuitions, but rather a desire to roam in Arden with them, or to join them at 'Roger de Coverley.' There were girls then, as there were boys. Alas, there are now neither girls nor boys, only nasty little men and women! I rather fancy that the easy descent of Avernus was begun when Thackeray drew Blanche Amory and Becky Sharp, and painted his good women without brains; for though Thackeray had been in Bohemia, and never quite forgot the soft sylvan susurrus of its green glades, he created a school of young cynics who have something in common with the young realists of to-day. Be that as it may, the time of cheap pessimism has come, and good cheer and animal spirits, poetry and enthusiasm, have now no abiding place in literature.

Next on my list comes the Olfactory Young Man, whom I shall deal with very briefly, as he differs from the Detrimental Young Man only in a few minor particulars, and, like him, is French by nationality. M. Guy de Maupassant, in his introduction to Flaubert's 'Correspondence with George Sand,' entreats us not to get angry with any one

artistic theory, 'since every theory is the generalized
expression of a temperament asking itself questions;' in other words, he contends that it is the
business of the artist, not to ascertain truth
absolute, but to describe the effect of social
phenomena on his own organs, his own temperament.   This being admitted, he contends, taking
his own point of perception, the only point of view
possible to his temperament, that it is a very
ugly and a very nasty world.   His sense of unpleasant odours in life leads to the most grievous
of all afflictions, Naresmia.   He goes through life
and literature following his unlucky *nose*.   All the
meaner phenomena of life, all its baseness, all its
triviality, allure and fascinate him, while he is
blind, and glories in being blind, to its subtle
suggestions, its higher meanings.   A critic and a
novelist, he parades his little gospel of realism,
and declines to subject either his thought or his
style to any disturbing influence.   But, after all,
the main thing in life of which he is conscious is
the sexual instinct, and the sexual instinct on its
most physical side.   His lovers find out each
other, like animals, by the sense of *smell*.   From
the scent of a rose to the perfume of a petticoat,
life is conditioned by its olfactory peculiarities;
beneath and within it all is the odour of decaying
moral vegetation, the stench, faint or overpowering,
of the human dead body, of the tomb.   I suppose
M. de Maupassant is an artist; he is careful to

tell us that he is. For my own part, I am
content, with only this stray reference, to pass him
by. A young gentleman who threatens to become,
like the famous Slawkenbergius of Sterne, 'all
nose,' would be very useful company for a sanitary
inspector or a member of the Board of Works, but,
fortunately, literature is much more than osmology,
and Humanity contains something beyond and
above its epidermis.

It is a relief, after discovering such subtleties
of refinement, literary and olfactory, to come face
to face with the good, square, honest, unintelligence of the Young Man in a Cheap Literary
Suit. Mr. James, M. Bourget, and M. de Maupassant are models of literary elegance, and would
look aghast on the loud, showy, every-day dress
of tweed which forms the literary attire of Mr.
William Archer, a young gentleman from Scotland
who has attained to the proud dignity of being
dramatic critic of the *World;* a saturnine and
severe young gentleman, a young gentleman who
has taken the Drama under his protection, and
writes in all seriousness about plays and players.[*]
I have on a former occasion, in a very rough
ad captandum fashion, described Mr. Archer's
literary gifts. It is a curious fact, not to be overlooked in the present survey, that while the critics
of twenty years ago were recruited from the ranks
of literary aspirants, with special gifts and ambitions

[*] 'About the Theatre,' by William Archer.

of their own in other directions, and while such critics were young men of enthusiastic temperament and with minds nourished on free literature, the most boisterous critics of the present moment are recruited from the ranks of the uninspired and unaspiring, are, in other words, young men who seem never to have studied seriously or felt profoundly any literature at all. A little knowledge, a very little English, and much pertinacity, are at any rate Mr. Archer's equipment, enabling him to pronounce judgment on works of art, to talk glibly about the drama and its professors, and to deliver a lecture on his favourite subjects at the Royal Institution. The pet object of Mr. Archer's aversion is Mr. Irving. Our young man began his career by an attack on that gentleman, consisting chiefly of ' Bank-holiday ' personalities. He qualified this attack a little later on by a pamphlet on ' Mr. Irving as Actor and Manager,' while his friend and quondam *collaborateur*, Mr. Low, laid at the popular idol's feet the dedication of a voluminous work on the drama. Still, Mr. Archer has nothing but scorn, open or disguised, for Mr. Irving as an actor, and for the ' poetical ' productions of the Lyceum. Ranging further afield, he inveighs against the ' fanfaronade ' of Victor Hugo, and finds his best dramas ' about on the level of Italian Opera ;' while in Zola and Flaubert he discovers the kind of beauty which enables him to exclaim : ' This is true ! this is real !' The public, it seems to Mr. Archer, ' is beginning to demand more and more imperatively that the dramatist shall be, not indeed a moralist (*that may come later on!*), but an observer, and shall give us in his work, not a judgment or an *ideal*, but a *painting;*' and on this score, and on the score that he finds indications among dramatists of increased observation, he thinks that the drama is ' advancing.'

Mr. Archer, in fact, is nothing if not ' critical '; that is to say, his cheap literary suit is worn by him as armour against all the shafts of imagination. He pines for a drama where there shall be no ' ideals,' and which shall be an absolute and accurate ' transcription of life,' and he sees hope for it, finds hints of it, when he contemplates such splendid experiments as Mr. Pinero's ' Lords and Commons,' Mr. Grundy's ' Snowball,' and the ' Great Pink Pearl.' ` Poetical and imaginative plays he finds, on the whole, dull and uninteresting ; not nearly ' knowing ' enough, or severe enough, for this generation ; and in his gloomy expectation of the hour when the dramatist shall be a ' moralist' (which is ' to come,' *mirabile dictu!*) he turns with all the eagerness of which he is capable to the latest dramatist of Scandinavia—to Ibsen, who is ' stumping ' the North of Europe in the interests of so-called Scientific Realism.

Shrewd, clever, fearless, individual if not original, Ibsen has produced certain pamphlets which he calls plays, and in each one of which he

advances one of those dreary ethical propositions
which the world is now receiving *ad nauseam.*
A⁻ quite loathsome piece of morbid pathology
called ' Gengangere ' is considered his masterpiece.
It is a story of heredity, showing with what has
been called ' relentless fidelity ' how the sins of the
parents are visited on the children—a thesis
chiefly illustrated by two characters, a miserable
and depraved young man who inherits insanity
from a dissipated father, and a perkish young
woman who takes her foibles from a mother who
' went wrong.' As a realistic experiment this play
is not uninteresting ; as a work of art, it is on the
intellectual level of De Goncourt ; for it means
nothing and is nothing, except a disagreeable
reminder of facts with which every thinking man
is familiar. A poet might have taken the subject,
and stirred us by it. A dramatist would have
made it live and move. Ibsen, after disgusting
and horrifying us beyond measure, leaves the
subject exactly where he found it—in the region
of dreary and dirty commonplace. And as this
arid writer deals with the subject of Heredity, so
does he deal with Sociology, with Morality, with
Religion, placing a smudgy finger on the black
marks which disfigure the map of life, but seldom
if ever assisting us with any flash of poetic vision.
Unfortunately for literature, his audacity in
attracting the modern young man has infected
a far nobler writer of his own nationality, the

Björnson who imagined what is perhaps the divinest love-episode in any language, that of Audhild in 'Sigurd Slembe.' Of late years Björnson has been drifting towards the shifting sands of realism, attracted thither by the false lights set by Ibsen *et hoc genus omne.* But not in that direction, not in the way of cheap science and hideous human pathology, lies the freedom of art or the salvation of literature. When the prose of truth has been said, its poetry remains to be told ; and when the great writer comes to deal with such themes as physical disease and moral responsibility, he will show us how impossible, how hopeless, how heartbreaking it is, to view these themes from the point of view of the pessimist or of the Modern Young Man as Critic. Fortunately, Shakespeare and fresh air remain, while the artistic progeny of Schopenhauer asphyxiate themselves in close chambers and try experiments on the dead or living subject.

If Ibsen is a great or even a good writer, as Mr. Archer and his friends assure us that he is, then the great writers of all countries have been from time immemorial hopelessly in the wrong— then we must accept M. Zola's dictum that the true method of literature is only just discovered. In that case, to be a great writer it is only necessary to be stupendously and supremely unimaginative, and to see nothing beyond the bit of tissue at the point of the scalpel. But Æschylus and

Sophocles, Shakespeare and Fielding, Balzac and
Victor Hugo (to go no further for examples) have
warned us that literature can glorify Science while
embracing it. Take a work of any of those
masters, no matter how gross or how revolting the
subject—choose the 'Agamemnon' or the 'Antigone,' 'Macbeth' or 'Lear,' 'Tom Jones' or
'Joseph Andrews,' 'Père Goriot' or the story of
Fantine—and what impression remains? The
terror, the sadness, the pity, or (as it may be) the
mad absurdity of life, but above all, its divine
suggestions. What holds true of the masterpieces
holds true of all literature which is sound and hale ;
such literature explains by insight what is dark
and horrible, redeems by insight what is base and
mean, and instead of leaving the wound of a moral
sore wide open to horrify Humanity, heals it with
the balm of a subtle interpretation. It is because
Zola justifies himself thus occasionally, that even
he, with all his banalities, is worth considering.

But, naturally, the Young Man in a cheap
Literary Suit, sunk in the self-satisfaction of being
completely though inexpensively rigged out, and
consequently overpowering, resents imagination.
Great is the truth, he says, and it shall prevail ;
but there is truth *and* truth, and what satisfies
the needs of a small critic is wormwood to the soul
of a thinker or a poet. A little culture is a
dangerous thing ; for it encourages a dull young
man of saturnine proclivities to decry the masters,

to extol the dullards, and to pose as a superior person. Writers like Mr. Archer assert that Art may go wrong through too much sentiment, too much imagination, and that photography has been sent to put it right. Yet the outcome of the teaching of all great literature is that, while Realism is the device of blind men and feeble intellects, Poetry, not Pessimism and Cynicism, is the living *Truth*.

It would be vain to follow our present young man through all the perversions caused by a hasty literary equipment and a morbid intellectual appetite. As the absinthe-drinker, rapidly losing the sense of taste, finds that only acrid wormwood will suit his palate, so Mr. Archer takes his Ibsen with a relish, and even thanks the gods for Mr. W. S. Gilbert. While he has not one good word for a Titan like Mr. Charles Reade, he waxes almost eloquent when his theme is a small cynic or a huge dullard. Great sentiments, great motives, great emotions, great conceptions, great language, alike repel him. By temperament and by education, he is, like his superiors with whom I have placed him in juxtaposition, wholly un-imaginative and unsympathetic.

One word, before I proceed, on a point sug-gested by the growth in art of that diabolic love of the Horrible which is to be found among the class of realists so much admired by Mr. Archer and his friends. To those who imagine, as I do,

that the world has been growing too cruel and
cynical to exist in any sort of moral comfort, there
is more than mere social significance in the occur-
rence of such hideous catastrophes as Whitechapel
murders and other epidemics of murder and mutila-
tion ; for they show at least that our social
philosophy of nescience has reached a cataclysm,
and that the world, in its despair, may be driven
back at last to some saner and diviner creed. The
lurid and ever-vanishing apparition known in the
newspapers as ' Jack the Ripper ' is to our lower
social life what Schopenhauer is to philosophy,
what Zola and his tribe are to literature, and what
Van Beers is to art : the diabolic adumbration of
a disease which is slowly but surely destroying
moral sentiment, and threatening to corrupt human
nature altogether. ' Jack the Ripper,' indeed, is a
factor to be reckoned with everywhere nowadays,
and it behoves us, therefore, to study him carefully.
To begin with, he is an instructed, not a merely
ignorant, person. He is acquainted with at least
the superficialities of Science. His contempt for
human nature, his delight in the abominable, his
calm and calculating though savage cruelty, his
selection of his victims from among the socially
helpless and morally corrupt, his devilish ingenuity,
his supernatural pitilessness, are all indications by
which we may know him as typical, whether in
literature or in the slums, in Art or among the
lanes of Whitechapel. Most characteristic of all

is his irreverence for the human form divine, and
his cynical contempt for the weaker sex. As the
unknown murderer of the East-End, he desecrates
and mutilates his poor street-walking victims. As
Zola or De Goncourt, he seizes a living woman,
and vivisects her nerve by nerve, for our instruction
or our amusement. To him and to his class there
are no sanctities, physical or moral or social ; no
mysteries, human or superhuman. He believes
that life is cankered through and through. And
as he is, let it be clearly understood, so is the
typical, the average, pessimist of the present
moment. Everywhere in society we are con
fronted with the instructed person for whom there
are no gods, no holy of holies, no purity, and, above
all, no spiritual ideals. Contemporaneous with
modern pessimism has arisen the cruel disdain of
Woman, the disbelief in that divine *Ewigweibliche*,
or Eternal Feminine, which of old created heroes,
lovers, and believers ; and this disdain and unbelief,
this cruel and brutal scorn, descends with the
violence of horror on the unfortunate and the
feeble, on the class called ' fallen,' which in nobler
times supplied to Humanity, to Literature, and to
Art, the piteous type of the Magdalen. To understand the revolution in human sentiment which has
taken place even within the generation, contrast
poor Mimi once more with even Madame Bovary !
With the decay of masculine faith and chivalry,
with the belief that women are essentially corrupt

and fit subjects for mere vivisection, has come a
corresponding decline in the feminine character
itself; for just as pure and beautiful women made
men chivalrous and noble, so did the chivalry and
nobility of men keep women safe, in the prerogative
of their beauty and their purity.

For myself, who write as a pure optimist and
sentimentalist, and still preserve the illusions of my
foolish youth, I see in the change around me only
a lurid and hideous nightmare. It cannot be real,
it cannot be the living waking truth, for if so, Life
is a lazar-house and a slaughter-house, and there is
nothing left but Despair and Death. I know (am I
not told so on every hand?) that this is mere
'sentiment.' I know that to believe in the Magdalen is almost as retrograde as to believe in the
Christ. I am referred, for my guidance, to a
whole literature dealing with the morbid pathology
of the female character, and am left free to consult
my Thackeray of the drawing-rooms or my Zola of
the sewers. Neither Becky Sharp nor Blanche
Amory, however, any more than Madame Bovary
or the wife of the painter Claude, has any power
to interest me, any skill to convert me. My own
experience, though poor and uneventful, has shown
me that womankind is *not* entirely composed of
silken monsters and ferocious tigress-cats. I have
with my own ears heard the cry of the Magdalen
just as certainly as I have listened to the bird-like
laugh of Mimi and have stood by the bedside of

Camille. I am aware, in a word, that what is known as the 'sentimental' view of evil is corroborated by my own knowledge of the world and of human nature. Pessimism is a lie; that basest of lies which is half a truth, it attracts, by its special pleadings, its triumphant reference to hideous facts, the half-instructed among human beings. It is a creed for the semi-cultivated, for the men of some knowledge and little understanding, and from the bulk of these issue our 'Jack the Rippers' —in Life, in Literature, in Art, and in Criticism.

I have now arrived at the bottom rung of the ladder, where Mr. George Moore, the last young man on my list, is waiting for me, ready, nay determined, to throw off the mask and let us see the Modern Young Man as Critic exactly as he *is.* It is doubtless a far cry from Mr. Henry James to Mr. Moore; but though the one is a barbarous and the other a superfine young man, they have certain typical qualities in common, as we shall discover. In a recently published masterpiece,* Mr. Moore paints his own portrait for a faithless generation. His book goes straight to the mark. Its vanity, its ignorance, its courage, is colossal. Its self-exposure amounts to the sublime.

I for one am very glad that, after all the lamentable want of candour characteristic of our Harrys with the 'H,' the world is treated at last to a complete revelation of the type which has

---

* 'A Young Man's Confessions,' by George Moore.

discarded its ' H ' for ever. The typical young
man of this generation, the 'Arry of the casinos and
the music-halls, has broken out in Criticism. A
problem well worth studying is this young man of
boisterous indecency, with his incidental acquaintance with the *argot* of Paris and the studios, and
his general incapacity for consecutive thought of
any kind—this young man who, like those others,
has never been young, and will never, we know,
be old or wise. I have read his book with no little
pleasure, for it is, at any rate, thoroughly candid
and representative. The high jinks of the excursion train developed into criticism in which
everybody is ' bonneted,' even poor Shakespeare,
the wild revel of the penny steamboat, the
Bacchantic romps of Hampstead Heath, are
expressed at last in a malodorous but honest work.
The Belshazzar's Feast of small beer and skittles,
the Bohemianism of bad tobacco, the exuberant
Cockney horseplay, all is here ; and, to crown all,
we have the portrait of the young man, not the
'Arry of the revels, but the penitent 'Arry of *next
day*, after the trying excursion to Gravesend or
Hampton Court, exclaiming to himself, ' Oh, I do
feel so bad !' The doleful 'Arry countenance, the
'Arry coat, the 'Arry tie, are all typical of the
young man who has never had a clean mind, who
glories in his uninstruction, yet who is so far from
happy ! A noticeable experience in his life has
been a holiday trip beyond the Thames, to Paris.

12

He has seen the photographs in the Rue de Rivoli, and visited the Eden Theatre. He talks complacently of his experiences and his predilections— of the great Balzac, of 'his friend' Zola (whom he bonnets, too, quite merrily), of girls, of artists, of pictures, of books, of a general ramble and scramble through cafés and bagnios, always ending in the same Elysium of unsavoury jokes and pipes and beer.

This young man was never a child, never had any eyes to see what ordinary people see. His earliest remembrance is of a miracle—'plover *rising from the water*'—so that even as a child he was incapable of observing correctly the simplest natural phenomena. In later life, his reading has embraced, among other works, a book called 'The Rise and Fall of Rationalism,' doubtless some *prophetic* history, which in his Wegg-like way he mingles up with a certain 'Decline and Fall of the Roman Empire.' If he has studied any books, he is completely fogged as to what books. He knows literature as he knows Nature, out of his own confused, ill-balanced head. He hates everything— Shakespeare, Art, Poetry, Religion, Decency — everything but pipes and beer. When he goes to the theatre and sees Mr. Wilson Barrett as Claudian, he beholds 'an elderly man in a low-necked dress, posturing for the applause of some poor trull in the gallery.' He brands Mr. Irving scornfully as a 'mummer,' and describes all actors and actresses as idiotic marionettes. His dream is that the tongue of the music-hall shall be loosened, and that we shall then have a New Drama, free, unfettered, primitive ; meanwhile he is careful to tell us that ' Whoa, Emma !' ' Charley Dilke,' and other ballads of the music-hall, are of far deeper artistic value than any more sober productions of the modern stage. For novelists and poets he has as profound a contempt as for ' mummers '; the only English writer he professes to admire being Mr. Walter Pater, whose jejune essays he assumes to have read with rapture. For himself, he frankly informs us that he is immoral and indecent, and asserts that those who pretend to be otherwise are simply ' hypocritical.'

Now, all this, horrible as it may sound, is better than ' trimming '—better, to my mind, than the superfinities of Mr. James or the literary pretences of Mr. Archer. The young man really respects nothing under the sun, and is honest enough to say so. His more ornate brethren respect and love quite as little, but, unlike him, have not the courage of their emotions. They accept themselves dismally, as omniscient spectators of the human comedy ; he accepts himself savagely, as a Cockney Bohemian of the Latin Quarter. But Mr. Moore is frank and fearless, while they are merely polite or saturnine. He goes on his trip to Paris, and thinks he is 'seeing life.' Truth, Reality, Naturalism is his cry, as it is theirs ; but while they keep to

12—2

the pavement, he dances in the mud, reels along mud-bespattered, talks and yells, and thinks, *C'est magnifique, et c'est la vie!* There is no nonsense about *him*—*he* does not pretend to be virtuous or literary—virtue particularly is all 'gammon'; every. thing is gammon, except indecency, except horse-play, except the jolly Bank Holiday and all its concomitant delights. The superfine and the saturnine young men secretly detest the proprieties of life and literature. *He* utters his detestation, and boldly pictures to us the literary future : 'Arry triumphant, the tongue loosened, the morals and manners free and easy, the old gods of letters set up for cockshies, the music-hall turned into a Temple of all the arts, and 'Arriett, *alma Venus* of Seven Dials, *hominum divumque voluptas*, at her apotheosis. Well, all this is infinitely refreshing, after so much disingenuous respectability. The age of Sham is over, and the new prophet of straightforward animalism is Mr. George Moore. We are at last returning to Nature, *viâ* Rosherville Gardens and the Alexandra Palace. The Young Man as Critic triumphs, after all. He is found everywhere, in varied forms : with Mr. James, writing little novels, studying the little masters ; with Messrs. Bourget and De Maupassant, studiously detrimental and avowedly olfactory ; with Mr. Archer, grimly in-tolerant of imagination ; at the Universities, lecturing on Art for Art ; on the newspapers, giving up Religion and Morality as a bad job ; to be known everywhere by his leading characteristics —a temperament which forbids enthusiasm, and a character which is heterodox, not merely by constitution, but out of predetermination to be 'knowing.' But this honest young man of 'A Young Man's Confessions' is the spokesman of all the rest. He, at all events, is not disingenuous. He, at all events, has shown his class as it is, in all the nudity of its cynicism, in all the plenary audacity of its unbelief. We ought not, therefore, to be very angry with him, after all.

So far as the Young Man as Critic is concerned, there is little more to be said. It is with him, under the various forms which I have described, and under others with which my readers are doubtless familiar, that the men of thought, the men of another and, I think, a nobler temperament, have to reckon. It is he who will criticise us or ignore us, praise us or abuse us ; from him the rising generation will learn, at least for a little while, how to estimate us. He it is who is talking imbecilities in a thousand magazines and newspapers. He it is who is filling the free air of literature with the chatter of the *salon* and the *argot* of the studio. He is fundamentally and constitutionally cynical and destructive, as opposed to those individuals who, be they small or great, are fundamentally and constitutionally sympathetic and creative. Fortunately for Art, for Letters, he is fast becoming a public bore, a crying scandal. But for this fact, which may ensure his summary extinction and self-effacement, this woeful Young Man might succeed in destroying creative literature altogether.

IS CHIVALRY STILL POSSIBLE?

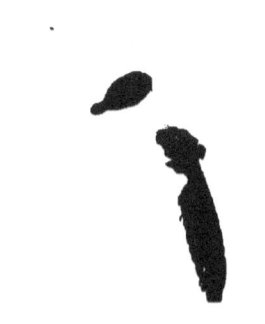

IS CHIVALRY STILL POSSIBLE?

To the Editor of the 'Daily Telegraph.'

SIR,

While congratulating myself on the complimentary expressions contained in your editorial article, on the subject of my paper* in the current number of the *Universal Review*, I am constrained to deprecate certain remarks in which you appear to class me with merely destructive critics, incapable of enthusiasm for anything contemporary. I know that I have been previously so classified, chiefly because I have thought it my duty on more than one occasion to attack popular reputations. I have invariably done so, however, on public—never on merely literary—grounds. But to say that I do not honour or glorify every contemporary is quite another thing to saying that I have depreciated all. My error, indeed, has been, in certain cases, on the side of enthusiasm. As one instance in point, I may mention the fact that I worked loyally twenty years ago to establish the literary reputation of

* The preceding article.

Mr. Browning, and that I have at this moment
before me a letter from that gentleman describing
me as ' the kindest critic he ever had.'   In short,
I hold him to be a poor critic indeed, or no critic
at all, who reserves all his idolatry for the gods of
the past, and can find no divinities, literary or
artistic, in the present.   This, however, is merely
by the way.   The matter which moves me to write
this letter ¡is of far higher importance than any
of my personal sympathies or antipathies—of far
more burning consequence than any subject merely
' literary.'   I have touched upon it *currente calamo*
in the paper you have criticised so sympathetically.
I am anxious to touch upon it again, with your
permission.

One of my strongest contentions against the
Modern Young Man as Critic—against, in other
words, the average half-educated, semi-cultivated,
small pessimist of the present generation—is that,
thanks to him and his, Chivalry is fast becoming
forgotten ; that the old faith in the purity of
womanhood, which once made men heroic, is being
fast exchanged for an utter disbelief in all feminine
ideals whatsoever ; and that women, in their turn,
in their certainty of the contempt of men, are
spiritually deteriorating.   As an illustration of this,
I state that the piteous type of the Magdalen,
which had so signal and sublime an influence on
life, on literature, and on art, is now put aside, not
merely as sentimental, but as practically ' inex-

pedient,' while the pent-up barbarity and savagery of the pseudo-scientist falls with all the violence of horror on the class called 'fallen.' As I write, one of your contemporaries proposes to get rid of certain midnight nuisances, which culminated a few nights ago in a disgraceful street scene, by giving absolute and practically despotic power 'to the police '—that is, to its individual members. Every day, in every club-room, we are told by men of the world that there is practically no such thing as 'seduction,' and that the hideous nightmare which haunts our civilization is really born out of the folly and the depravity of womankind. So that, it would seem, the only way to deal with the Abominable is to put it under the control of the guardians of the peace, and, while accepting its necessity, to take care that it does not trouble our social comfort.

Here, again, I am in serious disagreement with the quasi-scientific Pessimist of To-day. So far from having the Abominable hushed up and well regulated, I would have it flaunted publicly, in all its hideousness, till the real truth is understood— that it is a creation of the filth of man's heart, and that the class called 'fallen' is practically a class of Martyrs. Heaven knows, I am not writing as a would-be moralist and Pharisee ; Heaven knows, I am not blind to my own or my sister's infirmity ! But when the pessimist postulates, firstly, with Swedenborg, that this human sacrifice is a necessity, and, secondly, that women as a class wilfully and

cheerfully sacrifice themselves, I know out of my
own experience that he is uttering a lie !

We have consistently degraded Women. From
generation to generation we have denied them their
moral privileges. We have asserted that their
only function is parasitic, their best qualities less
intellectual than instinctive. But hitherto, while
complacently admitting their inferiority, we have
believed in their moral influence, in their divine
sympathy. Now at last, while Jack the Ripper
in Whitechapel desecrates and destroys the bodily
mansion, his kinsman, the Pessimist of To-day, pol-
lutes the tabernacle of Woman's Soul. He frankly
despises and persistently depreciates what was once
a temple where all strong men, all men who were
sons, husbands, or fathers, might meet and pray.
There is, he says, no ' seduction.' Women minister,
for the most part cheerfully, to our vanities and
our pleasures. Antigones, Cordelias, Rosalinds,
Imogens, Eugénie Grandets, are the mere dreams of
' poets.' A popular dramatist thinks he touches the
quick of the question by making comic capital of
' Woman's Rights.' Popular poets and novelists
swarm the bagnios of literature with Monsters,
which they label ' Studies of Women.' Certain of
contempt, certain of misconception, women at last
throw off their lendings, and become what men
make them. The Rome of Juvenal repeats itself
in the London of to-day. And masculine corruption, male deterioration, is, I contend, at the

bottom of it all.   The master, who once worshipped
his slave because she was beautiful, now scorns her
because he believes her to be base.   Let it not be
forgotten, either, in this connection, that those
women who most cheerfully accept the master's
supremacy, and wear with his sanction the raiment
of conventional morality—those women who are
bought and sold, not in the streets, but in the
higher marriage market—are the bitterest enemies,
the cruellest judges, of such members of their own
sex as sink to sorrow or try to escape convention.
The petted favourite assists her lord to hunt down
her less fortunate sisters.

This question is far too broad and world-em-
bracing to be discussed in a newspaper letter.
Some good may be done, however, by asking if it
is not possible, in the face of the grievous social
peril—the threatened loss of a Feminine Ideal—
for some few men, knights errant in the modern
sense, but full of the old faith, the old enthusiasm,
to remind the world, in the very teeth of modern
pessimists, of what woman has been to the world,
and of what she may yet become ; to keep intact
for our civilization the living belief which sanctified
a Madonna and a Magdalen ; to protect the helpless, to sympathize with the unfortunate, and, above
all, despite the familiar sneer of the worldling and
the coarse laugh of the sensualist, to reverse the
familiar adage now and then, and read it *cherchez
l'Homme ?* Quite recently, I am happy to say,

the man has been sought and found. We may find him much oftener, if we try! I for one, at least, look forward anxiously and hopefully for some glimpse of the old Chivalry, which set the name of Bayard high as a star in Heaven, and made even the eccentric Don Quixote a figure to sweeten human happiness and 'brighten the sunshine.'

ROBERT BUCHANAN.

[The preceding letter elicited a long and characteristic letter from Mrs. Lynn Lynton, from which I quote as follows :]

'Can anyone explain how it is that, when people discuss the Woman Question in any of its phases, they lose sight of proportion and take their leave of common-sense? The Idealists seem to hold women as altogether of a different race from men ; not only different in degree, but different in kind ; not only told off by Nature for certain special functions, whereby are emphasized certain common qualities, but as possessing intentions, faculties, characteristics with which men have nothing to do. To these Idealists women, *quâ* women, are semi-divine, where men are more than half bestial. The sex is sacred, and to be a woman is to be ex officio consecrated. To the Cynics, on the other hand, to be a woman is to be the source of all the evil in the world—where each daughter of Eve repeats her mother's folly and transgression, and where men are but the puppets whom she makes dance at her pleasure. Mr. Buchanan offers himself as an Idealist, and talks sentimental bunkum with splendid literary power. . . . Where has woman deteriorated ? Why, even the poor Abominables are less degraded than of olden times ; and the modern danger with respect to them is not of their oppression, but of their being treated with undue partiality—so that the good of the community is less considered than their un checked individuality. As for the Chivalry of which so much nonsense is talked and so little true knowledge is afloat—well, it may stand as a sign, *like any other algebraic symbol.* We need these signs and symbols in life—words which evoke ideas, no matter whether the root be real or not. The past of Chivalry was a very different thing from this all-embracing, all-suggestive, this verbal symbol for an impossible ideal. . . . Chivalry died because it became corrupt, affected, and unreal. The true hold that women had then on the respect and love of men was to be found in the bower and the hall—the house, where women reign, and where alone they ought to reign. Men came from the heat and passion of the strife to the rest and peace, the wholesome purity and order, of the house. Women were their solace, ministering to their needs, soothing their weariness, healing their wounds. The clash and din of battle were exchanged for the music of the bower, the peaceful

revelry of the hall.   Thus it came about that in
those rough fighting times women were indeed, in
a sense, sacred ; that the house was, as it were,
their temple ; and that, alternating as they did
with the rude life without the castle walls, they
were idealized and reverenced by the men who
died to protect them.   How this spirit will survive
the modern acceptance of warfare as part of
woman's life remains to be seen.   We have no
longer harryings and raids, burning of homesteads,
and lifting of cattle, but we have, instead, party
cries and political passions ; and when these have
invaded the home, and women are fighters with
their men and against their men, it is to be
feared the fabric of society as at present constituted will fall to pieces, to be built up again on
a different—but a better ?—plan.

'As for the degradation of women by men, that
applies to only one of the various relations between the sexes.   Do men degrade their mothers,
their sisters, their daughters, their wives ?*   Here
and there a few wretches may, just as here and
there a few women kill their children for the
sake of their insurance money ; but not the mass
—not the generality.   In that most tremendous
problem of how to reconcile *the imperative laws
of human nature* with the arbitrary requirements

* Most absolutely.   By the existing moral codes, they degrade
them.   Corruption begins in the household, and spreads thence
into the street.—*R. B.*

of society, women suffer, and must suffer. . . . The Magdalen is a very beautiful theme for art and poetry, but the poor drunken flaunting Professionals are stern facts—the results of poverty and passion combined—and white kid gloves are as much out of place when dealing with them as either art or poetry. Let that pass. Women have inflicted the deadliest wrong on their generation in connection with their unhappy sisters, but in a very different sense from that deprecated by Mr. Buchanan ; and I repeat it—the present danger is not in over-severity, but in over-petting and sentimentality, in maudlin pity and unjust partiality. If, as Mr. Buchanan says, men are the causes of all the misery of the world, and *cherchez l'Homme* ought to take the place of the familiar *cherchez la Femme*, are not men the direct and absolute creation of woman ? Built up day by day out of the very substance of her body, do they not also receive their first ineffaceable mental impressions from her ? As mothers, have not women unchecked power — absolute authority ? How foolish it is to differentiate the sexes on one ground only, and to judge of men and women simply on the platform of unlawful love ! For that is what the whole thing comes to. The wholesome orderliness of marriage, the dignity of the home and family, the domestic influence of women—all this is ignored ; and the wife and mother, mistress of her house and shaper of her children's minds and characters, is

13

forgotten for the sake of the poor Abominable
whom Mr. Buchanan wants us to idealize as the
Magdalen ! But, indeed, all this clamour about
woman, whether as ideals, as subjects for 'dissec-
tion,' or as very pitiful realities, is in itself
destructive of the virtues which should be specially
theirs before all of that modesty which was the
very core of her chivalrous ideal. And why all
this fatal incense of flattery ? Smaller than men,
with weaker animal instincts and weaker heroic
virtues, why should they be worshipped as superior
beings, too good for life as we have it ? If men
are to worship us, what are we to reverence ?
Ourselves—like the Buddha on the lotus-leaf?
Some already do, not to the edification of the
race at large ; while those who still frankly and
womanfully acknowledge their natural leaders in men
are treated as traitresses to the divine cause. . . .

E. LYNN LINTON.

To the Editor of the ' Daily Telegraph.'

SIR,

I was in hopes that Mrs. Lynn Linton's very
characteristic letter, published in your issue of the
27th, would have been answered by some authoritative person of her own sex. In common with
everybody else, I admire Mrs. Linton hugely, and
have done so ever since the days when she who
had sat at the feet of the old heathen Landor first
began scarifying her less accomplished sisters.

Who does not love a clever woman, even one with a bee—in this case was it a wasp ?—in her bonnet ? Who cannot forgive a brilliant woman, even when she becomes angry and describes male Chivalry as ' sentimental bunkum ' ? This gifted lady begins by asking in a tone of no little asperity, ' Can anyone explain why it is that, when people discuss the Woman Question in any of its phases, they take their leave of common-sense ?' Let me, in Scottish fashion, duplicate this question with another. Can anyone explain why it is that when ladies of a certain temperament discuss the characters of their own sex they take their leave of common charity ?

Mrs. Lynn Linton is a serious writer, and deserves to be dealt with seriously ; otherwise I should have looked upon her letter as a mere flash from the sombre spectacles of some Mrs. Pardiggle converted to the religion of the Hall of Science. Strangely enough, she, a woman of rare intellectual gifts, is on the side of those who would rivet the chains on womankind ; who sneer at men in whose opinion the ' sex is sacred ' ; who talk about the ' idealization ' of woman as ' absurd ' ; who think that the world is in danger, not of being too cruel to the fallen and the driven, but of treating them ' with undue partiality.' Well, I suppose she ought to know. George Eliot could never get over her hatred of pretty women—of poor butterflies like Hetty Sorrel ; and Mrs. Linton, if she spoke her mind, would no doubt say that all

13—2

naughty creatures deserve 'slapping.' Thus far, indeed, I can understand her ; but when she goes on to talk about ' the imperative laws of human nature,' and says that ' the whole question of the Abominable is one not of sentimentality, but of political economy,' I am lost in wonder. I remember on one occasion, many years ago, when someone was talking at the late G. H. Lewes's about a simple social question chiefly affecting the nursery, the voice of George Eliot suddenly intoned, 'Very true ; but, in that case, what is to become of our *Jurisprudence ?*' Jurisprudence was a good word, and so is political economy, but I have yet to learn what political economy has to do with Chivalry. And then, *mirabile dictu !* ' the imperative laws of human nature.' Is Sensuality, then, a ' law ' ? Just as much, perhaps, as Virtue is a ' law,' or Purity, or Philanthropy, or Misanthropy, or any other ' anthropy ' ; and in this case, I suppose, Mrs. Linton's ferocious Nymphophobia is a ' law ' too !

This is not the place, nor is the present the occasion, to discuss the interminable question of Woman's Rights. To many sensible people the very idea of social and political activity on the part of women is annoying, if not repulsive. For my part, I sympathize with any movement which may render Woman more happy, more active, more beneficent, and, above all, more influential. Woman will never be the equal of Man, because (*pace* Mrs. Linton) she is so infinitely his superior. Just as the reason of a human being transcends the instinct of an animal, so does the insight of a woman transcend the reason of a man. Deep in the nature of Hu manityabides a light which illustrates truth better than any syllogism, and this light burns brightest in the clear souls of the weaker sex. The great Positivist, as we know, admitted this. For what, after all, is Insight? Reason enlarged and glorified. And what, to proceed still higher, is Faith? Insight purified till it reaches the subtlety of Divination. Faith and Insight, the power of perceiving those verities which constitute Religion, are often denied to great men; they are seldom denied to a pure and perfect woman. This, of course, is the creed of Chivalry. In the eyes of a modern knight-errant Woman is the purifier of the earth, the creature

> ' Without whom
> The earth would smell like what it is—a tomb !'

Whatever sullies her, whatever degrades her to a lower level of thought and action, injures and hampers man's own progress upwards. I am now, of course, talking of the Ideal, not always, yet very often, realized in contemporary experience. Unhappy, however, is that man who has never realized such an Ideal at all ; who, after base moments of the strenuous sense, after misconception and moral backsliding, after the blows and buffets of the world, after all the efforts of his reason to solve the ever-present Mystery, has not been comforted and

strengthened by the faith and insight, the pure
benediction of a woman's belief and love. The
free-and-easy scientists, the patterers about ' heredity,' ' development of species,' ' laws of nature,'
' moral dynamics,' resolve the difference between
the sexes into a mere little matter of physiology.
Just so ; a little matter which, according to some
physiologists, gives Woman a second and supple-
mentary brain, or, according to sentimentalists,
gives her a clearer spiritual vision, the lens of a
finer-seeing soul. The votaries of Chivalry, the
preachers of sentimental bunkum, find in the
Ewigweibliche an abiding temple ; on its thres-
hold, kneeling prone, the Magdalen ; in its inmost
shrine, typical and supremely spiritual, the
Madonna.

Here, however, I would pause to deprecate all
misconception. When I wrote of masculine purity,
I was not posing as a moralist, least of all as an
Ascetic. I am not of that sect which macerates
the flesh, and pretends to find baseness in all
sensuous passion. I simply contend that the relations between the sexes, when not consecrated
by spiritual Love, become purely animal ; that the
buying and selling of what is the divinest posses-
sion given by God to human nature is a living
horror and a deadly sin. Personally, indeed, I
would rather be Burns than St. Simeon Stylites,
and should prefer, on the whole, to be lost with
Byron than saved with Mrs. Hannah More.

Chastity is the noblest privilege of Womanhood; it is more, it is a quality appertaining to Woman as light to the ruby, 'growing more precious as it nears the core'; but it does not preclude, it includes and sanctifies, Passion. A passionless heart is not necessarily a pure one; on the contrary, those hearts are the purest which can burn most ardently. In one suggestion, perhaps, Mrs. Linton is right enough—that we are all very human. For that very reason let us beware how we forget that the purest Soul who ever wore earth about Him was not only the greatest Sentimentalist, but the greatest Logician. He knew the truth so far as it concerns our poor human nature; and out of His infinite insight came the deathless Ideal from which Mrs. Linton turns to 'laws of human nature' and to 'political economy' —the Ideal of the Magdalen.

I am, etc.,

ROBERT BUCHANAN.

[To the foregoing Mrs. Linton replied as follows :]

Mr. Buchanan calls my letter 'characteristic.' I accept the term as meaning that in this, as in other matters, I have kept my head cool and level in the midst of the heated and sickly wave of sentimentality with which we are flooded for the moment—let us hope only for the moment! And

in this special part of the great, rampant, noisy
Woman Question, I trust that it is characteristic
in me to remember what the idealizers of street-
walkers do not, that we have our virtuous young
to care for even more than their poor erring sisters,
and that any class movement which weakens the
joints of national virtue is an evil to be fought
against by all who regard the general good.

Let Mr. Buchanan or any of his school consider
what is the likely effect of all this high-flown
idealization on the mind and principles of the
struggling hard-worked girl who resists the easy
temptation of the streets, and prefers, to vice and
champagne, chastity and a crust. She resists that
temptation importuning her at every turn, in part
for self-respect, in part for religious fear, but in
part also for that potent influence—the esteem of
the world, with its correlative, the loss of character
and consequent loss of consideration. But when
she reads of the women whose lives she has been
taught to loathe, talked of as only the pitiable
victims of man's brutality, held as themselves free
from moral blame, and as the fit objects for
admiration and pathetic idealization, how much
easier does that make her own hard struggle?
Difficult enough as things are—her fall offering
her all things pleasant to youth and womanhood—
this perversion of the wholesome moral law which
pronounced these women moral outcasts makes it
ten times harder. It takes away one of the

strongest of the props which support her poor fragile temple of virtue, and it undermines the others. There is no religious fear of offending God necessary for a woman who qualifies herself to be called the Magdalen—the beloved of Christ, whose sins were forgiven because she loved much. Instead of the contempt of the world she has the prurient petting of the men who stand and sigh over her—of the women who question first and exhort afterwards. Her self-respect receives no shock, for in her fall she is more cared for than ever she was in her virtue, and the joy of the angels in heaven over one sinner that repenteth is nothing compared to the excitement of which she is the centre. If she believes the newspapers and the idealists, she cannot condemn herself. She is a victim, according to some ; a martyr whose life was a sacrifice, and who is worthy of all esteem, according to others. That she preferred fine dresses, idleness, and the excitements of drink and adventures to close, dry, ill-paid work was no sign of a lower taste, but was all the fault of men—as, indeed, in one way it was, but not in the way meant by the idealists. I repeat it, and I know that thousands of kindly women and humane men will bear me out in what I say. This sentimental placing of prostitutes on an ideal pedestal as objects for poetry and pity only, and not at all as objects for condemnation, is one of the most disastrous things in all this flabby age, in view of the young who have to be kept straight against difficulties and in the face of temptations. Anyone who for over forty years has walked about London as I have done must have seen and heard things which take all the sentimentality about vice out of one. Good, generous, loving, and even essentially pure-hearted girls there are, one in ten thousand among the class ; but, as a class, to treat them with poetry and sentimentality is a wrong done to society at large, and an infinite wrong done to the virtuous.

On another account, too, I differ from the idealists. While seeking to enlarge the sphere of woman's influence and power—as some of us think, disastrously to the nation—they, in the matter of chastity, take from her the moral responsibility she has ever had as the conservator of virtue. It is the fashion now to say it is all the men's fault, and the women are not to be blamed if they fall— they are helpless to protect themselves. The men ought even to resist temptations offered to them. The conscience of woman says differently. Save in the case of the very young, whose ruin rests on the mothers who did not properly safeguard them, women are their own guardians. And ought to be. If they are to be held capable of governing the Empire, they should be made accountable at least for their own self-governance. If they are to be man's ' abiding temple,' they should of their own proper force keep that temple clean and pure.

It is emphatically in their own choice not to listen to serpents and not to eat forbidden apples ; or to lend a willing ear, and run the danger of the rest. To give them a broader political margin, and to narrow their moral borders, seems to me, and to many more than myself, a terrible inversion of good sense and right reasoning. . . .

I am, etc.,

E. LYNN LINTON.

[Like some ladies when they argue, Mrs. Linton *would* not see the point. I charged men with being the chief factors in the debasement of women, and she retorted that prostitutes must not be idealized, and that we must keep our women pure ! etc.

Perhaps recent revelations, such as the West Ham tragedy, may incline my matron militant to think men are not quite such superior creatures. If she still holds to that opinion, let her consult the Sisters of Nazareth who took under their protection two little children, of seven and five years old respectively. True, these things are not for common publication. The men who de-filed a public newspaper with the details of a bestial record must have been without conscience and without shame. But it is well not to blind ourselves altogether to the horrors of masculine Lust ; it is as well not to forget the failures of the Beast that walks upright.

Again, Chastity in itself is merely a negative merit. There may be, and is, infinite harlotry of the Soul even in so-called virtue. The poetry of life seduces nobody, and is *not* prurient. The prurient woman is she who hugs to herself the finery of her own purity, and scoffs at sentiment in connection with her driven sisters. Mrs. Linton is, so far as her present utterance is concerned, another example of my proposition—that culture and intelligence are lower in the moral scale than temperament, than sympathy. Reduced to the elements of Science, her opinions would fortify all the filth, all the destructiveness, of our social system.]

To the Editor of the 'Daily Telegraph.'
Sir,

Mr. Robert Buchanan asks you whether 'Chivalry is still possible'—meaning, as I gather, Is it possible to revive that ideal of conduct on the part of man towards women, which is designated, in strictly modern metaphor, 'chivalrous'? I say in metaphor, and in modern metaphor, because, as Mr. Buchanan is of course well aware, the ideal which men of later days have constructed for themselves in this matter has never had any complete historical realization in the past—the position of woman in the so-called age of chivalry being, in more than one respect, conspicuously inferior to that which she occupies even in our own unchivalrous times. Taking the word, however, in the meaning which Mr. Buchanan obviously intends us to assign to it, and asking ourselves the question whether it is possible to revive chivalry in this sense, it appears to me that we are at once brought face to face with two preliminary questions : First, did chivalry of this description ever exist at all, except among a comparatively small class of the community ? And, secondly, is it not to the limited extent of that existence still as flourishing and as little in need of revival as ever ?

That genuine examples of this noble habit of mind and lofty standard of conduct are, and always have been, to be found among us, I would be the last to deny. There have always been men of pure and high nature who have constructed for themselves an ideal type of womanhood, which they have not only reverenced as sacred in itself, but have regarded as extending its consecration to every individual member of the sex ; so that there shall be no woman, however humble or homely — nay, however sunken and degraded — who can be deemed to have altogether forfeited her title to some share of that exceptional leniency of judgment, that special gentleness of treatment, which chivalry recognises as the inalienable birthright of the whole sisterhood. Such men, I admit, have always existed. Colonel Newcome, their immortal representative in English fiction, is no mere fanciful creation in a novelist's brain.   Originals of that inspiring and pathetic portrait are to be found among us yet ; but they are few, and, with submission to Mr. Buchanan, they never have been, never will be, otherwise than few.   It is not given to the average man to idealize, to discern for himself the ' soul of goodness in things evil,' the indestructible element of purity in things impure ; and it is of the average man that Mr. Buchanan, I have a right to assume, is talking. If he is not, he on his part has no right to frame, as he appears to me to have framed, an indictment against society at large.   Such an indictment can only be sustained by showing that a general decline has taken place in the masculine conception of womanhood — that the average masculine mind is more sceptical than formerly of the existence of female purity, truth, and goodness, and less ready to do homage to these qualities where their presence is too unmistakable to be denied.

It is for Mr. Buchanan to produce proof, or at any rate, if absolute demonstration is, as it well may be, impossible in such a matter, to establish a reasonable presumption that such a change has taken place.   I cannot think that he has done so.   I cannot admit that his appeals to the cynical talk of ' club-rooms,' to the disquisitions of the ' quasi-scientific pessimist,' and to the ' analytical ' fictions of the day, prove anything.   As to the cynicism of the club-rooms, it is no doubt, so far as it is sincere, and indeed, to some extent, if it is insincere, a decidedly unlovely thing. But I altogether decline to treat it as a portentous sign of the times. Does Mr. Buchanan imagine that the walls of those apartments have ever listened to talk of any other kind since clubs, or the taverns which were their forerunners, first came into being? Does he suppose that the 'man of the world,' and still more the ' boy of the world '— if he will forgive my calling him so—has ever talked otherwise in any age; that the young bloods of Mr. Richardson's day did not think it fine to give themselves the airs of his Lovelace, and proclaim with many a ' damme ' their profound disbelief in the possibility of female virtue? It is no doubt true that even among the rakes of that time there were many too honest and too manly to feign an incredulity so dishonouring to the sex to which their mothers and sisters belonged. Tom Jones—to cite an example which Mr. Buchanan ought especially to appreciate—scapegrace as he was, held no such debasing view of women. His attachment to Sophia saved him from that, and his love for that young lady was no doubt a passion of the most purely chivalrous kind. But Tom, after all, would be a dangerous witness for Mr. Buchanan to call, for he would certainly be cross-examined as to his relations with Molly Seagrim and Lady Bellaston, towards neither of whom was

the element of chivalry very apparent in his be-
haviour. Probably he would have brought himself
under your correspondent's condemnation by citing
these two ladies in proof of the odious proposition
that 'Women minister, for the most part cheerfully, to our vanities and our pleasures.' No, sir;
I do not believe that cynical dicta of this kind
are at all more frequently propounded in our own
day than at any previous period. There has never
been a time when men, and especially young men
—and still more especially vain young men—have
not professed this ' delightfully wicked ' disbelief in
female virtue. It is a necessity of their own
conception of themselves, for how else could they
be the irresistible dogs they are? Men, however,
who have outgrown this little weakness, and have
no longer the character of Lotharios to support,
are as ready to recognise and to respect purity in
woman as ever they were; whilst their attitude
towards women of whom that feminine grace can
no longer be predicated has, I make bold to
say, distinctly changed for the better and the
more ' chivalrous ' in these latter days. Mr.
Buchanan seems to take peculiar exception to
man's present treatment of ' the class called
" fallen," ' as though it had undergone a change
for the worse. But surely it is matter of the
commonest experience and observation that the
class he refers to are, on the whole, treated nowadays with a forbearance and tenderness which our

rougher ancestors would have been simply unable to comprehend.

As to Pessimism and the modern ' naturalistic ' and ' analytical ' novelist, they do not appear to me to play anything like that important part as *causæ causantes* of the decline of Chivalry which Mr. Buchanan assigns to them. ' Naturalism,' or the discovery of the great fact that human nature consists wholly of the hideous, is a constant phenomenon in life and letters ; and its exceptional popularity and vogue at any given moment only shows that the writers who for the time being are the preachers of that dismal gospel happen to be preachers of exceptional directness and force. Byron made the same discovery in poetry, and, lo ! a wind of Byronism swept over the land, laying all young men's collars flat before it. Now it is Zola who makes the discovery in prose, and very unpoetic prose, and straightway follows the epidemic of Zolaism. Of course the great discovery is the discovery of a mare's-nest, and in their secret hearts the discoverers know it. They do not believe in their own theory of humanity. Only one man of letters ever did ; and he died mad, and is buried in St. Patrick's Cathedral, Dublin. Mr. Buchanan should seek consolation and reassurance in a pilgrimage to that sombre shrine. Jonathan Swift has preached the gospel that your correspondent abhors as no man ever preached it before him, and as none is ever likely

14

to preach it again ; and Mr. Buchanan may console himself with the reflection that a race which has retained its faith in itself , after reading the ' Voyage to the Houyhnhnms,' is not likely to be converted to the doctrine of despair by the author of ' L'Assommoir.'

As to the operation of Pessimism considered as a philosophy, and the grave injustice of Mr. Buchanan's attempt to fix it with responsibility for the decline of Chivalry and other mischievous consequences, there is much which I should like to say.   And some day, sir, when you can put seven or eight columns of your esteemed journal at my disposal, I may perhaps endeavour to say it.   I will content myself at present with asserting that the most complete acceptance of the philosophical doctrine of Pessimism is perfectly compatible with as complete a recognition and as anxious a cultivation of all that (in unphilosophical language) is ' pure, lovely and of good report ' in life ; and that, pending an opportunity of expounding and defending this truth at greater length,

I am, etc.,

AN INJURED PESSIMIST.

To the Editor of the 'Daily Telegraph.'

SIR,

Would that Fortune always sent me adversaries like your correspondent 'An Injured Pes-

simist,' who, while lightly and playfully tilting at
me, manages to make his gallant steed frisk and
curvet all round, to the discomfiture of my original
opponents ! I have only one fault to find with
him, which he shares with the famous knight in
' Ivanhoe '—that he comes disguised, and very
lugubriously ! In point of fact he is about as
much 'a pessimist' as Charles Dickens. I fancy,
indeed, that if he deigned to lift his visor, the
world would laugh merrily in recognition of one
whose name is a synonym for kindliness and
kindly optimism. He challenges me, however, to
prove my case further, and, since your insertion of
the challenge intimates your approval, I will join
issue with him at once. Let me premise, however,
by saying that the subject is one of unusual
delicacy, and could not be completed save with
the addition of evidence necessarily given *in camerâ*,
not in the columns of a newspaper ; nor would
even the six columns asked for by your correspondent afford sufficient space for its full and
absolute discussion. One can only select a few
points out of many, and leave all corroborative
testimony to the experience of our jury, your
readers.

Of course students of Modern Pessimism know
very well that, as a *philosophy*, it claims to be
beneficent. Its founder, Schopenhauer, and its
chief apostle and re-creator, Hartmann, feeling
profoundly for the sufferings of creatures emerging

into life and pain, have assured us that the only
comfort and joy of Humanity, so soon to perish, is
in acts of mutual service, mutual pity, mutual
love.   The blind Will or the blind Unconscious
(whichever name we give it) flowers up to its apex
of moral sentiment, gleams piteously, and dis-
appears.   These philosophers, like all others, testify,
of course, to the beauty of human affection ; and,
so far as I personally am concerned, I could as
easily find comfort in their gloomy Nirwâna as in
the mysterious Immanence of approved Pantheists
like Spinoza.   It is not with pure pessimistic
philosophy, however, that I have at present to
deal.

> ' When Bishop Berkeley said there was no matter,
>   And proved it—'twas no matter what he said,'

and there is nothing that Metaphysics cannot
establish, when we once grant its premisses.   I
spoke of Pessimism and Pessimists as they emerge
in Literature, I spoke more particularly of Pessimistic Realism.   Your correspondent's contention
appears to be that the phenomenon to which I
alluded is merely a familiar one, certain to emerge
from time to time, and equally certain to disappear.
To support this contention, he asserts, truly enough,
that a certain class of men have always been cynical
and unchivalrous, just as the majority of men have
always been impure.   Lovelace and his friends,
he says, talked much the same banalities as the
modern young men about town.   Quite true.   But

just then, in the person of the inspired little printer, in some respects the sanest and wisest soul of his generation, rose the Knight-errant of Literary Chivalry. It is the custom, as we all know, to sneer at Richardson. While the warm weak heart of Fielding awakens love, Richardson's piercing intellect almost repels it. Women, however, who are supposed to have no logic, recognised the great Logician of Morality, and cried, ' This man is our champion ! This man understands us—justifies us !' In the story of Clarissa Harlowe—tedious, monotonous, straggling, *bourgeois*—the great tradition of Literary Chivalry was carried on, and the world had the spectacle of a Chaste Soul, reaching its fulness at that moment when the martyred girl, with the libertine maundering at her feet and offering to make her ' an honest woman ' by marriage, turned quietly and proudly away, and passed through the portals of the tomb. Almost any English author, from that moment to this, would have satisfied himself and his readers by bringing down the curtain on the happy union of Miss Harlowe and the tamed, repentant Lovelace. Good, honest, virile Fielding would have done it, and chuckled over it. Richardson, far wiser, knew that, horrible as is the outrage of the body, still more horrible may be the outrage of the Soul; that for a Soul once violated, once disenchanted, there is no possible human reparation ; that for Woman cast from her sphere of purity, bereft of

her faith in Humanity, the only hope lies beyond
the shades of Death !

Which brings me to the heart of my sad argument. I have mourned the decay of Chivalry ; I
have asked if its revival is not possible. Your
correspondent—who loves Chivalry as much as I
do, who has bowed down as I bow down before
Don Quixote and Colonel Newcome—says, firstly,
that Chivalry never existed at all save in a small
class of the community. Yet it is admitted by the
realists that Literature represents the spirit of its
age—is, in other words, the adumbration of the
noblest temper of the community at large. What,
then, must have been the temper of communities
which, crystallizing in individual genius, produced
Iphigenia and Antigone, Beatrice and Francesca,
Cordelia and Imogen (to say nothing of the whole
female galaxy of Elizabethan drama), Eve and the
Lady of Comus, Clarissa Harlowe and Sophia
Western, Beatrice Cenci and the heroine of
Epipsychidion, Eugénie Grandet and Modeste
Mignon, Lady Esmond and Laura Pendennis,
Lizzie Hexam and Little Nell ? I should be
unjust, moreover, to the lights under which we live
if I denied that, even now, this tradition of purity
survives, that now and then Divine things come to
us, such as I found the other day when I read the
infinitely piteous episode of Lyndale in the 'Story
of an African Farm,' such as give modesty and
charm to the 'girls' of Black and Besant, and

power to the full-blooded women of Thomas Hardy, such as ennoble the stainless page of Mrs. Oliphant and brighten the gladsome books of Bret Harte, such as lend glory to the maidens of Alfred Tennyson, to the Madonna-like young mothers of Coventry Patmore, and to the Shakespearean women of Robert Browning. But, alas! most of the writers I have named belong to the last generation, and several of them are already voted 'old-fashioned.' The triumph now is with the realist, with the pessimist, with the young man who has never been a child, who has never dwelt in Bohemia. Why, the whole attempt of my original argument was to draw a comparison between the last generation and the one in which we live!

Your correspondent asserts, secondly, that after all Chivalry is still flourishing, and as little in need of revival as ever. Does he deny, then, that within the last decade, since the apotheosis of popular science and the spread of popular materialism, a very great change has taken place in the moral estimate of women? Of their social position I say nothing—that is another matter; but they, like the Irish nation, have won all that for themselves. It is not a question of whether we fear their power more, but of whether we honour and reverence them as much? The best proof of such honour and reverence would be the condition of our own morals, the purity of our own lives. Are we, then, so pure? I will turn away from the revelations of the Divorce

Court, from the reports of the newspapers, and just walk out once more into the midnight streets. What do I see there? Instead of the bold, painted woman's face of twenty years ago, I see the pale, thin face of a child! Instead of the coarse, robust young person from the country, I see the delicate young person, who has perhaps been a 'lady' and has known luxury. Let me tell, in this connection, two absolutely true stories within my own knowledge. A little while ago two pure young girls, daughters of a clergyman, left Yorkshire and came to London deliberately, out of choice, dispassionately, to throw themselves on the London streets! They did so, and were swept away into the great vortex. Here, certainly, we seem to have a proof in favour of the man of the world's argument that there is no 'seduction'; but the exception is meant to prove the rule. These young girls, well educated, familiar with modern pessimistic books, concluded that the world was impure, and, having lost all vital belief, followed their despair to a logical conclusion. My second story is of a young girl who, when I first met her, was a beautiful child of seventeen, reared in luxury, accomplished in music and painting, the idol of her home. She, too, became a reader of the new literature; she, too, had become utterly without faith, either in God or human nature, when, a few years later, she made the acquaintance of a married man, an officer in the army. This man deliberately set himself to under-

mine those moral instincts which still kept her
personally pure. He convinced her that society
was honeycombed through and through with liber-
tinism ; that there were no pure women ; that,
since life was transient, indulgence of all kinds was
wise and justifiable. Eager, like poor Lyndale, to
know, she came at last to as piteous and terrible an
end, dying in utter despair. Never shall I forget
the contrast between the bright, happy girl I first
met, all intellectual ardour, all moral purity, all
faith and hope, and the poor heart-broken woman
whom, only a few years later, I saw lying on her
bed of death.

My correspondent thinks the world is no worse ;
that Chivalry is no longer needed. Let him remember, however, that a generation ago the Devil
lacked his one last convincing argument which proves
to the weak and blind that there is absolutely no
God, no hope, no succour beyond these voices.
If Pessimism means anything, it means that.
Science corroborates it. Experience seems to justify
it. So that, after all is said and done, we come to
the final and irresistible conclusion that there is no
hope in this world because there is no faith in
another, and that Schopenhauer was right when he
described Death—*i.e.*, annihilation—as the great
and only Nirwâna. In that case, of course, it is
useless to trouble ourselves about what old-fashioned
people call the Soul. Let us legislate for something more substantial.

So the world is no worse?—nay, hints your correspondent, it is possibly much better, especially in this particular point of woman's condition. How, then, does he account for the fact—which I suppose he will not deny—that the ranks of the so-called 'fallen' (I say the 'driven') are now to so large an extent recruited from the educated classes, from those classes which are aware of the culture of the age? I speak within my own knowledge when I state that I have personally found, among the throngs who nightly haunt such places as the Empire and the Alhambra, women whose refinement of manner and purity of accomplishment would grace any drawing-room; faces which not all the fever of the gaslight could rob of the beauty and distinction which come of gentle blood. A generation ago these types did not exist on this side of the Channel. But now, as the satirist sings:

> 'Instead of Greece, whose lewd arts poisoned Rome,
> The harlot France infects our island home!'

and the educated girl who discovers that she has been brought up in a dead Faith, and turns her early accomplishment to use in the secret study of detrimental French novelists, soon loses the hallucinations which kept her pure. She, too, discovers that Divine sanctions are no longer needed. She, too, finds that Pessimism is the only creed thoroughly alive. Her father, possibly, is either an open sceptic or a person who still accepts religion because it is 'respectable.' Her brothers, perhaps, are young men about town, from whom she soon learns the *argot* of fast life. It is a horrible thing to say in this connection, but I have known many instances of pure young girls whose minds first became polluted through the conversation of their own brothers.

Now, Chivalry, as I conceive it, and as I hope and pray for it, might do something to remedy this grievous state of things, on which I have touched but very lightly. But Chivalry, unfortunately, means Religion—not necessarily the religion of any creed or sect, but that large faith in a Divine Power conditioning all we think and feel ; and even that nebulous sort of religion, as we know, is hard to find. Energetic Mr. Frederic Harrison, contemptuous of an anthropomorphic God, offered us his master's fetish, Humanity, the *Grand Être*, as a substitute, until quite lately a ferocious Professor, not to be humbugged that way, pulverised the Monster, to the general satisfaction (see Professor Huxley's diatribe against Positivism, *passim*). In all the conflict of the new discovery that the moon is made, not of green cheese, but of magnesium, there is not much time for reverence ; and, unfortunately, the scientists are even harder on Woman than the poets and romancists. How, then, shall Chivalry arise ?

In one way only. Through the physical purification of men. I am certainly not for turning the world into a moral seminary, for eliminating from life that Passion which alone, perhaps, lifts it towards divinity.   But the man who goes out into the market-place to *buy* the body or the soul of a woman is a leper, and as such he should be treated. Put a label on his breast, put a clapper into his hand, that all the world may know he is 'unclean.' My entire argument is that Man is the sinner here, and that Woman is the martyr.   I know well how my good physician and physiologist, Mr. Worldly Wiseman, will smile at my logic.   From time immemorial the Master has usurped the privileges of sensuality, while the Slave has been forced to acquiesce.   Only when the master has become a knight-errant, and has said to his ideal, ' Be pure, and I will emulate, so far as my coarser nature may, your purity !   Be good, and I will uphold your goodness before the world !' then, and only then, has Woman become glorified—no longer a Martyr, but a Madonna.

I have hinted pretty broadly at certain social phenomena which I allege to be taking place in our midst.   Thousands of your readers, if they cared to speak, could, I feel sure, corroborate me on such points as the decay of self-respect in women owing to male contamination, and as the want of Chivalry or purity in the young men of their homes.   With what your correspondent says on the abominations and absurdities of Naturalism I thoroughly agree ; but I open my eyes in wonder when I find him classing Byron among the discoverers 'of the great fact that Nature consists only of the hideous.' Byron was a romanticist pure and simple. He discovered that the world and society were full of shams, and he turned in gloomy pride to Nature, to the mountains and the sea. Bitter things said about mankind, sarcastic things said about the sex, do not make a Pessimist—in fact, Poetry and Pessimism are antagonistic terms. Byron's idea of Woman was not, perhaps, the highest, but it was a high one, nevertheless, and I only wish we had a few of his women now. To put the creator of Haidée in the same pillory as the author of ' La Curée ' seems rough-and-ready justice indeed ! Byron, with all his thoughts, was a Man, and when he revolted against what Mr. Morley justly calls ' the piggish virtues of the Georges,' Nature revolted with him and proclaimed him right. Had he lived a little longer, he would have become, perhaps, the noblest knight-errant that modern Chivalry has seen.

I am, etc.,

ROBERT BUCHANAN.

NOTE ON THE PRECEDING.—My question, ' Is Chivalry still possible ?' elicited, in addition to the letters of Mrs. Linton, a vast amount of correspondence, occupying the columns of the *Daily Telegraph* for some weeks. As usual, the discussion ended on the level to which all high things fall in this country—that of the comic paper ; and there the question arrived at its *reductio ad absurdum*, whether men who travelled in omnibuses were still sufficiently chivalrous to get outside to oblige a lady ? As a matter of fact, however, it was found impossible, in the columns of a daily journal, to touch the quick of the matter, which chiefly concerned Prostitution, classed by me with War, as one of the two hideous Sphynxes of modern civilization.

I may remark in this contention that my statements concerning the change of type among fallen women, concerning the spread of social disease to the higher classes of society, were corroborated by innumerable private correspondents, as well as by a letter of emphatic assent from the present Secretary of the Lock Hospital.

By far the most important published communications were the letters from the pen of Mrs. Lynn Linton, conveying as they did the anti-sentiment of that large class of women which is moved alike by the scientific spirit and the puritanical bias—in other words, by a desire to dogmatize in matters of feeling, and to be severe on the weaknesses of human nature. I do not dispute for a moment that Mrs. Lynn Linton's ideal of womanhood is a high one ; but it is an ideal based quite unconsciously on the British ideal of commercial virtue. Mrs. Linton sees in Woman only the type of chastity and maternity : I see in her the partner of Man's passion and Man's power. She sees a domestic machine ; I see an ever-present inspiration. She elevates conventional Chastity as the highest of female virtues ; I see in it only the unchastity of English legislation. She would limit the sphere of woman's activity and energy ; I would enlarge that sphere indefinitely. She has spoken of the inexorable Laws of Human Nature, and indirectly has drawn from these laws an inference that Prostitution is a necessary evil ; I, on the other hand, have affirmed that there are no laws to turn man from a rational being into a beast of the field, and have asserted that spurious Chastity, the puritanical bias in ethics and in legislation, is sacrificing the rights of one class of human beings to the vices of another. We are trying to appease the angry gods by a holocaust of helpless women. That holocaust would be recognised as what it is, an enormity, if women were made more free and men became more pure. The Passion of Love is not of necessity, as puritans affirm, an unclean passion. It is the breath of Heaven which sweetens and purifies every coarse necessity of Earth.

IMPERIAL COCKNEYDOM.

15

IMPERIAL COCKNEYDOM.

A REJOINDER TO CRITICS.

FOR an article by the writer who still lives, I am glad to find, to subscribe himself 'A. K. H. B.,' 'On certain Terms of Opprobrium' would be a felicitous title. Perhaps the most notorious manufacturer of such terms was Carlyle, following close in the wake of Goethe ; but the late Mr. Arnold ran him very hard, inventing many catchwords and nicknames which have passed into the current vocabulary of journalism. For example, everyone who did not agree with Mr. Arnold, or who called a spade a spade, was a 'Philistine,' and everyone who emulated him in the suppression of vitality possessed 'sweetness and light.' 'Anthropomorphism' is another epithet much in vogue with those writers who dislike the idea of a personal God ; it was invented for us, I fancy, by Professor Tyndall. Well, an epithet, be it opprobrious or complimentary, is to be valued in proportion to its aptness and suitably. Of course, such terms are coarse and trivial enough, and need

15—2

abundant qualification. Most living writers have
at one time and another, when uttering some
disagreeable truth, been called 'Philistines.' Some
of them, too, have been called 'Provincial'—a
term which has its antithesis in the other magnificent term 'Cockney,' invented by Professor
Wilson, but applied with singular ineptitude to
the school of Keats and Leigh Hunt. In the
present article I purpose to appropriate this term,
and for the first time, I believe, to apply it
properly. For, as I have suggested, a term or a
nickname, to possess any force and durability, must
be felicitous. When Mr. Andrew Lang, in view of
certain expressions in a recent article, calls me
'provincial,' the epithet has meaning. I am very
provincial, as I purpose to show, while showing,
at the same time, that Mr. Andrew Lang, though
Scottish by birth, is a Cockney of Cockneys.

For to be a Cockney, it is not after all necessary
to be born within the sound of Bow Bells ; the word
implies, not a nationality, but a temperament, an
environment, and a habit of mind. Charles Lamb
was a Cockney in the best and finest sense of the
word ; Hazlitt and Gifford were Cockneys in its
worst and earthiest sense. The true Cockney, like
the true Parisian, regards his own City as the
Centre of the Universe ; his own outlook as the
one outlook on life and literature ; his own taste
as the only taste to appreciate what is pleasant
and what is beautiful ; his own little pool of

thought and feeling as the one Ocean where a man-tadpole can comfortably push about. There has never been a great Cockney, but there have been shrewd and sagacious and delightful ones ; the type rises as high as Ben Jonson and sinks as low as ' Mr. Gigadibs.' The true ' Provincial,' on the other hand, is considerably sceptical as to the centralization of all thought and feeling, all brilliance and all activity, in any particular city, although, if he sinks very low, he may rather incline to the opinion that the centralization should take place in Birmingham, or Glasgow, or Stoke Pogis, or Kilmarnock. He has no particular bias towards any form of life or literature. For the narrowness of personal taste he substitutes the breadth of ideal principles, and is guided by those principles. He moves about this merry England, about the waters of the world, with a full consciousness of his own insignificance, yet with no disposition to take minnows and tadpoles for leviathans or even bottle-nosed whales. He, in a word, is ' free.' Shakespeare and Milton, Wordsworth and Byron, were glorified provincials. In the great periods of literature the men of light and leading have been Provincials always. In the little periods, *e.g.*, those of the Georges and Queen Anne, the victorious writers have generally been Cockney to the marrow. But Richardson was a true Provincial, and so, thank heaven, was Harry Fielding.

Are we getting near to a definition? If not, we may get quite close to it as we go on, and furnish contemporary illustrations. It is, by the way, a very certain sign of provincialism to say severe things of any *contemporary*, more particularly if he is a Cockney. The Cockney way, the way of ' sweetness and light,' is to take one's stand apart, to say nothing personal, but to depreciate by complacent innuendoes, and at any rate, if fighting has to be done, to do it in kid gloves. I can imagine nothing in literature more trivial and more spiteful than the late Mr. Arnold's comments on his contemporaries—but Mr. Arnold was jejune, and talked so much of 'culture' that many who read him thought him sweet instead of bitter. Then, says the Cockney, if you *must* attack, instead of taking your cakes and ale comfortably, for Heaven's sake attack only Things in General, Things which are helpless and incapable of self-defence ; it is very bad taste indeed to do as Byron and Shelley did, and 'name' your Southeys and Castlereaghs. This, however, with a reservation. If it is merely a ' provincial ' you have to deal with, call *him* what names you like. Call him, as they called Coleridge, a *genius manqué*. Call him, as they called Wordsworth, a ' driveller,' a ' Lakist.' Call him, as they called Christopher North, 'that damn'd Scotchman !' The whole vocabulary is at your service. Call him, if at a loss for an adjective, a scrofulous

Scotch, or Irish, or Manx poet. And then, should the poor Provincial, irritated by your ill-treatment of him, retaliate by calling you a fleshly poet, or a society journalist, or a chirpy smoking - room critic, or a Bank-Holiday young man, you are still free to hold up your hands and exclaim, ' How provincial ! how ill-bred ! how barbarous !' Your strong point is that the world in general still confounds the Cockney with the Londoner, and when the Cockney utters his fiat, is ready to accept it as representative of the great Centre of Opinion.* You are localized for the time being, you build your little nest, in the Temple of all the Sciences and all the Arts, London ; and so, if you are noisy enough, the sound you make may seem, not the caw of the jackdaw, but the voice of the Oracle.

Let us understand, clearly, however, what we mean by Cockneydom. It by no means follows that a Londoner is necessarily a Cockney. Your

---

* On the other side of the Channel it is still the highest possible compliment to call a man or an author 'a true Parisian of the Parisians.' Admiration even went so far as to apply the compliment to Balzac and (*mirabile dictu !*) Victor Hugo. But though Hugo himself said that Paris was France, and France was the centre of the Universe, every line he wrote under inspiration rebuked the absurdity. We are learning just now what to be a 'true Parisian' means in literature ; it means simply to be a *boulevardier*. A similar lesson is being taught us, here in England, as to the true meaning of the word 'Cockney,' though Cockneydom, of course, works by stealth towards imperialization, instead of vaunting it grandiloquently.

true Londoner, like your true American, is cosmopolitan; he is fortunately very numerous, and may still be found writing books, painting pictures, editing newspapers. In many cases, indeed, he is merely a transplanted provincial; in journalism, especially, the strength, the vigour and intellectual capacity is constantly supplied from the provinces; and because journalists are for the most part *not* Cockneys, but liberal men of the world, some of our criticism is broad, generous and fair. Cockneydom is to Cosmopolitanism what the Gironde was to Jacobinism. Its philosophy is epicurean, its humour is persiflage, its poetry is *vers de société,* and its wisdom is the wisdom of the clubs. Within its own little sphere it is triumphant, because it suits well the temperament of men thoughtless by disposition and busy in occupation. It has its libraries, its theatres, its journals. It exchanges for a provincial worship of Truth and Beauty, a lightsome admiration for the pretty, the elegant, the *comme il faut.* It quite objects to take life seriously. It regards Thought itself as an almost disturbing influence. It occupies itself with the manners of accomplished men and *nuances* of well-dressed women. A glorified Cockney is a sort of literary or artistic 'Buck' of the period, exhibiting himself in the *salon* or the club, showing to ordinary people the pink of literary manners, and accepting with easy complacence life as it really is, in London clubs. He has seen the

sea at Scarborough and Margate, and he has seen
the mountains from the door of an hotel in
Switzerland. As the degenerate Roman copied
the elegancies of moribund Greece, the Cockney
frequently apes the affectations of honeycombed
France. He has the light literature of Paris at
his fingers' ends.

And what has this glorified being to tell us?
About manners, much; about those questions
which determine the thoughts and feelings of
aspiring men, nothing. His inclinations are lightsome and practical, and his injunction upon us
is that, since life and religion and philosophy are
all a muddle, it is best to exist comfortably, to
ask no more of Providence than a good dinner,
a cheerful friend, a pleasant, well-printed book,
a picture or two, a newspaper, and a charming
woman to flirt with upon occasion. His motto is
laissez aller. Pessimist and epicurean in one, he
regards all conduct that is not ill-bred with
equal sympathy; with a ' one thing is as good
as another ' sort of criticism, forbearing in appearance if fundamentally heartless. Great deeds and
great thoughts have no real interest for him, but
he has a cultivated appreciation of them on the
æsthetic side. ' For heaven's sake,' he says to us,
' be calm! Things may be very bad indeed, society
may be rotten to the core, London may be a
warren of the poor and wretched, but all this
is really not worth troubling about; it will so soon

be over ! To excite yourself over the loss of a
Religion is like crying childishly over the breaking
of a toy. To protest against public nuisances is
to make *yourself* a nuisance. The most disinter-
ested Man that ever lived, the Man who your
teachers tell you was Divine, has been a puritanical
Bore for nearly two thousand years, and his
preaching and prosing has all come to—nothing !
You can't make the world better. You can't keep
the monkey-blood out of humanity. You can,
however, " sit apart, holding no form of creed,
but contemplating all." You can always find
a piano, or a flower, or a set of verses, or a bit
of scandal, or a pretty woman ; all of which make
life gladsome. And when it is all over, when the
lute is unstrung and the golden bowl is broken,
you can at least go comfortably to sleep !'

I am obliged, in this connection, to proclaim my
belief that the man who, more than anyone who
ever lived, wrote most about the Metropolis, was
not a Cockney. The cheeriest of all humourists,
Charles Dickens, whom the true Cockney is so
fond of quoting and yet underrating, was awfully
and hopelessly provincial, and was frequently
reproached for the fact by the *Saturday Review*.
An idealist and a dreamer, he found in this great
City, not Cockneydom, but Fairyland, and he was,
never tired of wondering at its piteous oddity and
delightful quiddity. Now a Cockney sees nothing
of all this, though it is all so near to him. Words-

worth had to come up from Cumberland, at the
very time when every clique and coterie voted him
an utter failure, and when every Cockney literary
man professed total ignorance of and contempt for
his works, before the world could realize the beauty
and solemnity of the Dawn seen from Westminster
Bridge :

> ' Dear Lord, the very houses seem asleep,
> And all that Mighty Heart is lying still !'

That Mighty Heart! which sends no pulsation
whatever through the veins of the contingent
poetaster.   Why, it required even a poor Glasgow
poet, whom the Cockneys first welcomed and then
stoned and killed, to produce even the fine lines—
describing London as :

> ' The terrible City, whose neglect is Death,
> Whose smile is Fame !'

That Mighty Heart!   The Terrible City !
How felicitous, and yet how provincial !   No
Cockney has ever yet expressed in literature the
mystery and the awfulness of this London in the
shallows of which he sports.   A fine old Cockney
once attempted it, and was told by his friends that
he was a great poet ; and indeed if all Cockneys
were like that honest, purblind, pertinacious,
prosaist, Samuel Johnson, how we should adore
the breed !   But in those days a Cockney had not
discovered that ' there is no God,' and that Life
means comfortableness and prettiness.   He had

only begun by discovering that the world is Fleet
Street, and that it is merry to hear the chimes at
midnight.   The rest has followed in the usual way
of Evolution.

The great Cockney organ of opinion is still the
Quarterly Review.   Many years ago the standard
of revolt was raised in Edinburgh by the Whigs,
and the *Edinburgh Review* was started ; but a very
short time sufficed to show that this was, after all,
a Cockney organ too.   Gifford and Jeffrey were
both arrant Cockneys.   They cackled endless
praises to Byron because he was a lord, but there
was not a stainless reputation, not one flower of
original genius, they did not pollute and try to
kill.   In their dotage, the good old Quarterlies,
once the watchmen of our literature, survive still,
but amid universal neglect or derision, as things
far too slow for the times.   Poor old Dogberry
and Verges !   Lanthorn and clapper in hand they
pop out of their pigeon-boxes, and months after
the henroost is robbed and the house burned down,
utter their wheezy cries of ' Fox ' or ' Fire.'   And
they are still Cockney to the marrow ; still cheerfully unconscious that the world is in earnest, still
ready to aim their paralytic blows at ' Deformed '
and other malefactors.   Only yesterday, Dogberry
told us that Mr. John Morley was the inheritor
of the character and temperament of—Rousseau !
The good old man had somehow muddled Rousseau
with ' Deformed,' and was quite unconscious that

he was comparing an inspired Deist, the one writer who kept the soul of men aflame when Rationalism had almost blown it out, with a belated Hume whose mind had been nurtured on the gospel of the Hall of Science, who printed God with a small 'g,' and who had descended from the azure of the Savoyard Vicar's prayer into the atmosphere of stump oratory. Only the other day, the same asthmatic authority told us that Lord Tennyson was 'no poet.'

For Cockneydom to speak in the name of London, then, is a preposterous impertinence. The chirp of the sparrows which nest in the ear of a stone Colossus is not likely to be mistaken for the voice of the giant. Fortunately for free thought, for literature, for art, for science, London remains cosmopolitan. The great journals, with notorious exceptions, are broad and eclectic. The best writers for the press are men of the world, many-sided, many-minded, free from the prejudices of clique or class. The most popular actor of the day, Mr. Irving, is so sublimely 'provincial' as to believe, in the very teeth of the Cockneydom which never ceases to decry him, in the ideal side of the Drama. Only very low down in the intellectual scale is heard the clamour of the cliques, the voice of eager Cockneydom.

If this article were political I might proceed to point out the Cockney statesman and the Cockney publicist. My readers, however, know them well,

and so I need not particularize, save to say that
they have more than once imperilled the honour
and threatened the ruin of their country.   A
thoroughly provincial politician, however, may be
quoted in the form of the late Mr. Bright, who
was abused throughout his whole career for his
anti-Cockney proclivities, who never feared to speak
his mind, and who was guided from first to last
by solid principles.   It may be remarked here,
in this connection, that on great public questions
involving the progress of humanity and the rights
of minorities, Cockneydom is nearly always on the
wrong side, and generally the last to be converted.
It was a great Cockney organ, the *Times,* which
steadily upheld the South almost to the bitter end,
when all sane men saw the inevitable issue of the
conflict between Nationality and barbaric Revolt
in the United States of America.   It was the
same organ which, to damage a forlorn cause and
destroy a martyred Nation, instituted an infamous
prosecution against the Perseus of Ireland, Parnell.
In Cockneydom alone the god St. Jingo has found
idolaters.   Mere provincials have passed him by
with contempt or indifference, and turned from the
clash of cymbals and the battle-cry of eunuchs to
the teachings of wisdom and the humanitarian
sentiment of virile men.

   Yet Cockneydom, not content with metropolitan
or even national triumphs, hungers to become
imperial, to possess, like Great Britain, an Empire

on which the sun never sets. For example, so far as current literature is concerned, its missionaries have completely converted, while its central powers have complacently annexed, the distant city of Boston. Mr. Henry James has become a Cockney. So has Mr. Howells, in spite of his contempt for Dickens. Through the cult of Cockneydom, spreading through mysterious channels of journalism, people yonder are beginning to think dubiously about those good old Puritan fathers, Whittier, Emerson, and Longfellow, and to welcome with complacence the *dii minores* of the Savile Club. In New York, and as far away as Chicago, Cockneydom spreads its propaganda ; so effectually, indeed, that young men have given no ear to the ' barbaric yawp ' of Whitman, know not even the name of Hermann Melville,* and have found little fascination in the Idylls of Dudley Warner or Charles Warren Stoddard. Of course, I know Americans too well to believe that the Gospel according to Cockneydom, expressed in easy essayism and patter-versification, will ever do for *them*. It fills certain of their magazines, but to

---

* When I went to America my very first inquiry was concerning the author of 'Typee,' 'Omoo,' and 'The White Whale.' There was some slight evidence that he was ' alive,' and I heard from Mr. E. C. Stedman, who seemed much astonished at my interest in the subject, that Melville was dwelling ' somewhere in New York,' having resolved, on account of the public neglect of his works, never to write another line. Conceive this Titan silenced, and the bookstalls flooded with the illustrated magazines.

these, in reality, they pay no serious attention
Omnivorous readers, they devour everything ; free
cosmopolitans, they accept in a friendly way even
Cockney missionaries ; but as the future masters
of the world, they are certain never to be annexed
en masse. Nearer home, at Paris, imperial
Cockneydom is likely to be more successful. Very
busy there has been the good Apostle, James, and
we find the Cockneys of Paris dedicating books to
him and writing articles about Cockneydom in the
Revue des Deux Mondes. My acquaintance with
the missionary reports of the new religion is not
intimate enough to enable me to say whether any
Cockneys have been converted in Tasmania or
New South Wales ; but I met a Parsee the other
day who confided to me his belief that all religions
except Epicureanism were equally nonsensical, and
that the greatest of English poets was Mr. Austin
Dobson.*

My article on the Modern Young Man as Critic
has at least done something. It has drawn Mr.
Andrew Lang, a very typical Cockney, from the
obscurity of his club and the anonymous sanctities
of his daily and weekly journals. Gently and not
ill-naturedly, calmly and not angrily, he chides me
(in the *St. James's Gazette*) for 'discourtesy,' for

* Here followed in the original article a description of Mr.
Lang's lecturing visit to Scotland, in which, by following certain
newspaper reports and comments, I appear to have exaggerated
or mistaken Mr. Lang's utterances. I therefore suppress the
passage.

(in House of Commons fashion) 'naming' particular offenders. He knows—no man knows better
—that the covert sneer, the lifted shoulder, the
smug innuendo, the depreciating smile, are far more
à la mode than plain speaking and rushing into
print. The former, however, has never been my
method of warfare ; I leave it to the cheery pessimists, and the prophets of modern Nepotism. I
call a spade a spade with the Philistines, and a
Cockney a Cockney with the provincials. For Mr.
Andrew Lang personally I have no little respect.
He is a gentleman and a scholar, and in certain
moments, when he forgets his newspaper and his
club, a poet. I have still ringing in my ears
certain lines of his about the ' Iliad ' and the
' Odyssey '—lines full of the swing of the early
periods of literature. Yet I am going to arraign
him on the very score of his natural abilities and
literary gifts. ' Sir,' I say to him, after the
manner of a certain famous justice of the peace,
' you are clever, well-educated, able-bodied, intellectual, instead of which you go about disguised as
a Cockney.' I blame him not, as others have
blamed him, for now and then showing the courage
of his opinions. I am with him even when he
vindicates the ' imagination ' of Mr. Rider Haggard,
and holds that one gleam of creative power atones
for a host of small technical imperfections. Never,
in my wildest moments, should I condemn him for
his occasional courage. My charge against him,

16

of course, would rather convict him of constitutional literary cowardice, of chronic anxiety to keep out of brawls and take things ' easy,' of urbane freedom from anything like real enthusiasm—in a word, of a desire, at the hazard of all disingenuous suppressions, to ' get comfortably along.' Even now, I apologize with all my heart for disturbing him in his pet studies of linguistic ' origins' and the manners of primeval Man.   But he is a journalist as well as a scholar, a clubman as well as a student, and in a moment of distraction he has put on his ' war-paint' and fingered his tomahawk.   ' Is this a free fight ?' asked the pugnacious American. Quite free ; and it is indeed a pleasure to find that Mr. Andrew Lang, not content with indulging in cynical ' asides' in the *Daily News* and elsewhere, has stepped out, armed at all points, to join the fray.   He, above all men, was the one we of the opposite faction wished to meet.   To attack him without some personal provocation, I, for one, had hardly the heart, for despite his literary offences he has often been kindly to a fault.   Now that he himself has voluntarily come forward, there can be no harm (and I am sure there will be no bitterness) in touching on certain matters in which he has urgent personal concern.

But before I join issue with Mr. Lang on these matters, let me refer to one or two points of his criticism of my article.   I may pass on one side his suggestion that the same charge as mine was

brought against the young men of the *last* generation ; that is a suggestion easily met by a reference
to the literature of the eighteen-sixties. His first
serious assumption is that I ought not to have
' mentioned individuals,' or have ' called them
names.' My reply to that has been given ; my
charge was specific, not general. Mr. Lang goes
on to say that about several of the gentlemen
I denounce one ' may easily be silent,' as ' it is not
given to everyone to keep up with current literature.' Very characteristic this, as we shall see
later on, of an author who, more than most of us,
watches every swirl and current of the literary tide.
Of course Mr. Lang knows these gentlemen as
well as I do, but they do not belong to his ' set,'
and he has no particular call to defend them. He
then goes on to say that M. Bourget, though he
may be a *ridiculus mus*, can ' interest us, in spite
of everything '; and he adds, lightly, that ' M.
Bourget has " done a murder very well indeed, with
pleasing circumstances of good taste." ' Here
again, as we shall see, is characteristic levity in
dealing with a serious accusation. Mr. Lang then
defends Mr. James, and vows that he has written
at least four admirable novels. I do not think that
I denied Mr. James's cleverness ; I said, indeed,
that he was very clever. My charge was that he
was superfined to the point of indetermination, that
he became feeble from supreme good taste and
overweening catholicity. My critic, then, with

16—2

growing irritation, refers to Mr. Robert Louis
Stevenson, a valuable reference, as we shall see.
I called Mr. Stevenson 'a hard-bound genius
in posse'; by which I meant that he was a genius
who had never expressed himself in creative work,
although Mr. Lang and his friends have attached
noisy importance to every one of his callow flights
in literature.   Mr. Lang refers me triumphantly to
'Kidnapped' and 'Treasure Island,' two excellent
books for boys, and (as a proof that this cannot
be the period when 'all young men never have
dreamed a dream or been children ')* to ' A Child's
Garden of Verse.'   I am loath to say one word
in deprecation of the praise Mr. Stevenson has
received from his contemporaries ; personally, he
deserves it all for modest gentleness and persistent
work ; and the exaggeration of his performances
would matter little if every such exaggeration did
not mean the neglect of young writers at least
equally deserving.   The late Mr. Jefferies, who
was a genius *in esse,* had to die miserably before
the fact of his genius was discovered ; and for
every word of praise he gained, Mr. Stevenson
received a thousand.   Mr. Lang, in his reckless
light-heartedness, has actually talked of the author
of 'Treasure Island' in the same day with Walter
Scott, but he has refrained from informing the
reader of such trifling matters as the bodily theft
of the young writer's leading character, the one

* Of course I said nothing of the kind.

striking character in the book, viz., the blind man, out of the pages of ' Barnaby Rudge.' For the rest, ' Treasure Island,' excellent as it is, is a story of ' reminiscences ' of better stories ; at its best, it is worthy (though that, indeed, is no little honour) of Mr. R. N. Ballantyne ; but work so trivial can never justify the serious language used concerning it by nepotic criticism. The ' Child's Garland of Verse ' is another matter ; as poor and made-up a matter, from any child's point of view, as one can well conceive ; and yet it has been treated as the work of a poet. The late James Thomson, who died miserable and neglected only a little while ago in the casual ward of a London hospital, and who wrote poetry which will live, would never have died, perhaps, so miserably, if he had received one modicum of the encouragement vouchsafed to Mr. Stevenson. Mr. Lang goes on to say that the value of my criticism may be estimated by my casual references to writers of another age, and of more settled reputation. I call Théophile Gautier ' insufferable '— Théophile, ' the joy of youth.' Heaven help the youth of whom this extraordinary stylist, who treats the flesh like a porkbutcher, and makes love like a cony of the burrows, is to be the joy ! Since Mr. Lang has faith in the ' golden book of spirit and sense, the Holy Writ of Beauty,' I leave him to his religion. Again, I have said that Zola is a dullard *au fond ;* and so I hold him to be in spite of all his genius (which I was among

the very first to praise), and so I hold every man
to be who believes, *au fond*, that baseness and
bestiality predominate in human life and character.
I called this pessimism ' dulness,' and sought no
harsher term.

A criticism of Mr. Arnold as a poet would be out
of place here. What I said of him dead I said long
ago of him living. He was a poet when he wrote
' Thyrsis ' and ' The Strayed Reveller.' He was
no longer a poet when he perpetrated his verses in
unrhymed Heinesque ; when he compared the
receding tide at Dover to the receding Sea of
Faith, and could find nothing better to say of a
sublime Humourist than that ' the World smiled,
and *the smile was Heine.'* This may be criticism
of life, but it is neither poetry nor even decent
imagery. *Au reste*, Mr. Arnold forgot that Poetry,
so far from being a dilettante's opinion or
' criticism ' of life, is the very Spirit of Life itself.

We shall get into deep waters if we discuss in
detail the correctness or incorrectness of my opinions
on literature. They have one poor merit—they
are at least my own. If Mr. Lang wishes to
understand them (and no man is better able if he
will try), he will learn that from my point of view
literary accomplishments are nothing, and literary
fame is less than nothing, when they do not imply
that spiritual insight which I believe to be the one
prerogative and proof of genius. I am not at all
what Mr. Lang calls me, a virtuous person. I am

not at all what he implies me to be, a person who
makes it a condition that anyone to be worthy of
admiration must agree with a certain view of life
and ethics. I find the spiritual insight I demand
in Herbert Spencer as well as Dr. Martineau, in
Walt Whitman as well as Lord Tennyson, in the
late Mr. Darwin as well as Faraday, in Byron as
well as the late Mr. Longfellow, in Burns as well as
Keble, in Mr. Bradlaugh as well as Mr. Gladstone.
I do not find this insight in any thinker who has
a retrograde, or a contemptuous, or a dilettante
view of human nature. I sit at the feet of no
bogus reputation, however magnificent; worship
no idols, however bedizened by criticism; follow
no particular religion, and assume no particular
morality. My cardinal literary crime, up to the
present moment, is that I do not worship Goethe;
that I hold him to be, with certain qualifications,
a tedious, a tiresome, and a dilettante writer; an
opinion based, not upon 'The Grand Coptha' and
his voluminous miscellanies, but on his popular
masterpieces. Thus it is clear I am not a hero-
worshipper, that I reverence no qualities in a writer
or in a man but Truth and Goodness. All this, I
am aware, is highly provincial, but I *am* a provincial, not a Cockney. If Mr. Andrew Lang can
give as good reasons for his prepossessions as I can
for every one of mine, he has my sincere congratu-
lation. They will be far more valuable to him in
a worldly point of view, since, unlike mine, they

will facilitate his philosophy of easy acquiescence, general discretion, and 'jogging comfortably along.'

Let us touch now in this connection on another question directly connected with the subject of the present article. There is no charge which so seriously affects the character of a contemporary, whether he be politician, poet, artist, or general man of letters, as that of Nepotism. Nepotism is congenital Trades Unionism; it is, in other words, an attempt in criticism at Over-legislation, or Providence made Easy—to those who *believe* in a literary Providence. Often, when proven, it has caused the fall of a great statesman; and I see no reason why it should not wreck the reputation of a small critic, or small body of critics. In literature it is a cruel crime, since it means the exaltation of mediocrity, and the perversion of the rising generation. Nepotism is the poison of which such men as Keats and Coleridge, as Richard Jefferies and James Thomson, miserably died. Read the life of Coleridge. Read the words which were written by the cliques of that great and good man up till a few months before his death, and note *en passant* that *Blackwood's Magazine*, which labelled him at the height of his living achievement as a dotard and a driveller, honoured him on his decease a few months afterwards as the greatest of English writers! Nepotism, of course, does not kill strong men. Wordsworth, we know, survived its endless persecution. But the weak, too gentle man, the struggling writer, the genius out of tune with the times, perishes by it daily. What comfort is it to him who starves for bread, who hungers for a little praise, who saddens for a kindly word, to be told that neglect and insult are the historic credentials of originality, and that he who does not humour and pander to the Cockney cliques must be persecuted by them? So long as little men band together, Cockneydom and Nepotism will always flourish. To be outside their barriers is to be a 'provincial.' To be within them, at the present moment, is to be a 'Cockney.' Pass the word round: Trades Unionism is rampant, and if the non-union man is not discharged, the unionists of criticism will strike *en masse*. We have to ask ourselves, therefore, if Cockneydom is to prevail in Literature, while it fails so miserably, as it has failed on every great occasion, in Politics, while it gains only a precarious and a doubtful victory in Art and even Science?

It is, as many contend, a small affair, a miserable affair, and he who comes forward to discuss it will doubtless be set down, as every reformer has been set down, as cantankerous. What does it matter, after all, how a few light-hearted gentlemen combine to criticise or ignore their contemporaries? That 'no man was ever written down, save by himself,' is the truest of all sayings. But *in the meantime?* At the beginning of this century Wordsworth was busily 'writing himself down';

so even was the prodigious Goethe, if we may trust the *Edinburgh Review*, just before Carlyle rushed in to 'write him up,' and to find in 'Wilhelm Meister' not a tawdry didactic essay, but a 'masterpiece.' Is it .not a little hard that mediocrity *plus* Nepotism should have all the cakes and ale, while originality *plus* dissent should be denied even a little bread? It is the weak, the unknown, the non-unionist, who suffer most by Cockneydom. If only for their sakes, it is worth inquiring how far literature is now suffering from the old disease.

There appeared some little time ago in a leading monthly review an article which caused the initiated infinite amusement; so naïve, so outspoken, so fresh and yet florid, was its impudence, so specious was its pleading on behalf of the gospel of literary trades unionism, that more than one reader exclaimed: 'Nepotism is at last to be vindicated as a literary religion; there are, after all, many gods, and Mr. Andrew Lang is their prophet.' We all knew the chirpy Prophet well; admired him for his abundant cleverness, liked him for his easy good temper, even when we most wondered at his temerity. He was one among a group of light-hearted and feather-brained gentlemen who had come to the conclusion that literature is not literature, but high jinks; who had adopted the moral philosophy of Mr. Puff and the worldly wisdom of Mr. Dangle, and who were resolved to exchange for the freedom of pure letters the trades unionism of a social club. Working out in practice a well-known theory of the great Balzac, that a dozen bold and unscrupulous writers might easily conquer criticism and occupy all its bastions, by religiously banding together and working for each other in and out of season, these gay fellows had for at least a dozen years been working hard for a common apotheosis ; and the result had fully justified the great Frenchman's theory. True, there had been moments of peril and hesitation ; heartburnings and backslidings caused by the occasional obtrusion of individual vanity and selfishness ; but on the whole the spiriting had been done so cunningly and so cleverly, the anonymous system of criticism had been utilized so judiciously, that the reading public—or at least the Cockney portion of it—had been converted to the belief that England was labouring under an absolute plethora of original genius—nay, even America had been invaded, and Boston itself had paraded in its newspapers and magazines the likenesses of the new gods of literature. Great little poets, great little novelists, great little essayists, great little critics and journalists, swarmed on the walls of our modern Babylon ; helping each other up, praising each other's prowess, singing each other's songs, sharing with each other the hot ginger of ambition, and chuckling to one another over their adventurous feats of warfare. Well, it was magnificent, but it

was not war at all. It was the mere skirmishing
of Nepotism. It needed only one piece of sound
artillery to put all the skirmishers to rout, and,
strangely enough, the Prophet of the new religion
provided that same artillery, and by bungling
turned it upon his own friends, when he recklessly
opened fire from the masked battery of ' Our
Noble Selves.'*

Let me now turn aside from the personal ques
tion to one broader and more cosmopolitan. My
article on ' The Young Man as Critic ' elicited,
among many other comments, one in the editorial
columns of the *Daily Telegraph*, in which the
writer, while expressing sympathy with my views
in general, objected that I was somewhat unjust to
the higher work of my contemporaries. I therefore
wrote and published a letter, under the title ' Is
Chivalry Still Possible ?'† pointing out that the issue
involved affected the whole fabric of modern society,
and more particularly the moral and social status
of the two sexes. The Cockney pessimist, I contended, had poisoned the wells of life and literature
to such an extent that Chivalry, by which I implied
the old-fashioned faith in female purity and goodness, was, like other religions, fast passing away.
The discussion raged for some little time, but of
the many letters which appeared on the subject,
scarcely one dealt logically, or even instructedly,

---

* See the *Fortnightly Review.*
† See *ante,* the section under that head.

with *my main contention. As usual, also, the subject had to be expurgated of all objectionable matter ; for I had touched on what is known as the Great Social Evil, asserting that its existence was the shame of civilization. The remedy I suggested was a higher standard of purity on the part of *men*—a remedy which every Cockney regarded with supreme derision. I took the sentimental view—the provincial view—which still regards 'seduction' as the great factor of public immorality, and I proclaimed my sympathy with the martyred class. At this point I had to join issue with Mrs. Lynn Linton, a lady who is intellectually an honour to her sex, but who has unfortunately sided with those who are sceptical as to the powers of womanhood. Mrs. Linton dubbed me roundly a 'sentimentalist,' and scouted the idea that women were to be 'coddled' and persuaded that they were superior beings. But my fair antagonist, like the rest, entirely lost sight of the premisses on which my argument had started—viz., that the true cause of feminine deterioration was masculine corruption, and that the real cause of masculine corruption was the omnipresent want of faith in spiritual, or in other words religious, ideals. I contended, moreover, and I again contend, that a man has no right to set up for a woman any personal standard of thought or conduct by which he is unable or unwilling to measure *himself.* If women are to be pure, I said, let men be pure too. I did not mean by purity the negation of human passion. Unfortunately, in the artificial atmosphere of Cockneydom any man who professes to be a logician is liable to be set down as a Puritan—even a 'prig'; and so I, who never had any virtue to speak of, who profess no particular personal piety, was taunted with being a virtuous and a pious person—a taunt which, if it had been applicable, would certainly have been complimentary. All I held was that men who are notoriously impure themselves have no right to persecute the individuals who minister to their impurity; that the man whose life is (as Goethe said of his walk) a series of falls, has no right to despise the woman whom he drags down with him. And yet, as everyone is aware, all the *onus mali* falls on the weaker sex—falls more especially on her whom I designated, after a Divine Ideal, the Magdalen. With curious want of logic, Mrs. Lynn Linton identified my Magdalen with the depraved, drunken, besotted creature of the streets and the gin-shops, battered by misery out of all human likeness; whereas the true Magdalen is the woman who, in spite of all physical degradation, brings her penitence, the spikenard and myrrh of her spiritual yearning, to the feet of a Redeemer. The modern pessimist contends that *this* Magdalen is an impossibility—that the true original is even as himself, evil because evil is of the very essence of her nature; and Mrs. Lynn Linton, a pure woman, a good woman, and a woman (I am sure) who is generous and loving to a fault, sides herself, I am grieved to say, with the modern pessimist.

Chivalry, as I understand it, is (1) the belief that the moral temperament of women is superior to that of men, and (2) that men should regulate their social conduct by the laws feminine insight has discovered.* Of course, this belief goes right in the face of modern Pessimism, not to say modern Science. A grim young pessimist confided to me only the other day his belief that there were no really 'good' women except 'fools'—*i.e.*, unintellectual persons ; and this belief is very common. Science fortifies it by asserting that woman has a smaller brain, a narrower understanding, than man; that in her case the sexual evolution dwarfs and narrows the mental evolution at every stage. And Mrs. Linton, herself a woman whose intellectual gifts it would be difficult to parallel among men— a woman who is careful to tell us that she has fulfilled all feminine functions and duties—scoffs at the equality of the sexes with the very accomplishment which refutes her theory ! Surely, some less disqualified person, not a woman of genius, should tell us that a woman unsexes herself when she

* I was delighted to note that Mr. Pinero, in a recent play, 'The Profligate,' upheld this view, but unfortunately he conciliated the Cockneys by his catastrophe, and made the pure woman, as usual, give her profligate a clean bill of domestic health. Reverse the positions, and how criticism would protest ! Yet I cannot understand for the life of me how any average man can dare to pronounce judgment on any woman, however fallen.

measures herself against man, and demands from
him equal rights and equal privileges ! My own
experience is that intellectual culture, so far from
making women hard and rectangular, almost invariably deepens their insight and makes them
more spiritual. If it occasionally renders them
'masculine,' it only does in the inverse ratio what
it does to some men, by rendering *them*, in the bad
sense, feminine. Intellectual culture, whether in
man or woman, is the poorest and meanest of all
accomplishments when it is not coincident with
spiritual development. What is called culture is
often only another word for narrow-mindedness, for
dilettantism. If a human being does not become
better and wiser through what he or she knows,
the knowledge is practically worthless. Supernatural cleverness did not create in Goethe the
enthusiasm of Humanity, but it created it in
Schiller and Richter, who were infinitely less
' clever,' infinitely less ' knowing.'

Chivalry, however, is, as I have discovered, quite
provincial. Imperial Cockneydom will have none of
it. The Cockney, with Mr. Podsnap and the editor
of *Truth*, puts all moral difficulties behind him ; the
discussion of the wrongs of women is ' unsavoury';
the great journal which opened its columns to that
discussion was ' pandering to a morbid appetite, in
order to increase its circulation.' Elsewhere, in less
discredited quarters, there is the same prurient tendency to ' hush up ' those agitations which imperil

the moral status of *men*. If you vindicate Marion de Lorme, you asperse directly or indirectly the character of the Cardinal, with a possible innuendo concerning the King himself! The Cockney sentiment—a sentiment existing wherever Cockneydom prevails—appears to be, that open discussion is inexpedient, and that, if left alone, the world (with Mr. Lang) can 'jog comfortably along.' Of course, there is a possibility of such revelations being made as absolutely corrupt and poison the atmosphere they assume to clear ; and this was notoriously exemplified a short time ago. ' Unto the pure all things are pure' is true enough as applied to grown men and women, whose purity is a matter of degree ; but many things which are pure enough from our point of view are utterly impure from the point of view of a maiden or a child. ' The young person' is a fact, even in the exaggerated caricature of a Miss Podsnap ; and her innocence is also a fact, with which even a publicist should reckon.

Perhaps, when all is said and done, there is a dash of the ' Cockney ' in us all ; in all of us, at any rate, who have lived in the great cities, and known little of the solitudes. I myself can remember being very much shocked at Mr. Bradlaugh when he first uttered those diatribes which earned him so unenviable a name, and I could not at once realize that I was listening to the best music in the world, the voice of an honest man. Cockneyism, after all, is only self-righteous-

17

ness and self-conceit, using a flippant vocabulary to cover envy, hate, and all uncharitableness. Cockneyism, imperialized, is completed social and literary vanity, extending from a metropolitan centre to organizations all over the earth. Yet the gospel of 'jogging comfortably along,' the art of conventional veneer, the methods of Nepotism, have always been more or less sanctioned by Society, while the bold Provincialism which calls things by their true names, and is always over-ready for martyrdom, has never been, and never will be, either profitable or fashionable.

IS THE MARRIAGE CONTRACT
ETERNAL ?

17—2

IS THE MARRIAGE CONTRACT ETERNAL?

To the Editor of the 'Daily Telegraph.'

SIR,

Mr. Gladstone's ideas on the subject of 'Marriage and Divorce,' as set forth in the current number of the *North American Review*, have been familiar to us all ever since the publication of his paper on the same subject which appeared among the 'Ecclesiastical Essays.' For my own part, much as I dissent from the views expressed, I honour and reverence them, as symbolic of a perfectly stainless and beautiful wedded life. I know that every word they contain comes from the bottom of one of the kindest hearts beating on this planet, and in presuming to correct so apostolic a person as Mr. Gladstone, a man who belongs to the high-priesthood of human nature, I am restrained by no little reverence and affection. But I know well, as all sane men must know by this time, that this great leader would prefer to any half-hearted acquiescence a firm yet respectful contradiction. 'Great is the truth, and it must prevail,' has been his watchword throughout his life,' and he will forgive now, for the Truth's sake, the denial of one who sympathizes, but who is *not* a disciple.

Veiled in the golden cloud of a happy destiny, crowned with the lilies and roses of that perfect conjugal peace which Swedenborg justly thought the noblest blessing of human life, Mr. Gladstone, confident of his individual happiness, forgets the conditions of human nature. His appeal to Christian documents, his erudite citation of the Christian Fathers, to prove a point which can only be established by human Science, may be gently set aside for the present as irrelevant. To contend upon Biblical evidence that Marriage is a Contract for Eternal Life, never to be entered into with a new individual after bodily and spiritual separation from another, is not much more tenable than to hold carnal Love itself a thing to be avoided because the Apostle Paul rebuked the fleshly appetites and held matrimony only a little better than concupiscence. Surely that Protestantism which Mr. Gladstone loves so well decided long ago that human Conscience is superior to any constituted authority ; and surely also Free-Thought, the heir male of Protestantism, has convinced us at last that Knowledge is antecedent to, and supreme over, the domination of any Documents. As I have elsewhere written, the man who says that a Book can corrupt his Soul ranks his Soul lower than a Book ;

and even when a Book is wise beyond the possibility
of corruption, it is poorer and feebler at best than
the human inspiration out of which it came. Unless
the sun of human intelligence, like the sun of
Joshua, has stood and is standing still, the later
inspiration must supplement the earlier, and the
Bible of Humanity remain incomplete, until many
another Book is written. Generations ago Milton
added to it one luminous page—that in which,
starting from Mr. Gladstone's side of the compass,
he vindicated the right of Divorce in the name
of the Christian documents ; and Milton, were he
living now, had he learned what Man knows now,
would have uttered truer, though not mightier,
words in the name of human inspiration.

For surely, the hour has come when the rights
and needs of human nature are no longer to be
decided by the straggling traditions, the vagrant
and often feeble utterances, of those who were
Martyrs and Apostles of Liberty once, but who,
were they living now, and waging the same conflict
against social science, would be regarded as fit subjects for Bedlam. Since the age of St. Athanasius
we have had the age of St. Servetus, whom I, for
my own part, value more highly than most saints
in the Church's Calendar. We have drained our
cities, reformed our manners, invented soap as an
adjunct to water, and become, if a little less
credulous of documents, a great deal more tolerant
to Inspiration. The Poet and the Philosopher may

now get in a word occasionally in the intervals
of pastoral homilies and domiciliary exhortations.
True, many of our discoveries, and a little even of
our inspiration, are of comparatively small value.
To find magnesium in the moon is perhaps not
much more precious than to ascertain, with Panurge,
that the moon is made of green cheese; while to
establish the caudal ancestry of man is merely to
corroborate the irony of Voltaire, and to verify the
fanciful flights of Lord Monboddo. Even Goethe's
discovery of the intermaxillary bone, though precious to sheer scientists, has had very little effect
on human knowledge. A larger and certainly less
doubtful discovery is the quasi-legal one—that no
contracts are really binding when the very nature
of a contract is unintelligible to the contracting individuals ; and since, *pace* Christian documents, the
Marriage Contract is very seldom made in Heaven,
and is very frequently entered into by practically
irrational persons, the corollary of our discovery in
this direction is—that such a Contract as Marriage
should certainly *not* be eternal.

To argue this part of the question thoroughly out
would far transcend the limits of a brief letter. Far
more important to the present issue is Mr. Gladstone's extraordinary suggestion that the laxness of
public opinion on the subject of the Marriage Contract is the main cause of the loose morals of Modern
Society ! Even here, up to a certain point, I am
with the modern apostle. I believe true Marriage

to be in its very nature Divine, but that is only another way of saying that conjugal Love is of necessity eternal. Well has it been said that ' he who loves once can never love again.' Perfect love between man and woman means complete fusion of two beings into one immortal Soul. But when this Love comes—and it does come, since miracles are daily wrought—we do not talk any longer of a contract ; it is abolished, it has vanished ; for the parties to it have no separate identity—they are

> ' Two souls with but a single thought,
> Two hearts that beat as one.'

Unfortunately, however, the miracle, if it happens at all, only happens once in a life-time, and after, in the majority of cases, many episodes of dis-hallucination. Are we to be told, in the face of experience, of reason, of knowledge in ourselves and around us, that, because a man or a woman has blindly signed one contract, has reached out loving arms and clasped only corruption, has awakened from a dream of Heaven to the realization of an Inferno, that he or she is to be precluded for ever from that moral redemption which Love alone can give ? Through the imperfection of even our present civilization many individuals commit in lawful marriage an innocent and pitiful adultery. Is the sin so committed, by those who in thought are sinless, to be ratified, to be eternalized and christened ' holy,' by any so-called Law of God, by any belated Spectres

of the Apostles? Is eternal solitude, eternal
isolation from all that makes life beautiful, eternal
misery and shame, to be the portion of the creature
who has been blinded, who has been hoodwinked,
who has been charmed by Circe, poisoned treacherously by the Siren, polluted shamefully by the
Satyr? If Christianity had taught this, it would
have long ago been cold and dead as the stones
of the Sepulchre. It has not taught, and it does
not teach it. At its highest point of aspiration
it embraces and uplifts, instead of corrupting,
misleading, and destroying, poor human nature.
It teaches us that the one Divine thing in
Humanity is Love. It convinces us that when
Love attains its apogee, it is not when stooping to
sign a contract, but when soaring to an apotheosis.

If the morals of modern society are lax (as Mr.
Gladstone premises, and as may possibly be the
case), it is precisely because we have elevated
Marriage, as an institution, as a contract, and have
lowered the standard of conjugal Love; it is because
there has come, following Man's conventional scorn
of Woman, Woman's revolt against and contempt
for Man. I do not myself believe that Humanity
has suffered in the least from the clear laws of
Rationalism; I do believe that it has suffered, and
is still suffering, from the miasma of moral Superstition. I have no respect whatever for the
Marriage Contract, for any contract, *per se*. I
want first to know the character of the contracting

parties, and their physical and spiritual relation to each other. When asthmatic January weds buxom May, I know the wedding-bells are being rung by the Devil. When two mistaken Souls embrace in the sanctuary, and discover sooner or later that Nature never meant them to mingle into one, I say, ' Tear that blundering contract ; put the poor creatures back to back, and let them march, far as the ends of earth, from one another.' When one Soul turns apart in cold disdain, and another Soul vainly tries to draw it back, I think ' all this is hopeless—say the sad word, Farewell.' For unless a union of Souls is consecrated by Love, that union is an embrace of dead branches on two withering trees. Shall the light and the dew and the pure air fall on neither—and for ever ? Set the trees asunder, and each may grow ; the eglantine shall come to one and the woodbine to the other, and both may become green and glad in the garden of the World.

True Marriage, indeed, is but the symbol (beautiful, like all symbols of things spiritual) of which the reality is Love. But reason teaches us, experience warns us, that there may be a symbol for things bodily as well as one for things spiritual. To the great majority of human beings the marriage contract means no more than a pledge to be kind and faithful, to resist temptation, to fulfil gently and affectionately the duties of the household. Such a contract is excellent, and suffices for the needs of large classes of the community ; but surely there is nothing in its nature to warrant the assumption that it cannot be broken, if by no slighter cause, at least by the death of the individual. Out of the Body it grew, and it perishes with the Body. Love had little to do with it, indeed nothing ; for Love is of the Soul.

I have no space, at least now, to traverse the whole ground of an argument which Mr. Gladstone carefully confines to the region of orthodox belief. The Dome of Heaven is wider than that of St. Peter's or St. Paul's, and the Bible of Humanity is broader even than the Old and New Testaments and the whole library of the Christian Fathers. It is sad, yet pitiful, in this nineteenth century, in the era of religious freedom and moral emancipation, to behold a great and good man gazing mildly backwards on the Fairylands of Palestine and Judæa, and in order to find some vanished star of Love, waving aside such cloudy apparitions as the countless wives and concubines of Solomon. Most strange of all it is to be told at the present period of social despair, that a Man or a Woman has only one solitary stake for happiness, and that, although the Bride is a Faustina, or the Bridegroom a Trimalchio-Cæsar, the Marriage Contract is nevertheless eternal !

ROBERT BUCHANAN.

To the Editor of·the 'Daily Telegraph.'

SIR,

I regret for many reasons that your correspondent 'Realist,' in commenting upon the subject of Marriage and Divorce, has imparted into the discussion that polemical bias which so often sets honest arguers by the ears. This is no question of Œcumenical Councils, of Papal influences, of Infallibility, of Agnostic Cardinals; it can be debated, I think, without awakening the religious prejudices of any class of believers. There are many Roman Catholics sound to the core who are in sympathy with the intellectual progress of mankind; nay, there have been far-seeing and saintly souls even at the Vatican. The hope and moral salvation of the world lie now in the fusion of the creeds into one High Creed of Humanity, and the healing of the world lies in its thousand nameless saints. Whatever my creed may be, I bow my head before Father Damien and that noble priest —truly, priest of God—who during the recent trouble which threatened our whole social system stepped bravely forward and proved the *one* infallibility—that of Goodness. Let us not drift backward to these old charges and counter-charges, these battles of the books, these vilifications of one creed by another. It is not merely because he is a dogmatic Christian, but because he is a thinker open to all the gentle influence of spiritual forces, that Mr. Gladstone has become the champion of Marriage as an Eternal Contract, never to be broken save at the risk of moral destruction. There can be no doubt that he would think as he thinks on this subject even if he were as free a rationalist as Mr. John Morley. It is his temperament, not merely his religion, which makes him regard the marriage bond as a holy thing. The documents in which he believes seem to verify his human instinct, that is all.

The history of the Churches is one thing ; the history of the Christian ideal is another. Baffled for centuries by the adamantine and indestructible logic framed by the Apostles, from John downwards—those Titans who scaled the very walls of Heaven, and only just failed in their attempt to set the Cross above the seat of Jehovah—Religion has at last resolved to seek its premises, not in any religious dogma, not in any metaphysical chimera, not in any crude physical discovery, but in the highest Science of all, that of human Sentiment. This Science—a product of all moral and religious inspiration—has established as one of its cardinal principles that nothing is really holy which conflicts either with the natural instincts or with the verified insight of human nature. It has rejected the dogma of Eternal Punishment because that dogma is repellent to common justice and common-sense, and it has rejected the no less dreary rationalistic

dogma that Man is only one of the beasts that
perish, because that dogma, too, though promul-
gated so eagerly by the philosophic undertaker, is
opposed at every point to common instinct. It
utterly refuses also, in the light of social knowledge, to regard Marriage as invariably and essentially sacramental. To accept a sacrament of any
kind a man or a woman must be purified, must be
' born again.' Beautiful indeed is Marriage when
the recipients of its happiness *can* accept it as a
sacrament. How many do so ? For how many is
to do so possible ? To the great majority of human
beings, Love is (as I said in my first letter) of the
Body. Now the time is long past when the Science
of Human Sentiment is content to assume that Man
is a spiritual being *only*, without flesh and blood,
without passions, without animal instincts, without
those corporeal attributes which are often the
beauty, and now and then the glory, of Humanity.
By his mouth is he fed ; by his appetites is his life
conditioned. ' Carnal, carnal !' cried St. Simeon of
the Pillar, and so cry the Saint's emasculated
modern descendants. But the very spirit of
Christian theology asserts in its supremest sacrament that Flesh and Blood may be themselves
divine. During the fierce asceticism of the early
centuries of Christianity (see the great historian of
Rationalism, *passim*) every human sentiment, every
natural affection, was repudiated as carnal, as
emanating from the Spirit of Evil. Fathers, to

prove their spirituality, dashed out the brains of
their little children; sons, to prove their purity,
turned in loathing from their own mothers. To
be indifferent to every human tie, scornful of every
human impulse, was to be certain of the hall-mark
of Salvation.

Well, that is all over. There is no danger to
poor human nature in that direction. Science,
which is only Religion veiled, has taught us to
reverence the abodes of flesh in which we dwell,
has proved to us that, so surely as we desecrate
them, so surely shall the House of Life fall in ruins
about our ears. We believe now that there is
sweetness and wholesomeness in every human
function, that neither Asceticism (which degraded
the body of man) nor Virginity (which became a
rock of wretchedness for women) is necessarily holy
in itself. Purity, like Love, attains its apogee
when the Soul fulfils, through the perfect organization of natural passions and instincts, the sane and
lovely laws of life.

As I write these words, there bounces in upon
me, flushed and fluent, the 'Wife and Mother'
who has told you, in resonant periods, that the
highest bond of love is all nonsense, and that she
is content, for her part, to take her husband as he
is (a very fragile specimen of humanity), and to
shake hands with him for ever at the gates of
Death. Now this frank, honest, dish-and-all-
swallowing matron pleases me well, as the rooks

in the rookery and the cattle in the fields please me. Right honestly she admits that the father of her children is a cleverer being than herself, and must, therefore, have plenty of rope to wander astray with.

> ' " Oh, naughty, naughty world !" she cries ;
> " Men are a dear, immoral set !"
> And flirts her fan and winks her eyes,
> And gaily turns a pirouette.'

She is, doubtless, one of those purely beautiful creatures who have made men what they are. Talking the other day with a friend of fair intelligence, I was assured by him that Man, being an intellectual being, was independent of the moral restrictions incumbent on Woman, who is not intellectual. Men of genius more particularly, my friend averred, were to be allowed to do exactly as they pleased. The question of the relative intelligence of men and women is too long to be discussed here ; but in a remarkable work recently published—Dr. Campbell's book on the ' Causation of Disease ' — the evidence will be found fairly weighed. I should say myself, from the little I have observed, that the average man is in no respect superior intellectually to the average woman, while the names of Mary Somerville, of Georges Sand, of Mrs. Browning, and of many others, are sufficient to establish that women of genius are tall and strong enough to stand beside men of genius now and for ever. But Genius—so called—is to me a very unknown

18

quantity. I deny that it has any privileges whatever, or that it can make any laws for itself outside the laws of love and sympathy by which the highest and the lowest live. So far as this very question of Marriage is concerned, our men and women of genius have often got into very serious trouble—not, I think, because they have erred in their interpretations of its sanctions, but because they have generally, in the face of public opinion, overlooked the contract and searched everywhere for the sacrament. Nothing proved so completely the necessity of a Science of human Sentiment, as opposed to the still lingering dogmas of unhuman spirituality, than the conduct of men like Shelley and women like Georges Sand. Twenty-fold intellectual power would not save them from condemnation. Unless Genius is a synonym for Goodness, it is a sham and a phantom ; and Goodness, the Soul of human sentiment, believes that no intellectual power whatever can justify the shameless profanation of any one human function, the cruel rending asunder of any one human tie.

The point upon which I am now touching is more important than it may seem at first sight. For many centuries Man has justified his infamies to Woman on the score of his intellectual superiority, while individual men of genius have considered themselves entitled—on the score of their flatulent ' inspiration '—to base their pyramid of greatness on broken hearts. Lacking the temper of hero-worship, and having little or no reverence for mere cleverness, I follow the records of certain famous lives with much the same feeling that I peruse the ' Newgate Calendar,' and I could, with little or no compunction, see Rousseau whipped at the cart's tail, or Alexander Pope put in the pillory. The right of indiscriminate and limitless aberration claimed for men of genius is claimed, in most matters of conduct, for men generally. Common-sense recognises neither claim. If his artistic gift does not render a man saner and wiser it is a false counter, worth nothing. If the superior cleverness claimed by men over women does not enable them to keep their souls saner and their bodies purer, it is only the cleverness of the parrot or the ape. Physiologists and Sociologists are very fond of telling us that since there is a radical difference between the two sexes it is absurd to lay down laws of conduct for both alike. While the wife sits at home among her children, the husband is free to amuse himself at his own sweet will. It is indeed in the very nature of things that, to quote the vulgarism, he ' may do as he darn pleases'! The majority of women accept this condition as inevitable. Even women of genius are found ready to proclaim the superior intellectual power, and the greater moral freedom of men. And thus, in the very land where a gray modern apostle proclaims that Mar-

18—2

riage is Eternal, we find the eternal parade of the two meanest of all privileges, that of Intelligence and that of Sex ; we find that to be a little cleverer than one's neighbour is only to be a little baser, a little fouler both in mind and appetite ; we find that to be a man, hailed as the highest of creatures, is only to exist on the same plane of passions as the beast. No wonder the world is getting tired of the religious ideal, of the faith which recognises only one privilege—that of truth, of goodness, of purity, both personal and spiritual. No wonder the laughter echoes from club to club at the mere notion that the Matrimonial Farce, the humour of which consists of jokes about male hypocrisy and female toleration, is to be played on for ever !

In asking whether Marriage is an Eternal Contract, we mean by the word ' Eternal ' simply the period of moral consciousness. Whether or not we believe in eternal Life is neither here nor there. It matters little whether a Soul is married or single when it has been absorbed into such abstract states of practical nonentity as the ' Immanence ' of Spinoza, the ' Will ' of Schopenhauer, or the ' Unconscious ' of Hartmann. Marriage, be it contract or sacrament, is a relation only possible to a state of individuality. The whole question, therefore, narrows itself thus, So long as we are conscious creatures, whether in this world or another, have we the right to marry a second time ? I have answered that question in the affirmative, while asserting that, when Marriage is really and absolutely sacramental, it must of its own nature be permanent. The fusion of two perfectly united Souls lasts for ever, survives all bodily conditions. This, I am aware, is regarded by the world in general, and by your merry 'wife and mother' in particular, as the very madness of sentimental optimism. Well, it is the optimism of the Science I am upholding, that of human Sentiment. Just as surely as the moment of supreme insight comes with the sacrament of Death, touching our tearful eyelids with the euphrasy of glorious pain, so does the moment of supreme Marriage come with the sacrament of Love. There are men who can stand in a death-chamber and see only the stone mask and the shadow of mysterious dread. There are men who can come fresh from Belshazzar's Feast—fresh from the very Handwriting on the Wall—and put on over their uncleanness and their impurity the white robes of the bridegroom. For such men Marriage may serve as a contract; it is all they need for self-protection, all Society needs for its security. To tie such creatures by a Sacrament is monstrous; they are incapable by very temperament of understanding its nature. But, over and above the lower strata of Humanity, there exist those who have seen Death transfigured and known Love unveiled; men and women, many of them, who are stained and fallen, who have experienced endless dishallucinations, who have been in revolt against the conventions—nay, even against the very sanctities—of Society. These men know that Love, like Death, comes to the Soul but once ; that Love and Death may come hand in hand, that once, together. Far, far more beautiful than the sight of a Shelley standing on Harriet Westbrook's grave, or running from his next wife's chamber to follow the frisky heels of homebred or foreign ladies, is the picture of poor Byron, besmirched with his own mad sensuality from head to foot, yet still dreaming of the sacrament, the sublime moment, the eternal passion, which never came. The old couple sitting side by side and crooning 'John Anderson, my Joe,' as gentle Death opens its arms to receive them, are diviner still. In a few short hours* all England will be looking reverently on while the body of Robert Browning is committed to its native dust. The crown and glory of that great man's life was its consecration to one serene and sacramental passion. Through all these years of loneliness, amid literary detraction or coterie fume and incense, in the midst of the busy world or out of it, in the silence of his own chamber, Browning listened to that immortal voice which sings of eternal love :

> 'O, lyric Love, half angel and half bird,
> And all a wonder and a wild desire !'

Thus, for the instruction and beatification of humanity, the supremely great remained the

* Written just after Browning's death.

supremely good, and in his great song his great goodness, completed in a transfiguration of Love and Death, eternally survives. It is better, perhaps, even in these days of unbelief, to listen to the song of the poet than to the purr of the contented Matron, who looks cheerfully forward to the inevitable moment of saying, ' Good-bye, old fellow ; we've got along very comfortably on the whole, and we part on the best of terms.' Poor little Matron ! Does she really live, or is she only a male cynic masquerading in a petticoat ? If she lives, I see no reason why she should not be very happy. The legal contract was made for her, and suits her admirably. I see no reason, moreover, why she should not, if occasion offers, renew it just as often as she pleases. The Sacrament of Love is another thing.

ROBERT BUCHANAN.

NOTE ON THE PRECEDING.

MR. GLADSTONE'S ECCLESIASTICAL ESSAYS.*

Essay-writing appears to be a lost art, or at least an art in which few people now take any interest, except those scattered individuals to whom the *Quarterly* and *Edinburgh* and other old-fashioned reviews still form an inspiration. Instead

---

* 'Gleanings of Past Years, 1851—1875,' by the Right Hon. W. E. Gladstone, M.P. Ecclesiastical, vols. v. and vi. London : Murray.

of the essay proper, with its air of superhuman insight, its rapid generalizations, its bold survey of its subject as of mankind ' from China to Peru,' we get now the fragments of Experts, on whom there sits that priggish profession of infallibility which is even more irritating, sometimes, than the once popular assumption of omniscience. I confess frankly that I miss the old style, of which Johnson was the forerunner, and Macaulay the supreme and imperial outcome. It was royal in its massive impudence, splendid in its glorious marshallings of fact and fiction, viewy, broad, blatant, and very entertaining. Now, the new style, whatever its other merits, is not so entertaining. It is far too correct, microscopic, technical, and neglectful of what we may call the grand manner of English prose. Your old-fashioned essayist might be, and generally was, a humbug, knowing little of details, smelling the paper-knife when he was dealing with a book, scornful of truth when he was dealing with things and men ; but what ground he managed to cover ! how fine was his verisimilitude ! how well oiled his periods! how fluent his general eloquence ! how brilliant his particular flourishes of rhetoric ! how bright his occasional flashes of wit ! Add to this, that he did his best to make his essay exhaustive of the subject. When Macaulay had done with Johnson and Boswell, the topic was squeezed dry ; there was no necessity even to go back to Boswell's

life. The reader, omniscient like the critic, knew
all about it! When Jeffrey had disposed of
Wordsworth, Wordsworth was sentenced; the
reader knew all about *him*, and there was an end.
When so much knowledge could be gained at
secondhand, it was quite unnecessary to go to the
fountain-heads. Of course it was all very stupid,
very blatant, and very unjust; but on the other
hand it was so thoroughly judicial! Nowadays
we get only little bits of literary special pleadings, instead of grand, swinging, overpowering
summings-up.

Mr. Gladstone's manner, in these so - called
' Ecclesiastical Essays,' is, to my thinking, a compromise between the old style and the new. Like
the old style, verbose, rotund, fluent, and at times
omniscient; like the new style, careful, watchful,
accurate, and zealous of correction. Born under
the protection of the old gods of Edinburgh and
Albemarle Street, Mr. Gladstone has lived long
enough to recognise the later pantheon of scientists,
experts, and professional doctrinaires. As the
world well knows, he is a man of much knowledge and many gifts, with a good deal of the lost
grand manner, modulated by a fine modern feeling
for truth and verification. In an omniscient generation, like that of our grandfathers, there would
have been no question of his critical greatness; he
would have sat upon the Olympian hill of criticism,
and felt the world tremble at his nod. In a

generation like the present, divided between moods of paralyzing caution and states of total nescience, his hand is weakened, and his influence almost doubtful. He would fain pronounce judgments, but he is too conscientious ; he would limit himself to special pleading, but as a special pleader he is very roundabout indeed. Seen as he here appears before us, in half a dozen representative essays, he strikes me as a writer of eager authoritativeness, who, under happier circumstances, would have made a first-class Bishop, but who suffers peculiar discomfort from being compelled to inhale the too clear atmosphere of modern advanced ideas.

Perhaps the most characteristic of these Essays is the one on ‘ The Bill for Divorce,’ reprinted from the *Quarterly Review* of 1857. It commences in the old way, with a lordly outlook on Creation and the period in general. ‘ The age in which we live claims, and in some respects deserves, the praise of being active, prudent, and practical : active in the endeavour to detect evils, prudent in being content with limited remedies, and practical in choosing them according to effectiveness rather than to the canons of ideology,’ etc., etc. ‘Canons of ideology’ is good, even if it means nothing. We have not read much further before we know what side the writer is on ; that he is, like all the omniscient school, on the side of authority and the powers that be. Very familiar indeed are the phrases—‘ the fences which enclose the sacred

precinct' (Marriage), 'general decay of the spirit
of traditionary discipline,' 'the relaxed tone of
modern society.' Mr. Gladstone, like a very
Bishop, asseverates that marriage is a life-long
compact, 'according to the Holy Scripture,' which
may sometimes be put in abeyance by the separation of a couple, but which can never be rightfully
dissolved, so as to set them free, during their
lives, to unite with other persons. As might be
expected, his arguments are almost entirely Scrip-
tural, though he is not above passing references to
the Greeks of Homer, to Athenæus, and even to
Gibbon. Nothing could be more idle than his
examination of those passages in the New Testament which touch upon the question of Marriage
and Divorce, unless, perhaps, that other portion of
his essays where he cross-examines the mediæval
authorities and Church dignitaries. I have no
concern here with his argument, which it is no
business of mine either to support or refute; but
surely no one not saturated with the spirit of the
Old Church could talk in this way on so solemn a
topic, quite oblivious of the fact that no such topic
can be settled without an occasional reference to
Science, to Philosophy, and to Physiology. In some
places, notably where he alludes to the 'adamantine
laws of grammar,' and examines a Greek abstraction
with the solemnity of a pedant, Mr. Gladstone
almost passes the limits of human patience. He
himself talks of arguments of 'that deplorably

fatuous description which almost makes a man despair of his age, if not of the whole future of his kind.' Conceive the man who could despair of his age, not to speak of 'the whole future of his kind,' because doctors and divines differ as to the nature of Marriage, and its character as a 'Sacrament'! With quite forensic fervour Mr. Gladstone tells of the 'pestilent ideas' of Milton. 'That for which he (Milton) pleads is a license of divorce for aversion or incompatibility; the wildest libertine, the veriest Mormon, could not devise words more conformable to his ideas, if, indeed, we are just to the Mormon sages in assuming that they alienate as freely as they acquire !'

The other essays in the volume are on such themes as 'The Functions of Laymen in the Church,' 'The Church of England and Ritualism,' 'Ward's Ideal of a Christian Church,' and 'On the Royal Supremacy.' They are none of them, perhaps, quite so earnest or quite so wrong as the essay on the 'Bill for Divorce'; but they all evince the same confusion of the old style and the new. They are all conscientious, careful, ornate, and fairly liberal of view. They are all old-fashioned in the sense of a dictatorial manner and a lost style ; all new-fashioned in the sense of intellectual uneasiness and indisputable zeal for truth. But they are none of them above the average episcopal or clerical intellect ; they none of them possess the higher sort of literary or spiritual insight. If I knew Mr. Gladstone by these Essays alone, I should think him a very able and zealous, but by no means extraordinary, person ; knowing him, as I do, as one of the most prominent political figures of the day, I can now clearly understand why he has become the great disorganizing force, the most disturbing and contradictory influence, of the Liberal Party.

FLOTSAM AND JETSAM.

FLOTSAM AND JETSAM.

I.

WHAT IS SENTIMENT?

In a recent number of a new publication called *The Speaker*, there is an article on 'Sentimentalism,' in which it is contended very justly that the *Aberglaube* of hysterical emotion is a sham thing by the side of true pathos ; but very falsely, that the air of the present day is overcharged with 'Sentiment.' The writer thus confounds what is real with what is true—Sentiment with Sentimentalism ; and the confusion is one which has been made from time immemorial. Sentiment, I conceive, is the power which generalizes the experience of mankind, the verification of long centuries, concerning the links which unite members of the human family surely and remorsely to one another, and which thus justifies Poetry (in the words of Novalis) as the only Reality. Sentimentalism, on the other hand, is sentiment perverted and overcharged — in other words, become unscientific. While objecting somewhat

19

to his terminology, I cordially agree with the
writer of the article I have named in the distinction he draws between true and false pathos
in literature.   I fail altogether, however, to follow
him in his contention that either Sentiment or
Sentimentalism are much in the air at present.
I believe, rather, that cheap Science and cheap
Cynicism are destroying, or trying to destroy, both
the sham and the reality.   Men nowadays do not
feel too much, but far too little.   Thanks partly to
the influence of the baser portion of the public
Press, the era of completed ethical obtusity seems
fast approaching.

The man who endeavours, as I shall endeavour,
to treat Sentiment as an exact science, stands at
a strange disadvantage in these days of troubled
materialism, when the nobler emotions are old-
fashioned and unpopular, and even Conscience is
likely to suffer from being classed as a complica-
tion of brain secretions.   I may fairly say, however, that I have never wavered one hair in my
doctrine on this subject, from the day when I
wrote the ' Ballad of Judas Iscariot ' to the day,
only just past, when I dramatized the ' Clarissa '
of Richardson.   The late Lord Houghton said
to me many years ago, ' The English people
are practical, they do not care for Sentiment ;'
to which I replied by quoting several extraordinary
instances of popular success secured entirely by
what is conventionally known as Sentiment, and

especially the instance of Mr. Gladstone. It was quite clear, however, that Lord Houghton attached the ordinary meaning to the word under discussion, while I attached to it a meaning by no means ordinary. I wish, therefore, to put the question, ' What is Sentiment ?' Does it mean, as certain scientists and many of the general public contend, a false and distorted, a transcendental and hysterical, conception of the relations of life—a general distribution over thought and feeling of what is known as Sentimentalism ; or does it mean, as I have long maintained, the absolute experience of Humanity in the process of reduction to a Science ?

Of one thing we may be quite clear, that there was never a period in the world's history when the mere word Sentiment awakened in the thoughts of the classes called cultivated a fainter sympathy than now. Luxury on the one hand, and materialism on the other, have done their work so completely that large numbers of men can witness without emotion of any sort even the Dance of the Seven Deadly Sins. The Rome of Juvenal is, as I pointed out years ago, reproduced in the London of to-day. The spirit of a spurious and empirical ' scientific ' philosophy, adopting as its shibboleth a certain specious jargon of experimental ethics, mental culture coincident with moral degradation, the avarice of the rich and the misery of the poor, just as surely contradict the

stern old English type of character as the same
phenomena contradicted, in the time of Juvenal,
the power, the integrity, and the austerity of
ancient Rome.

> 'Et quando uberior vitiorum copia ? quando
> Major avaritiæ patuit sinus ?'

The parallel might be pursued down to the smallest
detail, but to pursue it is not my purpose. I
merely desire to remark, *en passant*, that the
present social crisis is not unprecedented, but has
occurred more than once, and once phenomenally,
in the Evolution of Mankind. The Gospel of
Sentiment shook the world eighteen centuries ago.
The Science of Sentiment, verifying the instinct
of that gospel, will stir it now.

The Science of Sentiment, then, adopts as
its cardinal principle that the evolution of human
ethics has proceeded in direct ratio with the
growth or the suppression of the individual
capacities of love and sympathy—sympathy seen
dimly in the affinities of the lower organisms,
shown largely in the lower animals, evolved
wonderfully by human aid in the domesticated
animals, notably in the dog, and attaining to the
power of self-knowledge in the Mind of Man. The
law of this Science, the condition on which it exists,
is, like that of all other sciences, that of verification. To verify it completely would be beyond
my power. I shall therefore confine myself to one
position only, which is a paradox—that Love and

Hate, attraction and repulsion, in the human creature, are practically equivalent forces, although divergent, and that the object of the Science of Sentiment is to reconcile and assimilate them.

An illustration comes to my hand in a play from my pen produced at the Vaudeville Theatre. One of my critics has assured me that I stultify my moral teaching by suffering the libertine Lovelace to profane by a touch, even for a moment, in her dying delirium, his victim Clarissa. He has sinned past all pardon, he has isolated himself from all humanity, by a hideous act of violation ; and so, indeed, the poor girl tells him, in the supreme *Aberglaube* of her exaltation. Her last clear words are of eternal renunciation, eternal farewell. He says he will 'atone.' 'You cannot, sir,' she answers ; 'it were as easy to turn the world upon its course and bring all Eden back.' This, the critic says, is final. It is so from an unscientific point of view. But the Science of Sentiment instructs us that though individual Man cannot bring back the lost Eden, God can. God, the eternal Law, the loving Force in the heart of physical and moral evolution, completes a miracle of creation in a daily miracle of moral interchange and interaction. Lovelace is lost—that is certain. He is to be saved ; but how ? By the very act which destroyed him, but made him abject in contrition. The fire which purifies, the punishment which cleanses the conscience of the world, which is irresistible, and

the acquired insight of humanity, which is indestructible, leave him linked for ever with the lot
of the angel he has wedded in the lurid halls of
Hell. There is no escape for him otherwise. Even
God cannot save him, except through himself;
and thus through *her*. The moral interchange is
thus inevitable.

Another paradox. Next to the man I have
blest, the man I have cursed is nearest to me
of all human creatures. So surely as I am bound
to the man I love am I bound to the man I hate.
He has become a part of me; though all the rest
of the world may be a blank to me, I am certain
of *him*. Every struggle I make against my
enemy, every blow I strike him in the face,
brings him closer into my life. This, indeed, is
Sentiment, but it is Law. It is a thought for
fools to laugh and scoff at, but it is as scientifically
verifiable as any law of Selection based upon the
fossils of extinct species. And the closer my
enemy clings around me, the more I shudder at
what seems to me his moral hideousness, the more
terrible grows his power upon me. In my despair
I curse him, I curse Humanity, I curse the cruel
Law of Life. I struggle upward, and he holds
me down; and I find that to rise at all I must take
him with me. At last, out of my despair, comes
insight. I see that he, too, is struggling, downward perhaps, but struggling inevitably in the
throes of Evolution. I see my own sorrows, my

own meanness, my own misery, reflected in him ; nay, I see my own 'self,' as in a mirror, *looking out* of him. There is no other way—I must take him with me or perish utterly. His life has become a part of mine. Then we cling together, and cry for help, for mercy, for Light! Darkly, dimly, I begin to know that he is helping me, that he, too, feels the piteousness of our repulsion for each other. I save him ; I have saved myself. The deadlier the wrong that I have done him, or that he has done me, the more inextricable become our thoughts, our conditions. This is the Law of Sentiment which saved Lovelace. This is the Law of God which made the violated and the victim man and wife. This is the paradox which redeems the world.

'Very foolish, very absurd!' says the young lady, who, my critic tells me, will not go to a theatre unless she is to laugh, not to cry ; in fact, as she adds, 'very sentimental.' But the theory is not one developed *a priori;* it is founded on what Professor Huxley terms 'grovelling among facts.' No living man has yet struck a blow which did not injure himself more than its object. I myself am 'indifferent honest,' fond of tussles with the enemy, but this same Science of Sentiment has instructed me that I have never had one real enemy except myself. But, the young lady perhaps adds, 'The idea is so impracticable!' Well, so is the Christianity which it formularizes, and

Christianity, apart from the dogmas which disfigure it, is recognised even by modern philosophy as the highest Ideal of the human mind. Very possibly, and often very certainly, I do *not* love my enemy ! Well, as the Yankees express it, I have *got* to reckon with him. So long as I fail, says the Law, I shall stand still. And putting bad temper and violent passion aside as really ephemeral, the task of recognising the equivalency of Love and Hate is, to a thinking man in his sane moments, fairly easy, after all.

It is difficult, it is often impossible, to live up to our ideals ; none of us, I fear, do that, and least of all the present writer. If the issue depended on our own *conduct*, on our own practical recognition of ethical principles, Sentiment would be vague as the Chimæra. Happily the law of Evolution works independently of human consciousness, and he who thinks all things evil is quite as surely at its mercy as he who thinks all things good. The clearest teaching of this age affirms that the evolution of the race, conditioned universally by the influence of individuals upon each other, is an evolution *upward*. It is no mere cant of little Bethel, therefore, which tells us that we should love our enemies ; we *do* love them when we most hate them, through the inexorable laws of moral interchange. As the poor fellow said in the story, ' It all comes reet i' the end,' and the transfusion of antagonism into its equivalent affinity, of repulsion into its equivalent attraction, is the moral business of the world. Sentiment, then —the insight which enlarges the area of human sympathy, which reconciles the divergences of human character, which equalizes in the long-run the results of all human effort — is nothing if it is not verifiable or scientific ; but since all true Science is another word for Religion, Sentiment is spiritually Sacrament—the crowning Sacrament of daily life.

II.

EMMA WADE'S MARTYRDOM.

In May, 1879, there was lying in the county gaol of Lincoln a young girl just respited from a sentence of death. Under what possible delusion the jurymen who convicted her were labouring when they found her guilty of murder in the first degree, I cannot explain ; possibly, however, they were bewildered by the summing-up of the Judge, who, according to the reporters, ' reminded the jury that their verdict must be based, not upon their feelings, but their judgment.' It seemed to me, at all events, that the verdict was very cruel, rash, and wrong, and that, while exhibiting little feeling, it showed no judgment whatever. The facts were very simple. Emma Wade, a domestic servant and the daughter of a police-constable, contracted an attachment for a jeweller's assistant in Stamford, was seduced by him, and gave birth to an illegitimate child. At the time of the birth she was residing at home, and the evidence showed that she was gentle, dutiful, and affectionate, both to her parents and to the child. Her father seems to have treated her kindly, with the patience of love, but it was proved that the mother subjected her to just that kind of persecution, seasoned with taunt and insult, which drives a feeble girl to despair. She was daily taunted with her shame, and urged to return to service. On the evening of April 18 her sister, hearing a scream, rushed upstairs, and found Emma in mortal agony. 'Take the baby,' she cried ; 'I have poisoned it and myself.' Medical assistance being called in, the mother was recovered, but the infant died, traces of strychnine, Prussian blue, and wheat flour (elements of a poison called 'Battle's Vermin Killer') being afterwards found in its stomach. Previous to taking the poison the distracted girl wrote to Scarcliff, her lover, a long letter of farewell, which I quote at full length, certain that it forms in itself a stronger appeal for mercy than any words of mine :

　　　　　　　　　　　　　　　　'Stamford.

　'DEAR HARRY,

　　　'I am sorry to write to you. Dear Harry, I return your portrait with a heavy heart. It's sadder than I can express to anyone ; but I have borne my mother's treatment till I can't any longer. Dear Harry, it is all because father won't turn me out in the streets. The words she uttered about me and the baby— they are too cruel to express to you. Dear Harry, I love my child as I love my life, but I can't go through the treatment I am going through now ; my life is a complete misery, and my child's too. Dear Harry, I wish to bid you farewell in this world, but I hope to meet you in another, never to part again. I hope the Lord will forgive me and take me to a home of rest. Harry, I have one comfort ; and that is I know my child will be happy. So now, dear Harry, you must pass me out of your mind and look for something brighter. Dear Harry, I wish to tell you it is nothing on your part. Dear Harry, my love is never vanished : I love you now as I loved you at first ; you (have) been in my thoughts from morning till night. So now I must bid you farewell for ever. I hope you may enjoy happiness in this world and the next, too. My heart is too full to speak all, so good-bye for ever.

'EMMA.

'Respect Mrs. Weatherington. She has been a kind friend to me. I have sent you a piece of baby's hair. You won't forget her name— Constance May Scarcliff.'

It seems to me, taking all the circumstances into

consideration, that a more beautiful letter was never written. In its infinite simplicity and pathos, in its gentle dignity and sorrow, it is a wonderful production for the pen of a domestic servant. Note the tenderness of the thought, 'I have one comfort, and that is I know my child will be happy,' together with the last piteous words, 'I have sent you a piece of baby's hair.' Yet with this document before them, with the poor heart-broken martyr herself facing them, the jurymen, listening to their 'judgment,' not their 'feelings,' brought in their verdict of wilful murder.

I am no apologist for Infanticide. I have no sympathy for the mother, however troubled and distressed, who to save herself from ignominy or inconvenience destroys her helpless child. But for the poor, bewildered, distracted girl, herself almost a child, who loves her babe so passionately that she cannot bear to hear it despised and spoken of with cruel scorn, and who, having no earthly hope, cries to God, 'Forgive me, take me—take us both —to a home of rest,' I felt, as every true-hearted man must have done, pity which is too deep for tears. The law of this country, with curious inconsistency, pronounces suicide to be a criminal offence, and at the same time connects with every suicide an exculpatory explanation of 'temporary insanity.' The sentiment of this country pronounces that there are a thousand things so hard to bear, so terrible to understand, especially amongst those classes on whom the pinch of life comes sorest, that suicide is sometimes the only escape from a great and seemingly endless difficulty. The poor, unfortunate, 'weary of breath,' and 'sick of life's mystery,' has the sympathy of every thinking being, whether her story be told by a penny-a-liner in a mere newspaper paragraph or by a great poet in an immortal song. Put the case only altered a very little : If a broken-hearted mother, clutching her child to her heart, were to leap over Waterloo Bridge, and if when they drew her forth still breathing the child were found to be dead, who would not sympathize ? and if afterwards the mother were tried for murder and condemned to death, who would not feel his soul rise in passionate protestation ? Now, it really makes very little difference, save to a poet treating the subject, whether the means of suicide is found in the Thames by moonlight or in a wretched packet of 'Battle's Vermin-Killer.' The offence, the motive, the moral responsibility, is the same. Emma Wade's was a case of Suicide pure and simple. The poor girl wished to die, and she loved her baby far too passionately to leave it behind her. In a moment of delirium, she clutched it to her, and sank, as she believed, to slumber, confident in the mercy of God. Her last thought was of her darling babe. 'I have sent you a piece of baby's hair. You won't forget her name— Constance May Scarcliff.' Her last thought was

to give it *his* name, to lend its poor memory that
shelter which she could not legally claim.   Picture
her agony, her despair, when they drew her back
out of the very Shadow of Death, when she awoke,
not to God's mercy, but to man's judgment; her
babe dead upon her breast, her heart broken, her
brain still stagnified from its fatal sleep.   If ever
woman was punished for her sins, if ever woman
drank the cup of man's cruelty to the dregs, that
woman was Emma Wade.   Tortured back to life,
dragged to prison, pitilessly tried, what must she
have suffered in those dreadful days, until the hour
came when the Judge assumed the black cap, and
sentenced her to be hanged by the neck till she was
dead !*

III.

THE APOTHEOSIS OF THE GALLOWS.

ON Tuesday morning, February 25, 1879, at eight
o'clock, was performed the last scene of a drama in
which the British public had taken an unprecedented interest, which eclipsed in its attractive
horrors even the exciting news from the Cape, and
made all minor records of the prison or the Divorce
Court seem comparatively stale and tame.   This
drama might be entitled ' The Life and Death of
a Convict ; or, The Apotheosis of the Gallows.'
Beginning at Bannercross, in Yorkshire, with about

* Emma Wade was respited.—R.B.

as coarse and clumsy a bit of murder as ever
awakened ignorant admiration, it passed into a
series of episodes of the most every-day brutality,
until it glided from utter commonplace into sudden
romance under the very shadow of Death. A
more uninteresting ruffian than Charles Peace can
scarcely be conceived. A less dignified criminal
never paid the extreme penalty of the law. There
was nothing in him to awaken either attention or
admiration, save his courage ; and that courage,
disintegrated into its component elements, seems to
have consisted of unparalleled obtuseness and
gigantic self-confidence. Yet of this poor wretch,
who has scarcely one trait of redeeming manliness,
and whose moral ugliness was without any sort
of grandeur, the public Press actually manu-
factured a Hero. I say the Press advisedly.
Save for the elaborate reports in the daily papers
and the wild and wondrous inventions of the
pictorial weeklies, Charles Peace would have gone
out of this world ignored and despised even by that
great criminal class to which he belonged. But
ever since the memorable occasion when he tried
to escape from the railway carriage, he had been
consecrated to the penny-a-liner. He had been
described in various forms of disguised panegyric
as the Admirable Crichton of Housebreakers.
Because he could play a little on the fiddle and
had brought together one or two musical instru-
ments, he was represented as a perfect Paganini

and a splendid amateur collector of violins. Because he had some little cleverness in mechanics and had within him the amateur engineer's morbid passion for ' patents,' it was given out that his gifts of invention amounted to little short of genius. Because he had had one or two dirty liaisons, and in the sanctity of his private life always had a trull at his elbow, he was pictured as a criminal Don Juan, surrounded by Odalisques of splendid infamy. His character fascinated even philosophers. One gentle newspaper, the *Spectator*, accepted the penny-a-liner's chronicle, and preached a beautiful homily upon it. There was something beyond measure alluring in the idea of an unclean old man with tremendous intellect and sublime courage, setting all the forces of the Law at defiance, by living all day the life of a respectable elderly gentleman with one arm, and all night the life of a truculent assassin with a fatal weapon. For all these pictures, for all these mercies of the mendacious, we have to thank the penny-a-liner. There was no deity but Peace, and the penny-a-liner was his Prophet. So the great sensation drama throve, though its production on the public scene, with all the advantage of big posters and capital letters, could be regarded as nothing short of a public calamity.

Now, the entire thing would have been an utter failure but for the introduction, in the last scene, of the Gallows. Till the Shadow of Death was actually upon him, till it became known that he was really to be *hanged* for his misdeeds, Charles Peace lacked the crowning consecration. I am certain that if he had not received the capital sentence, if he had been simply relegated to his life of penal servitude, the public would have been utterly disgusted with him, as with one who was in some measure an impostor ; would have read with more or less weariness the account of his super-human talents, and would have waited patiently for the advent of some other sort of ideal. But the Apotheosis of the Gallows was to come, and with its coming the wretched man was to be transfigured. To the minds of the criminal classes, and to the minds of large numbers of people who may any day become criminal, the condemned murderer was one of the great Heroes of the earth. His passage from the prison bar to the condemned cell was a triumph, to be envied, to be emulated ; his passage from the condemned cell to the Gallows was a splendid transfiguration, to which few human crea-tures might aspire. In one of the woman Thomp-son's letters she talked of her name and that of her paramour living in the ' History of the Earth'! That was too glorious a forethought, with which few could sympathize ; for in the eyes of the criminal classes, a momentary apotheosis, with the white cap over the face, and the chaplain uttering a prayer, is enough. To fear neither man nor God, to have one's hand against all men, and to

'die game'—these are the conditions of such fame
as the Gallows can give. Fulfilling these conditions,
despite the little bit of religious talk at the last
(which many of his admirers possibly looked upon
as a delicious specimen of 'Charley's gammon'),
Charles Peace touched the heights of criminal
greatness. Anyone passing through the by-ways
of London after the execution might have heard
the popular expletives at every corner and in every
public-house. 'Poor old Charley!' 'Well, he's
gone at last, and he died game.' 'He was a rare-
pluck'd one, he was!' 'It'll be a long time before
we see such another!' Not a Bill Sykes in Seven
Dials but drew a great breath, and asked himself,
'Shall *I* ever cover myself with such glory, and
have all the newspapers talking about me, and all
the shops full of my portraits?' Yes, the last
scene was an ovation. The effect of the Gallows in
the background was stupendous, and the triumph
of the Hero of the Drama was complete.

If anything could add to Peace's glory in the
eyes of his tumultuous audience, it was his own
last confession—that he had been guilty of another
murder, and, with delicious humour, had managed
to get another man sentenced to death in his
place! Better still, the murdered man was a
policeman! True, there was a little weakness in
confessing at all; it would have been more heroic
to have died holding his tongue, and leaving the
other condemned man to his fate. But, taken

altogether, the thing was a rich joke, and a crowning feather in 'Charley's' cap. He might now say, with Shakespeare :

> 'If 'twere now to die
> 'Twere now to be most happy; for, I fear,
> My soul hath her content so absolute
> That not another comfort like to this
> Succeeds in unknown fate.'

Thenceforward immortality was secure ; even the penny-a-liner could not make it any safer. The path to the Gallows was 'roses all the way.' Nothing more was needed than to 'die game,' and the *dénouement* would approach sublimity.

It is no part of my present purpose to open up the old discussion concerning capital punishment. My present concern is rather with the state of journalism which renders the apotheosis of the Gallows possible. When nearly every one of our leading dailies devotes more or less of its space to recording the daily sayings and doings of a commonplace criminal ; when one penny-a-liner vies with another in piling on the agony, and making what is essentially vulgar and hideous assume the hues of poetry and fascination ; when the affairs of the Nation and the state of the Empire sink into insignificance (in the newspaper proprietor's eyes) by the side of the maunderings of a poor murderer, it is really time to protest. The Fourth Estate has a duty to perform. If it is to be respected as a power in the country, it must learn to respect its readers, not to

regale them with the garbage of the 'Newgate
Calendar.' The conductors of the sensational
papers aver that they are bound to give such
records because readers demand them, and
because they would in any case be given elsewhere. The answer to the first statement
is that readers are only too willing to accept
whatever is given to them by their journalistic
guides ; to the second, that readers who love
garbage should be left to find it, for themselves, in
the literature of the slums. But the truth is that
no one gains by the apotheosis of the Gallows save
the newspaper proprietor and the penny-a-liner.
I regret to say it, but these two worthies are in
a conspiracy to prostitute the Press, and to sow
crime broadcast, by glorifying the criminal. We
cannot now tell what evil seed their latter-day
performances bring forth ; in the meantime, the
character of Journalism is degraded, and no English
journalist can remember without a feeling of shame
and humiliation the glorification of Charles Peace.

IV.

THE DEFEAT OF THE TOTAL ABSTAINER.

THAT lively old water-drinker of genius, Mr. George
Cruikshank, who played 'Hamlet' *en amateur* at
fifty, and could dance you a break-down and double-
shuffle in his grand climacteric, would have been
hotly indignant if he could have lived to become

familiar with certain recent aspects of the great
Temperance Question. In a picture which combined a maximum of moral truth with a minimum
of artistic taste, he tried to drive poor humanity
once and for ever away from the Bottle ; and he
was not much daunted when a wine-loving humorist
retaliated with an equally horrible caricature
representing the hideous creatures to be seen in a
Drop of Water magnified under the microscope.
For a considerable period the teetotalers have
really been having the best of it. Their wonder
of stump orators, Mr. J. B. Gough, having by
strictly abstaining from stimulants attained a
patriarchal beard and a stentorian power of lung,
had made the licensed victualler tremble, from
Land's End to John o' Groat's. Following in the
wake of this noisy platitudinarian, numberless bad
and good physicians have had an epidemic of
abstinence. Physicians, like other people, or,
rather, more than other people, are subject to
periodical crazes. Now it is a craze for bromide
of potassium, or some other panacea ; again, as
recently, it is a craze against all sorts of intoxicating
liquors. Happily, the reaction has at last set in,
and the leading doctors of the day have banded
together to put down that most irrepressible and
pernicious of all propagandists, the Total Abstainer. After the remarkable series of articles
which appeared in the *Contemporary Review*—a
series which must have done incalculable good, and

for which society has reason to be grateful to the able editor—the advocates of Total Abstinence can scarcely have another word to say. When such high living authorities as Sir James Paget, Sir William Gull, Dr. Risdon Barnett, Dr. Radcliffe, and Mr. Brudenell Carter, all spoke more or less in favour of alcohol, the consensus of testimony was overpowering; and it is to be hoped that after this, and at least for a time, we may be spared the familiar legend of the Total Abstainer who died triumphantly in his bed at eighty, after having kept all the commandments, and drunk nothing stronger than toast and water.

And yet, in reading those remarkable articles, I was struck by nothing so much, at a first glance, as by the overmastering moral influence of that fierce and frenzied being, the Total Abstainer, over even the tolerably impassive medical experts. So potent is enthusiasm, and so great is organization, that the doctors of the day felt strange diffidence and hesitation in giving Total Abstinence the lie direct. Sometimes, conscious of a wild water-drinker's eye upon them, they became almost timorous, and murmured with Sir William Gull, ' But though the use of alcohol in moderation may be beneficial ' (he had just asserted roundly, by the way, that it *was* beneficial), ' I very much doubt whether there are not some kinds of food which might take its place '; and he adds, vacillating feebly, ' If I am myself fatigued with overwork, I eat raisins, instead of drinking wine.' Sometimes, on the other hand, they gathered courage to boldly defy the water-drinker, and cry with Dr. Moxon, and Ecclesiastes,, 'Be not righteous overmuch, neither make thyself overwise.' But in all the cases under consideration, one perceived how strong, almost intimidating, was the power of the virtuous teetotaler over the respectable medical profession, and how much courage it required to speak the sober truth in the face of such a tremendously black-coated combination. This did not prevent Dr. Moxon asserting roundly that Teetotalers, as a body, are 'sensitive, good-natured people, of weak constitution !' For my own part, I rather quarrel with the adjective 'good-natured.' Your un-compromising, proselytizing, pugnacious teetotaler is too much of a murmuring and too little of a good fellow. He approaches the collective in-telligence of the community as a priest too often approaches the blacks, and arguments failing, is ready at any moment to resort to excommunication.

It is not to be supposed for a moment that the doctors expressed any doubts of the destructive effects of alcohol in excess. What, for example, can be more terribly true than the following picture of the fate of the inveterate drinker ?—

'When the sot has descended through his chosen course of im-becility, or dropsy, to the dead-house, Morbid Anatomy is ready to receive him—knows him well. At the *post-mortem* she would say, "Liver hard and nodulated. Brain dense and small ; its covering thick." And if you would listen to her unattractive but interesting tale, she would trace throughout the sot's body a series of changes which leave unaltered no part of him worth speaking of. She would tell you that the once delicate, filmy texture which, when he was young, had surrounded like a pure atmosphere every fibre and tube of his mechanism, making him lithe and supple, has now become rather a dense fog than a pure atmosphere :—dense stuff, which, instead of lubricating, has closed in upon and crushed out of existence more and more of the fibres and tubes, especially in the brain and liver : whence the imbecility and the dropsy.'

The only comment to be made on this, perhaps, is that inveterate tea-drinking might produce quite as lamentable a result; nay, that it might be induced even by too persistent a course of the hot buttered toast so much loved by Mr. Chadband. But Dr. Moxon, the physician to whom we owe that terrible picture, and whose paper, with all its wild and sometimes foolish language, was the finest of the whole series, only dissects the demented sot in order to martyr the delirious teetotaler. He tells us, with sly unction, of the case of the gentleman who, having consulted a 'great authority,' and been told to 'live on fish and wholemeal bread and to drink water,' had done so for two years, with the result that he *looked* a compound of water, fish, and wholemeal ! He tells us also, with no little ire against the Band of Hope, of the 'honest working cooper,' who injured his ankle with one of his tools, whose constitution became involved in fever, and who, when ordered to take stimulants, refused to touch anything containing alcohol, and died in consequence in a few days. Dr. Moxon is, as I

suggested, a wild writer, and his article was verbose
and eccentric, but he uttered terrible truths.   His
picture of the effect of alcohol in 'weakening
common-sense in opposition to individuality' was
masterly.   'The power of alcohol in this world,'
he affirmed, ' is due to the fact that it keeps down
the oppressive power of others, and of their
common-sense, over the individual sense, and so
makes a man better company to himself and others.'
He followed out the argument in a style as
convincing as it was luminous ; and I think his
reasoning had more effect on thinking people than
many of the pregnant truisms which seemed to
form the philosophy of Drs. Paget and Gull.

V.

THE CARNIVAL OF ROBERT BURNS.

ON the 25th of January, 1759—that is to say,
a little over one hundred and thirty years ago—one
of the most free and precious Beings that ever was
born to wear the poetic mantle first drew breath in
a humble cottage in the near neighbourhood of the
Scottish town of Ayr.   He himself has recorded
the event in one of the most spirited of his songs :

> ' Our monarch's hindmost year but one
> Was five-and-twenty years begun,
> 'Twas then a blast o' Janwar win'
> Blew hansel in on Robin.

> ' The gossip keekit in his loof,
>   Quo' she, " Wha lives will see the proof,
>   This waly boy will be nae coof—
>   I think we'll ca' him Robin." '

The remainder of the song, with its references to ' misfortunes great and sma' ' to come, and the love the poet would bear to the female kind, was singularly truthful and characteristic. Robert Burns lived to enjoy a little tawdry personal fame, to be overridden by misfortunes in their most squalid and wretched shape, and to leave to his country a great legacy of noble Song. But one fact I wish particularly to dwell upon, for in it lies the moral of this brief note : Burns was too free and true for his generation, and he died of a broken heart on account of its neglect. Who has not read, and who does not remember, that infinitely pathetic anecdote told by Mr. Lockhart, as told to him by David Macculloch, of how, one summer day, Burns was walking alone on the shady side of a street in Dumfries, while the opposite side was gay with groups of ladies and gentlemen going to a county festivity, not one of whom would recognise him. Macculloch accosted him, and asked him to cross the street ; but Burns answered, ' Nay, nay, my young friend—that's all over now'; and then quoted in a broken voice the lines of Lady Grizzel Baillie's ballad :

> ' O were we young, as we once hae been,
>   We suld hae been galloping down on yon green,
>   And linking it over the lilywhite lea,
>   And—*werena my heart light, I wad dee !*'

Only a little time before the poor Ploughman had been the lion of the hour ; but, as he truly said, that was 'all over.' The ignorant gentry and drunken squircarchy of the south of Scotland were tired of his splendid manhood, his fearless honesty, and his simple, independent ways.

Now, Robert Burns was a great man and a great poet, and the influence of his truly tremendous satiric and lyrical genius has been one of the great factors in the disintegration of Scottish superstition. The 'Unco Guid' still exist, but his colossal caricature of them has thinned and is thinning their ranks year after year. Indeed, it is difficult to imagine what Scotland, with its gravitation towards the Sabbatarian and the sunless, would have become, without such forces as scatter fire all over the poems and songs of Burns and his pupils. Unfortunately the very strength of this poet, and the very excess of his revolt against convention and other-worldliness, led to some literary performances of doubtful value. Perhaps the least interesting of his poems are those which are purely Bacchanalian. It was quite natural for him to sing defiantly and wildly in praise of 'guid Scots drink,' and to pledge openly, in brimming poetic bumpers, the cause of Freedom and Plainspeaking. He was a convivial creature, and his conviviality was that of a fearless and liberal nature, overflowing with love, and honest as the day. But what was to some extent a virtue in him has become, to my mind, a very curious

vice in his disciples. The fact is, Scotchmen seem
to have granted Burns his apotheosis chiefly on
account of its being an excuse for the consumption
of Whisky. So they celebrate his Birthday. So
they fill their glasses, hiccup 'Auld Langsyne,' and
cry in chorus :

> ' Robin was a rovin' boy,
>   Rantin' rovin', rantin' rovin' ;
>   Robin was a rovin' boy,
>   Rantin' rovin' Robin !'

The drunken squirearchy, whose progenitors broke
the poet's heart, and who, if the poet were alive
now, would break his heart again, are full of
enthusiasm for his memory. Even some of the
more liberal-minded ministers of the Gospel join in
the acclaim. Farmers and shepherds, factors and
ploughmen, all come together on the one great
occasion to honour the bard whom everybody can
understand, because his synonym is the Whisky
Bottle. They weep over his woes ; they smack
their lips over his satire ; they shriek at his
denunciations, and they murmur his songs. Burns
or Bacchus—it is all one. The chief point is that,
now or never, there is an excuse for getting ' reeling
ripe' or 'mortal drunk.' It is poetic, it is literary,
it is—hiccup !—honouring the Muses. Any frenzy,
however maniacal, is justifiable under the circumstances. ' Glorious Robin !' Pledge him again
and again, pledge him and bless him ; and when
you can't pledge him upright, pledge him prone, as

you lie, with your fellow Burns-worshippers, under
the table.

I am sorry to say it, I am sorry to utter one
word which might seem to deny the beneficent
influence of noble poetry and a surprising poet, but
I believe this Burns - worship to be worth —
exactly the amount of bottles emptied in its
celebration. I will go further, and affirm that
Burns himself, were he living, would be the first
to launch his fiery satire at such a sham. The
sham brotherly-kindness, the sham tears, the sham
unction, and the sham sensation of being poetic,
mean no more than other forms of tipsiness, and
so far from bringing honour to a poet make his
apotheosis a farce. I know well that deep in the
heart of Scotland there lies a well of pure and
abiding gratitude to Robert Burns, but I doubt
very much if those who love the poet best and
study his works most tenderly are to be found in
the ranks of those who stand before his shrine in
the public-house. I may be wrong, and if so I
speak under correction, but I should fancy that
Scotchmen might discover other and better opportunities for exhibiting that queer conviviality
which does not abide in them gently, as in other
men, but seizes them spasmodically on festive
occasions, like a kind of St. Vitus's Dance. It
seems to me that it is just this dram-drinking side
of Burns's genius which they ought to conceal, or
at least to forget. No one with any tenderness can

think of Burns's story—of his ghastly fits of
conviviality, of his cruel wrongs, of his broken
heart—without real tears, not the maudlin tears
of semi or complete intoxication. I am scarcely
overstepping the mark when I add, what all men
know, that the weakness of Burns was his own
readiness to yield to the same kind of false enthusiasm which is in vogue among so many of his
disciples. He himself sounded the shallows of his
own nature well, though he said little of its divine
depths, in his own 'Epitaph':

> 'The poor inhabitant below
> Was quick to learn, and wise to know,
> And keenly felt the freendly glow,
>   And softer flame;—
> But thoughtless follies laid him low,
>   And stained his name.'

He too often mistook excitement for inspiration,
and rushed into revolt for its own sake; but he
would have been the first to perceive the folly and
the cruelty of selecting for admiration and imitation
only one side, and that side the worst, of a great
man's character. If he could be present in the
spirit at a few of the gatherings held annually in
his name, and if he could then flit away to some
annual gatherings of the 'unco guid,' he would be
troubled to perceive that both those who love and
those who hate him are worshipping the same fetish
—a whisky bottle. It is a pity, a very great
pity, that so much enthusiasm should be spilt about
on a single evening, or on special occasions. Were

I a Scotch poet, living or dead, I should prefer a very little sober appreciation to any amount of drunken idolatry ; and I should not care to gauge the height of my success by the depth of degradation into which I had plunged my votaries. Be that as it may, the poet who taught, as the flower of his human experience, that 'prudent, cautious self-control is Wisdom's root,' should have some fitter temple than a tavern, and some kindlier consecration than the maudlin applause of maniacs in all stages of alcoholic delirium.

VI.

BENEFICENT 'MURDER' (1).*

AMID the storm of popular indignation over the horrors of the recent execution by electricity, one curious—and to me most significant—circumstance appears to have been overlooked. Simultaneously with the news of Kemmler's judicial torture in the interests of Science, we have received from America the news that Count Tolstoi's 'Kreutzer Sonata,' and other 'immoral' books, have been suppressed in the interests of Morality. It has not, possibly, occurred to many that there is any other than an accidental connection between those two recent events ; but to my mind they are only

* The two letters under this title are reprinted from the *Daily Telegraph*, where they appeared immediately after the execution of Kemmler.

two aspects of the same social question, two strange results of the same political force which I have on a former occasion called 'Providence made Easy.' Both the conduct of life and its duration are regulated, for the time being, by the pragmatic sanction of the Legislator. All other sanctions are temporarily abolished. The reverence for human life, for the human body, has departed with the reverence for the Soul, for Freedom, for individual hope and aspiration ; and, under the same cloak of empirical knowledge, Morality and Science shake hands. Was I not justified, then, in asserting that our modern Trades Union of scientists and materialists was merely a survival of the old Calvinism—that Calvinism which, ever since honest John triumphed in the burning of Servetus, has been 'cruel as the grave' ?

How much further will the appetite for carnal knowledge, the lust for verification, lead the creature who loudly vaunts his descent from the anthropoid ape, and who looks forward to the dawning æon of the new god, Humanity ? Everywhere the beneficent Demagogue, who would regulate the growth of individual evolution, who would experimentalize on the living subject, from the beast that crawls to the beast that stands upright, is busily at work, and the voice of the Legislature says, 'Well done !' While the cynic in the market-place loudly proclaims the death of all human hope and aspiration, while even the Judge on the bench accepts the destruction of Religion, but utters a pharisaic 'If we can't be pious, let us at least be moral,' the scientific jerry-builder constructs his lordly pleasure-house out of the stones of dead creeds. The ethics of the dissecting-room and the torture-chamber replace the instincts of the human conscience, which conscience, if *forced* evolution continues to prevail, will soon become a mere register of average human prejudices. Meantime, having disintegrated all laws in succession, we remain at the mercy of the empirical laws of Demogorgon. To talk through the telephone or to talk into the phonograph is to penetrate the mysteries of Nature, and, heedless of the bolts of Zeus and kindred gods, we exult over Mr. Edison's bottled thunder.

All this would not matter much if the tyrannical will of the new Science and new Morality would suffer us to breathe in peace, and if the New Journalism, talking the shibboleth of Science and Morality, would leave our *personal* evolution alone. But we are being legislated for, not only in the Senate, but in the Vestry; not only by the County Councilman, but by the Penny-a-liner. With what result, may I ask? With the result that every day men and women are growing more indifferent and more mechanical, and that a nation of freemen is being transformed into a nation of sanitary prigs. If I may use the expression, we are becoming

21

Teutonized; the peculiarity of the Teuton being that, although free, he forges his own fetters, and voluntarily accepts his slavery as a moral and political machine. For my own part, I find that I cannot procure certain books without police supervision; that I cannot see a play or write one without being guided for my good by a legal supervisor; that I cannot put my hand in my pocket to assist a beggar without being looked at askance by the Commissioners of Lunacy; that I cannot use my own judgment even in a literary contract without being pounced upon and bullied by a trades union of authors; that, in a word, I can do nothing, think nothing, be nothing, without some sort of organized social intervention. As for the right of private judgment, it is rapidly becoming a farce. Men no longer think or judge for themselves; they do it all by machinery. There are cheap manuals, mechanical guides, to classify and regulate even my tastes and likings. Little trade unions innumerable make up the corporate trades union, the State. And the individual member of society, the thinking and seeing man, becomes either a martyr or part of a Machine.

The apogee of the moon of Dulness, of Mob Rule, of Beneficent Legislation, is reached at last, when the free people of America, in their zeal for the public good, furnish the world with the edifying spectacle of a judicial murder and torture by electricity, and when, in the same breath, they consign the work of a daring thinker to the civic pit for rubbish. Let me say in this connection that I have no personal sympathy whatever with the diseased views of human passion taken by Count Tolstoi. Morality has made the man, as it makes the Council and the Legislature, raving mad. Science, Christian or un-Christian, renders the individual, as it renders the State, insane with the pride of empirical discovery, with the zeal of impious verification. And, after all, we can verify so little! What does it serve the lover to know that his beloved moonlight is made of green cheese or magnesium? How does it help human nature to learn that the beauty it yearns for fattens on corruption? to be told that every happy instinct, every function of the flesh, is dangerous, and to be summarily repressed? The new scientific Calvinism would turn the many-coloured picture of the world into one common black and white; would teach the maiden to analyze her first blush, and the boy to dissect his first love; would turn pure natural impulse into prurient inquiry, and put glass windows into everybody—as in the famous surgical case—to show us the mean processes of the Unconscious. Men who, like myself, were not born 'moral'—men who refuse to measure themselves by the common standard which regulates social conduct, and who, above all, would secure for their fellows perfect freedom of moral evolution, stand wondering in the darkness of eclipse, while Puritanism and espionage conspire against human nature.

Now, more than ever, at this crucial point of the world's history, it behoves all thinking men to cry, with Virchow, *Restringamur!* Do not permit Empiricism to go too far, either in the destroying of sanctions, or in the formulation of enactments, or in the legalizing of experiments ; but let every man who thinks he has a message speak with a free tongue, and let Art, above all—in which may lie the salvation of the world—live a free and natural life. The example of Kemmler should be a warning to everyone of what beneficent legislation may yet do for us in the interests of the State, of Science, and of Morality !

VII.

BENEFICENT 'MURDER' (2).

IN view of the reproaches of some correspondents, who contend that they do not quite know what I mean or what I am complaining about, I find it necessary to add a few further words of explanation. I never posed as a Gnostic, as 'one who knows,' and if I show scant respect for authoritative opinions, I feel quite as little respect for any opinions of my own. I invariably try, however, to make these opinions clear. Since I appear to have failed in the first instance, let me try again.

I am not, to begin with, a Socialist in the ordinary sense of the word, and I distinguish in both the moral and the political world between sympathetic co-operation and arbitrary trades unionism. I will combine with no man, with no body of men, to dictate absolutely to others how they are to think and act. True Socialism I believe to be the self-protection of minorities against the despotism of majorities, the self-protection of individuals against the tyranny of mob-elected legislators, against encroachments on the part of the State, of the Church, of Capital, of the working as well as of the governing classes, and of Society. False Socialism I believe to be the combination of organized classes or communities to limit the free action of the individual, and to force unnatural evolution all along the line. A true Socialist accepts patiently the inevitable limitations put by the community on his personal activity. He is perfectly well aware that government is necessary, and that, if his fellow-men are to be comfortable, he cannot do just as he pleases. If he protests against taxes, it is only when he considers them iniquitous—*e.g.*, taxes for foolish wars, for the support of discredited institutions, of unnecessary offices, of sinecures. He cheerfully contributes to the lighting and draining of cities, to the wages of a necessary police, to the support of the helpless and deserving poor, to the necessary institutions of the State. But there he pauses. Having done his duty as a citizen, he retires on his rights as a man. He complains if he has to support a Church in which he has ceased to believe, and contends that if his neighbours require the services of a clergyman they should not ask *him* to pay for them. If he seeks entertainment he elects to choose it for himself, without legislative super-vision. If he likes statues and pictures of the nude (as I do), he contends that he has a right to enjoy them, despite the fact that they create nasty sensations in ' moral ' people. So with Books and with the Drama. He claims a free choice in their selection, no matter how many ' young persons ' may be peeping round the corner. Despite the Priests in Absolution of the New Journalism, he protests against combinations which make life hideous—*e.g.*, the inquisitorial Newspaper. But even here he does not interfere ; he only smiles, and prays that God may send poor Humanity a better religion and better literature. And so on, and so on, to the end of the chapter.

I hope this is very simple. Well, in the present condition of affairs, how does the true Socialist— or, in other words, the rational, peace-loving citizen —find himself treated ?

He finds, in the first place, that false Socialism, using the shibboleth of the ' greatest happiness for the greatest number,' is, both here and in Germany, bolstering up the tyrannies of an all-present officialism. He finds that powerful organi-

zations of men are trying to legalize in our cities
what is in his sight the abomination of abominations. He finds that the finest course of action a
Government can adopt to repress crimes of murder
and of violence is to imitate them, or even, as
lately in America, to excel their horrors. He
finds that, by our marriage laws, men and women
are chained like beasts together, and that their
very despairing effort to escape from each other is
called 'collusion.' He finds that everywhere in
Society, wherever the Puritanical bias prevails, the
simplest and purest natural functions are looked
upon as unclean ; that Morality despises the body
now, as Religion despised it long ago. He is told
of the spread of education ; he finds that he is
being told merely of a spread of half-instructed
ignorance. He finds our leading scientists justifying
War and Appropriation, as our leading Spiritualists
and Churchmen used to justify them. He finds
it dangerous, or at least incompatible, to express
his real opinion of any existing institution, particularly if that institution is either 'moral' or
'religious.' He is not led to the stake, but he
is 'boycotted'; he is a discredited and suspected
person. He finds, in one word, that at every
point of his individual advance he is confronted by
the mass of organized cruelty and unintelligence.

All this, of course, is no new thing. As a
child, I saw Robert Owen stoned for saying that
Marriages were not always made in Heaven !

But at no period of history, except that period when false Christianity was most dominant, have individuals been so much at the mercy of a false Morality. In literature especially the extent of completed ignorance is something scarcely credible—ignorance not only of the uneducated, but of the cultivated and the superfine. To illustrate it I need go no further than a recent number of the *Quarterly Review*, where conventional Morality speaks out loudly as a trumpet on the subject of the French nation and of French fiction. Even the School Board, it appears, has not killed the insular prejudice that every Frenchman is a sensualist and every French book an outrage on decency. But what is to be said of a writer (the mouthpiece of a large class, or we should not find him in the *Quarterly*) who lumps Balzac, Flaubert, and Zola together as writers of the same calibre, and actually affirms that ' Balzac was a materialist, who did not believe in God' ? Poor Balzac ! who swore by Godhead and the Monarchy, and was so mercilessly roasted for his leaning to these aristocracies. ' His (Balzac's) only faith was faith in money ; he is the supreme artist who excels in consummating the type of the ignoble, even of the cadaverous. His characters are always intrinsically vicious, and he anticipated the worst things of Zola.' And this of the writer who gave us ' Eugénie Grandet,' and ' Cousin Pons,' and ' Modeste Mignon,' and a hundred other imperishable types of human beauty and goodness. Is it any wonder that the wretched poor flock to hear the tumult of the Salvation Army, when the rich and cultured combine to support such dismal howling as I have quoted, such utter ignorance of the subject, such spasmodic stumbling, as of the blind leading the blind ?

For myself, I still find in France the centre of the World's free thought. The mad political craze, the whirl from one system to another, is nothing ; the bold and fearless freedom of the great French writers, from Diderot downwards, is everything. No matter if they have now torn open the sewers, as long ago they tore down the superstructures of society. They have taught men to *think* and *feel.* Even Zola among the shambles is better than Chadband among the churches, better than the easy English novelist who cloaks up the ulcers of society, better than Mr. Chaos-come-again and his army of howling teetotalers and Sabbatarians.

But I find I am wandering away into criticism. What I wanted to point out was, that it is not the freedom of individuals we have to fear, but the combinations of classes—the trades unions of well-intentioned political moralists, culminating in the tyrannies of the Legislature. England under the new Radicalism is growing as terrible as Sheffield under Broadhead ! We have too much legislation and too little individual responsibility. Men who used to fight for their own hands now cling

tremulously to the skirts of officialism, and cry,
'Help us ; instruct us. We are too weak to help
and instruct ourselves.' Small wonder that, in
their extremity, they turn from the conscience im-
planted in them by God to the legerdemain of
Providence made Easy. If we want to know
whither a large portion of the community is
drifting, let us glance for a moment at General
Booth's view of the Millennium, given in a
publication called 'All the World.' 'First, we
should have Hyde Park roofed in, with towers
climbing to the stars, as the world's great, grand,
central temple ! . . . And, then, what demonstra-
tions, what processions, what mighty assemblies,
what grand reviews, what crowded streets, im-
passable with the joyful multitudes marching to
and fro ! . . . Five million hearts would turn to
God with voices of thanksgiving and with shouts
of praise !'*

Far be it from me to underrate the good work
General Booth is doing in some directions ; but
take such a proclamation as this, and it is an
attempt to turn Humanity into a huge barrel-
organ, with an accompaniment of 'shouting' per-
formers. And herein, as we are aware, lies the
secret of his triumph. Knowing how little is done
to amuse the masses, seeing their utter wretchedness and dulness, he shows them how to exercise

---

* See, further on, the remarks on the Social Aid side of
General Booth's scheme.

their bodies and use their lungs by organizing for one universal Shout. Out of this tumult, to which the ' tom-tom ' of the poor savage is music, peace and salvation are to come. Looming in the near future is the Golden Age, when any individual who refuses to join in the general noise will be regarded as anti-social, as an unsympathetic member of the community. In the face of this and kindred horrors, we are asked to believe that beneficent and philanthropic Organization is everything, and that individual peace and personal freedom are of little or no consequence.

VIII.

BOOKSELLERS' ROMANCE.

MR. RIDER HAGGARD, whose own work in fiction is at present delighting all who take pleasure in the marvellous, and who possesses in a certain measure the imagination of a poet, has published in the *Contemporary Review* a diatribe against the novel of the period, the moral of which appears to be : ' If modern fiction fails to content you, try back to " Robinson Crusoe ;" and if home scenery fails to inspire you, go to Africa.' Now, it is no part of my business to defend our modern novelists from their latest critic, any more than it is to deny the novelty and the charm of Mr. Haggard's own flights into easy romance ; but in this particular instance I looked for a Daniel come to judgment, and I

find only a Jeremiah. Leaving out of sight all
that my clever contemporaries have done in fiction,
work at least equal to the finest ore ever dug out
of the Dark Continent, I want seriously to ask
if Mr. Haggard, in the heyday of his sudden
popularity, is not rather overestimating the prodigy
of his own advent; and whether, after all, true
Romance has very much to do with those wild
fancy-flights which transport the booksellers for a
season, but alarm the quiet students of human
nature? Romance, if I understand it rightly, is
the art of idealizing the splendid *facts* of life, of
seizing human nature at its highest, and present-
ing it in types of poetic beauty, rather than the
art of telling tales for the marines, and disseminat-
ing the philosophy of the preposterous. If the
hope of the English public lay in Mr. Haggard's
way, we should have to recognise Jules Verne as
a fine romancist, and place the fairy taletellers
right over the head of Shakespeare; snatch the
Bible from its shelf and substitute the ' Arabian
Nights ;' and instead of Walter Scott and Charles
Reade, Dumas and Victor Hugo, content ourselves
with the author of the wonderful adventures of
Peter Wilkins. I am not, let it be borne in mind,
underrating the author of ' King Solomon's Mines,'
although, if I were to pronounce an opinion, I
should say that a commonplace, vivid, truthful
bit of work like ' Kidnapped ' was really more
imaginative; but even Mr. Louis Stevenson would

be the last man to maintain that his work in this
direction was a new departure. The point I wish
to insist upon is that great fiction, instead of
escaping from the realm of common-sense into
that of pure fancy, throws the light of imagination
over that realm of common-sense in such a way
as to make of *it* a veritable fairyland. Nor is
Mr. Haggard in any way justified as a romancist
because, in the manner of M. Verne, he puts in
the centre of his domain of fancy a few exces-
sively prosy and old-fashioned realistic types, such
as the wonderful Englishman with the white legs,
the wandering African chief, and the hideous
sibyl of innumerable story-tellers. He is quite
within his right in escaping human character, but
if he were a true romancist he would certainly
not escape it ; and, again, if he were a new as well
as a true romancist, he would leave on the mind a
higher and nobler impression than is to be derived
from the literature written for, and beloved by,
the boys of England. In his story of ' She,' he
certainly does show imagination ; but surely the
whole work is marred and spoiled by the inconsistency which blends a good poetical idea, worthy
treatment in verse, with the commonplace associations and stereotyped characters so long familiar in
books of the modern marvellous written for Pater-
noster Row, and published with illustrations. The
idea of ' She ' is fine ; the treatment, in spite of
its cleverness, is not far beyond the method of

M. Verne. Instead of truth irradiated by idealism, we have beauty degraded by commonplace ; and as a consequence, the tale, in spite of all its clever workmanship, leaves the impression of a large canvas painted to order. This, of course, does not prevent it from being very amusing ; only the fact of having written an amusing book does not justify an author in affirming that amusement is to be the prime vocation of the novelist of the future.

To compare great things with small, Æschylus is a true Romancist. When he deals with the great issues of life, he uses the supernatural only as a background ; but his ideas and his pictures would be quite as true, and just as noble, if his supernatural were merely an atmosphere, as it often is. Homer, perhaps, is more to the point ; his tales of gods and men have all the strength of early fable, none of the mixture of ancient and modern moods. Dante writes romance in colossal cipher, never mean and never small. But to come down to modern times, Swift is a romancist, and Defoe is a realist ; each in his turn is too wise to mix with foreign matter the elements peculiarly his own. Sublime human Romance attained its zenith in Hugo, who accepted Nature as she is, and craved no fable, but found in Nature's own bosom the god, the godlike man, as well as the monster and the chimera. It is cruel to Mr. Haggard to mention him in connection with these masters, but the man who coolly relegates Zola to

the Limbo of the Unclean, and who indirectly in-
dicates his own form of art as higher and purer
than that which produced 'Une Page d'Amour,'
must at least *aspire* to be a master. And with all
that has been done in England even in recent
years, Mr. Haggard is discontented. He has no
good word to say for any of his elder brethren—for
Charles Reade, for Walter Besant, for the author
of 'Lorna Doone,' or even for the author of
'Alice in Wonderland.' All to him is leather and
prunella, except Robinson Crusoe, African cram,
and the merry boys of England. Unto this last
we are coming, he says, since the good Howells
avails us not, and the bad Zola grows more and
more insufferable. The romance of the future is
to justify, not Shakespeare, not Scott, not Dumas,
not Hugo, not Dickens, not Reade, but M. Jules
Verne, Mr. R. M. Ballantyne, and Captain Mayne
Reid. For five shilling *pot-pourris* we are to
exchange the oldest school of Idealism and the
newest school of Naturalism! The panorama
business, the book of travel business, the highly
coloured showman business, is to take the place of
human nature and human passion; and poetry
and prose jumbled together are to supplant the
literature of patient imagination. Really Mr.
Andrew Lang and the *Saturday Review* have
much to answer for, unless Mr. Rider Haggard,
whom their praises have persuaded to this deliverance, is laughing at us in his sleeve.

IX.

PROFESSOR HUXLEY'S MIRACULOUS CONVERSION (1).*

I HAVE only just read, with feelings of mingled surprise and delight, Professor Huxley's letter to the *Times* newspaper on the subject of the Salvation Army and General Booth. It is so sweet to find one's self a true prophet; and did I not prophesy some little time ago, in a contemporary, that Professor Huxley would soon be converted 'like another Saul'? The Arch-Sociologist, the denier of the natural freedom and equality of man, the upholder of 'a statute of limitations in matters of wrong-doing,' the denouncer of Freedom as *laissez-faire*, the preacher of Providence made Easy and special Governmental supervision in all departments, now wheels round in the very face of Mr. Spencer, and cries : 'I said so ! Organization is dangerous ! the safeguard of society lies in the freedom of the Individual !' And all this because one man of untutored intellect, with limited reasoning powers and miraculous powers of organization, has done in a few short years what all the Churches, including the Church of Pragmatic Science, have utterly failed to do—has awakened the imagination of the British Philistine to the fact that the miseries of the social deposits must be reckoned with, and has, in a measure, pointed

* The first of the following letters appeared in the *Times* and *Daily Chronicle*, the second in the *Chronicle* only.

out 'the way.' Why, only a while ago the militant Professor was stumping the magazines and advocating the possibility of advancing evolution by force from without and from above ; was 'persecuting' the faithful who clamoured to be saved or damned in their own fashion ; and here he is, already struck down by a Light from Heaven (or some other dwelling-place of the aristocracy) proclaiming that he, too, is of the Faithful, of the poor persecuted remnant which 'believes' !

I was severely rebuked when I dared to defend Mr. Herbert Spencer's doctrine of absolute ethics against the savage attack of Professor Huxley ; because I questioned the reasoning powers, while fully admitting the ingenuity, of my opponent. I am now, therefore, on the horns of a dilemma. Either Professor Huxley was always rational, or he was, all along the line, inconsistent. If he was rational, he failed to express his ideas logically ; and if he was inconsistent, like most persecutors, he needed, besides logic, fuller light and edification. With what fervour did he argue (in his favourite metaphorical manner) against the fatuity which would place the guidance of a Ship in the hands of the crew, instead of those of the Captain ; against the 'reasoned savagery' of those who would, it seemed to him, uphold the natural 'rights' of even the man-eating tiger ! *Then* we wanted leadership, organization, espionage even, and scientific police ; *now,* all these things are

22

perilous, and General Booth, with his tom-toms and his military orders, is threatening the lives of 'individual' men. Yesterday Professor Huxley was championing that Over-legislation which would mean the slavery of all mankind; to-day he is protesting against the strong men, and questioning the would-be legislators. A little while ago he was Mr. Herbert Spencer's deadliest opponent; just a pirouette, and here he is at Mr. Spencer's feet. Truly a miraculous conversion! All our fears were vain. The protector of the loaves and fishes, the peripatetic Providence incarnate, will harm us no more. Only a few steps further, and the Saul of the *status quo* will be the St. Paul of Individualism.

Frankly, however, I distrust both this Saul and that other of the New Testament as persons possessing neither great logic nor trustworthy insight into human nature. The converted Persecutor is sure to lapse backwards during the very process of edification. And now, to my poor judgment, the Professor Huxley who refuses to disgorge his friend's thousand pounds, on the ground that he will not countenance any form of social or religious 'tyranny,' is fully as suspicious a figure as the Professor Huxley who avowed that 'the equality of men before God was an equality either of insignificance or imperfection,' and that there was a strong argument for supposing that Force, reasonably applied, was an indispensable factor of our civilization. Am I wrong in suggesting that, now as always, the pragmatic temperament and the anti-theological bias has far more to do with Professor Huxley's attitude than any real conversion to the Individualism he has hated so cordially and so long? I may be wronging a true convert, but I cannot help believing that Professor Huxley would be far less shocked by the Salvation Army if it used the shibboleth of Science in lieu of that of Christianity—if it were beating its tom-toms in the name of David Hume instead of that of Jesus of Nazareth. Your scientist will endure a good deal of noise, a great deal of fussy organization, when the object is secular, and not religious.

It is no part of my purpose to uphold the scheme of General Booth ; I have not studied it sufficiently to justify or condemn it. So far as it involves a tyrannous organization, an interference with the right of private judgment, an upholding of effete superstitions, it has no sympathy of mine, and not all the approval of all the Churches would induce me to utter one word on its behalf. But the merest tyro in history must see that Professor Huxley's attempt to liken it to the schemes of Francis of Assisi and Ignatius Loyola is simply absurd, illogical, and uninstructed—worthy, in fact, of the mind which justified Jacob against Esau on the ground of 'practical expedience.' For if one thing is clear, it is that the religion of General Booth, whatever its crude forms and ordinances

may be, is at once unsectarian and beneficent,
practical as opposed to dogmatic. The use of the
Christian *vocabulary* is a detail. I have nowhere
read that the General troubles himself about
Christian dogmas. His cry has rather been, 'A
truce to your dogmas, and even to your moralities ;
let us see if we cannot save the "submerged
tenth" by making it conscious of happy responsibility—by enabling it to *live.*' The comparison
with Mormonism is equally unfortunate ; and, in
any case, Mormonism is an institution which has
existed with few or no crimes, no Wars, no Brothels,
and no 'Hells'—all accredited ornaments of our
higher civilization. Say what we may of General
Booth—and I myself (horrified by the clamour in
the street) have said some hard things—he has
struck a chord of beneficence which vibrates round
the world ; he has cried to the rich and powerful,
'Lo ! these also are your brethren' ; he has succeeded in startling the Bishops from their arm-
chairs, and the priests from their confessionals ; he
has said, 'What *you* for eighteen centuries have
failed to do—what you have scarcely even cared
to do—I, an individual, a man of the people, will
at least *try* to do.' And in the face of this man,
whose hand is open to the outcast and the fallen ;
who turns his back on no human creature, however
base ; who knows the world far better than any
scientist that was ever born, Professor Huxley
buttons up his pockets, purses up his lips, and

tries to escape from the imputation of inconsistency, of inhumanity, by avowing his adherence
to Principles which he has been opposing all his
life.

But no ; Professor Huxley is *not* inconsistent.
He stands where he has always stood, among those
who are by temperament deprived of the true
philosophic vision and the real enthusiasm of
humanity. A genuine scientific student, capable
of much careful verification on a low plane of
inquiry, he cannot generalize and cannot organize.
He has vindicated centuries of wrong-doing ; he
has upheld the tyrannies of Force and Convention;
he has sided with Society against the Individual on
the ground of utility, and with the Strong against
the Weak on the score of necessity ; and so, after
all, even this last miraculous conversion—a sham,
like all things seemingly miraculous—cannot save
him. He is condemned out of his own mouth as
the Pharisee who passes by, while General Booth
is justified, by his own act, as the Samaritan who
at least endeavours to heal and bless.*

* Professor Huxley's only comment on this was a protest that
I utterly misstated his views, and that I was, he believed, merely a
writer of ' works of imagination.' The good Professor's contempt
for his opponents, for all who dare to question his empirical
statements, is notorious. To him, even Mr. Spencer was only
' an abstract Philosopher.'

X

PROFESSOR HUXLEY'S MIRACULOUS CONVERSION (2).

In the *Times* of December 9, 1890, appeared another letter from Professor Huxley, written in the same vein as his first diatribe, on General Booth's scheme, and attached to it was the letter from my pen, which was printed in the *Daily Chronicle* (and the *Daily Chronicle* only) on the previous day. Now, my letter was issued to the public Press on the previous Sunday, but several of the dailies passed it by without insertion, on the conventional ground that the letter of which it was a criticism 'had not appeared in their columns.' The *Times*, however, with characteristic unfairness, published it a day late, in order that, when my protest was seen and read, Professor Huxley might have another opportunity of raising false issues on the subject. These, as we all know, are the usual tactics of the great organ of British Philistia. It cannot be fair and honest, even in so small a matter as the printing of correspondence. From the day when it fought on the side of Slavery during the American Civil War to the day when it organized the Pigott forgery, and from that day to the present, when it lets loose the quasi-scientific Boanerges to fulminate against the Salvation Army and talk half-instructed twaddle about Simon

Magus and the Mendicant Friars, it has been
steadily posing as the enemy of human progress
and human enlightenment.

It is not, however, with the *Times* I have to
deal, but with the gentleman in full 'useful-know-
ledge canonicals,' who now, as heretofore, refuses
to give General Booth his blessing—for which, I
am sure, the General never prayed. By what
right of achievement or attainment Professor
Huxley assumes to speak authoritatively on social
questions I have never been able to discover.
Both he and Professor Tyndall, who steps forward
to support him, have done very little to justify
any faith in either their sympathy or their insight.
But both, we have to bear in mind, have one
mission in common—to translate the jargon of
Carlyle into the easy patter of Cheap Science, so
that ' he who runs may read.' Professor Huxley,
on the grounds of his recent ' miraculous conversion' to Spencerian principles, now poses as an
Individualist ; but we must be careful to distinguish between such individualism as his and the
deeply reasoned individualism of the Philosopher
he has denounced so often and so long. We must
remember that his warning is not philosophical,
but empirical ; that he has on previous occasions
committed himself to a defence of the present
social cosmos, or chaos, as opposed to the aspira-
tions of human freedom ; that, in a word, he embodies the kind of opinion which would oppose to

the Enthusiasm of Humanity the dreary conventionalities of the Pragmatic Sanction.

For what, after all, has this self-canonized lecturer on useful knowledge to say on the subject at issue ? What is his criticism of the Man who, like his great Prototype, has actually descended into Hell, hoping to snatch thence the submerged ' tenth ' of our population ? Firstly, that there are many philanthropies in the world, and that General Booth's is only one of them. This, surely, we knew already. Secondly, that earlier labourers in the field of Socialism had no army organization, no beating drums, no general fanfaronade, and that such organization belongs rather to the raving mystagogues of the East than to the steady social workers of the West. In this connection, curiously enough, the empirical Professor, always inconsistent in argument, while ever consistent in temperament, sighs for the old-fashioned and quiet ways of the Apostles, about whose ' quietness,' by the way, he might have learned something by a few more visits to the British Museum. It is surely news to all the world that the early Christians were peaceful, non-revolutionary, non-organizing persons, in no way troublesome to persons of opposite opinion and lovers of *laissez faire.* Thirdly and finally, Professor Huxley, while recognising the fact of human misery, asserts that General Booth's scheme to check it is likely to do ' more harm than good.'

And then he begins to tell us 'why.' Then, for the first time, we begin to get at what he really *does* mean. ' It is primarily and mainly for the sake of saving the Soul,' writes General Booth, ' that I seek the salvation of the Body.' This means, according to Professor Huxley, that ' men are to be made sober and industrious mainly that, as washed, shorn, and docile sheep, they may be driven into the narrow theological fold which Mr. Booth patronizes.' Does it mean anything of the kind? I, for one, have about as much belief as Professor Huxley in any religious dogma or Christian formula, but I have never gathered from General Booth that he bases his scheme on any foundation of abstract theology. But, if he did, surely the man who, with any formula whatever, *can* make the wretched millions 'sober and industrious,' is achieving fully two-thirds of the objects of all human science, of all human regeneration. Here, again, Professor Huxley is illogical ; for once make a man 'sober and industrious'— once make him to some extent a rational creature —and be sure you will not 'drive' him very far. You have given eyes to the blind; those eyes will *see*.

' I have been in the habit of thinking,' proceeds Professor Huxley, 'that self-respect and thrift are the rungs of the ladder by which men must surely climb out of the slough of the despond of want, and I have regarded them as perhaps the most eminent of the practical virtues.' *Après?* Has

General Booth ever denounced self-respect and thrift? No, admits the Professor; but he has said that 'envy' is the corner-stone of our competitive system, and that the sufferings of starving men are the consequence of 'the sins of the capitalist'! Here we get a fine glimpse of the good Professor who defended the *Status quo* on the score of expediency, and who demanded for the landgrabber and the capitalist, enriched by centuries of wrong-doing, a certain statute of limitations. Does anyone but an empirical scientist, confusing the survival of the socially successful with the natural survival of the fittest, doubt for a moment that 'envy' and greed *are* the crying sins of our generation, and that many men starve because their fellow-men refuse to feel? Read, in this connection, the solemn and beautiful words of Mr. Henry John Atkinson, printed in the very number of the *Times* which contains the Professor's grisly diatribe: 'I cannot sit still in warmth and comfort when I know that many of my countrymen are wandering about London without food or shelter all through these inclement nights, and that General Booth and his corps of workers wish to help them, and cannot get the means. My wife and I will give £300'—while Professor Huxley, who would cheerfully, no doubt, contribute to a scheme for the extension of Vivisection, buttons up his trousers-pockets and keeps his friend's 'thousand pounds.'

Further on, Professor Huxley pushes his objection further home by citing a case of so-called 'persecution.' A girl was 'seduced twice,' and applied to the Salvationists, who thereupon 'hunted up the man, threatened him with exposure, and forced from him the payment to his victim of £60 down, an allowance of £1 a week, and an assurance on his life of £450 in her favour.' Intimidation with a vengeance, very Jedburgh justice, says the Professor. Let us not be quite sure. Let us not assume too hastily that the case was not fully investigated. Let us reflect at the same time what the precious Law would have done for the victim of this seducer. It would have enabled her to take out a summons, perhaps, and, if there were a child, secure a weekly sum of *half a crown* while that child was of tender years! Professor Huxley thinks that, in all possibility, it was a mere question of relative moral delinquency between the parties, and that the man, so brought to book, was as much a 'victim' as the woman. Excellent Professor! True upholder of masculine law-making and the survival of the culpable fittest! May we not in all seriousness wish Mr. Spencer joy of his last proselyte?

When all is said and done, all that Professor Huxley can advance against the Salvation Army is that it is 'noisy'; that it uses the vocabulary of superstition; that it reproaches the rich for the sorrows of the poor; and that whenever it can,

it tries to bring delinquents to justice ! Well,
admit every one of the indictments, and what is
proved ? That every beneficent scheme has some
little drawbacks, but that every such scheme must
be judged by the totality, by the entire moral
efficacy, of its influence. What the Salvation
Army has done is this—it has, first of all,
awakened the sleeping conscience of the world.
It has told Dives that he must not sleep so long
as Lazarus starves ; it has proclaimed that there
is hope for every man, even for the basest, if he
will try to be ' honest and industrious' ; it has
held out hands to the Penitent Thief (as it would
hold out hands to the penitent Professor), and it
has broken bread with the Magdalen. Then think
for a moment what Cheap Science, with its demagogues of the dissecting-room, its peripatetic professors, has done, or tried to do. It has prattled
glibly of Natural Law and the Survival of the
Fittest; it has cast in its lot with the *Times* and the
governing classes; it has paraded forged documents
to enslave the Irish people and discredit a nationality ; it has countenanced the ' unco' gude ' and
joined in the holy horror against the destroyers
of national institutions, such as War and Prostitution ; it has contented itself with Carlyle's Gospel
according to the Printer's Devil and the faith
which confuses natural Freedom and Equality with
' reasoned savagery' ; and last, and greatest of its
achievements, it has instituted the beneficent

tortures of Vivisection. Well, if we have to choose between Simon Magus and Professor Huxley, or between General Booth and Professor Ferrier, let us give our vote to those who are the friends of both man and beast—with the workers who are tender to the weak and merciful to the fallen, not with those who turn with complacency to acts of beneficent legislation, and — let the lost go by ! As for Professor Huxley, he is only our old friend the Priest in another guise, as unsympathetic, as bigoted, as retrograde as anyone who ever wore *soutane* or cowl. Even in his new aspect as a convert to Individualism, he will convince no sane man that Folly and Enthusiasm are synonymous terms.

XI.

'THE JOURNALIST IN ABSOLUTION.'*

WRITING neither as a person having authority, nor as one of the scribes, I wish to put on record, if you will permit me, my complete and absolute sympathy with Mr. Parnell. He may, or may not, be an Adulterer—that, in any case, I consider a detail chiefly interesting to himself ; but I contend that his technical and legal guilt is no proof whatever of his moral turpitude. No question involving the relation of the sexes can be absolutely decided in the tainted atmosphere of

* First published just after the divorce suit of O'Shea *v.* Parnell.

our foul Divorce Court, and the case of ' O'Shea
v. Parnell' was established by the unworthiest of
all evidence, that of prying chambermaids, prurient
lodging-house keepers, and all the miserable human
fry who swim in the unclean shallows of the legal
puddle. To my mind, Mr. Parnell's stern and absolute silence, his determination not to be dragged
through the obscene mire, is negative evidence in
his favour. He has chosen, like a strong man, to
let the blow fall on his own shoulders, and the
result is that Mrs. O'Shea has been spared and
almost forgotten, while all the moral wolves are
clamouring for Mr. Parnell's blood. But even if
Mr. Parnell is guilty, no man can tell in what
degree. That, as I have said, is a matter chiefly
concerning himself. What concerns us, men who
stand as simple spectators of a persecution unparalleled in the history of Politics, is the means
which are being adopted to hound a great man out
of public life.

It is on record, I believe, or at any rate it has
been stated, that immediately after the decision of
the Divorce Court a well-known Journalist waited
upon Mr. Parnell and informed him that unless
full ' confession ' was made at once, and the leadership of the Irish Party simultaneously resigned,
the said journalist would appeal to the Puritans of
England to ' let loose the dogs ' of moral War.
Whether threatened or not, the thing has been
done, and Mr. Parnell has been hunted down, not

by honest public opinion, not by British virtue, not even by the British Matron, but by the Journalism of the Sewers on the one side and the Journalism of the Back-kitchen on the other. For whence chiefly arises this ferocious clamour of prurient Morality, this talk about the sanctity of the household, and the eternal symbolism of the bed-post? Firstly, from the source out of which arose the publication of a scandal so infamous, and described so infamously, that the very air of Nature was polluted as by a cesspool, the stench of which penetrated like poison into every household of the land. Secondly, from the individual who invented the journalism of Paul Pry, who has violated all the privileges of social life, while haunting the back-kitchens of the aristocracy, and counting the candle-ends of the governing classes; and who, finally, proposed not long ago in the House of Commons, to the manifest satisfaction of a crowd of fellow-demagogues, to pollute the ears of his fellow-members by opening up in broad day the sewer of another foul and loathsome scandal. The other attacks on the character of the member for Cork may be set aside as purely political. The attacks to which I draw attention are specifically 'moral.' It is the latter to which I wish to confine your attention, while demanding whether we are to substitute for the old and discredited priesthoods, the priesthood of the Journalist in Absolution?

No 'Confessional Unmasked' has yet, to my mind, furnished so sad an illustration of human prurience as the new Confessional of the Journal. Manifold as are the injuries which Journalism in general has done to Society, to Literature, and to Art, by fostering the uninstruction of the general reader, and parading the ephemeral judgments of the hour, those injuries are small to the crimes committed by the Journalism which masquerades in the guise of Morality, which deals in household garbage, and, in the interests of vulgar curiosity, institutes a Public Confessional. Dismal indeed is the lot of the human being who, like Mr. Parnell, sits in the confession-box, with the Priest of Prurience on one side and the Priest of Scandal on the other. If he refuses, as Mr. Parnell has done, to make any kind of utterance, woe to him and to his generation ! The flood-gates of denunciation are opened ; the whole army of back-kitchen moralists and scandal-mongers is arrayed against him ; the standard of the Cross is raised, and men prepare for the luxury of the *auto da fé.* Honest citizens bar their doors, and peep from their windows in terror. Everywhere, ushered by the newsboy with his 'latest edition,' walk the agents of the Inquisition.

To most men who would live their lives in peace, Journalism is merely Babbage's Organ in the Street ; they stop their ears, and try to think and work in spite of it. But to all men who

value the security of their homes and the right of
private judgment, the New Journalism, with its
aggression, its tyrannical bias, and its shameless
indecency, is the old Priest in Absolution forcing a
way into every household. Tartuffe and Melchior
live again in the columns of the inquisitorial newspaper, while the Scapin of Politics walks hand-in-
hand with the Mawworm of Morality. At this
moment, therefore, when a wave of prurient
Puritanism is rising higher and higher to destroy
all that makes the world sweet and wholesome, it
is with no common interest that we who are
neither inquisitorial nor 'moral' watch the fate of
Mr. Parnell. If he stands like a rock, refusing to
be doomed by the Divorce Court, and defying the
clamour of penny-a-lining Pharisees, there is still
hope for Society. If he falls, bestraddled over
by the rampant Journalist in Absolution, we who
loathe his would-be Confessors may well despair.
I shall say nothing here of his public services, of
his power and prescience as the one man capable
of interpreting the hopes and wishes of the Irish
race ; nothing of the constitutional bigotry which
has led even so honest a man as Mr. Gladstone to
join in the cry against him. It should be remembered, nevertheless, that Mr. Parnell retains his
position, not because he is privately virtuous, but
because he is politically *puissant,* and that Mr.
Gladstone, despite all his noble disinterestedness,
is a retrograde moralist, who repudiates Divorce

under any circumstances, and founds his repudiation on the diseased ravings of mediæval monks and saints. I for one believe that issues far deeper than any issues merely political will be determined by the ultimate position of Mr. Parnell. I for one refuse to accept the discredited disclosures of the Divorce Court, and the obscene comments of the Journalist in Absolution, as any final test of human life and character.

XII.

THE COURTESAN ON THE STAGE.

I HAVE recently read, with no usual interest, a clever and trenchant article on 'Stage Courtesans.' To 'shatter the sentiment,' as the writer expresses it, of such plays as the 'Lady of the Camellias,' is a task which even his able pen is quite unable to accomplish; for that sentiment, I believe, is founded on some of the strongest instincts of human nature. Moreover, the type of Camille is, according to my small experience, quite as common as the type of Cora Pearl; and from the days of the Magdalen to those of De Quincey's Ann the street-walker, the class named 'unfortunate' has claimed, and claimed justly, the sympathy of all mortals except a few supervestal virgins and a large proportion of matchmaking matrons. I am not, however, vindicating in this connection the morbid psychology of the sentimental school of the early Empire. I am simply contending for justice to a type of character which, with all its depravities, is full of irresistible artistic fascinations.

The ethical question involved in the article I have named is far too involved a one to be discussed in the space of a brief note. All I wish to do is to protest against the Pharisaism which, both in life and literature, describes certain characters and certain subjects as unfit for the treatment of dramatic art. In England, only those situations and characters are held justifiable which have received, or are likely to receive, the sanction of Mr. Gilbert's young lady of fifteen ; and the result is a Drama which, to my thinking, leaves out of sight at least the half of human life, and supplies us with the barest possible profile of human nature. In the field of pure literature the result is dispiriting enough ; in the field of dramatic art it is simply stupefying. I believe myself that playgoers would be a healthier race if their morals were less tenderly taken care of; that even morbid psychology is a healthier thing than morbid prudery or 'Podsnappery'; that before the stage can be a great literary influence, its tongue must be set free and its moral speech unfettered ; that, in a word, we want a breezier atmosphere and a saner method if our stagecraft is to grapple at all with the great problems of life and religion.

The courtesan is the creature of society—pure

and noble, as in the case of Aspasia; bold and vicious, as in the case of Nell Gwynne; sad and hectic, as in the case of Marguerite Gautier; or simply carnivorous, as in the case of Nana and Cora Pearl. As long as she exists, either as a worker of that social safety-valve recognised in the execrable ethics of Swedenborg, or as a sad 'necessity' created by the evils of modern society, she will have her fit place in literature as well as in life. Those who know the Courtesan best believe that Cora Pearl, who, when her lover destroys himself, simply thinks of the stains on her carpet, is a monstrosity—that is, true to a certain monstrous form of womanhood as Faustine or Messalina. For one creature of this sort there exist a thousand creatures who are not the avenging furies, but the victims and martyrs, of an infamous social law. Far distant be the day when personal purity and chastity is not recognised as the highest quality and prerogative of woman-hood—when we forget to desiderate in all noble women the qualities we respect in our mothers and our sisters. Yet, since the Courtesan is what the sensuality of man has made her, let us, if we are in the mood for stone-throwing, aim our mis-siles, not at her, but at the men who have created her to minister to their appetites. Do not let us, above all, simulate indignation when we see her momentarily transfigured on the page of a poet or behind the footlights of a theatre; but let us remember in connection with her the infinite pathos and tenderness with which she has been surrounded for eighteen hundred years, through the sagacious beneficence of the law-abiding Founder of Christianity.

XIII.

GOETHE AND CRITICISM.

WHEN Goethe found his sheep's-head on a common, and proclaimed his discovery of the inter-maxillary bone, he was doing better work for Humanity than when, in his minor poems and romances, he preached the retrograde gospel of Egoismus. Science may possibly have gained something by his anatomical generalizations, but Literature has lost everything by his successful sermonizing. To a belated idealist like myself, the whole work of Goethe is a clumsy pyramid on the world's highway. By one solitary effort of true imagination the great pagan saved his soul for posterity, and just where he was most primitive, most conventional, least egoistical, did he achieve his poetical success. A commonplace story of seduction, relieved by the cynical asides of a conventional Devil, remains as Goethe's masterpiece. Meantime his mean and selfish gospel has sunk deep into the souls of little men, emerging from time to time to paralyze sentiment and imagination,

and creating literary monsters as hideous as the
Frenchman Zola and as crude and unfinished as
the Scandinavian Ibsen.   That this same gospel
of Egoismus appeals to a certain order of intelligence may at once be conceded; it is a fact
proved by the vitality of Goethe as a literary
influence.   Although that influence has been
mainly in the region of criticism, and although,
in spite of it, the great humanists Balzac and
Hugo have emerged triumphant, it is still a force
to be reckoned with, more especially as in recent
manifestations it combines itself with the inchoate
force of Science.   It is, however, in its very
essence *anti-literary*—a statement easily proved
by a reference to the literary history of this
century.   Goethe has begotten a whole race of
Critics, but not one modern Poet, not one modern
writer of genius, has turned to him for paternal
inspiration.

XIV.

'DRAMATIC CRITICISM AS SHE IS WROTE.'*

'If an English school, which heaven forefend!
should be moved to attempt a similar pleasantry'
(p. 9).   Mr. Archer means to say the reverse of
what he writes.   In English the sentence would

* Extracts from a book called 'About the Theatre,' by William
Archer. See *ante*, 'The Modern Young Man as Critic.'

run : ' If an English school should be moved (which heaven forefend !) to attempt a similar pleasantry.'

' Which of our countless humiliations was it that broke the camel's back, and made it morbidly eager to balance matters by splitting its sides ?' (p. 13). How a ' humiliation' could ' break' anything, how a ' camel's back' could be ' morbidly eager,' especially to ' split its sides,' I must leave my reader to explain.

' A Lyceum first night has now become a solemn " function," which peers, millionaires and honourable women " intrigue to see " ' (p. 4). Mr. Archer must indeed be considered superhuman in his insight ; he can ' see' a ' function.'

' This genus all' is Mr. Archer's elegant translation of *hoc genus omne.* Yet we are authoritatively informed that Mr. Archer has been to school, in Scotland.

' The audience knows perfectly well he is intended for a bishop, accepts him for one, and (such is *their* reverence) laughs at him accordingly' (pp. 147, 148).

' The theatrical critic who desires to write, I do not say a good style, but English of moderate purity, has a hard time of it' (p. 203). We had always imagined literary style to be a quality of something written. To ' write a style' is a phrase as full of meaning as ' to paint an art' or ' to sing a tone.'

' Though the logical difference between this case

and that of the "ensemble" may not be apparent, I believe that even the Americans have trusted to their ears rather than their logic, and *have accepted the one and rejected the other*'! (p. 207). Does Mr. Archer mean by this that the poor Americans have accepted a certain 'logic' at the expense of the rejection of their 'ears'?

'It (the Censorship) is destructive, because it takes out of the people's hands a power that they alone can wield, and thus deadens their feeling of responsibility for the morals of the stage' (p. 157). Imagine the 'feeling of responsibility' for theatrical morals conceived by the 'people's hands'!

But I hear my readers cry, 'Hold, enough!' Mr. Archer's book is full of flowers such as I have transplanted.

FINAL WORDS.

FINAL WORDS.

I.

THE PARADOX.

THE paradox of this book, permeating it throughout, is the one stated in the letters entitled ' Are Men born Free and Equal ?' to the effect that true Socialism is another name for Individualism. A little reflection, however, may convince us that it is perhaps no paradox at all.

Personally, I should be grieved and disheartened if any friends of mine should class me with the enemies of the higher Socialism, which has all my sympathy and all my prayers. My contention is in favour of the right of individuals to agitate for purposes of self-protection, to destroy false economics, cruel monopolies, tyrannical inter-ferences with the conduct of life. For example, in the admirable series of economic and historical statements published by the Fabian Society, there is scarcely a word from which I should dissent, if I were allowed to qualify the preposterous con-clusions based upon those statements. Rational

Socialism has worked wonders for society; but how? By protecting the weak against the strong, the worker against the capitalist, the average man against the organization of hereditary monopolists. But surely such Socialism is only the fruit of the labours performed by temporarily discredited minorities — in a word, by aggressive and self-assertive Individualism? Latter-day agitators are very fond of regarding those who disagree with them, about the extent to which democratic legislation should be carried, as selfish and anarchic faddists—men who would leave the 'strugglers for life' to take care of themselves, and who use as mottoes, *Laissez faire* and *Laissez aller*. These Socialists base all their hopes of a social cosmos on a system of State organization, worked by a democratic majority, which would gradually average the laws of life for all men, and suppress all individual development.

Yet it is here, I think, that my friends are themselves paradoxical, for I would be quite content to canvass them on most of the questions discussed in the preceding pages, and abide by the result. They, surely, would contend for the natural freedom and equality of Man, as *I* understand it; for the emancipation of the weaker sex; for the freedom of art and letters; for the right of private judgment in matters moral and religious; for the repression of scientific or quasi-scientific experiments on the lives of human beings and helpless animals;

for the destruction of War and Prostitution. Yet
here, as may readily be shown, they are contending
with the minority, they are fighting for individual
liberties and privileges which the State at present
denies them. Their power in the land is already
great, and will be greater as time advances. The
abstract principles they are preaching will slowly
leaven the mass of misery and crime. But why?
Not because they are waging a mad crusade against
Society as rationally constituted, but because they
are organizing, under able individual leaders, to
disintegrate the present too common social evils;
because, in one word, they are proving that every
sane human being is not merely a member of
Society, but an individual possessing natural rights,
liberties, and privileges.

This, I say, is the Paradox, the Riddle of the
Sphynx: How to preserve the freedom of Humanity
while preserving the freedom of individual men?

On one point there can be no dispute, and has
been no dispute. The present system of Society,
it is admitted, includes structures honeycombed by
centuries of wrong-doing. It is indisputable,
nevertheless, that such wrongs as have been
redressed already have been redressed less by
mob-organization of any kind than by the free
and unfettered primary action of martyred *individuals*. It was the Five Members who, to their
own great peril, destroyed the social and political
prerogatives of the Right Divine. It was Milton

who, in the face of English Puritanism, established the Liberty of Unlicensed Printing, the right of men to save or lose their Souls by literature in their own way; and it was the same Milton who vindicated, against the Christian Socialism of his own age, the liberties of Divorce—liberties still denied to us by the advocates of the *status quo.* It was the pertinacious Lord Shaftesbury, then Lord Ashley, who passed the first Mining Act; it was the unconventional Howard who reformed our prisons; and it was Robert Owen, an unpopular 'faddist,' who passed the Cotton Mills Act in 1819. In the eyes of his own generation, each of these men was looked upon as an eccentric Individualist, as an enemy of the social organization. Nay, are not many of our own energetic philanthropists themselves considered, by the majority of their countrymen, as individuals accelerating the period of absolute social anarchy? To be called 'a Socialist,' even nowadays, is to receive a name of opprobrium, and to be discredited by the great majority of human beings.

No more extraordinary example of the futility of generalizations can be found than the manner in which many modern Socialists confuse Capitalism with Individualism—a confusion based apparently on the fact that certain individuals have become enormous capitalists! I should have conceived myself, in following the arguments intended to establish so absurd a proposition, that the history of Capital is simply the history of successful attempts to place each individual labourer at the mercy of Capital. Surely Individualism means the moral rights of individuals, not the right of any one individual to steal, to amass money, to do no manner of work but to live on the labour of his fellows? Capitalists themselves are strong only when, like banditti, they league themselves together, and utilize the very machinery advocated by the friends of Trades-unionism. From which point we return to the statement that the true Socialist is an absolute Individualist—one who establishes his own rights by clearly defining the rights of others, by limiting accumulation and oppression in any shape, by asserting, on the plea that each labourer is worthy of his hire, his own plea to possess the results of his personal activity.

Socialism, again, is not to be confounded with Democracy, or Mob-Rule, and the Rational Socialist, therefore, invariably distrusts the Demagogue; but these facts do not altogether imply that State interference is not desirable within limitations to be determined by the conscience of Individuals. The question may perhaps be stated thus: So long as Socialism is a condition of active revolt, qualifying the conditions of political order, and ameliorating abuses, it is practically beneficent; so soon as it becomes an overpowering State organism, paralyzing individual resistance and asserting a claim to absolute power, it is likely to become tyrannical. Now, as always, the strength and justice of a people lie with the intellectual minority, and that minority at present is, in my sense of the word, individualistic.

II.

THE SOCIAL SANCTION.

INDIVIDUALISM, however, is not to be confounded with unlimited freedom of personal conduct. In exact proportion to the duty Society owes to the Individual, is the duty owed by the Individual to Society.

The late Thomas Carlyle, in that wild chaos of vague assertions and unreasoned socialistic prejudices which humorists call his 'philosophy,' preached, following his master, Goethe, the worship of successful Individuals, men of genius, men of 'worth,' but in doing so lost sight of the rights of Humanity in general, and wrote a succession of variations on the glorification of so many Jonathan Wilds. Individualism, like Socialism, protects the weak, and insists that even Genius possesses no privilege entitling it to disregard human responsibilities. The worship of mere intellectual or physical power, the moral *carte blanche* given to an aristocracy of intellect, the argument which justifies the selfishness of a Goethe, or the sexual hysteria of Goethe's worst disciples, is essentially as irrational and anarchic—at once as anti-individualist and anti-social—as the worship of our aristocracy or our plutocracy. To say this is not to say that men of genius are to be judged by the sham conventions of Society; but neither are any individuals, however free of genius, to be so judged. It is well to remember that there is, at the present moment, both in literature and art, a great and growing tendency towards sham, as distinguished from true, Individualism—a tendency to represent Society as entirely wicked, and Revolt as of necessity commendable. The modern school of literary reformers has not as yet improved very much on the Weimar standard of ethics, and the result is that revolt has remained self-conscious, self-seeking, and self-conceited. Curiously enough, many of our leading Socialists have distinguished themselves by sympathy with the new births of sham literary Individualism—the intellectual prig, the super-moral female, the self-analyzing pessimist, *et hoc genus omne*—a fact which, while it establishes my postulate that Socialism and Individualism are convertible terms, also shows that Socialism hardly understands as yet the meaning or the consequences of its own propaganda. For a moral or intellectual aristocracy is as much to be feared and dreaded as a political one; and the man who conceives he has an intellectual privilege to put himself above or beyond the just standards of conduct is as dangerous as the man who claims a class-privilege

24

to avoid the just standards of natural competition.

Society is impossible if we have no ethical standards at all; if any given course of conduct is regarded as quite as good as another; and if human Society is considered, as some writers appear to consider it, necessarily false and conventional. The problem is, how to separate what is false and conventional from what is true and necessary; in other words, to learn those laws of common well-being which may fairly be termed absolute. Kant's categoric imperative may possibly serve us here. No law of conduct should be made compulsory which the individual would consider arbitrary and cruel if applied to his own case; and to define such laws, it is essential that individuals should agree as to certain absolute ethical standards, free of Empiricism on the one hand, and free of Convention on the other.

III.

THE OUTCOME IN MINOR LITERARY CRITICISM.

SINCE the first publication of 'The Young Man as Critic,' and of the correspondence which in this book follows it in sequence ('Is Chivalry still Possible ?'), at least two of the persons severely censured have made both my criticism and myself the subject of continual animadversion, or, rather, recrimination. This was only natural, and to be expected. I have now, therefore, to revise my judgment, as every honest writer is bound to do, and to indicate those particulars in which I feel myself to have exaggerated the truth. It appears to me, then, on reflection, that I have been unfair to some of our young men, in so far as I have accused them of a want of any intellectual ideal whatsoever. Further familiarity with their writings convinces me that they have certainly the virtue of sincerity, and that, allowing for the aberrations of personal malice, they are conscientiously endeavouring to criticise literature according to their lights. Their belief is that our literary salvation lies in the direction of absolute and trivial Realism; their conception of a work of Art is that it should be an unimpeachable transcription 'from the life.' They have faith, also, like their teacher, Goethe, in the power of Womanhood as a force to disintegrate social convention and moral superstition — a faith, by the way, which (*pace!* these gentlemen's reproaches) I have been preaching all my life. On the whole, then, I conceive that the difference between writers of this class and myself is temperamental rather than intellectual; that, different as our methods and our sympathies may be, our conclusions are not always diverse.

And, further, it appears to me that little or no harm can be done to the literature of Imagination by any hostile critic who is thoroughly in earnest. To find edification in the dreary family anecdotes and dingy back-parlour chronicles which are now called 'dramas,' and to conceive life as drab-coloured and lugubrious throughout, is far less harmful than to have no taste for novelty and no zeal for humanity. The present apotheosis of what is mean and trivial and cheaply scientific—the present conception of Art as a series of dingy amateur photographs taken in the scullery during sunless weather —is only the inevitable reaction following the great period of loose and unfettered Ideality through which we have just passed. Presently, no doubt, it will be discovered that there is even more falsehood to Nature in a bad photograph than in a wildly-executed painting; that no amount of truth to outlines and to shadows, no obtrusion of minor details, can compensate for the glow of light, of colour, of imagination. In the meantime, the craving for Photography in Literature may serve some good purpose if it leads men to be zealous for general truth of presentation. There will always be critics who are colour-blind. There will always, on the other hand, be writers who find in Nature not merely one common black and white, but all the radiant colours of the prism.

It is on ethical grounds, however, that the minor critics of the new photographic creed claim to be finally judged. They claim that Morality should have a foremost place in Art, particularly the art dramatic; and the morality they parade is the anti-social morality of Egoismus. Now, Egoismus, as

I conceive it, is Individuality under diseased conditions. Falk and Nora in Ibsen's dramas, for
example, are types of violent moral crudity in revolt
against the 'conventions' of society. The one is
a sulky provincial Byron, who, out of cowardly self-
love, refuses his happiness when it is offered to him;
the other is a petulant little monster, whose eccentricities are only comprehensible on the score of
some obscure epileptic disturbance, and who is
equally detestable when sucking lollipops or suggesting syllogisms. The minor criticism applauds
these and cognate monstrosities as phenomenally interesting and important to literature; in point of
fact, they have neither human interest nor any
literary importance, save as indications of the fatal
influence that morbid self-analysis has had on
thought and on expression.

Egoismus is a literary complaint first contracted
by the men who drank too deeply of the poisoned
waters of Weimar. Its signs are feverish dissatis-
faction with society, irritation at social trifles, sus-
picion of all sanctions, and incapacity for honest
laughter. In its worst examples it bereaves the
literary organism of all colour but black and white,
and gives to its victim the complexion either of the
negro or the albino.

IV.

ALTHOUGH the type I am attempting to describe may be traced far back in history, the chief modern example is Goethe*; not the Goethe of 'Faust' and the 'Divan,' but the Goethe of 'Wilhelm Meister' and the 'Elective Affinities.' In spite of all that wise critics have said to the contrary, I have always contended that Goethe, so far from being an 'Art for Art' philosopher, was permeated through and through with the self-consciousness of a haunting non-moral Morality. It was he who first among moderns began to analyze and to dissect his own sensations, and to reduce his heart-beats to a science. In his case, however, it was a strong and healthy man condescending to that self-analysis which, in less vigorous natures, develops into anæmia and vainglory. The result was to be found less in the giant himself than in his numerous literary progeny—a tainted and exhausted breed still lingering among us, chiefly in the form of the albino.

In cases of this kind it is of little consequence whether the personal bias is moral or whether it is what is called 'immoral.' The impeccable albino

* See my article, 'The Character of Goethe,' in 'A Look Round Literature.'

Mr. Howells is just as much tainted with Egoismus as the nerve-shocking negroesque M. Zola. The self-analyzing and hypercultured young lady of Boston is as disagreeable in her superfinity as the nevrose heroine of 'La Curée' is in her sexual mania. In either case Morality has poisoned and perverted Art. Here, as in other developments of the disease, I see in the so-called Gospel of the Ego, not a new reve-lation, but the last slimy trail of the Goethe system of ethics, shown in productions which, like the for-gotten and worthless portion of Goethe's work, were devoid of imagination and true human sentiment. What is new and immense to the young men of the ferociously 'moral' newspapers has been familiar and detestable to me from the first moment I began to think and write. Where they find literary salva-tion I have found only the last dregs of a Devil's gospel which has corrupted almost every branch of modern literature, and which, had Heaven not sent the world its literary knights errant in Victor Hugo and Dumas, would have long ago destroyed all poetry in the world. To them the moral of the Ego is novel; to me it is as old as the 'Elective Affinities' and Goethe's self-culture, with little new in it, and that little untrue, and delivered without a gleam of consecrating insight.

V.

'MORALITY' AS LITERATURE.

THE literary character is curiously inconsistent. A
little while ago we were being assured on every
hand that Art had nothing whatever to do with
Ethics, and a large number of intelligent writers,
in order to vindicate that theory, were joining together in a wild revel of indecent exposure. The
reaction has come. We are now assured with equal
vehemence that the functions of Art are ethical or
nothing, and an equally large number of intelligent
writers are flooding the world with sermons upon
questions of Morality.

Now, the truth lies in the *via media*—the way
between two absurd theories. It makes all the
difference whether, in a work of Art, we place
edification in the first place or in the second. In
reality it exists in all true Literature, but there its
place is secondary, and it is subservient, even incidental; it is the perfume, not the body, of the
flower. Directly it assumes the first place, as in
Goethe's inferior writings, in the albino or negroesque novelists, in the chamber-dramas of Ibsen and
Björnson, and in the recent imitations by English
novelists and dramatists, Art becomes diseased and
stultified; all its free and vigorous life is gone.

The tendency of English literature generally, as

of the English life and character, has been towards
edification. For a long time under the old sanctions
this edification was religious; at present, under the
new Providence made Easy and the new literature
made moral, it is ethical. We have banished all the
superior gods, but the Furies and the Eumenides
remain, and shriek the new shibboleth of 'Heredity'
and 'Evolution.' The cant-phrase of our most destructive propagandists, the last word of both
Atheism and Positivism, is, 'Since we know Religion to be fiction, let us assure ourselves of the
one fact, Morality.' Hence, in literature, the dreary
latter-day treatises of George Eliot; hence, on the
stage, St. Ibsen's Epistle to the Young Men as
Critics; hence, over there in France, the vivisection
of human nature to verify theories of hereditary
moral diseases and of the survival of the morally
unfittest; hence, yonder in America, the hyper-
æsthesia of Moral Cock-Certainty, the nervous
exhaustion of the well-conducted Man-Milliner.
We are anxious to be 'good,' but do not yet know
how. We think we can cozen the Devil (in whom
we still religiously believe) by a system of self-
examination and self-dissection. And in our despair
of individual success we turn to Sociology for 'facts,'
and to practical Politics, the Limbo of the Legislator, for inspiration.

The outcome of late in literature and in the
drama has been a series of stories and plays in
which the characters are moral chameleons, who,

both in act and deed, shock nature and belie experience, and who are just as like life as the ' edifying '
creations of the Religious Tract Society.   Quite
recently, in an egregious drama by Messrs. Henley
and Stevenson, acted at the Haymarket, we have
had the last ethical flavour of ' edification ' imported
into the story of a *beau* and *roué* of half a century
ago ; and to hear Mr. Beerbohm Tree, in the costume
of a Beau Nash, talking the patter of Ibsen, and
listening to the reproaches of an Ibsenite young
woman in the Dresden China costume of our grand-
mothers, was a sight for the gods to smile at.   If
Shakespeare in his tragedy of ' Romeo and Juliet '
were suddenly to turn Juliet into an oracular Miss
Blimber, or in his tragedy of Othello should make
Desdemona just before her strangulation lecture
Othello on the moral-philosophical disadvantages of
marrying a person of colour, we should find Shakespeare doing on occasion what the modern literary
moralist does almost invariably.   Such feats of
psychological legerdemain may please a small section of the public ; but why, because those persons
like to turn the theatre into a museum of moral
monstrosities, should every writer who has tried to
give innocent amusement to his countrymen be vili-
fied ?   Why should I, for example, because I think
the ' Doll's House ' is a literary crudity, be attacked
for upholding ' Institutions,' taunted with a belief in
the ' conventionalities ' of personal honour, honest
humour, and natural affection ?

One of my critics has abused me roundly for describing Ibsen as 'a Zola with a wooden leg.' Another writer avers that 'A Doll's House' is the only play which has not 'bored' him within the last few years, and adds (what is more to the point) that the nightly 'storm of discussion' over Ibsen's 'ethics' is a proof of the dramatist's genius and originality. Now, as a matter of fact, nothing is so easy as to outrage commonsense, and so arouse discussion and opposition; nothing is so difficult as to please, to refine, and to charm. A playgoer witnessing the great masterpieces of dramatic literature does not become polemical; he carries away with him the pathos, the solemnity, and the calm of life itself. He has been to a theatre, not to a debating-room; he has been enjoying a work of Art, not a feverish and irritating platform controversy. It has ever been the aim of the great dramatists, from Sophocles downwards, to magnify the divine meaning of life, to depict that truth which is beautiful and spiritualizing. The mission of prosaists like Ibsen is the mission of dullards like Zola—to shock and to revolt us with the meannesses of life, and to assume that those meannesses most abound where Religion and Morality are most powerful. My callow critic is not merely disgusted with the modern dramatist; he describes the average home as a 'harem,' the domestic affections of average men and women as stupid and conventional, the religious instincts of average humanity as instincts 'he grew out of before he was born.' The same jaded and foolish creature who sees in Ibsen's Nora a living woman representing Woman in the Abstract, would see in the banalities of ' La Terre,' if produced upon the stage, a glorious lesson convincing us of the monkeydom of humanity. We want no such lesson, for we have had it of late years *ad nauseam.* We have not yet arrived at the point of believing that every institution is vile merely *because* it is an 'institution.' The collective sentiment of Humanity has formulated a religion of Altruism, not of Egoism; it has felt from generation to generation that only by our faithfulness to those who love and depend upon us, our forbearance to those whom we think weak and helpless, our tenderness and compassion, our supreme pity for others, can we save ourselves. In the eyes of rational beings, not infected with the poison of the egoistic gospel, the woman who would save her own soul without first seeking to save those of her little children is, under any circumstances, a monster of selfishness and self-conceit; the man who thinks redemption comes through mere self-culture is a man ignorant of the world and its lessons ; the dramatist who represents society as an aggregate of moral ' prigs ' and self-conscious feminine ' cads,' catching from the common sunlight all the colours of the chameleon, is not merely unfamiliar with human nature, but ignorant of the first elements of that art which still keeps Shakespeare a triumphant certainty.

VI.

THE OUTCOME IN IDEALISM.

I AM perfectly prepared to meet any charge of inconsistency, made upon the ground that I am at once an advocate of Socialism and an advocate of Individualism. I would destroy false Individualism by the socialistic test, and I would destroy sham Socialism by the test which is converse. One half of this book is devoted to proving, with Mill, that individuals have a natural right to free, unfettered, and even eccentric development; while the argument of the other half is that individual development, being often crass, anarchic, selfish, and harmful to Society, has to be carefully watched and qualified by the corporate conscience.

There is no more amusing illustration of the silliness of ultra-individualism than the favour shown by a certain portion of the public to that recent gospel of Egoismus to which I have alluded. Modern writers, indignant at the very constitution of Society, and exaggerating its evils, have presented us with innumerable types of character illustrating, unconsciously, the intellectual crudity of self-love. 'A man has first of all to save his own Soul,' say these writers, following their master Goethe. How far this precious zeal for spiritual self-preservation may be perverted may now be seen in the sunless

pages of numberless saturnine writers. It is needless to say that the true Individualist, despite all his
opposition to social and political conventions, is well
aware that no man can save his own Soul *alone*, or
without the help of his human environment. 'We
live by admiration, hope, and love,' says the poet.
Liberty and equality do not preclude responsibility
or exclude the social sanction; on the contrary,
they determine the one and postulate the other.

There is no doubt that at the present moment
the Enthusiasm of Humanity, which has worked so
many miracles of love and healing, is just temporarily
receding here and there (fortunately not everywhere) like a great tide, and leaving dry and arid
shores of dark Reality, over which we are invited to
wander, searching for the shells and bones of fact,
and examining the shallow pools for living speci-
mens. Moral philosophy, and abstract philosophy
of all kinds, is out of fashion, and Poetry paddles
through the mud. Little cynics run about with
their toy spades, building up a politics and a literature of slime and sand, and getting very dirty in the
process. Nevertheless, the great Ocean still exists,
and in a very little while the tide must turn. But
in the meantime we may be satisfied that our time
is not being absolutely wasted, and that the present
interest in morbid psychology and pessimism, like our
present faith in State nostrums, will not be without
its good fruits. After the reaction we shall be
curious and accurate, as well as sympathetic and

enthusiastic. Truth will receive more justice, and Beauty more verification. True, the houses of mud and sand will crumble away, and the ephemeral names written on the shore will be effaced. But when all around us has 'suffered a sea-change,' whatever is great and imperishable in Thought and Sentiment, as well as in Society, will remain.

VII.

' POOR HUMANITY.'

HUMANITY, at the present moment, may be compared to a Hypochondriac, to Molière's own 'Malade Imaginaire.'

His chief concern is with his own personal ailments, some of them quite imaginary. With the aid of the microscope, he examines his own secretions ; yet he still plucks at the entrails of beasts to consult them as an augury. He swallows all new panaceas indiscriminately ; bolts his door against the old charlatans of Religion, but admits by the side-entrance the new charlatans of Useful Knowledge. His firm conviction is that his disease is incurable, that he has soon to *die!*

And only a little while ago, in the robust faith of his youth and strength, he believed himself immortal! The physicians of Positivism and cognate creeds assure him that he is *still* immortal, in the abstract ; but abstract consolations are of no use in hypochondria ! In a fit of disgust at his own body, he becomes super-moral, disgusted at every natural appetite, afraid of every natural function. In a mood of sexual madness, he becomes indecent, and descends to all the banalities of self-exposure. Nothing to him is innocent or clean during these aberrations. He thinks all Society, and every institution, rotten at the root. He has invented the Modern Newspaper, that he may gloat over the obscene details of his own case, over the general diseases of his social organism ; and he has fabricated the modern Novel, that he may discover other hazy diseases, never to be classified by Science. With all this, he is not in such a bad way as he imagines. His hypochondria is only at the early stage, and not yet chronic. To cure him, only freedom, good food, and fresh air are necessary. Free exercise of all his functions will put him right —at least, let us hope so. He will cease to contemplate his secretions, to be haunted by thoughts of his own excrement. He will cease to prate about ' morality ' and ' immorality.' He will know how absurd he looks, eternally feeling his own pulse. And then, when he is renovated by free oxygen, he will burn his treatises of domestic medicine, his tractates of empirical knowledge about Morality and other ailments, his illustrated books of disease-germs enlarged by the microscope, his prescriptions of Providence made Easy and of State Socialism, and look heavenward once more for sunlight and consolation. Then the lost Gods may appear again, radiant and beautiful as ever, and the lost Poets will be re-born with the lost Gods. Before this happy change, however, will come the crisis of a *real* illness, some of the features of which I have tried to foreshadow in these pages. Humanity will sicken almost to death; but after all, the old creed of Youth, and Hope, and Light is a true creed, and Humanity, so far from dying yet, will live to a good old age.

THE END.

HILLING AND SONS, PRINTERS, GUILDFORD.